I0743367

# THE COMPLETE SYLVAN INVESTIGATIONS

## LAURA ANNE GILMAN

Copyright © 2020 by Laura Anne Gilman

Cover Design: Natania Barron

Production: April Steenburgh

Ebook ISBN 978-1-951612-26-9

Print ISBN 978-1-951612-27-6

Miles to Go first published 2013

Promises to Keep first published 2013

Work of Hunters first published 2016

An Interrupted Cry first published 2016

All rights reserved.

No part of this book may be reproduced in any form or by any electronic or mechanical means, including information storage and retrieval systems, without written permission from the author, except for the use of brief quotations in a book review.

**Miles to Go:** It's an ordinary day, another ordinary job, when Danny's approached by a young woman with information he needs to solve a case. With a life – or more – on the line, it's hard to turn down help. But the cost of that information will change Danny's life...forever.

**Promises to Keep:** A boring snoop-and-scoop infidelity case, the kind of thing that pays the bills and keeps everyone fed, should be a piece of cake. But his new partner sees something more in the scenario...and what she sees is deadly. To the client – and to them.

**The Work of Hunters:** Ellen's most recent vision strikes a memory for Danny — one that quickly turns deadly. Soon, they are racing the clock not only to stop a new killing, but to find justice for the long-dead.

**An Interrupted Cry:** A blackout hits New York City. Already reeling from one of her visions, Ellen discovers that Danny has gone missing, leaving a violent scene behind... And the city is in the dark about what's coming, in more ways than one.

# CONTENTS

# MILES TO GO

My back hurt, my horns itched, and I was pretty sure that burrito for lunch had been a mistake.

"You're bluffing," I said.

"Danny, oh Danny." The miserable fucker had the balls to smile at me. "You know I never bluff."

It was summer. Some places in the city, summer's nice. You get out by the water, maybe Orchard Beach or Coney Island, or even the Seaport if it's not too crowded, and the salt air and breeze touches your skin and you're seventeen again. And the Green, what humans called Central Park, was a blessed respite, even on the worst days.

But inside the city itself, locked within the henge of buildings that reflected heat and cast it back to the pavement which in turn shoved it up into living tissue, summer was miserable. I wanted to be somewhere with clean air, cold water, and a colder beer. Instead, I was stuck on a park bench in midtown Manhattan, watching tourists pile on and off those damn tourist buses.

The last round had been a mistake, last night. So had the

first round. I'm not much for drinking – my years on the force showed me how badly that could go wrong, and my father's genetic inheritance makes me prone to...overindulgence. But an old friend was getting married next week, and the least I could do was go along with the bridal shower, make sure nobody got in trouble.

Everyone, of course, had. And now I was paying for it. At least the sweat was soaking the toxins out of my system, right?

Anderlik, next to me, smiled again. His teeth were perfectly capped, his skin naturally tanned, and his eyes flat and ugly as the pavement. His hands rested on his lap, and I noted that the creases of his pants were perfectly pressed, even in this heat. Bastard.

"So, if you're willing to negotiate", he went on, "I think we can come to an amicable position that leaves everyone satisfied."

One of the double-decker buses I'd been watching pulled up and disgorged its passengers, overwhelmed families tumbling off onto the sidewalks, fanning themselves with cheap folding fans, hats, and folded brochures, their faces red with sweat and bright with excitement. Mothers and sons, fathers and daughters, young lovers and wait for it, a pack of teenaged boys, out on a lark, not minding the heat. Sixteen, tops. They came off the bus last, already looking for their next big thrill, their body language practically screaming 'fresh meat.'

"Danny? Can we talk terms?"

I saw him then, oozing his way through the crowds like a proper snake, eyes beady and tongue practically scenting his prey in the air. Another two-three minutes, and he'd be on them, dropping lures and seeing what he could catch.

Not this time, I thought, standing up. "Danny!"

My fist was almost an afterthought, hitting Anderlik a solid three-quarter blow on his perfect nose.

"The photos haves already gone to the PUPs," I told him. "You're going to have to negotiate with Venec. Have fun with that."

I walked off, my gaze focused on my prey, Romeo Anderlik already forgotten. I moved through the crowds, aware that I was getting looks as I went. Tourists always looked; the Department of Tourism should send me a check every month. I had an actor's face, a friend once told me, and I'd be cast as Every New Yorker Ever; sardonic, weary and just a hint of amusement left in my eyes. The bastard love child of Jimmy Stewart and Woody Allen.

Slime had found his prey: he was leaning against the hip-high white barricades the DoT had put in to keep cars on the road and pedestrians on the sidewalks, his body language oozing smarter, cooler older guy. Two of the boys were buying it, the other three not so much. I'd have to wait: if they walked away, I'd have nothing, no proof.

Part of me wanted them to be smart and walk away. The rest of me wanted nothing more than to get this slimy skin-seller out of business.

Something – someone – was pacing me. Tall, taller than me, dark, and female. Clearly pacing me too, with a mind to intercept, rather than just moving in the same direction.

"Excuse me?"

She was talking to me, yeah. My momma raised me to be polite, most especially to women. I kept an eye on the knot of potential boy-toys ahead of me, and turned just enough to see who was trying to get my attention.

She was tall, dark, and strong-boned, with black curls pinned away from equally dark eyes and a nose like Cleopatra might've had. Not a beauty, but New York's values aren't LA's, and I've always been a sucker for an interesting face.

All right, I've always been a sucker, period. "Danny Hendrickson, right?"

Ahead of me, Slime was leaning in, trying to close the sale.

Next to me, a dark-eyed woman knew my name.

"Honey, it's gotta wait," I said, and stepped forward. She followed.

I was a long pace away from the boys when two oversized individuals in regrettable matching outfits passed in front of me. I dodged, came around, and saw that the majority vote had won: the boys were backing away, several of them looking somewhat nervous. Good, and damn it. I stopped, and something tipped Slime off, because he looked up and saw me standing there.

He had no clue who I was, but his slimy instincts told him *what,* as much as if I'd still carried a badge. And that was enough to make him disappear like a Salamander on a frosty morning.

"Mister Hendrickson?"

I exhaled, let the irritation go, and turned to see what the hell was tapping me on the shoulder.

"Mister Hendrickson." "Danny."

She nodded, gravely. Looking at her straight on, I could see her skin had an ashy tint to it, and she was sweating. Okay, we were all sweating, but I didn't think the heat was what had her shaking.

"My name is Ellen. Bonnie...Bonnie told me how to find you."

New York City was a big town. Bonnie knew a lot of people. But there was only one Ellen I knew about, who Bonnie Torres might have sent my way.

I'd heard about Ellen. Heard enough to be damn cautious. She licked her lips, and raised those scared eyes to mine, and said the words that were always my damned downfall. "I need your help."

One of these days, those words were going to get me killed.

Might even be today.

---

WE DECAMPED to the nearest coffeehouse that wasn't Starbucks, which in this case was the venerable Café Cafee. It's been around since 1952, and looks it. Even the repeated clean-ups and gussy-ups of Times Square couldn't touch CC's.

She wrapped her hands around her coffee mug like it was the last source of warmth in a stone-cold winter. She had long fingers, broad palms, the kind of hands that looked capable, like they could saw a body apart or sew it back together, whichever she had a mind to.

She looked, in fact, like a sturdy, well-built girl, the kind who took up wall climbing or hiking, something physical, was maybe too chunky as a teenager, and has been turning it to muscle ever since.

She didn't look dangerous.

I'd heard enough to know better.

Ellen. No last name, no known background that anyone had heard of, suddenly appearing thirteen-fourteen months ago on the scene in the company of Bonnie Torres and her crew.

The so-called CSI of the magical community excelled at digging out details – and keeping those details to themselves. So I didn't ask. None of my business, no matter how curious I'd been.

And then a few weeks later, The Wren, one of the most powerful Talent currently alive on the East Coast, had taken this unknown girl to mentor. Gossip had flared immediately, of course. But when young Ellen didn't seem to be moving in her mentor's larcenous footsteps, nor in fact, doing much of note at all, the talk turned to more interesting, immediate things.

I hadn't pried, but I hadn't forgotten, either. Sudden changes and unexplained actions were relevant to my interests. Lines of mentorship were incredibly important to the Talent community, more so than blood. Why had Wren taken an unknown Talent to mentor, seem- ingly out of the blue? Something hadn't quite added up, knowing both Bonnie and Wren the way I did. The two of them taking an interest in this girl meant something.

What a little careful poking around turned up was that Miss Ellen No Last Name had no training, hadn't even known she as a Talent until recently, and that fact made the PUPs, Bonnie included, nervous as hell. That, to a trained investigator like, say, myself, meant that Miss Ellen also had power. Power that The Wren had been asked to shape – or control.

And now powerful Miss Ellen had come looking for me.

I suddenly wished for a shot of something stronger than caffeine to pour into my coffee.

If I was nervous, Miss Ellen was clearly terrified, but she wasn't going to let that stop her.

"Bonnie said...she said you help people."

She was too young to get the pop culture reference that went through my head, so I kept my mouth shut, nodded, and waited.

"There... someone needs your help. I just don't know *who*."

All right: that was a different song than I usually got. I leaned back, stretched my legs out in front of me, and studied my damsel in distress. I'd gotten pretty good at judging human ages: she was twenty-three, tops. Maybe only twenty-one. Legal, by the Null world's standards. But to the Cosa Nostradamus, she was a Talent in mentorship, and that made her, in all the ways that counted, a minor.

"You know they need help, but not who it is that needs my help." Being a PI wasn't all that different from my years as a beat cop: sometimes you had to walk people through it before they'd get to the point and tell you what they wanted you to know. Small words and long silences worked better than trying to ask questions before they were ready.

"You know who I am."

It wasn't a question. She'd been in this world long enough to know that the *Cosa* gossiped like a granny on meth.

"You don't know what I am."

"Talent." A human with the ability to manipulate current, also known as magic. That was a no-brainer: human Nulls weren't part of the *Cosa Nostradamus*. Most of them didn't even know we existed.

My mother had been a sensitive Null, aware but not part of.

My father... we don't talk about, much. Ever.

"I don't know anything about that. I don't know anything about any of it. Genevieve's been trying to teach me, but..." Genevieve, huh? Most days I forgot that was Wren's legal name. She swallowed, gathering courage, and I could feel something cold touch the base of my spine. Here it came, whatever it was.

"I see dead people."

Whatever I'd been expecting, it wasn't that.

"You mean like Bruce Willis?" The words just slipped out; my mouth is like that sometimes.

Ellen had a touch of steel to her little-girl-lost routine; the glare she gave me over that proud nose would have made my momma proud.

"I see people who are going to die," she clarified. "In the current. I don't ask for it, it just... comes."

"And you saw someone." She nodded.

"Someone you know?"

She shook her head, and then hesitated, nodded. I took a deep breath, let it out. "You saw me."

She nodded again.

"Just me?" I doubted it, and I was right.

"No. There were others. But that doesn't mean... I don't know how to read what I see yet. Bonnie uses scrying crystals, but she says my visions aren't like hers. They're... more. She says I'm a – "

That sound you heard, the metallic ping of a penny dropping? Yeah. "You're a storm seer."

She nodded, looking miserable. I didn't blame her.

No wonder they'd been keeping her quiet. The only reason I knew about storm seers was because my mother, once she figured out about my old man, got her hands on everything she could find about the *Cosa Nostradamus*, which included a lot of junk but also some of the real histories, all the way back to Founder Ben's time. Ben Franklin had codified the laws of current, helped shift it from some random hobledygook of superstition and woo-woo into a practical system that could be studied and ordered. For humans, anyway. The fatae – the non-humans – didn't use magic, they *were* magic. So it was different for them.

I was half-human, half-fatae. Didn't happen too often. Most of the time, a woman found herself with a fatae child, she drowned it, if she couldn't take care of the problem beforehand. My mother had made a different choice. I didn't think she regretted it, but I never asked, and she never told me.

If she'd asked me, I might have chosen differently, but, well.

This wasn't about me, it was about the woman sitting in front of me.

Storm seers, according to what I'd read, were a legend.

See, magic exists, but it's cranky. It doesn't like being touched, and most humans try to manipulate it, it'll fry them up like bacon. But some humans, they've got the gift. Talent. That's what they have and that's what they're called, and they're the rest of the *Cosa Nostradamus*, along with the non-humans of the world. I'd grown up with Talent, counted most of my friends among them, but they were a mystery to me, in a lot of ways.

A storm seer was that mystery wrapped around dynamite. A storm seer, according to legends, could take wild current, the magic that hums throughout the world, emerging from the core of the earth or coming down from the sky in lightning, and <u>see</u> what was coming. Cassandra-style seeing, not just a touch of kenning or precog.

Apparently what my girl saw was death. Specifically and relevant to my interests, *my* death.

---

ELLEN HAD THOUGHT he would be...scarier. Or larger. Or not seem so...human. In her vision, her kenning, Bonnie called it, his face had been more drawn, his cheekbones more pronounced, and his chin – clean-shaven now – covered with stubble. And his horns...

You couldn't see his horns, now. His brown hair was a tousled mess, curly but not in any kind of styled way, more like he washed it and dried it and then forgot he had it, and you had to look carefully to see the tiny curved points peeking out.

About the size of her thumb, she figured. Maybe smaller: she had large hands. But very real.

Faun. Half-faun, Bonnie had said. Fatae – not human. That still blew her mind; she'd only just learned that the *things* she kept seeing out of the corner of her eyes were real, that the *things* she saw and felt and could do were real. After twenty years of being told she was imagining things, and then being told that she was crazy, reality didn't quite feel real to her.

She knew enough not to reach out and touch those half-hidden horns, though. She wanted to. Badly. Badly enough that her immediate suspicion was that it wasn't her wanting, exactly. "Danny's a heartbreaker," Bonnie had said that morning, casually, like it wasn't anything important. "It's the whole faun thing. He can't help it."

Ellen licked her lips, and tried to focus on the vision that had sent her here. But that didn't help any, either. Her visions scared the fuck out of her, more and worse than anything else. Especially now that she knew they weren't just bad dreams or hallucinations, that she wasn't crazy, and it was all real. Everyone she saw dead, died.

"Not all."

"What?" He looked at her, and she realized suddenly that she's said it out loud. She swallowed, and it felt like something sharp was stuck inside her throat.

"Not everyone I see, the ones who call to me, dies. I'm fifty-fifty, so far."

"Well. That's reassuring." He didn't sound reassured. But he also wasn't trying to pretend he was reassured, the way everyone else did. Genevieve and Sergei, even Bonnie and the others, they all tiptoed around her, careful and cautious, and she knew why. It was because she came late to this, to knowing she was a Talent, and she was supposed to have learned all that before, when she was a kid, and she didn't and that was bad.

"I saw you." She had to get it out before she was too scared to talk. "Last night. You were wet, like…like you'd gotten caught in the rain. And you looked really tired. And there were these…" she fumbled, trying to remember the details of the vision from nearly twenty four hours before. "Kids? Teenagers. Three of them. Behind you. They were all wet too, and they looked weird, but I can't tell you how. And you were all dead."

There was something in his expression when she started to describe the other people she'd seen. Like he didn't much care about himself being dead, but other people bothered him.

She understood that.

"First, relax," he said, leaning forward a little. "You're not going to be able to remember anything important if you're tensed up and stressing about remembering the important things."

He had a nice voice. Not too deep, but broad and warm, like... like... she didn't know what it was like, but the voice more than the words helped her muscles loosen, her stomach unclench, and she leaned back into the booth, resting her hands on the table, even though her fingers remained clasped together maybe a little too tight.

"Tell me about where you were, before."

"Before?"

"Before you saw me. Where were you?"

She had been in Wren's living room. They were supposed to be having a class – she thought it was a class, anyway. Mostly, it was Wren telling stories, stuff that happened to her, or to her mentor. Sometimes older stories, about things that happened hundreds of years ago. The sky had been clear that morning, a sharp blue, with only a hint of clouds when she walked from her little studio apartment uptown to where her mentor lived. The air had felt...strange, sort of tingly, but there was so much that was new to her, she hadn't thought anything of it.

"Wren was telling me about how she learned about being a Retriever. About how her no-see-me was part of her, and since she couldn't turn it off, she had to learn to use it."

That story, at least, had been obvious. She might be new to this, and kind of clueless about magic, but she wasn't dumb. Being a storm-seer was part of who she was, and she couldn't shut it off, either. So she had to live with it, or...

"And then... I felt weird. Like I had too much to drink, or like the building was moving under me, moving and spinning. And thunder cracked, right overhead, even though it hadn't been raining, and I heard Wren swear, and then everything went black, like it does when a movie's about to start, and I saw..." she remembered what Bonnie had told her that first time, about stepping back from what she saw. "I saw a figure, a man. Ordinary clothes, jeans and a T-shirt, a red T-shirt. And soaking wet. The way you get when you're caught in a storm, and your umbrella gets trashed by the wind. Tired. He looked tired, and worried, and there was a streak of something on his face, something... blood."

She hadn't remembered that before, but now it was clear as that first vision, a streak of muddy brown from ear to chin. Not a scratch, more like he'd tried to wipe his face and smeared it off his hands.

"And horns. I remember the horns. Your hair was matted, and they showed through, and I said something to you about it and you were annoyed and then the others appeared."

She hadn't remembered that at first, either. Had it happened in her original vision, that sense of being there, of knowing him, or speaking to him? Or was it coming up now because she knew him, had spoken to him? She didn't know.

Too much she didn't know, and only one thing she did for sure.

"Three teenagers. Two girls and a boy. All wet, and tired, and.... I don't know. I can't see them as clearly, they're already fading. There's something about them, something strange. It's like something's taking bites out of them? Something hungry, nibbling." Her voice faded for a moment, then came back, stronger. "Mouths of steel biting at them, a bite at a time. But that might be a metaphor. I still don't know how this works, exactly. At all. But they're angry, not scared. Really angry."

"Who are they angry at?" Ellen shivered. "I don't know."

She tried to hold onto the vision, tried to wring something more out of it, prove she could be good at this, but it was fading, the split-second of clarity gone.

"That's all. I had the vision, and then the rain came down like crazy, and it was gone."

Lightning triggered it. Not lightning itself, but the energy within the lightning, the current – magic – that ran through every bit of electricity in the world, her brain reacting to it somehow. That was what they told her. That's why they called her a storm-seer.

"I didn't sense the storm coming," she said to herself. "I wasn't ready. I need to learn how to be ready."

She felt her hands covered by something warmer, and opened her eyes to see his hands on hers, the skin several shades lighter, but the flesh so much warmer. She was cold all over, all the way down to her bones.

"It takes time," he said. "You did great. Thank you."

Then, as though he'd just realized he was touching her, his hands were gone, his arms crossed over his chest, and he was looking away, calling the waitress over for more coffee that she didn't want, but took anyway, because that made the mug warm enough to hold, warm enough to rewarm her.

"I don't know where, or when, though," she said. "Or who. Last time..."

Last time, she had seen her mentor, whom she knew now, but not then. And the man who had died, Bonnie's boss, whom she had never met, but they had known, the minute she described him. She'd told them he was going to die, and then he did.

"You've known about what you are for, what, a year? Less? And this is your second storm vision?" He sounded like he was making notes, even though he didn't write anything down.

"My third." The second one had been induced, her mentor calling down lightning – the most terrifying experience she'd ever had, including visions, had been standing on the rooftop watching that happen – and she'd seen half a dozen people, but none of them had called out to her. None of them had forced her to find someone, and tell what she had seen.

Genevieve had said that maybe those were natural deaths,

or older deaths that had already happened, or a dozen things that were supposed to make her feel better, that maybe not every vision she'd have would involve terrible things.

But those people were still dead, or going to die. And she couldn't do anything about it.

"Third. And you're handling them – upright, sane, and still verbal. I'd say you've got nothing to be ashamed of."

When Sergei, Genevieve's partner, said things like that, she knew he was trying to make her feel better. When her mentor said it, she was trying to build up her confidence, make her willing to try another test, learn another thing, listen to another story. And both those things were...nice. No, more than nice. After a lifetime of people -her own family- thinking she was lying, or crazy, the reassurances were a lifeline, and Ellen was smart enough to grab on with both hands.

But this man... he said it casually, almost off-handedly. Like of *course* she was managing it. Ellen wasn't sure how to deal with that.

"They're still dead," she said. "I was only able to save some of them."

That got his attention. He looked at her – straight at her, those hazel eyes looking more green than brown, and sharp as flint – and smiled. It wasn't a particularly happy smile, though.

"That's why you came to me."

---

I'D GIVEN her my best shot, reassured her of my competence, and not quoted her a fee – this one was going to be on the house, and Bonnie had known that when she sent Valere's pet Seer to me. I'd expected the girl to gasp out some thanks, grab her bag, and flee.

Instead, she sat there, staring at me like she expected me to get up and dance, or turn into a goat, or something.

I resisted the urge to check my hair, to make sure my horns weren't showing, and waited.

"I need to see this through," she said, her voice small and uncertain. Then her jaw moved again, like she was chewing something over, and she said it again, this time stronger. "I need to see this through."

Oh. Ah, hell. I worked alone. All right, sometimes I worked with the PUPs, when they called me, or if our cases collided, the way they'd done once or twice, but on my own, my own time, I wasn't a team player. My duty sergeant had made that point clear, several times during my tenure with the NYPD. My partner had been a patient man, but when he retired... yeah. Not a team player.

It wasn't just about having to hide what I was, either. Since leaving the force I'd been more or less out – not that I'd been all that "in" back then, either. I liked my space, mental and physical.

I could probably say Boo! and she'd run. She had that edge-of-skin look to her, like she was terrified but holding on through sheer grit.

Damn it. I respected grit. I thought it was dumber'n hell, but I respected it.

And if she was seeing that scene play out behind her eyes... I knew something about that, too.

"You need me," she said, her voice desperate and a little too fast. "I know what they look like. I know..."

"It's all right, girl," I said, not even pretending to be happy about it. "You don't have to convince me. If I say no you're just going to get into mischief on your own, probably, and then I'm going to have The Wren breathing down my neck, and no thank you."

Bonnie I could sweet talk and explain. Wren Valere...

Valere scared me, just a little. I had no shame in admitting that. Valere was a little crazy herself, where it mattered.

"I won't be any trouble," she promised. I gave that the once-over it deserved, and she blushed, her cheeks darkening like she knew it was a promise she was bound to break.

"I need you to agree to three things, though." I pulled my cop voice out from the box I'd shoved it in, fixing her with the "don't make me tell your parents" look that my old partner had perfected after two decades on the street. "One, that no matter what I say, no matter how it sounds, if I tell you to do something, you do it."

A single wisecrack or hesitation, and I'd hog tie her and deliver her to Wren's front door, if I had to.

She nodded.

"Two, if I decide, for any reason, that I'm doing something alone, you accept that, without back talk."

She nodded again, although with a faint hesitation. I wasn't sure I'd have believed her, if she'd agreed without hesitation. I love women, individually and as a gender, but there wasn't a one of them that accepted anything without argument. Most days, I counted that a plus, but not on the job.

"Three. You don't use current unless you clear it with me. I know you Talent, you do it like breathing, but the people we're talking to, they're not always comfortable with it, and I can't have you spooking them, or pissing them off."

I didn't expect her laugh, and didn't expect it to sound so...sweet.

"That, I can promise," she said.

Right. She was new to all this. Current probably still freaked her out worse than it did a half-headblind Null.

"Good," I said, dropping the bad cop routine. "Let's go."

I threw down enough cash on the table to cover the coffee, and stood up. She took longer to unfold herself – she was taller than me, if only by an inch or so, but it was mostly leg, like watching a giraffe find its balance, except that made her sound ungainly and she wasn't. Just... unsure.

Useless in a fight, I decided. Hopefully, it wasn't going to come to that. She'd seen me dead, not herself.

Me, and three teenagers.

If Bonnie were here, she'd point out, logically, that I might not be in danger at all if I walked away. Yeah. It wasn't a choice: I'd do whatever it took to find out who those kids were, where they were, and how to get them out of whatever danger they were in.

Bonnie knew that. Anyone who knew me, knew that.

Outside the coffee shop, I held up a hand, and then pointed with two fingers. "Go stand over there."

She looked puzzled, but did as I said, just like she'd promised. Once she was a safe distance away, I pulled out my cell phone, and turned it on. Hanging around Talent as often as I did, you learned to power down your electronics when you weren't using them, just in case. Current might run with electricity, but they didn't like sharing the same track, and current usually won.

I hit number three on my contact list, and waited until the other man picked up.

"Didier. It's Hendrickson." Not that Sergei Didier answered his phone without knowing full well who was on the other side, but my momma had drilled manners into me. "Just wanted to let you and your bird know that I've got possession of your fledgling."

"Good." Didier was his usual urbane self, but I'd known the human long enough to be able to detect relief in that smooth voice. "I assume she has told you what is bothering her?"

"Oh yes. I've decided to take the case."

"I thought that you might." There was a pause, almost imperceptible. "And I should tell Genevieve that her student will be available for lessons, or is she otherwise engaged?"

That got a laugh out of me. "She's determined to play hooky." I slid a glance at her. She was still waiting, patient the way people who've spent a lot of their life waiting get. Her hands were at her sides, not fiddling with anything, her eyes were soft and her face almost relaxed. She looked almost passive, but I could feel the tension in her body. It was just coiled down deep, and under an almost scary level of control. Whatever I might have to worry about her current, leak wasn't going to be part of it.

"Danny." And there was Wren on the other end of the line: even if I hadn't known, the static filling the spaces between words a dead giveaway. A Talent, agitated, near electronics. I hoped Didier had a spare phone handy.

"Valere."

"She shouldn't be out and about."

If half of what I'd heard and suspected was true, Valere was right about that. "She's invested in this. I send her back with a pat on her head, tell her not to worry about it.... How well would you have taken to that?"

There was a long, dire silence; even the static went dead.

Then: "You take care of her, Danny. Keep her safe."

I closed my eyes, feeling an impossible weariness wrap itself around me, all the way down to my bones. It was a too-familiar feeling, these days. I didn't need a shrink to tell me I was on the edge of burnout. For every kid I found and brought home, five more went missing. I was starting to wonder if any one person could really make a difference. But making a difference was the only sanity I had.

"Understood, Valere."

I ended the call, turned off the phone, and put it back in my pocket. I turned and studied my new temporary companion. She looked back at me, still waiting. Tall, yeah, and not lean, and not graceful exactly, but there was power coiled under there, like the lacrosse players I'd see out in the Green, sometimes, or the field hockey girls. Potential, that was the word I'd been looking for.

"What do you see?" she asked, finally. Her voice carried without stress across the sidewalk, despite the usual ceaseless noise of traffic and sirens and the construction they were still doing up on 53rd.

"Trouble," I said honestly.

For some reason, that seemed to please her.

---

ELLEN KNEW it was rude to stare – and in this world she'd fallen into probably dangerous – but she couldn't stop herself from looking at him, even if she had to turn away every time he looked back, like some dumb, giggling teenager. His words – she shouldn't feel flattered by them. She'd worked so hard all her life, not to be trouble, to stay out of trouble, not give anyone – her parents, her teachers, the few friends she could keep – cause to turn away, that his words should have hurt.

But he wasn't like her parents, or her teachers. He wasn't even like the other Talent, not the woman who had lured her away with promises of being "special" and then abandoned her, not even like Bonnie and Genevieve and the others, the ones who were showing her how to use current, teaching her how to control it. And he wasn't *normal*, wasn't...what did Genevieve call them? Wasn't a Null, thinking that she was crazy because she saw things, felt things, they didn't.

He wasn't human. Like the...the other things, the things she saw out of the corner of her eye, the ones Wren said were called fatae. They were real, she wasn't crazy. But most of them were.... Too weird. He looked human, if you didn't see the horns, or look too closely at his face, the way his ears weren't quite rounded, and his cheekbones were too high.

But his eyes were kind, and his voice was soft, even when he was obviously annoyed, and there was something about him that made her feel like for once, she didn't have to be careful, that she wasn't going to break something, ruin everything.

That he wouldn't turn away, no matter how badly she fucked up.

Ellen didn't trust that feeling. But when he called her trouble, it felt like...like something that didn't hurt.

And maybe, she didn't quite dare to think, if she could help him, if her vision saved those lives, saved *his* life....

She couldn't think that far, what that might mean

THE HOME BASE of Sylvan Investigations wasn't all that, but it was in a good enough part of Manhattan to reassure clients, and a boring enough part of town that I could afford the rent without dipping into my pitiful excuse for a pension. Mostly.

My shadow looked around the front room without a comment. I tried to see it through her eyes: windowless, painted an allegedly-soothing shade of cream that wasn't aging well, two broad-leafed plants in the corner that needed repotting already. There was a wooden secretary's desk dead center, three-quarters of the way back, with a scattering of papers and a hand-sized intercom system set-up, even though I'd never hired a secretary in my entire career. The look, overall, was bare bones, but that was okay: the people who hired me weren't looking for pretty. They wanted competence.

Shadow finished sizing the place up, and if she had an opinion, she didn't show it. "What now?" she asked.

"Now, we go to work. Or rather, I do. You're going to be useless right now." I meant it jokingly, but the expression on her face reminded me that this wasn't Bonnie I was talking to. I had to watch myself, watch my words.

"You know about current, and electricity?"

She bit her lip, and was obviously thinking carefully

about what to say. Good. Caution wasn't a bad trick. "Current and electricity run together, come from the same sources, have a lot of the same properties. We - Talent - can channel both of them, they won't harm us, but current's the one we can shape and use. It's the stuff they used to call magic in the old days."

"Yeah. Which means that you people are pretty much shit out of luck when it comes to things like computers, because that ability to channel also means you're walking, talking lightning rods. But I find them, computers, damned useful in my job."

"So what do I do?"

I nodded at the secretary's desk. "There's a pad of paper, and pencils, maybe even a pen with ink. Sit down and write out everything, and I mean *everything* you can remember from your visions. Visuals, feelings, hell, even what you were tasting in your mouth at the time."

"You think that's important?" "I don't know that it's not."

She considered that, letting it settle in her brain before nodding. I was starting to like the girl; she had a solid brain between her ears. With Valere's mentoring and Bonnie's guidance, she just might make it.

"You want coffee?" I asked. "The machine's old, but it does decent enough work."

"I don't drink coffee," she said, and my opinion dropped a little. I also wondered how the hell she was surviving, living with Valere. Maybe she teamed up with Didier and drank tea?

"I like my caffeine carbonated," she said, almost apologetically.

"Oh, right. There's some soda in the fridge but I don't know how old it is. Does that stuff go bad?"

"Not that my taste buds ever noticed." She went to the little fridge tucked under the far counter, and pulled out a can, frowning at it. "Yeah, that'll do."

My obligations dealt with, I opened the door to the back office, and went in. I left the door open, just in case.

I'd upgraded to a sweet little laptop a few months ago, which was one of the reasons I was leery of letting a Talent – especially an untrained one – anywhere near it. The older desktops were easier to ground. Nick, one of Bonnie's team-mates, said that tablets were actually safer around Talent – he used one, when he did his Talent-hacking thing – but my hands never fit on the keyboards.

"All right, Chinjy, give me what you've got."

The Child in Jeopardy site was a relatively recent thing, compiling every Amber alert, every state's child welfare filing, every missing person's report filed on a minor, swept and sorted into a database that could be broken down by gender, location, description, and type of abduction, and multiples of same. You had to be licensed and accredited to get access, hoops upon hoops set in place to prevent abuse and satisfy the privacy rights advocates. But the retrieval rate for missing minors had gone up seven percent since we - private investigators and other non-government interests - were able to use it, and that made all the hoops, and the yearly fee, worth it to me.

The sheer number of names in the database always made me want to drink. I'd learned to do a tunnel vision sort of thing, only look at the ones who fell within the parameters of my case, and never, ever for fucking ever look when I wasn't on a case. I focused on the girls, narrowed down the parameters, and still got over thirty kickbacks just in the past six months. I needed more.

"Hey-" and for a second I couldn't remember her name, only "Shadow", and I didn't think that would go over well. But before I could remember, she was in the doorway, hesitant, like she wasn't sure she was allowed in.

Computer. Right. I'd warned her off.

"How you coming with those notes?" I asked.

She held up the pad, and I could see that it had been filled with writing and a not-bad pencil sketch of three faces. "The moment I started, it all kind of fell out."

"Talk to me. What's most significant, most memorable about them?"

She hesitated, and I realized that her body language wasn't just about proximity to the computer, or me. Something else was going on. Then something clicked for her, you could see it in her face. "What?"

It took a second for her to put the thought into words. "The kids. The ones I saw. They... their skin color was off, and it threw me. I'd thought there was a scrim between us, or they were blue from the cold, but the more I tried to remember, the more I... their skin was weird. And they had gills. On their necks." She raised her hand and placed it on the side of her own neck, like you would if something bit you.

Well, hell. I closed the laptop and stood up, palming the taser stashed in the desk drawer. "Right. Time to do a different kind of research."

---

I FELT BAD, dragging Shadow everywhere, but I didn't even suggest her staying back in the office. First, I was under orders to keep her safe, and while I didn't think anything was going to go down in my office – I'd been working there for six years now and the most excitement we'd ever had was when a rabid squirrel decided to take up residence in the bathroom down the hall – I couldn't say for sure trouble *wasn't* going to suddenly show up.

And anyway, she wasn't going to stay put, not when we might have a lead on the missing kids. I knew that already. She might be a mouse, but if you poked her, she roared.

We took the 5 line downtown. It was the start of rush hour,

so we didn't catch seats, but there was room to railhang without getting squashed up against other people. I'm a New Yorker through and through but I hate the subway, especially when it's crowded. People tend to cluster toward me, not even realizing it, and I've got a touch of clausto to begin with. My mom might've spent most of her career before me on a ship, but my fatae genetics were geared more to open hillsides and relative solitude. I never did understand why I stayed in New York, except I couldn't quite wrap my horns around leaving.

Shadow swayed a bit, swinging toward me, then catching herself. She had that slightly dreamy look on her face, one I recognized from long exposure: she was jamming with the current that ran through the underground tracks, looping around the electricity that powered the trains, the lights, streaming through stone-carved tunnels, winding in around itself and just waiting for a Talent to come siphon it off, just a little bit, a hit to sooth the stress of a long day.

Or so I'd been told. All I could feel was the rackety-clack of the rail under us, the occasional hitching scream of the brakes, and random cold bursts of the train's straining air conditioning. But it was nice to watch her face, see the tiny stress lines around her mouth ease. She had a nice mouth, wide, and full, but not pouty or posed. You could describe it in crude terms, yeah, but my mother did her best to raise me to not be a dick. Anyway, all I could think was that she probably had an awesome smile. If she ever smiled.

"What are we – where are we going?" she asked, not opening her eyes.

"What, you're not going to just trail after me like a good shadow, trusting my decision-making?" The moment the words fell out of my mouth I wished I could recall them, remembering how badly she'd reacted before. Her eyes opened then, and she stared at me, judging something.

I guess I passed, because she shook her head, and closed

her eyes again, letting her body sway as we slid around a curve in the tunnel. "I don't trust anybody anymore," she said. "But I'm good at following."

There was something in that, some depth in her words that lost me. I'm usually pretty good at sounding the depths, too. I decided to focus on the hunt, and worry about my shadow later.

"Yeah, you proved that earlier," I admitted. "We're going to talk to some people, best you stay quiet and just pay attention. If you see anything, or you remember anything, tuck it into your brain and tell me when we're alone."

She clearly remembered her earlier promise, because she just nodded once, and followed me up out of the station at our stop, down John Street and into the chaos of the South Street Seaport. Home to some of the most comprehensive kitsch in all Manhattan, outdoing even Times Square on summer after-noons when half the world and three-quarters of Wall Street were there for the view, the booze, and the mingling. I'd spent more than a few hours here himself, killing time and a few beers, watching the tall ships and the tourist boats.

This time, I bypassed the flurry of the Seaport itself, dodging buskers, tour-hawkers, and tourists, Ellen at my heel. Under the overhang, and down past the old fish market, where the East River greenway began.

This had been easier when it was still run down and dingy; nobody questioned a guy sitting on the bench, talking to himself. But then, I wasn't by myself, now.

That would make it easier, and possibly harder. "Sit."

She sat, legs stretched out in front of her, and damn the girl had some legs. She leaned back against the bench, her elbows braced, and lifted her face to the sun, then looked at me when I sat next to her.

"Whatever happens, just pretend I'm talking to you."

"Whatever," and she lazily waved a hand. It wasn't a perfect act, but it was pretty good. I turned so that it seemed as though I was facing her, and watched the walkway over her shoulder.

"I'm here looking for information. You know that I pay fair for whatever I get."

She shook her head, and smiled. Two men came along the path, talking to each other; one of them noticed her legs, the other kept yakking, and then they were gone. To my right, something in the sparse shrubbery between the walkway and the street made a rustling noise. It could have been the wind, or a squirrel, or a rat.

"Come on, don't waste my time." I played irritated, annoyed, no time to waste. Truth was, I'd be willing to sit here all night if that's what it took. I'd done it before.

"More children gone walkabye?"

My shadow jumped a little; the voice was right by her elbow, way too close, and way too loud for a whisper. I might have jumped too, if I hadn't been expecting it.

If someone weren't paying attention, they'd think that a bush had overgrown the verge, greenstick branches reaching over the bench, buds of leaves too small for full-summer and the faintest hint of fading yellow flowers. Then they'd realize that the branches were too thick, the leaves and flowers moving with a slow, steady pulse, and then, if they were paying attention, they'd see the eyes, heavy black orbs, and the small, sucker-shaped mouth.

"You know me," I said, keeping it casual. The trick to dealing with fatae was to never let them think that you needed them. Humans liked to be needed, got off on it, could be flattered into giving it away. Fatae saw it as a chance to build obligation, accumulate debt they could turn around and use for themselves.

Of course, they want to be needed, too. The desire to show off how much smarter you were is universal to every species that could communicate.

"We know you," it agreed. "Animal, vegetable, or mineral?"

"Fish," I said.

"Ah."

One branchlet touched Ellen's shoulder, and she managed not to jump or shudder. Her expression wasn't too happy, though.

"Talent," it said. "Shiny-sharp."

"Valere's," I said, and the branchlet paused, squeezed once, and fell away. Her eyes were wide, but she didn't react. Someday – soon, I was betting – she'd be able to singe grabby hands on her own. But for now, a mentor's protection was… well, part of why Talent had mentors.

"You have anything?" I didn't want to waste time.

"Wrong time, right place. Fish go missing, weeks ago. Think first it was prank or school-joke, but they not come back. School scared, swim back north. Think shark got 'em."

Close enough, if not the kind of sharks the school had been thinking.

"You're a pal," I said, and passed something flat-palmed over Ellen's shoulder, where it disappeared into the leaflets.

<hr>

ELLEN FOCUSED ON BREATHING. If she kept breathing, she'd be all right, even when that…thing touched her, sticky-sharp pressure on her shoulder, on her neck, and she wouldn't turn around to look, didn't want to see anything more than what she'd already glimpsed out of the side of her eyes. She focused instead on Danny, on his face, his hands moving as he talked. He had nice hands, strong ones. They looked like they'd be capable of doing a lot more than hailing a cab or typing. She moved her gaze up to his face, the rough lines of his jaw, the curls plastered now in the summer heat against his forehead. He had cute ears. She noticed that in passing, not letting herself smile at the thought. His attention was on whatever was touching her, talking to it, listening to the hot whisper that she didn't dare listen to, or she would turn to look at it, and she knew if she did it would be over, she would freak, she would break her promise to Danny, and right now that promise – that she would follow, and she would tell him everything, and he'd find a way out of the nightmare of her vision, was all that was keeping her intact.

"*Feel your core,*" Genevieve had told her. "*Reach in, down into where you feel the most centered, the most* real *and shove your hands into that, feel what's there.*"

Ellen'd spent so many years being told she was crazy, just looking for attention, imagining things…. When the Central Park cult leader had told her she was special, that she had something, and then cast her out, Ellen had decided that they were all right, that everything she felt, everything she saw, thought she'd seen, just meant she was crazy, broken.

She still wasn't sure she wasn't. But when she breathed deep and reached, the way Genevieve had taught her, the static prickle of warmth and comfort that greeted her, stinging up her arms and spine, down her legs, connecting her to every inch of her body and the static waiting beyond….

It made her feel like broken was another word for amazing.

And then the *thing* touched her again, and her eyes went wide, instinctively falling into her core the rest of the world fading to a blur of grey sounds, wrapping herself in the static, the *current* that rested inside her, and suddenly she could see the three teens again, the blue tinge of their skin, the dampness of their clothing, the faded, haunted expression in their eyes, not hurt or angry but lost, so lost, and she needed to find them, she needed to wipe that look away and if she just reached, she knew that she could find them, could-

"Ellen."

She opened her eyes, not remembering having closed them,

and Danny's hands were on hers, his face inches away, his eyes intent enough on her to be scary. The thing behind her was gone, she knew that without looking.

"It wasn't going to hurt you. It was just curious. You're strong, we can all feel that. Some of them get a little grabby, but... "

She almost couldn't remember what he was talking about. "I saw them again."

He pulled back, his expression changing from concern to something sharper, more hungry. "Another vision?"

"Not a new vision, it was... I saw it again, only closer, clearer.More details, things I missed last time."

"Is that normal?"

She almost cried at the absurdity of the question, and his face changed again as though realizing that yeah, she had no idea. It was subtle, something around his eyes and mouth, the way they tensed and relaxed, but she could read them like signposts, and somehow that let her breathe more easily.

"You'll remember it now, though?" he asked.

"I...yes." Before, the visions had been like nightmares, fading wisps that couldn't be clutched at, disappearing almost the moment she became aware of them. This time it was different.

Different worried her, but she thought maybe it was the way Genevieve had said, that the more control she got, the better she'd be at this, more able to control it. Control was the name of the game.

Danny stood up, slipping sunglasses back on, pushing them up the bridge of his nose and looking away, over across the water. "My snitch confirmed that several merfolk disappeared from here, so we're on the right track."

"Mer...mermaids?"

"Don't ever call 'em that if you want to step into the ocean without fear, ever again. Merfolk, or mers."

She nodded, storing that information away with everything else she'd been learning. "They disappeared from here?"

"Under this very dock, it says."

It being the thing that had been behind her, that had touched her. She resisted another shudder, and instead got up off the bench - noting as she did so that what she'd thought was a bush was now gone, as though it had gotten up on its roots and tip-toed away - and walked across to the railing overlooking the water. Not really the ocean, if she remembered the maps right. The end of the East River and the start of the bay, waters mixing and mingling with the tides. She tried to imagine beings swimming underneath, living in those waters, and was surprised to find that it was easy enough. She'd already been introduced to a woman who lived in, no, *belonged to* a tree, after all. Why not mers?

"Danny?"

It was the first time she'd used my name. That was my first thought, even as I got up to join her where she stood along the railing. The slightly briny air made me even more aware of the sweat on my scalp and back, while her skin practically shimmered in the sunlight, bringing out dark copper highlights along her cheekbone. First Nation blood in there, maybe. Or just that I don't know enough about human races to catch the clues; they were all so much alike, compared to the fatae, I found it difficult to take the divisions seriously.

"Did you remember something else?" I asked, resting my hands on the wooden railing, and looking not at her, but the ocean spread out in front of us. If I narrowed my gaze enough, I could block out the boats and the buildings, and almost imagine the city didn't exist around us, just for an instant.

"No. I...." She kept looking out across the water too, her

head turning slightly, scanning from left to right, with the longest hesitation toward the right. "I can feel them."

"What?" Okay, that wasn't what I'd been expecting. I didn't know seers could do that. "When you say feel, you mean...?"

"I don't know. You, ah, you feel different. You, the...the thing that touched me, PB – all the fatae I've met so far, you all feel different, but when you're near me I can feel you, recognize you. I can feel them here, too. Or, something, anyway. Something that feels like what I saw in the vision." Her forehead crinkled again, trying to get the right words. "Mers, I guess, but specific. Familiar feels."

Talent, I'd been told, could pick up signatures, the feeling current got after it's been wrapped around another Talent, or something. But it took training, and a level of skill there was no way Shadow had, not yet. Still, she'd already had them in her head, their current, and their fate, zapped into her brain. That could be enough of a connection. Maybe.

Magic. I might be part of it, but that didn't mean I understood it. Not really. I didn't let that stop me, though.

"Can you follow it? The feeling?"

"I... yes. Maybe. Yes." Her breath hitched, and she nodded.

Yeah, she could do that.

From what I'd already figured about Shadow, she didn't have a hell of a lot of self-confidence, and doubly so when it came to what she could do, what she *was*. So 'maybe-yes' was enough for me. "But we need to get out on the water. I can't follow it from here."

Oh, I so really hadn't wanted to hear that.

---

Once I'd accepted the fact that we were going to have to get our toes wet, metaphorically if hopefully not literally, we had to find a way to get out there. I considered and then discarded the idea of renting one of the two-person kayaks that people took out on the Hudson - with my luck we'd capsize and drown, and no thanks. There were half a dozen charters and ferries that worked the rivers, but they all kept to a regular route, and I wasn't going to rely on Shadow's scent trail, such as it was, sticking to regular routes. If our missing kids had been taken, odds were low it had been on a registered passenger ferry. So I went an alternative route. Or tried to, anyway.

"So, you want to hire me, but you don't know for how long, or where you want to go?" The guy leaned against the wooden sign advertising his fishing boat, and shook his head. "Sorry, no."

"It's nothing illegal. Or even immoral." I'd already showed him my PI license, but that hadn't impressed him much. To be fair, it didn't impress many people. I might look like the quintessential ideal of a New Yorker, as filtered through Hollywood, but I didn't look much like a hard-bitten PI, I guess. Maybe I should switch out the baseball cap for a fedora, or something.

"Ffffft." The captain made his opinion of illegality or immorality clear. "S'not the laws it's the cost. Fuel's too expensive to be doing that. You want to wander, you want a smaller boat. Or a sailboat."

Those were actually two things I really didn't want. But he had a point.

"Got someone in mind?" I asked. Recommendations were always useful, even if I didn't take them.

"Talk to Tal Berthiaume, captain a' the *Mercy Me*. They've got a slip up at the Basin. *Mercy Me* doesn't do charters, but you're interesting enough a request, Tal might bite."

---

I'D NEVER ACTUALLY BEEN to the Boat Basin - it was out of my usual range, as far on the Upper West Side as you could get without actually hitting New Jersey. It had the usual blend of rundown and very expensive that you get at working marinas, but the view up and down the Hudson was definitely million-aire's row. I could see why people lived here, year round.

Shadow, and I needed to stop thinking of her as that before it stuck, was, well, shadowing my heels without a word, her gaze taking everything in. Clearly, she'd never been here before, either. "Can you imagine living on a boat?" she asked, her voice sounding younger and more gleefully innocent than it had been before.

"No." I could, actually, but it wasn't a pleasant thought. Give me a nice apartment in a nice building, where the bathroom has room to turn around, and you don't get seagulls crapping in your morning coffee.

"That's the *Mercy Me*," she said, pointing down one of the wooden extensions, clearly a lower-rent section of the Basin.

She was a sailboat. Maybe there was a technical term for the size or how many sails or whatever, but "sailboat" summed it up for me: sails the color of, well, canvas run up on masts, the ship itself sleek and clean, painted a dark blue, with pale yellow trim. The railings were varnished wood, and you could see the care that maintained them, even from here.

"Anyone home?" I called, as we reached its berth.

"Hang on," a voice called, and then someone appeared from below the floor – the deck.

Legs. Long legs, but not skinny, curving under shorts that came a respectable way down the thigh, connected to a torso clad in a white T-shirt, arms just as long and curved, and my gaze connected with the face that went with that body, and it was looking at me with bemused patience.

Next to me, Shadow let out an unkind snicker.

"I was told you might be agreeable to a day-hire," I said. If they thought getting caught staring was going to discomfit me, they were in for a surprise. I might not give in to the more basic urges of my faun genetics, but lack of shame was one of the things I'd found useful.

"Today? Local charter, out and back again by sunset?" When I nodded, the ship's master went on, "Cash, in advance. Five hundred. There's an ATM at the dock, if you need it."

"You don't want to know-"

"Nope. You're hiring me to take your lady on a romantic cruise around the island, that's your business. I got rent to make. The money gets you on-board, soda and water included, but if you want food you gotta bring your own. No glass, no drugs, no booze. If the cops board us and you're not clean, I'll hand you over to them without a second thought."

"Got it." I turned to Ellen, meaning to give her my ATM card and send her to get the cash out while I discussed any further terms with our captain, then realized that handing my ATM card to a Talent – a powerful and mostly untrained Talent – was one of my less thought-out ideas, unless I wanted to have to stop by the bank and get a new card after her current had demagnetized the damn thing.

"I'll be right back."

---

BY THE TIME I got back – after having a slight panic about leaving enough money in my account to cover the bills that would be paid in the next day or so – Ellen and our Captain had settled in, Shadow curled up on a wooden locker that was doubling as a bench, and the Captain doing competent-looking things with ropes.

I hesitated, then gave myself a hard shove, and climbed, rather inelegantly, onto the ship itself. The moment my feet hit the deck, my entire body swayed once, a slow rolling movement I felt from the soles of my feet all the way up my spine and into the back of my head, and it took every bit of stubborn I had not to turn around and get the hell *off* that boat.

My mother might have been a sailor, but water and I did not get along.

"Captain Tal says all I have to do is stand in the front of the ship and point, and she can get us there," Ellen said.

Tal – I was guessing it was short for Talia, or something – shrugged. "You're paying, you get to choose. If we start to get somewhere we shouldn't be, I'll tell you."

"I could always use some help with that," I said, not even meaning to turn on the charm, but Tal's face reserve a little, the way people always did.

If I'd been full-blood, she might have offered me more than a smile. If I'd been full-blood, I wouldn't be here in the first place.


Tab Berthiaume – Tal was short for Thea Anna-Louise, Ellen had learned while I was gone and no, the good captain apparently hadn't forgiven her parents yet – was a good sailor, and the *Mercy Me* seemed to be a good ship. I spent the first hour trying not to throw up, and the second hour wondering why I hadn't let myself throw up more often.

"You're really crap on boats, aren't you?" Ellen seemed surprised, and not inclined to tease, although I suspected it was less having to do with kindness and more not being sure how I'd react. Someone had told her to sit down and shut up a load too often, but I didn't have the energy to do any reassuring just then.

"Yeah well, I'm built for ground." I took a sip of the ginger ale Tal had provided, trying to ignore the rise and dip of the boat as we cut through the water. We couldn't go exactly the direction Ellen pointed at, but the winds seemed to be behaving, far as I could tell, taking us sideways in the direction we wanted.

If all else failed, we'd been told, there was an engine that would get us there.

"Landlubber?" Tal had used that phrase first, less kindly than Ellen did.

"I'm half-faun." She knew I wasn't human, but she was still learning the *Cosa Nostradamus*, and even Talent had trouble with all the various breeds. Hell, I wasn't sure I could name them all, and it was my *job* to know 'em. "Named for the god Faunus, although we could just as easily have taken Pan's name. Woodland revels are more our thing, not seaborne hijinks."

Woodland revels, meaning indulgences of all sorts, especially sex. The few cousins I'd met over the years took the "life is a party" philosophy to heart and groin, and they were charming enough to make humans – and a lot of other fatae – go along with them. Unfortunately, they matched charm with an utter and absolute inability to think about consequences, long or short term.

I didn't spend a lot of time with my cousins.

The *Mercy Me* hit another swell, and I had to interrupt my explanation with another bolt for the bucket.

"Nice impression you're getting of me," I said wearily. I'd done worse, in front of more people – the first dead body we found on my first month on the job, in mid-summer, was high up there – but this wasn't so good for my ego, either.

"Actually, it is kind of nice," Ellen said. "Everyone I've met in the city so far is so... competent. It's unnerving." She swallowed, her throat working visibly, and looked away, like she thought she'd said too much and didn't know how to take it back.

I just laughed. "Yeah. Seeing as who you've been hanging with, I can imagine the competence level has been nauseatingly high." Maybe I should have used another word... but no, my stomach stayed quiet for the moment. "If it helps any, Valere unnerves *everyone*."

"She didn't want to take me. I know that. I don't know why –" She broke off what she was saying, coming to point like a rescue dog catching scent of a live one.

"There."

I followed where she was looking, and sighed. "South Jersey. Well, could have been worse, could have been Staten Island." I don't usually indulge in the time-honored borough-bashing so beloved of my fellow citizens, but I'd a grudge about Staten Island that wasn't going away any time soon.

———

Danny had Captain Tal cruise along the coastline, just outside the markers that showed where they shouldn't go, until Ellen could say for certain where the trail led, and he marked it on a map he'd pulled out of his jacket pocket. Then Danny nodded at Tal, and the *Mercy Me* headed back to the Basin, where the captain saw them off with an invitation to hire her any time again. Apparently, having someone spend most of the day throwing up in a bucket wasn't enough to put her off, so long as they paid in cash.

The investigator still looked a little green, and he was staggering rather than swaggering as they walked down the pier, but Ellen wasn't going to point out any of that. The sway of the boat had actually felt a lot like current, the outsides finally matching the way she felt inside during a thunderstorm, or when Genevieve had her try to draw down current from a man-made source and then reshape it to her own needs.

She wasn't going to say any of that, either. But she held the knowledge to herself, that sailing was a thing she could do. It was a small thing, probably a stupid thing, but it was *hers*.

"So what now?" The more she focused on the connection,

the more the need to find those three teenagers chewed at her. Now that they had an idea where to go, she wanted to go *now*.

"The fact that you were able to pinpoint them probably means that they're still alive," Danny said. "And the fact that they're still alive means that whoever has them intends to keep them around for a while longer."

Ellen listened to what he was saying, and thought that she heard something else, underneath.

"But what do they want them for?" she asked. "And..." And what is being done to them? She didn't finish that question out loud. She knew enough to know that it probably wasn't good.

Danny sighed, and shook his head, removing the baseball cap and wiping his arm across his forehead to clear away the sweat. His curls were sea- and sweat-damp, the fine lines around his eyes more visible now than they'd been under direct sunlight. If you could ignore the horns more visible through his damp curls, he looked a hundred percent human, and really tired.

"I want to look at a better map, see if I can pinpoint exactly where you were targeting, and also figure out the best way to get there. I don't suppose you drive?"

Ellen blinked. "Of course I do."

That got a laugh out of him. "Right. Suburban girl, right?"

"City boy" she retorted, the words slipping out of her mouth before she realized it. She knew – she *knew* – he wasn't going to yell at her for sass, or get pissed off, but her breath still hitched for a second, her body bracing itself.

"I can drive," he said, mildly. "Only last time I did, it was a patrol car, and my instincts are not what you want out among civilians."

She was diverted, trying to imagine him in a uniform. "Did you ever do a high speed chase?"

"Never once. But I do occasionally forget to stop for red

lights. Or stop signs. It's safer just to not let me behind the wheel."

"I don't have a job, to rent a car, though." Ellen felt she should make a clean breast of everything. "I don't even have a bank account, or a cable bill, or anything. They ask you for all that, when you rent." She'd come to New York with a friend, who had rented their car, and she remembered the excess of paperwork that had been required.

"So I rent, and we put you down as a driver. You're staying with Valere?"

"No." She had slept on the couch for the first month, until Genevieve got her office cleared out to use as a second bedroom. Now she had her own place, an off-the-books sublease, but it was so tiny, and she spent so little time there, she'd never gotten around to acquiring Stuff. Not that she had much; she'd left home with just her backpack, and living in the Park the way she'd done, you didn't keep much in the way of belongings. Even if you tried, they'd disappear pretty soon.

"Hrm." He made a noise she didn't understand, but then they were on the street and he was raising his hand to hail a cab, and she didn't want to ask any more questions while they were in public, even if it was only one cabbie listening in.

"How urgent does it feel?" he asked, out of the silence. Ellen was taken aback – she'd slipped easily into follow- the-lead, and wasn't expecting to be put on the spot again.

"Urgent," she said. She didn't know what not-urgent felt like; the people she Saw were about to get dead, so urgent was the only way she knew to feel. Then she thought about it a little more. When she'd Seen Genevieve and the guy who had died, Stosser, it had felt urgent, too. But nothing had happened for a couple of days after, and Genevieve hadn't died at all, because... because something had changed. Because she had changed something, by telling them.

So. Urgent, yes. Death was always urgent. But maybe they had time.

"They're not dead yet." She was pretty sure about that, especially after what Danny had said. Pretty sure, but not absolutely. She licked her lips, trying not to think about the cabbie who might or might not be eavesdropping. She tried not to think about her mother, who had told her all these things she said she saw meant that she was crazy, or lying. She tried not to think about anything, except the sense of three figures, ghostly but real, lingering in her brain.

No, not her brain. Genevieve had explained that. Her core. The place where current coiled inside, the magic everyone had access to, but only Talent could handle, channel, and manipulate. Only Talent, like her, could hold inside.

She was a Storm-Seer. She Saw things in the current that even other Talent couldn't. She saw Death, and the dying. She wasn't crazy, she wasn't lying, and Danny needed her in order to find them.

Had Genevieve felt different, after the other one, Stosser, had died? Yes. A subtle, slight difference, like feeling silk under your hand instead of silky cotton, but there. Maybe. If that's what the difference was.

She needed more visions to learn what they meant, but she never wanted to have another vision, ever.

"Can you feel anything more than that?" He was pushing, but he wasn't pushing *her*, he was pushing for *them*. That made it okay.

"Hurt. Weak. Angry. Afraid. Angry most of all." That was what had reached her, their anger and fear; they did not want to die.

"At risk?"

She thought, reaching mental hands down the way Genevieve had taught her, stroking the waves of current in her core, letting the ripples run over invisible fingers until the knowledge reached her brain.

"Yes."

"Do you need to get anything from your apartment?"

He was taking her with him. He'd promised, and yet the confirmation was equal parts relief and fear. Relief, because she needed to do this, needed to see it through, to know that yes, she had helped, that it wasn't just chance, that there was a *reason* that she Saw all this. And fear because... well, she might be crazy but she wasn't stupid.

"No." She'd spent days in the same clothes, before. She could buy a toothbrush and a comb, if needed, and they weren't about to go hungry. Everything else was just details.

"Right. I need to get a few things from the office, and," he checked his watch, "yeah, there's enough time to swing by and rent a car."

Ellen decided not to tell him that the *Mission: Impossible* theme just started playing in her head.

---

WHEN WE GOT BACK to the office, I sent Ellen off to pick up some road trip essentials – water, soda, sandwiches, and a stack of whatever daily newspapers were still on the stands. We could have picked all that up once we were out of the city, but there was something I needed to do that required her being out of earshot.

But the voice that picked up on the other end of the line was male, not female.

"Exactly how fucked up is she?"

To give Didier credit, he didn't hesitate, or ask what I was talking about, or who.

"We don't know. Bad, but not broken."

"If I'd thought she was broken I wouldn't have let her stick around," I said impatiently. Jesus, did they think I was an idiot, or that masochistic?

"A purely clinical assessment?" Sergei went on. "She's got some serious self-worth issues, probably inevitable from second-guessing her sanity for the past ten years, once her Talent kicked in and nobody told her what was happening. She then fell in with a group that first told her she was special and then rejected her, and was then informed that she was not only not-crazy, but she had a skillset that was going to direct her life for, well, the rest of her life. Within those parameters, she's not fucked up at all."

"Within those parameters." Like saying a cobra wasn't dangerous, within the parameters of it being able to kill you with one shot if you disturbed it, and oh guess what, you won't see it until you step on it.

"Is there a problem?"

"No." I was used to working with high-res Talent, and poking at temperamental fatae, and going toe-to-toe with the least-appealing of humanity. Relatively speaking, this was a piece of cake. "I just wanted to know where the stress lines were."

"So we shouldn't expect her home tonight?"

And damned if Didier didn't have the Big Bad Daddy voice down perfect. I almost felt guilty.

"I need her to keep me on track, to find these kids." I could do it myself, but it would take longer. And, I'd promised her.

"If she can help you, it will help her."

"Yeah."

"Tell her to ping Wren if anything, and I mean *anything* goes to hell."

I blinked, and cursed myself for an idiot. Just because I couldn't use the ping, and neither could a human like Didier, that was no reason to ignore a damned useful tool.

"I'll do that."

The external door to the office opened, and I reached across my desk for the box I'd pulled out of the lower drawer before Didier had answered the phone. "Gotta go. Give the little woman my best," I said, and hung up before Didier finished laughing.

"Danny?"

She came into the inner sanctum's doorway, but didn't pass the threshold. She wasn't carrying anything, so I assumed that she'd put the bags down already.

"Checking in with another client," I said, lying smoothly. If her self-esteem issues were as serious as it seemed, then the idea that I was checking in with her mentor – okay, her mentor's significant other – wouldn't help any, no matter how normal a thing it was.

Normal if she were a normal teenaged Talent, I reminded myself. She wasn't normal, and she wasn't a teenager. I was painfully aware of both facts just then, as she leaned against the doorframe, for once not over-conscious of herself, and watched me.

She was a long drink of water, strong-shouldered and nicely tapered, and when she stopped worrying about other people noticing her, she had a regal sort of grace that matched her face. She was young, yeah, but in no way shape or form a child.

Fortunately, I was older and had learned how to put a lockdown on my libido before she was even born. No matter her age, she was damaged; the usual flirt-work pattern I had with Bonnie was not the way to go here.

"Car's reserved. There's a toiletries kit in the bathroom, under the sink. Grab it and let's go." I opened the box in my hand, and took out the extra case of bullets. I hadn't needed to shoot at anything other than a target in years, but I never assumed that was going to be the situation going forward.

"She's doing what?" Wren Valere put down the set of locks she had been playing with, and looked incredulously at her partner. "She was supposed to tell him what she Saw, and then come home, not run off playing Private Eye."

Sergei didn't disagree with her, but Hendrickson had been telling him what was going down, not asking permission. "Danny said that she was helping him track down the missing teens, something about her vision maintaining a thread?"

"Huh." Wren considered that. "A variant on a signature, maybe?" She wasn't all that interested in the hows of current, just so long as she could make it work. "Okay, I can see that, and why he'd take full advantage. No dummy, our Danny. But–" She bit down on what she was going to say. "No, I'm overreacting. Danny's a perfectly responsible adult, most of the time, and he won't let her get into trouble. And it's good that she get a first-hand look at the fatae community, right?"

"Right."

Sergei didn't quite trust her calm. His partner, normally unflappable, had been decidedly flapped ever since she accepted the mentorship of a half-grown, totally untrained Talent, and this should have sent her into a small panic, not calmed her down.

"And he'll be able to take care of her. Unless they run into another Talent. If they do, she's helpless. She barely knows how to maintain her own core, she's barely at first-level cantrips, and if she gets hit with another vision? She's a sitting target when that happens."

Wren Valere took a shallow breath, and leaned back against the sofa, staring out at the brilliant view out her apartment windows. Sergei waited.

"I'm doing that thing where you roll your eyes and tell me every mentor in the entire history of mentoring has had the exact same doubts and panics."

"You are."

"And Ellen's smart, and reasonably savvy, and oh by the way not an idiot teenager amuck with hormones and the need to show off."

"Exactly."

"And the best way for her to stop being afraid of her visions is to see, first-hand, that they can be used in a proactive way, too. That she's not helpless, she's actually incredibly powerful." She knew that already: Ellen had been part of the circle that caught a serial killer team. Admittedly, Bonnie and the other PUPs had been in control but it was Ellen's storm-seer sense that had allowed them to harness the storm.

"And if she really needs help, she will ping for it." Wren frowned. "She will, won't she? She won't go all stubborn and independent and decide she can handle it herself?"

"What, you mean like you would?" Sergei's lips twitched as she glared at him. "No, I don't think so. Even if she hadn't seen how well Bonnie and her crew work together, Danny won't let her."

But inwardly, shoved far below even the levels his partner could read, Sergei wasn't so sure. Ellen had something she needed to prove, even if she wasn't vocalizing that need yet. And, he knew all too well, a Talent with something to prove... sometimes took stupid risks.

---

ONCE ELLEN HAD IDENTIFIED our probable destination, I'd started working on a plan. Like most plans, it depended on a dollop of luck, a smidge of skill, and the smile of the gods. But then, that was pretty much the MO of the boardwalk, any given night.

My shadow, apparently, had never been down the Shore. "Wow." Ellen had a strange look on her face, like she wanted to grin, but was afraid it would be impolite. "It really is.... It really *is*."

I looked around, trying to see it through her eyes. "Yeah, it really is." The boardwalk was transitioning between day and night, some sunbathers still sprawled out on the sand even as the workers in the game booths began their calls, to win a prize and impress your girl. I could remember coming here as a teenager, and it had seemed exactly the same, back then. Even the people seemed the same: the teenagers in packs, the families with a small child wide-eyed and babbling with excitement, the occasional senior citizens walking slowly, and every now and again the bright "beep beep beep" of an electric cart bringing people from one end of the boardwalk to the other, almost but never quite running someone over. The booths were garish and overly-bright, the darkness hanging over the ocean somehow comforting and threatening all at once, the sound of the cold Atlantic surf a scarce murmur under the many voices.

I'd worked one of those booths as a teenager, lived in a house off the beach with seven other guys, worked all night, slept most of the day, not worried about anything except saving enough of my paycheck that my mother didn't kill me at the end of the summer. Hadn't been back, since.

This wasn't a vacation. The clock was ticking, a metronome in the back of my head, driving me on. Lives at risk, and I was the only one looking.

"How are we going to find anyone, or anything here?" Ellen asked. "It's a zoo."

"Ask a zookeeper," I said.

Ellen had to show I.D. at the bar, which was a difference from when I'd been down here, but the inside of Doblosky's was what I'd been expecting: bare wood walls and benches, a long bar that would be three-deep by midnight, and bartenders who already looked tired. We moved up to the bar, and I leaned against it, removing the baseball cap and ruffling the sweat-damp hair so that my horns didn't show through. Ellen leaned in at my side, not too close but clearly with me.

The bartender took a professional look, the kind that didn't see anything but remembered everything in case it was needed later. "What can I get you folks?"

"Yuengling, draft."

"Two," Ellen said. I was pretty sure she wasn't a drinker, but Yuengling was a good basic lager: decent enough to not get you sneered at, common enough that nobody would think you were trying too hard. And if she left it half-drunk it wasn't going to break the budget.

The bartender nodded once. "PI?"

I spread my hands, fair-caught. "After a while, it starts to show." Actually, it didn't, not on my face. The bartender was good, and experienced – he might even have been here twenty years ago when I did my time. "I bet you get a lot of that down here."

The guy shrugged. He had hands like baseball gloves, and a torso to match, but his face was more like a college professor's: narrow, with dark hair slicked back, and thoughtful eyes.

"Missing kids, mostly. Sometimes a missing spouse."

"Kids. Late teens. Two girls and a boy."

"Runaways?"

"Maybe. Probably not."

The bartender finished pulling our beers and set them down in front of us, hearing what I wasn't saying. "This ain't back when. Not much like that going down here."

"Not much isn't none."

Ellen stirred next to me, but only reached out to pick up her beer, and take a sip. I wondered what she'd been about to say, and why she'd stopped herself.

The bartender went down the line, dealing with other customers, and Ellen let out a little sigh.

"What?"

"How do you know what to say? How do you know if something's too much to tell them?"

"Experience." That probably wasn't what she wanted to hear, but it was all I had.

"If it was just boys, I might have something for you," the bartender said, coming back like the conversation'd never been interrupted. "House downtown is the place for that, lost boys end up there. But girls aren't their thing and the cops are watching too close for anything else to go on right now."

I looked sideways at Ellen, who was staring down into her beer like answers to a test she hadn't studied for were written in the foam. Anyone would have thought the faint shake of her head was her reaction to the taste. I wasn't anyone.

"They're together, last we heard," I said. "So yeah, probably not our scene." I made note of it, though. Prostitution was, my way of thinking, a valid lifestyle choice – hell, I sold my physical skill and a breed of comfort too, if you wanted brass tacks – but only if the people involved were of legal age and consent. A few unofficial pokes into the house's business would determine if official notice should be taken. I'd been a city cop, not Jersey, and I'd never worked Vice, but I still knew who to call.

"Nothing else floating under the surface?" I paid for our drinks, an additional two twenties folded into the tab.

"The usual graft and corruption, but it's been under control for a couple-three years by now. Bad business to let anything else in. You know how it is."

Yeah, I knew. The casinos had taught everyone else how to keep their backyards clean, the better to rake money in through the front door. If you kept under their radar you could survive, but pop up once....

"Thanks."

"Good luck," the bartender said, and one of my twenties came back to me, along with a handful of dimes in change. "I got teenagers, myself."

I nodded, and drank my beer.

"So what now?" Ellen had gotten halfway through hers, and then pushed it away, reaching instead for the bowl of bar-mix. "Got more bartenders to hit up, or are we going to pile back into the car and drive around randomly until we find them?"

My shadow had claws. Tiny milk-claws, but claws. That was good to know.

"We could do a survey of all the bars," I said. If the missing kids had been human, that's what I would have done. But what she'd Seen changed that plan. "But no to both of your questions." I'd stopped here to eliminate possibilities. Now it was time to open them up again.

Unfortunately, I'd have to wait until full dark for that. Some of the fatae could wander the beaches and boardwalks without being noticed – all right, some of us in bathing suits would probably make people do a doubletake or three – but the one in particular I needed to question raised a massive fuss every time, and I was in no mood for fuss. So there was some time to kill.

We stopped outside the bar to pick up dinner – a hot dog for Ellen, two slices of cheese pizza for me – and an extra pastrami sandwich, hold the slaw and mustard. The guy gave me a doubting look, but made the sandwich anyway.

"For later?" Ellen asked, as we walked away, heading not down the boardwalk but toward the nearest ladder down to the beach itself.

"For bribes."

The sand was almost too soft to walk on, courtesy of all the sunbathers, but we took off our shoes and slogged toward the water, a dark glint in the distance. I could see the city's lights, and something that was probably Staten Island, plus a couple of larger ships out beyond the markers. And, off to the side, the movement of something sliding through the water, then disappearing again.

I decided not to mention the shark to Ellen. It wasn't like we were going to go in all that deep. Just enough to be polite.

I took the sandwich out of the waxed paper bag, and peeled off the bread, shoving it back in the bag – no use wasting good rye, after all.

"What are you doing, going fishing?" She wasn't being snarky: she really had no idea. Valere had been slacking on this side of her education.

"Not exactly. But kind of. Stay here."

I left her ankle-deep in the surf, and moved forward, holding the meat in my left hand. With my luck I'd end up either getting nibbled at by a shark, or hit on by an inquisitive fendha. Neither of those would be useful, right now. Or, actually, ever.

"I'm looking for information," I said, trusting the night air and ebbing tide to carry my words. "No tricks, no traps. Looking for information on a trace carried in these waters, from Manhattan to here. Three traces, unhappy or angry or scared."

No answer. I didn't want to influence the witnesses – you never gave them any info they could build off, so nobody could say you led them – but a little glide for the ride could be overlooked. I shook the meat gently, letting the smell of it carry on the night air. "I'm offering dinner, to seal the trade."

There was no response, although I could hear something slapping the surface a few meters out. Unlike in the city, when I could play on my rep, I had to be more cautious here. This wasn't my turf, and the politics of who answered to whom could tangle me up badly, if I wasn't careful.

Still. Not as bad as the time I had to go to Denver.

"Nobody out there knows anything? I guess the Shore's reputation is oversold, then."

When in doubt, insult the fatae. It's not advice I'd give to humans, but I've found it remarkably effective over the years.

A louder slap on the water, and then something moved under the dark waves, a too-large mass coming too fast at me.

I held my ground. Sand. Whatever.

The mass stopped just shy of ramming into me, and a darker, more solid shape rose from the waves. The head was the size of a football, and shaped about the same, with a neck that managed to be both muscular and sinewy at the same time. The shadow underneath suggested that a more massive body was attached to that neck, but I wasn't going to poke it to find out.

"Yes." The voice was high, but masculine. As far as you could make assumptions about that sort of thing, anyway.

"Yes, what? Yes you have information, or yes, nobody knows anything?"

"We know."

I had no idea what breed this kid was, but it was clearly a groupthink type. Or maybe kid here was a split personality. So long as one of them had the info to share, I didn't give a fuck.

We stared at each other for a bit – or I stared, and it waited. If it had eyes, they weren't immediately obvious, just long whiskers dripping from either side of the football, the entire thing covered in gleaming black scales. Even its mouth was a narrow slit, the jaw dropping when it talked, but no teeth visible.

That didn't mean this thing wasn't dangerous, though.

"You want?" I held up the meat carefully, trying not to give any invitation for it to snap it out of my hand – and maybe take my hand along with it.

The head lowered slightly, and it took the meat from me like a cat tasting treats, soft and steady. One second the chunk of corned beef was in its mouth, hanging over the side, and the next it was gone, swallowed whole like...well, like a snake would snork down a mouse. I guess the analogy made sense, all structural resemblance considered.

It wavered back and forth in front of me like a damned sea-cobra, either digesting or getting ready to strike, and then it said, "Five night ago. We heard them screaming."

I tensed: screaming was never good. But "heard" was open to interpretation, especially coming from a breed that didn't seem to have ears. "A little more detail than that, please?"

"We were feeding. Over us, a ship. Not-large, not a barge, but larger than the usual ones that come here."

This was a public beach; anything larger than a two-person sailboat would probably get waved off by the lifeguards, assuming they didn't get grounded on a sandbar. But if this was late at night, there would be no lifeguards, and if they came in at high tide...

"And you heard screaming." The serpent stared at me.

"Were those screaming on the deck, or-?"

"From inside. We heard them, as they passed over" Vibrations. Of course. I'd save feeling dumb for later.

"The water shivered with their fear. We followed, as far as we dared, but there were too many humans. Too much light and noise, when they come to shore."

"Thank you," I said. "I am sorry the meal was so small."

The serpent stilled, like I'd insulted it, or it had no idea what the hell I'd said, and then it slid back into the water, barely a ripple marking its passing, and the dark shadow writhed and roiled back into the depths.

That hadn't been its body, I realized: that had been its entire school. I'd been surrounded. Jesus fucking Christ.

I turned around and sloshed back to shore, picking up Ellen along the way.

"Was that...another fatae?"

"Yeah."

"What kind?"

"I have no idea. The sea-going breeds are kinda standoffish.

Swimoffish. Finoffish? They don't come hang out with landfolk often."

"But it had something useful?"

"Yeah." I didn't know how much to tell her. I wasn't used to working with a partner – the times I'd done work for PUPI, I still worked it on my own, and reported back, mostly, and NYPD protocol was laughably useless here.

"Five nights ago, a boat came in, unloaded bodies that might or might not be our kids. I'm guessing they are, since there's no reason fatae would be interested in ordinary humans being hauled out."

"And?"

She was looking at me so expectantly, the lights from the boardwalk catching the turn of her head, the cant of her body, that I felt like not being able to say "So here's what we're going to do," was an utter and absolute failure of myself as a human being.

Since I'm not entirely human, this didn't bother me as much as it should have.

But it still bothered me.

"And...I don't know," I admitted. "'A boat' is too vague, and it's not like there are eyes on the beach we can hack. I'd been hoping they knew something more specific. Right now, the trail ends here. Unless we pick up something new, or you suddenly get a flash of something..."

The clock ticks on every missing kid case. These were older teenagers, and there were three of them, together, so the clock would slow down a little, but every day that went by, the damage risks went up until the difference between retrieval and failure was not much difference at all.

I didn't say any of that out loud, but I'd figured that Shadow was pretty good at reading the silence.

"They're going to die. I only see people if they're going to die."

"Valere didn't die." I put my hand on her arm, not curling my fingers around, just resting them on her skin. If she wanted to move away, she could, no resistance. "Wren Valere is alive, and well. You see a possible future. Yeah, it's the most possible, the most probable. But nothing's set in stone. Nothing's foreordained. You know Bonnie, I'm sure she's talked to you about kenning."

"Yeah." She didn't pull away, didn't move. She didn't sound convinced, either.

"Bonnie sees the highest likelihood of events coming together. But even one push can bring it all down, or send it in a different direction. Bonnie's like...like a shove. You're a battering ram. Just your Seeing has the potential to change things."

I sounded smooth, persuasive, convincing. Fact was, I didn't have fucking clue how much impact she had, although what I'd said about Bonnie was truth, far as Bonnie had explained it to me. But what mattered was that Shadow bought it.

"You're full of shit."

I probably shouldn't have laughed, but I couldn't help it. She wasn't mad, she wasn't offended, she was just so matter of fact, it was funny.

"I am. But I really do believe that the fact that you started people looking, started *me* looking, that we're asking questions, has the potential to change things."

"Change it enough?"

I sighed, and let my hand drop from her arm as we started walking again toward the lights and noise of the Boardwalk. "That, yeah. That's the question, isn't it?"

"So...we keep looking," she said. Yeah. We kept looking.

---

DANNY WAS USED to working alone. Ellen had known that,

figured that she'd be a tagalong, useful for... well, she didn't know what she would be useful for, actually. But she wasn't going to be left behind, to sit and stress and not know what was going on. Not this time.

And, unlike Genevieve, and even Bonnie and the other Pups, Danny Hendrickson didn't seem to think that she needed to be sheltered and protected, or act like she was some kind of bomb that was going to go off if someone spoke too loudly, or said the wrong thing. She'd made a Hulk joke, once, and only Sergei got it, which was just sad.

If being a Talent meant giving up pop culture, Ellen wasn't sure she wanted any part of it. Except she didn't have a choice, apparently. This was the road she'd been put on, and she had no real choice but to walk it. So she would.

While she was shaking sand off her feet, Danny had cornered a bunch of teenagers by one of the hundred and seven pizza places that lined the boardwalk, and was asking them questions, showing them the sketch she had done of the three faces. The teenagers were shaking their heads: another dead end. Ellen considered them, and then considered how little the hot dog had done to fill her stomach, and let instinct and hunger lead her to a different pizza stand, a long counter facing the boardwalk, with tables and plastic chairs arranged in the back. It wasn't busy, so she leaned her elbows on the counter the way she'd seen Danny do in the bar and waited for someone to notice her.

The guy behind the counter was old, maybe in his forties, and looked like he should have been cast in a mob movie. But his eyes were tired, and kind.

"A slice and a Diet Coke, please."

"Pepsi okay?"

Ellen made a face, and the guy laughed. "How about a root beer?"

"That's good yeah, thanks." She pulled out her wallet, and

counted the bills, then handed them to the guy as he shouted her order to the younger guy by the ovens, and handed her a drink. It was pre-made, and the ice was melting already, but the salty air and the walking and the beer almost two hours ago had left her thirsty enough to not care.

She turned to watch Danny, who had let the kids go, folding the sketch back into the inside pocket of his jacket.

"You work here long?" She turned back and asked the guy, as he slid her pizza across the counter, the grease already seeping through the two white paper plates underneath.

"Twenty-seven years this summer," he said proudly. "Family business, still."

"Nice. I bet you get a lot of regulars."

"Some. But there's always turnover. Kids, you know?" He said it like she wasn't barely five years older than some of the kids he was talking about – and some of them might even be older than she was. She felt older, though. A lot older.

"Three of my friends were down here, last week." She had no idea what she was doing, but she'd been watching Danny, and listening, and maybe it was time to be more than just a tagalong. "We were supposed to meet them, but... " She shrugged, tried to make it seem both important and no big deal. She'd been blown off before, dumped by people she thought were friends, who would have her back. She scooped up some of that bitterness, held it in her stomach, and let it blend with the worry she had for the three faces she had Seen in her vision. "If they took off and didn't tell me, I'm going to kill them."

The guy laughed, and leaned on the counter, mimicking her pose. "It's summer, it's the Shore. Stuff happens. You can't reach 'em on your cell?"

"It goes straight to voicemail. All three of them." She let a little more worry creep in. "You don't think anything bad happened to them, do you?"

"Bad things can happen," the guy said. "But no, I suspect you're right, they just flaked, and you can kick their asses all the rest of the year for it. But hey, hang on. Justin!"

The kid by the ovens turned, and she saw that he was younger than she'd thought, maybe sixteen at most. "Yeah?"

"C'mere," the guy said, and swung his arm. "This is my son, Justin. He notices faces better than I do, especially at that age. Maybe he saw 'em."

Ellen started, her mind suddenly going blank. "I—"

"Here," and Danny was next to her, his hand sliding the sketch across the counter. "Visuals help better – El's been known to forget what color her own eyes are, much less someone else's."

"Hey," she protested, and felt his arm reach around her waist, pulling her close. It should have felt awkward, but it didn't: she was reassured, and warmed in a way that had nothing to do with the air temperature, or the sweat already on her skin.

"You know it's true," Danny was saying. "Anyway, nobody's seen them, so if this is a dead end too, I think we're going to have to admit defeat."

The pizza guy had looked up at Danny, then back at her, and he looked like he was going to say something, and then shrugged. Ellen could guess – Danny wasn't that much older than her, maybe a decade? – but it was enough to raise a few eyebrows, the way Danny was playing it. Definitely not "older brother" style, or tagalong not-quite-partner.

"Nah," the kid, Justin, said. "I didn't see 'em. Sorry."

Out in the distance, over the water, there was a flash of heat-lightning, zigging from one cloud to the other, less a threat of rain than a reminder that it was still summer, that changeable forces still loomed overhead. Ellen didn't see the flash behind her; she didn't have to. She felt it, knew exactly where it was, how far away, how powerful, although she had no science training or instruments to measure it. She knew because the vision hit her like an icepick, bypassing her walls and digging right into the softest part of her brain.

Genevieve had taught her how to make it easier, how to let the visions in rather than having them knock her barriers over. It helped, a little: like diving into a tornado instead of being swept off your feet, she supposed, and then there wasn't any time to think, her mind sorting through what she Saw, trying to put it into some kind of order.

She felt Danny grab her arm, leading her away from the noise and bustle of the booths. Her body followed automatically, but the rest of her was inside a room filled with shadows. Her visions didn't have smell, and rarely sound – when they called it Sight they weren't kidding. So she *looked*, and the shadows became distinct shapes: boxes, and tables, mostly. She was in a storeroom of some kind.

Then one of the shadows moved, coming toward her, and there was a hand reaching out to her, pale and slender, palm turned up. There was webbing between the fingers, and something glittered faintly on the skin, even in the dim light.

Then the scene changed, wrenching Ellen along with it, and she was in the middle of a street, dark and abandoned. Rows of neat little houses sat along either side, with cars parked at the curb. She looked up, all the way down the street, her sight telescoping in a way that made her want to throw up, and she saw the beach, and the ocean. Too far away. Too far away to be safe.

"Safe from what, Ellen? Safe from what?"

She tried to walk toward it, but something had her by the ankles, and she couldn't move, couldn't step forward, only back, the weights pulling her back into the shadowed room, and she knew if she went back there she would never escape.

"Ellen?"

She made an irritable noise, and tried to flap her hand at

him, to tell him to shut up. He must have taken the hint because he didn't say anything more, although he still had a hand on her arm, somewhere outside the vision.

The street was nice, the houses in decent repair, what she could see in the night. Was it tonight? She looked up, and checked the moon, hanging high in the black. Tonight, or close enough. Tonight or tomorrow. But where?

She needed more. Needed to see more.

Unable to move from where the vision had dropped her, she couldn't turn to see the cross-street, but it was narrow, almost like an alley, and had more houses on it, smaller ones, almost like cottages. Carlyle, she read off the nearest street sign, squinting to read the letters.

Not enough.

*You're a storm-seer.* Genevieve had explained it to her, the two of them sitting on a bench in Central Park. The sky had been bright blue, the air clear and cool. Genevieve had said it was safer to talk about it then. *We all pull power from current, the magic that run along electricity, but you have an extra gift. Current carries things with it. Memories. Images. You can see them. You can pull them from the current, before they even happen.*

More current. She reached for the power she could feel racing overhead, riding along those lightning flashes out at sea. All those years of denying she saw anything, trying to fit in, it seemed almost wrong how easy it was to find the current, bring it in toward her...

Too much, too many conflicting sparks. She fell to her knees, the current prickling painfully up and down her spine, unable to settle, and the vision was lost.

"Ellen. Ellen, come on. Come with me. No, it's okay," and he was talking to someone else now, his voice pitched away from her, "She's ok, I think that last beer did her in."

She wanted to protest, but her knees felt like rubber and her head was burning and all she really wanted to do was lie down somewhere until the fireworks scrambling inside her settled down and behaved.

"You did something with current, didn't you? And it burned you. It's okay, you're going to be okay."

Yes. She knew that. She was the Talent here, not him, and she opened her mouth to say that, but all that came out was a harsh gasp.

"Come on, sit down." And she was being lowered onto a bench, and Danny was sitting next to her, his arm around her shoulders.

"I Saw," she said, barely a whisper. "I saw...her. One of the girls. She's alive, she'll be alive, but I don't know about the others." The last time she had seen someone twice, it had been Genevieve...and the one missing from that second vision had already died, although she hadn't known it at the time.

"And I saw... outside. Outside where she is." Although she didn't know for certain the cellar was on that street, why else would she be seeing it? "A street. Hamlin? No, Carlyle. Carlyle Court."

She felt him shift, reaching for something, and then he swore under his breath. "You scorched my cell." There was no condemnation in his voice, just resignation. "No way to get a new one before morning. But the street, it's near here?"

She nodded. "Yeah. Not here, the town's not like this one." The town they'd driven through had cottages the same size, but they were clearly rentals, more run-down, nowhere near as carefully tended. "I could see the beach from there, sort of. Down the end of the road. A private beach? Not like this."

"Beach town, nicer, Carlyle Court. Okay." His arm left her, and she opened her eyes to see him watching her intently, his face in shadows from the streetlamp hanging over them. "You okay?"

"Yeah." The current had settled, finally, and she no longer

thought she was going to throw up. She didn't want to try standing up just yet, though.

"All right. Hang tight for a minute."

She wasn't sure what that meant, to hang tight, but she was all right with sitting there while he went off, approaching an older couple walking past them. They spoke for couple of minutes, and then Danny held up his phone as though showing it to them. The woman laughed, and the man nodded, and took out his own phone, entering something on the keyboard. They spoke a little more, and then Danny was coming back, his body language saying he had something, a direction, a scent to follow.

Oh yay. She forced herself to sit up straight, pretending that she was ready to go, not a burden at all.

---

SHADOW LOOKED EVEN MORE like a shadow, like someone had taken an eraser to her sharp edges. If I had an inch of compassion and any sense whatsoever, I'd throw her into the car and go back to the city, leave her there and come back tomorrow, alone.

I was pretty sure that her reaction to that wouldn't be pretty. And she'd be right. She was wrecked, but she'd been the one to see the missing kids, and she had a right to be in on it. If she wanted.

"Light Bay," I said.

She lifted her gaze enough to look at me. "What?"

"The only town around here that has a Hamlin Court, according to the Internet, is the town of Light Bay. It's about fifteen minutes north of here. You game?"

"Yeah. I... Yeah."

She wasn't. But she wasn't going to admit it, either.

"C'mon, tiger," I said, reaching out a hand. "Get to the car and you can sleep the rest of the way there."

I ended up half-carrying her the rest of the way. She'd gone silent and loose, like a little kid sullen with exhaustion, and only pride was keeping her upright. I didn't remember if this was normal for Talent – the ones I hung with tended to be, well, tougher than this.

"You okay?"

"Yeah." It was more of an exhale than an actual word, but she was buckling herself in, and her eyes were open. "Genevieve says that pulling wild current is harder than man-made, and the storm was pretty far away. I don't think I should have done it."

"So why did you?"

She shrugged, and looked out the passenger side window. "I don't... it's not like it is for everyone else. I don't always have a choice."

I started up the car and pulled out of the parking spot, careful to avoid the gaggle of drunk teenagers trying to cross the street in front of me. "The visions?"

"They come when they come. All I can do is..." and she waved a hand lazily in the air, "ride it."

She seemed to be waiting for me to say something. "That sucks."

Her laughter was bright, unforced, and an unexpected surprise, even if it didn't come with a smile. "Everyone else says I'm rare, or special. I spent my whole life wanting to be special. But yeah. It sucks."

***

SHADOW FELL asleep in the car. She slept like a little kid, her head lolling forward, snoring faintly. I kept the radio off, and drove through the night. I took route 35 up, rather than getting onto the Parkway, and had to focus on where I was going. Even so, my mind wouldn't let go of the case, and the echoes that every case invariably, inevitably, stirred.

Every case I take, when kids are involved, I hope to hell that they're runaways. Runaways, there's a reason they left. You can deal with reasons, whether it's getting them help, or getting them out of that situation and into a healthier one. You don't always get a happy-ever-after, but you get a better-for-now.

And most of my cases *are* runaways. Just not all of them.

This one could have been – three teenagers ditching a bad situation or boring relatives for something they hope will be better, in the relative wilds of the summer shore. Fatae teens were dumb as human ones. Even with Ellen seeing people in death's way, it could have been accident, or random chance... but it didn't feel like it.

These kids had been taken.

There were three reason why teenagers are abducted, as opposed to the myriad of reasons little kids are abducted. None of them were good. Some of them were worse. The fact that these kids were fatae didn't change any of that. In fact, an "exotic" would probably bring twice the money, for the discerning predator.

One, they were taken for the sex trade. Horrible as that sounded, it was almost the best option, because I could find them, then. And, assuming they didn't put up too much of a fight, they wouldn't be permanently damaged. Physically, anyway.

I had to unclench my fingers from the steering wheel when they started to hurt. Calling that the best option was only relative to the others. Option Two was that they'd been taken as slaves. The slave trade could be sexual or non-sexual, but there was less value, more turnover there... the moment a slave became trouble, they'd be killed. Three....

I'd never run into the third, but I knew about it. There was a small but very profitable market for victims. Disposable flesh, designed only to be hurt. When I was a cop, I'd seen the end result, fished out of basements, and buried in a closed casket.

Ellen had only seen one of the three in her most recent vision. The other two might have been asleep, or taken elsewhere. But they could also already be dead.

"There."

Ellen's voice was sleepy, but she was alert enough to catch the signpost I almost missed. Three quarters of a mile later, we were taking the exit for Light Bay.

"I don't suppose you have any sense of where to go?"

"It doesn't work that way. But it was residential, and near the beach. So away from downtown."

Such as downtown was, a single street of storefronts, all closed and dark for the night already. This wasn't a hotspot. In fact, it was barely a warm spot on the map. I could imagine, in the daylight, it was cozy and quaint, the ideal place to take your pre-teens for a week down the shore, eat ice cream every afternoon and everyone's in bed by 10pm. The year-round locals were probably blue-collar, solidly working class of all races – probably a fair sprinkling of fatae, too. Two or three generations in one place, and the ones who leave probably come back, eventually, because once you've seen the rest of the world, this starts to look pretty good.

"This looks right," Ellen said, after I'd gone a few blocks east, driving slow enough to see but not so slow a late-patrolling cop would think to stop me. The local boys might be useful, but more likely we'd waste time and energy on territorial markings. "The houses look right."

They were seaside cottages, probably two bedrooms and a front parlor that could hold a pull-out bed, maybe another bedroom shoved into the attic. But they were all well kept-up, even in the moon and lamplight, the yards tended and the streets recently repaved. We drove along, and her attention scanned back and forth, not so much with her eyes but that weird blind look Talent got sometimes, the one that could seriously weird you out if you didn't know what they were doing.

I didn't plan it, but my right hand left the wheel, and reached out to touch her leg. Just a touch, my fingertips barely resting on the cloth, but it was enough to catch her attention. She looked down, smiled, just a corner of her mouth and a rise of her cheek, and then she went back to scanning.

"Anything?"

"It's not like a whatchamacallit, a GPS."

"You use a GPS?" The higher res a Talent, the less they were able to use tech. I'd thought that Shadow would be high res enough to warrant a strict low-tech ruling – and her lack of training would make the situation even worse.

"My dad. At least now I know why it never worked properly when I was in the car." Her smile was gone, now. "He was right to blame me."

I'd already gotten the picture of her life before Bonnie and her crew dragged her in, but confirmation was always a kick in the gut. Bonnie said I had a white knight syndrome thing going, always wanting to rescue the helpless. She was only half right. I wanted to rescue *everyone*.

"Yeah, you guys are hell on electronics." There wasn't any point in candy-coating it: her parents hadn't been winners on the support front, but expecting them to know, or understand, what was happening...might as well ask a dog to do your taxes.

"They're gone."

"What?" I might have overreacted a little, because Ellen's hand covered mine suddenly, pressing down in reassurance. "Not gone-gone. Not here, gone. The feel of them's faded."

"Do you know where?"

She frowned, her eyes narrowing. "This would be easier if they were Talent," she said. "I think I've touched them enough, I'd be able to follow their signature."

I'd only ever heard the PUPs talk about signature, the feel of an individual's personal current. She'd learned that from Bonnie, not Wren.

"But you can't do that for fatae?"

"No, like I said, you feel ...different. And this isn't signature, what I feel through the vision. It's... deeper, and softer, and... signature's something you follow. This is, it's leading me."

I wasn't Talent, I didn't give a damn about the technical aspects of current. From the look on Ellen's face, though, I suspected she was going to be cornering the PUPs, the *Cosa's* technicians, when she had a chance. "So they are fatae?" I was pretty damn sure, just based on her sketches, and the fact that the serpents had bothered to hear them, but...

"They feel... human but not. And the gills? So, yeah. Close enough to pass..."

"Like me?" We were still cruising the streets, although with less direction now. I came to the end of one road, facing the low seawall that kept the shore from the city, and pulled the car over to the curb. "What do I feel like, to you?"

It was a stupid question. I didn't even know why I was asking, or what she was going to say.

"Wood and wine, and a warm dirt road."

Okay, I absolutely hadn't expected that. From the look on her face, neither had she. I rolled the words around in my thoughts, and laughed. "Yeah, close enough. My genetic donor was a faun, so that makes sense. I-"

She wasn't listening. She'd gone glassy-eyed again, her fingers convulsing around my hand, her body bending over tense as a bowstring. Even I could feel the current crackling over her, even as I heard the book of heat-thunder in the distance out over the ocean.

"Ellen?" I didn't know what to do, if I should hold onto her, or pull away, or talk to her. My instinct was to protect her, to shield her from whatever was slamming into her so hard, and I couldn't, all I could do was sit there and watch.

I'm not good with being helpless. Never have been, that's why I ended up a cop in the first place.

"Danny. Danny, no."

She wasn't talking to me. Or, she wasn't talking to the me who was in the car. I unhooked my seatbelt and turned sideways, ignoring all doubt to yank her into my arms, holding her the way you would someone just yanked off a ledge, arms curved around her, keeping her steady without actually holding her down. One of the few things we learned in the academy that was actually useful on the street. That, and learning how to duck, mainly.

Slowly, her breath came back to normal, and she pushed away, a gentle request to back the hell off. I let go, but stayed alert.

"I saw you. Alone this time. At a...carnival? There were lights, booth lights, like the Boardwalk but it was...grubbier, and daylight. And banners flying and.. a gun."

"The other three?" I kept my voice soft and low, like I used to coax kids out of hiding places. Me and a gun, well, it wouldn't be the first time.

"I didn't see them. Only you."

"So we have no reason to believe that anything has changed. They're still alive," I said, although truthfully this could be taken either way. But hope keeps us moving, and she looked like she needed to move. "Let's go."

---

IN THE END, finding a carnival somewhere near Light Bay was easy. Danny pulled into a diner, they slid into a booth, and he asked the waitress. Between the menu being handed over, and Danny's second cup of coffee, they had not only directions, but gossip about how long the carnival had been coming around, who they probably had to pay off to keep those rides going, and how many times the local church had tried, and failed, to get them shut down for moral offenses, etcetera.

"Seriously?" Ellen's eyes were wide in a combination of awe and too-much-information as the waitress, finally, left them to their coffee in peace.

Danny nodded. "Seriously. People, mostly, want to tell you things. If someone doesn't want to talk, they're scared. Take the toughest, most morose bastard on the face of the earth, and give him a platform, and he'll talk for hours. They might not answer your questions, but they'll let enough slip that you can draw conclusions."

Despite the hour, the seriousness of everything, and her utter exhaustion, Ellen felt for the first time like they had a chance.

"Drink your coffee," Danny said, letting his lips curl in just the hint of a smile, suggesting that he felt the same way. "We have our destination."

───

AT NIGHT, the fairgrounds were near-magical to little kids and love-struck couples. During the day, before the lights came up, it was probably borderline seedy, worn and workmanlike. This early in the morning, with dew glittering on the grass and canvas tents, the sun just barely lighting the sky, dark purple streaks fading away to pale blue, it had an unexpected, calm beauty.

"I used to love county fairs when I was a little kid," Ellen said. "We'd go once a year, morning to midnight, and we got to run wild. Ate such disgusting things..."

"I'll buy you a deep fried something," Danny said.

"Yeah, thanks anyway." She couldn't quite work up a real

smile, not with the vision of him, and the gun, and the sensation of death still creeping around in her head, but she did appreciate the effort. "I suppose we...what? Go knock on the door?"

"You already did."

She yelped a little, jumping back as two men appeared in front of them. One of them was lean and long, the other low and square, like they'd been designed to be a salt and pepper set. The lean one was covered in a soft grey fur, like a pelt, and had a feline face. The squat one was softer, like a beanbag chair with feet.

"So you're here, and you have our attention. What do you want?" The *human* was silent in their question, but the way they were looking at them said it, pretty loud.

"My name's Daniel Hendrickson," Danny said, taking off his baseball cap and running his hand though his hair. It could have been the mark of nerves, if you weren't paying attention. Or, if you were, it would highlight the horns showing through the curls, shutting down the accusation of human in their tone. Ellen tried to shrink in on herself, calling on years of staying invisible, unseen, unnoticed. She wasn't a Retriever, though; it only worked when people wanted to discount and ignore her.

"Yeah, so?"

"I'm a private investigator," Danny went on, lifting his right hand to indicate he wasn't making a threat, while he reached into his back pocket and pulled out a little fold-over wallet, opening it one-handed to show the laminated card tucked inside.

"Yeah, so?" the fatae repeated, unimpressed without even looking.

"So you can either help a cousin out, quietly, or I can walk away and come back with a lot of official paperwork that will make your life more difficult than it has to be," Danny said, matching him tone for bored tone. He wasn't threatening, exactly, Ellen thought. He was...*promising*. Not bravado: a fact, backed by confidence. She wanted that, she wanted to learn how to do that so badly it made her teeth hurt.

Danny tilted his head a little to the left, and almost-smiled at the two figures blocking them. "And we both know that even a hint of red tape is going to screw your day a lot worse than answering a few uncomfortable questions."

"We'll take that chance," the second fatae said, finally speaking up. "Town and us have an understanding."

In other words, they'd paid off enough people that they weren't worried. Ellen might not be a trained PI but she knew enough to understand that. Danny could try to force the issue, but even if they could get backing from the cops, it would be at least a day and she didn't know what would happen to the kids then; the tension she'd felt during each vision, the knowledge that death was sliding its fingers around them, just waiting for the right moment to yank them into its domain.

The thought shivered in her core, and there was an odd echo of that shiver on the soles of her feet. Frowning, Ellen glanced down. They were standing on ordinary dirt, hard-packed and worn from a summer of foot traffic. Using the sense Genevieve had taught her, Ellen clicked over into mage-sight and tried to look again.

Ordinary dirt...but deep below, there was something that pulsed, a thick shimmering rope twisting like a slow heartbeat, running under her feet and off into the distance.

A ley line. Current ran with electricity, both man-made and natural. Most Talent looked in the air, but it was under their feet, too.

She pulled a strand of current from her core, letting the dark blue thread curl around her mental finger, and then sent it down the way she'd learned, letting the leading end touch the ley line.

It was a different energy than what she felt when a storm

touched her: thicker, less a jolt than a shove. It felt... like Danny, she realized suddenly. Solid, steady, and weirdly calm for something that was inherently unstable. Storm-current was harsh, unpredictable, as likely to burn your core as fill it, if you weren't careful. This... ley lines were easy enough to find, but harder to draw on, Genevieve had said; harder, and less powerful, diluted through the earth the way they were. That was why most Talent didn't bother using them. The power flowed through it, Ellen could *feel* it. Only, rather than forcing power into her the way air-current did, the flow enticed her in, surrounded her, soaking down into her core like rain.

Her visions, unlike most other usage, didn't drain her core because they came in from outside, an external force. Still, the sensation of topping off the tank was like an endorphin kick, making her feel competent and capable, too... or at least able to bullshit others into thinking that she was.

Five seconds, that had taken her. But in five seconds, things had gone from casual to tense.

"So why don't you both get back into your car, and drive back somewhere safer?" the squat fatae said, and it didn't sound like a suggestion. "This is our space, and we don't want you in it. *Cousin.*" He smiled, showing teeth like a shark's, and the lean fatae next to him took a step forward, bring a knife up out of nowhere. He held it casually, but Ellen had no doubt that it could become a threat as easily as it had appeared.

For an instant, she thought about using some of the cantrips that Genevieve had taught her, maybe to call fire, or levitate something. But she couldn't think she had enough control to do more than piss the two fatae off, and maybe making things worse. But she needed to do something: the thought that the missing kids might be here, and they were going to be turned away, was too much for her to bear.

Something inside her core clicked and turned, the ley-current sliding into place and her eyes glazed over even as she stepped forward, in front of Danny, and placed her left hand, palm out, on the chest of the first fatae.

It took a lifetime to sort through the possibilities rushing at her, instinctively not looking too closely at anything but waiting until that right moment in time came to her.

"Cancer," she said. "It's already in you, moving through your body. Nasty."

Before he had time to react, she turned to the other. He tried to evade her, and her hand closed on his shoulder, instead. "Car wreck. Drunk. You won't die immediately though."

She let go, not wanting to keep the vision any longer than needed, and stepped back, blinking at them. They both looked like frogs, mouths open and eyes blinking.

"You want to know what else she can find out about you?" Danny asked, and that soft voice didn't disguise any of the menace underneath, this time. "No, I don't think so. Why don't you just let us in, walk around, ask a few questions...and nothing has to get ugly."

Ellen breathed in and out, letting the current surge through her. Ordinary humans – Nulls – couldn't actually see current, but even though the fatae didn't use, it they could still sense it. That was what she'd been told, anyway, and from the way Tall and Squat were backing up, she was willing to believe it.

Nobody had ever been scared of her before, not even when they thought she was crazy. It didn't feel as good as she'd thought it would.

"Anyone complains about you, out you go," Squat said, like he was trying to regain ground.

"We will be as polite as your granny," Danny said. "Thank you, gentlemen. Have a lovely day."

The thugs backed off to what seemed like a safe distance, and they walked through the gates, and onto the carnival grounds proper. Ellen felt the ley line fade as they moved away, and pushed the last lingering bits of current back into her core. The tingling in her skin faded, and she made an involuntary but heartfelt noise that sounded a lot like "ugh."

"I don't know what the hell you did back there, but you did good," he said.

"I don't know what I did back there either," she admitted. "Can I not have to do it again?"

Danny wasn't a Talent. He couldn't understand – it wasn't just that the visions were painful, or that she was tired of death aiming for her like cupid with his bow – she was a Storm-Seer, according to everyone, and it was like being an epileptic or color blind or something, just a thing you dealt with and adapted for and she got that she really did, but-

"I don't want to know that much about other people. I don't want to know what's going to happen to them. It's too much." She could still *see* it in her head, even though she'd tried not to look, tried not to notice anything, but it was all there. Death called the most strongly, limned itself with fire and frost, but every end result of every act and inaction was still there, hanging in the current around everyone.

And then Danny's hand was on her arm, curved around the crook of her elbow, and the fire dampened, the frost melted, and all Ellen felt was tired.

"Come on, Shadow," he said. "Time to be eye candy while I do some work."

That was just ridiculous enough to make her laugh.

---

MY QUIP HAD COVERED up hell of a lot of uncertainty. I wasn't quite sure what the hell had happened back there at the gate: everything I'd ever heard of Storm-Seers, which admittedly wasn't a hell of a lot except what Bonnie had told me after Ellen showed up on the scene, said that they were only able to read the future randomly, when the current spikes were strong enough, and never in a particularly directed manner, the way she just had, by touching them.

I had a passing thought that maybe she'd made it up – I mean, who the hell would know – but I knew the signs of current-exhaustion well enough. Whatever had gone on, it had drained her significantly. And she looked unhappy enough for it to be real. There were folk who could fake me out, but Shadow wasn't anywhere in their league.

The sun had finally gotten up high enough that the overnight lights were flicking off, and people were up and moving. The livestock areas were bustling – horses and bears and whatever else they had there didn't like to wait until a decent hour for their breakfast, I supposed. But while their handlers might be the most awake, I didn't think that was the best place to start, since they'd also be the most distracted, and probably armed.

Sometimes, distraction was good, it got you information they didn't want to give, either verbally or through body language. But trying to wrangle a large-ish animal meant that any distraction could get someone hurt. I didn't want to risk that, not when we had other options.

The midway, with its games of chance, was still shut down; it wouldn't come to life until mid-afternoon, when the gates opened to the public. And I wasn't quite ready to go barging into the living areas...not yet, anyway. Not unless we had cause to.

"Are you picking up anything else?"

"No. Just... we're in the right place. This is what I saw. But I don't, I can't *See* anything else."

"All right." I was getting soft, relying on her visions, anyway.

Time to prove I deserved my license.

"Hey!" I raised my voice, and called out to a figure up ahead, carrying a long pole with what looked like a lash at the end. "C'mere a minute."

The boy turned and looked at us, and then with a shrug that clearly said whatthehell, walked toward us. He was in his late teens, sullen-faced and muscled in a way that suggested he didn't spend most of his day in front of the television – or a book, for that matter.

"You cops?"

Oh, the suspicious mind of a migrant worker. "If we were cops, we wouldn't have gotten this far."

The boy grunted, and gave Ellen a once-over. Her chin went up and she stared him back. His gaze dropped first. Whatever issues Shadow had, giving the other gender shit for sexism clearly wasn't on the list.

"We're supposed to find someone, figured you might know where they are."

"Maybe." Sullen didn't sound hopeful. "What's their name?"

"Don't know," I admitted cheerfully. "Don't know where they've been assigned, either. But they're mer." As I spoke I pulled my cap off and ran my hand through my hair.

It was a risk – this kid was human, not even Talent, and he might be a pure Null for all I could tell. But the fact that two fatae had been assigned gatekeepers meant the probability that this was an integrated crew was high.

"Mer?"

Bingo. The boy was playing dumb but his body language gave him away: he was ready to sprint in the opposite direction if I made one wrong move.

I spent most of my days passing – cross-breeds were rare enough that the fact that I'd lived as human my entire life trumped the obvious fatae aspects of my appearance. But I knew how to switch that out, at-need. I'd never look wholly faun, but there was no doubt that I was fatae.

Especially to a teenaged kid who – despite his sullen act –

was no fool. His gaze flicked from my eyes to my horns, and then did a quick once-over, skimming along my body as though he were trying to adjust his initial perception. Then his gaze came back to my face, and I smiled. It wasn't, I admit, a pretty smile. In fact, I'd spent a lot of time practicing it to display just the right amount of arrogant shit.

"Mer," I said again. Two girls and a boy, teenagers."

There was a flicker, an awareness, and then something fell behind his eyes, and he took a step back. "I'm sorry. I don't know anyone like that here. Not too many of your folk around here, and none of 'em my age."

"Never said they were your age," I said softly. "Just teenaged. Wide range, there." I could have been wrong, it could just have been the normal teen ego assuming everything revolved around them. But I didn't think so.

"Mister I swear, I don't know anything. There's nobody like that working here now."

"But there was, before?" I could feel Ellen tense beside me, but I didn't dare take my eyes off the kid to check on her. Some of the fatae, they could wring the truth out of you, like it or not. That wasn't my skillset. My glamour was hail-fellow-well-met, and it wasn't effective once they'd gotten skittish.

"Lots of kids come through. They think it's a glee, an easy gig for the summer. That they can drink all night and sleep all day and make money and then go home again when the summer's done. Most of 'em don't last a week. Mer wouldn't last a day, unless they were working the dunktank."

He wasn't wrong. But we also weren't looking for someone who was working here. Not willingly, anyway.

"Who does the hiring and firing?"

Passing the buck, Sullen could do. "Perkins. His office is back of the back, the one with the flags flying, that means he's in. I can go now? I gotta get to work."

"Yeah, go," I said, and he was halfway across the lot before I'd gotten the second word out of my mouth.

Ellen had seen me dead, too. And maybe dead here, or at least in danger, here, with a gun.

"How much control do you have?" It was way too goddamned late for me to be asking that.

She licked her lips, and rubbed the bridge of her nose, like it itched. "More than I did six months ago."

Not much of an answer.

"The first thing Genevieve did was teach me defensive spells. She said there were enough people eyeballing her and Sergei, I had to be ready to duck and cover without her worrying about me, just in case."

That was a better answer. I reached around under my jacket, and pulled out my Glock. I hadn't needed to use it even for show in almost a year, and I didn't think I'd need it here... but the moment you weren't ready was the second you'd need it. And if she was seeing a gun, I'd rather it be mine than someone else's.

The grip was warm and familiar in my palm, my fingers curling around it as easy as clicking a mouse. I'd had the damn thing since I was in the academy, same as the boots on my feet. The boots had seen more use.

I checked the chamber, then reholstered the pistol. "Can you Translocate?"

She shook her head.

"Damn. Would have been useful. All right. Stay low and quiet."

I should send her back to the car, but that probably would be worse – I didn't trust the goons out back not to be stupid again, if they saw her alone.

THE TRAILER WAS AS ADVERTISED – four flags hanging limp over the roof: one American flag, one MIA, and two I didn't recognize. The door was open, a concrete brick holding it ajar. I knocked anyway.

"Yo, in."

The thing you learn, after a few years, is that most stereotypes and clichés become stereotypes and clichés for a reason. Perkins might've singlehandledly created the cliché of the stogie-smoking, scowl-faced carnie owner. I hadn't expected him to be Korean, but that was a minor dissonance in the cluttered, dingy office that also looked like the cliché of every carnie office, right down to the three generations out-of-date computer and the pile of fast food wrappers.

Perkins had a thing for Arby's.

"What can I do for ya?" He looked me up and down professionally, and I returned the favor. "Cop? Not local. Who're you looking for? I don't hire runaways, they're more trouble than they're worth."

I believed him. That didn't mean I trusted him.

"Not a cop. Private citizen." If he asked, I'd show him my I.D. but not unless he asked. He didn't. "Looking for three teenagers, traveling together. They came through here, we know that already so don't waste my time denying it. I want to know where they went."

There was a sound behind me, and Ellen stepped forward, not quite stepping in front of me, but fully visible. Out of the corner of my eye I saw her hands moving, a palms-up gesture that would have looked like a peace offering if you didn't know she was Talent. If you did, it looked an awful lot like she was gathering current. Perkin's gaze went to her hands, then to her face, and he let out a curse in a language I didn't know. Then, without warning, he broke.

"Bad crowd. Damned bad crowd. But the locals, they like their cut, and they're going to get it somehow, and a man's got to make ends meet, so I lease them space, every year." He scowled at me like it was all my fault, and a few things suddenly made sense.

"Cost of doing business," was all I said, though. Whatever deals he'd made with the locals, cops or criminals, human or otherwise, wasn't my business except if and as it led me to my targets.

"Yeah." His expression was sour, but his voice was as matter-of-fact as mine. Cost of doing business. When both cops and criminals require payoffs, what's a businessman to do?

"I threw them out, mid-season. Got to be too much, no matter how much money it brought in." He was sulky, not apologetic. I suspected they'd tried to undercut him, or something had gotten too expensive to pay off to cover up.

"So, my kids were with these people you didn't want hanging around your show. What were they doing?" The list of things a legit carny owner would spit at was pretty short, and matched with my expectation of where this case was going, but I wanted to put him on the burn, just a little.

"I don't know. I didn't go into their tent. I didn't want to know." His body language flashed from annoyed to distinctly uncomfortable, and back to annoyed again.

"Don't ask, don't tell?" Ellen said, not really a question. "You knew something bad was happening, and you looked away."

There was something dark in her voice that hadn't been there before, not even when the current was flooding her system, speaking through her. My skin prickled, and I felt the urge to step away.

"El..." I said. Not a warning, not a question, just a reminder. We were in an enclosed space, a *metal* enclosed space, and she'd admitted that she didn't have all that much control yet.

"I saw them. I *Saw* them. And he looked away." She took a step forward, now ahead of me, standing between me and

Perkins, and things had suddenly gone from in control to not in control.

"Where did they go?" I willed the idiot to answer me, and in detail. As much as I didn't want to cause a fuss here, I wasn't sure I'd be willing to get between a pissed-off Talent and her target, either, especially since she had a damned good point. If I thought it would do any good at all, I'd take him outside for a little come-to-Jesus myself.

"I don't know." His eyes shifted to the left, and I coughed. "I swear. But they've got winter quarters outside town. An old warehouse. I've never been there, never wanted to go, but it's all I got."

"Thanks ever so much for your help." The darkness was still in her voice, but it was tinged now with a note of snark that was pure Sergei Didier. Wren might be Ellen's mentor, but her partner was leaving his mark, too.

That was both reassuring, and unnerving as hell.

---

WHATEVER I'D BEEN EXPECTING to find at the warehouse, this hadn't been on the list.

"A sideshow?"

"A freak show." I considered the neon sign, leaning against the car and crossing my arms against my chest, aware that – in my boots and baseball cap and leather jacket – I probably looked as disreputable as the building I was studying. Ellen was next to me, trying to mimic my pose and failing. It looked easy, but took years of practice.

"You think they have them there...." She looked puzzled. "Maybe... a front for prostitution? Or drug-running?"

"Maybe." I'd be surprised as hell if there wasn't some of both of that going on here. "But they've got an interesting cover. Freak shows are better suited to carnivals, not somewhere like this, where you don't get a lot of casual traffic. Even if they wanted to set themselves up for off-season customers, why not somewhere closer to a tourist area, where you get casual traffic? God knows, I doubt zoning laws would get in their way, if they're able to throw money around."

Ellen tilted her head, and made a face, understanding that this was a test. "Because there's something about this location that's important. Or they want to stay under the radar, here."

"And how do we find out?"

"We go in."

She didn't sound thrilled. I understood: when you're a freak yourself – and we both were, to the rest of the world – you were cautious about gawking at other freaks. Never mind that this was probably no different than any other Barnum-inspired funhouse with Fiji mermaids and mummified monkeys, and maybe a down on their luck fatae flashing a little wing or tail for the Nullbies.

"Seventeen bucks. There had better at least be an egress," I muttered. Ellen gave me a confused look, but the woman taking our cash almost-smiled. I do appreciate a woman who knows the classics.

The first few rooms were the basics, the expected mummified monkeys, and what I was pretty sure was a piskie skeleton mislabeled as a tooth fairy. The thought of one of those kewpie- troll-doll menaces acting as tooth fairy was almost worth the

$17 right there.

"Is that..." Ellen poked one finger at a glass case leaning over it to see better. "Is that a serpent's skin, like the one we talked to?"

"Yeah. They shed on a regular basis, when they're young. Might have washed up on the beach, or even been traded for something. Pretty, isn't it?"

"Prettier than when it's on it," Ellen said. She wasn't wrong:

in the artificial light, the old skin glinted with a definite irides-
cent shimmer that the sea water had muted.

There was a scattering of other people walking through the
rooms, one group of teenagers gathering around one case,
giggling nervously, a father and daughter pair, dad making sure
to keep her smaller hand in his, no matter how she tugged to
rush ahead, and an older couple, moving slowly, with evident
pleasure, through the exhibits. And a woman, leaning against
the far wall, near a sign that did, indeed, say "This way to the
egress."

The employee saw me looking, and smiled. It was a carny
smile. I sighed, and put on my best dumb mark expression.

"You like our exhibit?" she asked as I wandered over in her
direction. Her nametag said she was Kerry, and she was good,
mixing her professional shiller mode with an undercurrent of

bored-with-this-job and a hint of actual physical interest.
Just the thing to hook a male mark who needed his ego stroked
by a little casual flirtation.

"It's okay." Casual, playing it cool, too cool to give in but
definitely interested, even though I was there with someone.
She wasn't human. She thought I was, though. "None of it's
real, though, obviously."

"Yeah?"

"Please." I invested the word with male dismissive behavior,
guaranteed to irk any female with a brain.

Ellen wandered up slowly, hanging back like she wasn't
sure that she was welcome to join. I had a bad feeling that she
wasn't playing – that she really was that unsure of her place,
even now – but it worked too well for me to wave her closer yet.
I'd apologize and explain later.

"You want to see something that'll really blow your world
away?" Kerry said, her tone a come-on and a challenge, paired
with one raised eyebrow.

I narrowed my eyes at her and cocked my head, playing the overly-confident rube. "And how much is it gonna cost me?"

She laughed, leaning in like she was going to tell me a secret. "High-rollers pay thousands, because they're suckers. For you?" She gave me another once-over, not even trying to be subtle. "For you, ten bucks more, that's all. Another ten dollars for the stuff tourists don't get to see."

It wasn't the best hook I'd ever heard, but I'd have bit no matter what. I pulled out my wallet, and counted out twenty dollars, handing it to her. She took the cash, and leaned back to press open a door that had been hidden in the wall behind her. "Go on in," she said. "Enjoy."

The door led into a landing, and then a short flight of stairs leading down. The stairwell was barren but well-lit, and the steps were clean and in good repair. I tensed up anyway, and reached back to take Ellen's hand, squeezing it once in warning before letting go. The door closed behind us, and I had the Glock in my hand, dipped down but ready. I didn't think this was a trap, but I didn't know *what* it was. Prepared was better.

---

At the bottom of the stairs there was no ambush, no guards, and no goons of any species waiting to get shot. There were, however, cases. Large cases and small ones, a dozen or so, each lit with professional quality lighting.

Gun still in-hand, I stepped forward and looked into the first case. A face looked back. My breath caught, even as part of my brain was categorizing what I saw, the way I used to scan a crime scene. Ridged forehead, pearlescent skin yellowed with age, eyes wide and milky-white, and a jaw that, dropped open, showed a double row of sharp, shark-like teeth.

A Nagini. Just the head, and a chunk of her neck: the

muscled serpent's body missing, maybe lost, maybe cut off for easier display.

My throat tight, I moved on to the next case.

"Danny?" Ellen's voice was too small, too quiet, and I abandoned the display of what looked like a centaur's forearm to see what she had found. She was standing in front of one of the full-sized cases, at the back, and her hands were palm-flat on the glass, as though trying to reach inside.

The case was set up like a diorama, with a painted backdrop of leaves, green and vibrant, while a three-dimensional tree trunk filled the center of the case, and in front of that...

No, not in front of. *Nailed* to the tree was the body of a woman, her skin smooth and brown, her arms twined above her head, her hair falling over one shoulder, down to her hips, her face...

God, her face.

Most people – Nulls, maybe even some Talent – would assume this was more of what was upstairs, frauds expertly done. I knew better.

"A dryad," Ellen choked out. "They did this to a dryad."

And another fatae had sent us down here, knowing what we'd see. Not that we had any great claim to the moral high ground compared to humans, overall, but... I'd trained myself to hold back emotion, to never let the anger interfere with the job. This took a hard shove, but it stayed down.

"Come on." I used my free hand to gather Ellen in closer, and we moved away from the ghoulish display, moving toward the back of the room, where a short hallway led us to another room, both of us bracing to find our missing trio, even as I prayed that I was wrong, that this wasn't what it was.

There were four exhibits in this room, each in a full, floor to ceiling case. And they were moving.

My first instinct was to break the cases, to free the beings inside, but Ellen's hand on my arm held me back. I looked back, and her face was strained, stressed, her eyes too wide and intently focused.

"Current," she said, looking at the half-dozen piskies fluttering around inside their case. "They're not alive, not really. Just...moving."

Magic. A Talent did this. Not that I had any particular love for the squirrel-sized tricksters of the fatae, but not even piskies deserved this.

And the other cases....

Ellen let out a harsh cry, and fell to her knees, a howl rising out of her throat that made me want to kill something, anything, just to feed the bloodthirst I could feel in that sound. The rage that escaped my control, finally, was cool and hard, implacable, and in need of something to hit.

In the other case, the largest one, were three mer, one perched on a rock, combing out her long green hair, the other two half-submerged, their tails flicking underwater, as though they were telling each other stories, or competing for her attention.

Ellen keened, and I dropped to my knees beside her, trying to keep my gun out and ready while still trying to offer some useless support, some reminder that she wasn't alone, my arm over her shoulders, holding her to me the way I would any injured, frightened child.

Too late. Far too late to save them; whatever Ellen had seen must have been echoes of their road to this place, this end. "Are they aware?" I didn't want to know, didn't want to ask, but I needed to.

"I don't..." She choked back a sob, the sound thick with phlegm and sorrow. "I don't know. There's..." She stared at the case as though trying to memorize it. "There's current there, but it's wrapped around them so tightly, I can't tell if anything's beneath any more."

Current was kin to electricity. Life ran on electricity, too, the pump of hearts, the tingle in our brains. The thought that they might be aware, turned into conscious waxwork displays to horrify and titillate... it was worse than any horror movie I'd ever seen, because it was real.

"Why?" So much pain in that voice, so much anger. "Why do I see things I can't change? What's the point?"

Everything she'd hoped to do, tagging along with me, had shattered. I wanted to comfort her, but there was no comfort in this room.

"We know what happened to them," I said. "There's no more uncertainty for their families. Sometimes, that's the best we can do."

It sounds weak, but being able to give a family closure can be enough. When you know it's not going to end well, having it end with even a small kindness...you take the gifts you get.

"Not enough. They change out the exhibits, the sign on the door out front said, new ones every six weeks." Ellen's voice was raw but clear. "This is new... they had others before. They'll have others again."

She looked up at the mer display, and something in her face changed, like the ocean had washed under her skin. "This is wrong."

On so many levels. But this misuse of magic, and fatae involved with the actual freak show, from the security to the door guard... it was going to get messy.

"We can sic the PUPs on them, but for now we need to keep moving." I could feel the time ticking down again – not for the teens, but for us. At some point, someone was going to start talking, and this place was not exactly the kind of place that liked official notice. If we wanted to bring them down, we had to make sure they didn't spook.

And I hadn't forgotten that she'd seen me dead, too.

"All right." Ellen got to her feet, wobbling a little, but her back straightened and her chin went up, and I didn't know how far it would carry her, but it was enough for now.

We made it as far as the exit – and this one had an actual exit sign on it, not egress – when someone came in through the out door.

"Not so fast," the person said. Perkins. And he had a gun, too.

"Oh, fuck me," I said.

———

ELLEN HAD GONE THROUGH TOO many emotional switches already. She'd been scared, and sad, and horrified, and too many other things she wasn't quite able to grasp. When the carny owner confronted them, she reacted without thinking, following not instinct – to hide – but the way Genevieve had been training her, to grab hold of her current and let it flow through her, opening herself up to it so that she was ready to defend herself.

And when she did that, something pushed at her. Something large, not powerful in and of itself, but large enough to make itself known. It didn't feel like current, but it didn't *not* exactly, either. She tried to ignore it, keeping her gaze on the man in front of them, trying to see what Danny was doing, in case they had to make a sudden run for it, or if she was supposed to drop or-

That something pushed at her again, enough to slide through, a tendril, no, a gnat, biting at her, shoving something into her awareness, finding a tiny hole and forcing its way through.

"You bastard." She knew, suddenly, as though the mers had told her, their last whispers in her ear. "You sold them. You told them they'd have jobs, lured them here, and then you sold them!" Once she opened herself to it, the whisper grew into a wave, swamping her, explaining everything without having to say anything at all. The other fatae in the cases were too weak, their awareness too faint to start, or gone too long. But the mers were fresh, the magic animating them keeping electrical impulses running in their brain, too, enough that she had *Seen* them, *Seen* their despair, their sense of betrayal, the way they'd been moved from place to place…

They had called her here. Nobody else could hear them.

Nobody else could do this.

Current hummed inside her, making her feel queasy, like she was going to throw up, but at the same time like she could do anything, explode into violence like the ninja whatevers in the old movies her mother loved. Genevieve had warned her about that, about how dangerous is was to let current take control, that she could do more damage than she meant to.

She wanted to do a lot of damage. But Danny was next to her, and there were people upstairs, and she didn't know *how* to hurt only the right people.

"Just you?" Danny was saying, and she was confused at first, distracted by the current-hum, unable to focus well on the two armed men in front of her.

"Son, I don't want to be here," Perkins said, lifting his weapon until it was pointed directly at Danny's chest. "All you had to do was walk away, and nobody needed to be here, nobody needed to get hurt," he continued, like they were having a friendly little chat. "I told you the truth – I didn't want this anywhere near my show."

"But not out of any moral bias," Danny said, and his voice was dry, dry as paper, dry as winter air. "Just because things were getting too hot. Maybe the local inspectors got complaints? Comments that couldn't be ignored? There's always a small percentage of suckers who get too disturbed, who start to think, instead of reacting, and maybe some of them knew about the fatae, knew that your 'side show' was too real to not be real?"

"All it takes is one weak willy," Perkins said, "and the bribes cost more than what you're taking in. But I didn't like it, not once I knew about," and the tip of the gun moved slightly, taking in the entire basement, "this. Doesn't matter, didn't matter. Once you're in the game, you don't get to walk out again."

Ellen could *see* it all now, not the moment of death but just before, in that basement in the house by the Shore, the moment of realization when the girl cried out, desperate for something, for someone to know what had happened to her, to them, and the current had carried that call, dropping it into her brain, her core. It had all come from that, everything that brought them here.

There was no meaning to it, there was no hidden purpose.

It was all chance, all random, who she heard, who she saw, flickers in the current-line, roads taken or not-taken.

Danny had moved in front of her, a subtle but clear protection, for all the good it would do, and was still talking. "So you're here to kill us, is that it?"

"Of course not," the man said. "Killing a human? That's illegal. Oh, wait. You're not human, are you?"

Fatae had no protection, because they didn't exist, legally. He thought she was fatae, too. But he had felt her pull current... Ellen realized, suddenly, that Perskins didn't know about Talent. He knew about fatae, but not magic. He thought they were all the same, and his business partners had never told him anything else.

They were going to die. Die, and Danny would end up in one of these displays, and -

*genevieve* She didn't know if she could ping loud enough, over this far away, but she didn't know what else to do.

*bonnie!*

The current sizzled and snapped around her, demanding that she do something. Something *now*, not waiting for someone else, hoping someone else will fix everything.

Random chance. But random chance that ended with her, *here*.

"Don't be a fool," Danny said, his voice tight and angry, but not scared, he wasn't scared, and he stepped forward and the gun went off, too loud in the basement room. Ellen dropped instinctively even before Danny's body hit hers, taking her to the ground, and then there was another gunshot, or maybe the echo of the first, and terror ripped through her, loosing the current in her core without any control whatsoever.

The glass cases shattered, and all she heard was screaming. Some of it might have been her own.

---

I HATE GETTING SHOT. Never happened while I was on the force, but since then? Three times: twice in the leg, once in the shoulder. This made a third time in the leg, and it never hurt any less. The fact that I was pretty sure he'd been aiming for my chest wasn't much consolation.

The noise seemed to have died down, so I lifted my head and risked looking around. Underneath me, Ellen made a noise, and tried to get up, too.

"No. Stay down." I put my hand on her head, and kept her from looking. She didn't need to see this.

I couldn't use magic, but I could feel it. I was pretty sure head-blind Nulls a mile away would have felt this.

The glass cases were all shattered, the lights overhead likewise. The room was lit by a handful of emergency lights, the red glow adding to the surreal hellishness.

Perkins lay in front of us, face up. Or what was left of his face, anyway. Something had gouged at him, torn him apart, and left him in a puddle of... watered down blood.

I was pretty sure, without bothering to test it, that it was seawater. Poor bastard. He'd gotten too deep in bad things, but as much as I despised him, he wasn't the one who'd done this.

He'd been the one they could reach, though. Maybe. They? Maybe my Shadow had done this on her own. I didn't think so, though.

I'd leave figuring it out to the PUPs. My responsibility was to the living.

"Come on," I said, sliding my hand down to Ellen's shoulder. "Close your eyes, and come on. Trust me, and don't look."

She got to her feet, still shaking, and slid her hand into my other one, twisting her fingers with mine. I tried to project as much reassurance as I could into my voice and touch, and slowly her skin warmed, her shaking eased.

"Your leg..."

"Hurts like hell, needs to be looked at, yeah. But not here.
Let's go."

I'm not sure who was supporting whom, but we walked out of the exit and up into the lobby of the building. A few people stared, but nobody stopped us, as we walked out into the sunlight, and the car.

---

MOST OF MY CASES, I get to see the wrap-up. I'm the one who delivers a missing kid home, or tells the client good news about whatever they'd feared... or brings them the news they're never prepared to hear. Sometimes it's the best moment in the world, sometimes it's the worst, but there's always a sense of closure, that the agreement I'd entered into had been fulfilled.

I didn't have that, here. We'd gotten back to the city without incident, dropping the car off at the rental place and cabbing it, not back to my office, or the emergency room, but directly to the PUPI offices uptown. Bonnie'd been waiting, as had Valere and her partner, hovering with a mix of fear and anger. Valere had been almost maternal, swooping down on Ellen and wanting to know what had happened, if she was okay. The girl put up with it for a few minutes, stoic as an oak, and then broke down, wrapping her arms around her knees and putting her head down in a clear do-not-ask warning sign.

I didn't blame her a damn bit. I was tempted to myself. But Bonnie and Venec were waiting, and I needed to give them my report, so they could go do whatever it was they could do, to make sure this mess didn't get swept under anyone's' rug.

That's what PUPI was there for, to make sure magical crimes didn't get excused, explained, or otherwise forgotten. And if that meant that I didn't get to be in on the final moments... I was all right with that, for once. There wasn't anyone to tell: I knew that the sideshow'd already moved on,

and finding them would be damned near impossible. Word would go out, because the *Cosa Nostradamus* would know, once PUPI was done. People – our people – would be alert, now.

Only what happened before I could say anything was that their office manager/medic took one look at me, and had me flat on my back and pantsless in under three minutes, possibly a world record. Only after she'd pronounced me bullet free and luckier than I deserved, and stitched me up, was Venec was allowed to take over. He was the thorough bastard I'd expected, wringing the last detail out of me until I almost wished the bullet had done more damage.

By the time I was turned loose, Ellen had been swept away by her mentor. I stood in the office lobby, my leg aching like a bitch, and feeling weirdly bereft. She had only shown up, what, 36 hours ago? If that? How had I gotten used to having a shadow, so quickly?

I hoped that Valere was able to help her deal with what

she'd seen what she'd done, and headed home to a date with my case notes for the job Ellen's arrival had interrupted, a stool to put my leg up on, and a bottle of gin.

---

I DON'T DRINK OFTEN, but when I do, it's with the intensity and fierceness of my faun kin. And twice in one week added up, even for me. Which meant that when someone slammed on the door of my apartment at WTF early the next morn- ing, I wanted to tell them to fuck off and die. Instead, I made sure I was wearing shorts - I was - and staggered to the front door. I didn't get hungover as easily as humans did, but there was some definite dehydration-exhaustion happening in my cells.

"Open the door, Danny."

I opened the door. My shadow stood there, looking about as good as I felt. But she was fully dressed, and carrying a box of what smelled like pain au chocolat.

"Come in," I said, but she was already in, handing me the box and stalking into the apartment like she owned it. I closed the door behind her, and leaned against it, holding the pastry box. Definitely pain au chocolat. My mouth watered, even as my brain demanded coffee. And my body wanted painkillers.

"Genevieve says twenty-four hours with you did more good for my control than a month of training," she said without any kind of hello or how are you. Although the latter was probably pretty obvious. "She says you're Earth to my Air, whatever the hell that means."

"Current and grounding." I knew that much about Talent, anyway. Air was current, earth was...well, earth. I looked down at the pastries in my hand, and saw not Valere's hand in this, but Sergei's. I didn't think well in the morning, but even I knew something was up. "Why are you here?"

Ellen turned and stared at me from across the entry foyer of my apartment. She seemed to suddenly notice that I was considerably underdressed, let her gaze drop to my feet, flushed slightly, and then kept her gaze trained on my face.

"It's all random," she said. "What I see, what I hear, it's not God sending a message, or people picking me because I'm me. There's no point to it except whatever meaning I can give it."

If she'd figured that out, she was well ahead of most of the world.

So, I see the dead. No. " She collected herself, started again. "I see those who're going to die, violently. I can't stop that, for whatever reason. And Genevieve...she can't help me, not with that. It freaks her out a little. It freaks everyone out. Except you." She swallowed hard. "I don't know why you're not scared of me, but you're not."

---

MAYBE BECAUSE I didn't understand it, all the potential she carried inside her, the way other Talent could. Maybe I was an idiot. But she was right: I wasn't scared of her, or what she did, or what she could do.

I should have been. If I'd any sense...

No, that wasn't right. I had plenty of sense. Maybe even too much of it. And Valere – and Didier – knew that. Fuck.

"I'm no mentor," I said.

"I have a mentor." She stared at me, not arguing, just waiting for me to figure it out on my own.

This was a really bad idea, on so many levels. I worked alone, she had no training, no license. No idea what she was asking for.

"This job hurts," I said. "Rip-your-guts-out hurt, sometimes."

"I know. God, I *know*. I don't want this. I never wanted this any of this. But I can't just," and she waved a hand in the air, unable to articulate whatever it was she couldn't do. "I can't not."

We stared at each other, while I tried to find a comeback to that, and failed.

"*Only one way to screw up this game, rookie.*" My partner's voice, my first day on the street. "*And that's thinking whatever you do don't matter. Because everything we do, matters.*"

"Fuck."

I may have said that out loud, because Ellen almost cracked a smile. I remembered the pastry box in my hand, and handed it to her. "Kitchen's over there. Go put these on plates and pour me some coffee while I put some damn clothes on."

Looked like my shadow was going to stick around.

## PROMISES TO KEEP

The Thursday morning train was crowded, the weather was miserable with just enough rain to be, well, miserable, and we were coming up on a full week of non-employment. While I normally would never ill-wish anyone, it would not have bothered me if someone'd had something or someone go missing. At this point, I'd even take a stalk-n-snap job, just to have something to do.

Our office was a full block from the subway entrance. The rain had paused, but the air was still so damp with humidity, it almost didn't make a difference. My boots – acquired from a supply store in Oklahoma a decade ago – kept my feet dry, but my shirt was sticking to my back, and the cuffs of my slacks were soaked. At least I didn't have allergies. It seemed as though every other person I passed was sneezing and red-eyed from pollen.

I got off the elevator on our floor, took off my baseball cap and shook the dampness out of my hair, and checked my watch. Exactly seven fifty-eight. Well, at least I wasn't going to be late.

"Hey boss," a cheerful voice greeted me as I walked through

the door at exactly seven fifty-nine. "Coffee maker's broken."

I stared at my secretary-slash-assistant-slash-not-quite-apprentice, and sighed. Of course it was. And the look on her face told me *why*. "What have I told you about using current in the office?"

"I didn't." Ellen sat behind her desk, the very picture of injured innocence, which, considering I was the one out a coffee maker was just damned unfair. "Your new client did. But I ran down and got you some from the corner cart."

I hung my hat and jacket on the tree, while she picked up an unmistakable blue-and-white food cart cup from her desk and offered it to me. The coffee smelled of heaven, and had cooled down enough for me to hold the cup easily. Good girl. Not her fault thcurrent – magic, if you're old-school – wrecked havoc with most appliances.

"New client, huh?" The day was looking up, busted appliance notwithstanding. I took a sip, and then looked around as though she might have stashed the client somewhere, ready to leap out at me once I was caffeinated.

The office still looked the same as when I'd opened Sylvan Investigations seven years ago, after taking my twenty-and-out from the NYPD. The front room was clean but no-frills, a few potted plants clumped in the corner, waist-high and thriving, despite the fact that there'd never been a single ray of natural sunlight in this room since they put the walls up. The floor was scuffed hardwood, the walls were painted a non-industrial shade of sage green, and the wooden desk I'd bought at a fire sale for twenty bucks still sat in the middle of all that.

The difference between when I'd first set up shop and today was that the desk was now covered with manila folders, a dozen different colored pens, an antique but still workable electric typewriter plugged into the best surge protector my money could buy, and anywhere from three to seven cans of soda in various stages of empty, depending on the hour of the day and how bad a day it had been. And the girl behind the desk, abuser of both the typewriter and the soda.

We'd been working together for four months now, since Ellen's vision of three missing mer-children first brought us together. And by "brought" I mean she came to me asking for help, and I was dumb enough to give it.

Ellen was Talent, one of the magic-using humans of the Cosa Nostradamus. What in earlier days had been called a witch, a warlock, a sorceress. Me? I'm...not. Magic-using, or human. Despite that, we'd worked that first job together well enough

that her mentor, Wren Valere, had decided working for me on a regular basis would be part of her training.

Valere hadn't asked me first, of course.

"Drink your coffee, boss. Your horns are showing."

I don't know who'd taught her that was the fatae equivalent of calling someone a ditzy blonde, but I had my suspicions. If my office evoked a vague echo of the seedy-but-competent detectives of the 1940's – and I'm not saying it did, intentionally or otherwise – then Ellen could have swung the faithful Girl Friday. She wasn't particularly dishy, although she was young, and her style was more jeans and a sweatshirt than tight skirt and heels, but she had the sass down damn near perfect.

When it was just us, anyway. Other people came into the picture, and the uncertain, beat-down-too-damn-much shadow I'd first met made an unwelcome reappearance. But we were working on that, too.

"So," I prompted Ellen, leaning my hip against her desk. "New client?"

"In your office." Ellen handed me one of the files from her desk, while I, obedient, took another sip of coffee. "Mrs. Christina Eloise McConnell. A Ms. O'Sullivan sent her."

I remembered O'Sullivan. Her secretary had been hanging out with some rather nasty people who took things that didn't belong to them. She had been professionally grateful for my help - apparently enough to send her friends along, too. I'm fond of former clients like that.

"What's the deal?" I asked, even as I flipped open the folder and scanned the top sheet. Ellen had better-than-decent hand-writing, but she typed everything out so I could scan it into the files later. Having an assistant who was Talent - and therefore as likely to short out the entire office as get a file saved - meant I did more work, not less. Fortunately, she had other skills and abilities that made up for it, when they weren't getting us into more trouble, anyway.

But this seemed like a standard-issue referral, not what I'd come to think of as a Shadow Special, where her foresight got us involved. "Missing husband," Ellen said, and then let me read the rest.

"Missing a full twenty-four hours, from.... He disappeared from the roof?" I looked up from the report, surprised.

"Uh-huh."

"Well, that's different. And I take it her distress translated into our coffee maker going spoffle?"

Even when she smiled, Ellen looked serious. "Actually, she was detailing what he was supposed to be doing up on the roof, instead of disappearing, and it went spoofle. I don't think she's too happy with him."

"I can't imagine why," I said dryly, walking past the desk and opening the door to my inner office.

Mrs. McConnell was proof that you couldn't put a stereo-type on Talent. She was in her late fifties, well-preserved in the way suburban ladies of a certain income level get, dressed in a tasteful suit and carrying a bag that you could have hid a mid-sized Chevy in. She was from Westchester County, where the wealthy don't-quite-flee NYC, though, so it was more likely a Prius, or a Volvo.

She didn't turn in her chair to look at me as I came in,

waiting until I walked past her to my desk and introduced myself. Her gaze could cut glass, but her body language said she was more than a little embarrassed.

"I believe I owe you a coffee maker," she said.

I waved it off, pulling my chair out and sitting down behind my desk. "It happens. I take it you're calmer now?"

Either way, I wasn't going to take my laptop out of the shielded drawer until she left the office.

"Yes. I am sorry," she said, and looked it. I guess it was bad manners for a nice suburban lady to bust up a guy's coffee maker without having even met him yet.

Apologies offered and accepted, I was all business. "So, what can I do for you?"

Sylvan Investigations was, on paper, your basic private investigation firm. That meant that I took pretty much all comers, so long as they didn't smell too badly of trouble, and tried to find whatever it was they were missing, or track down what they feared was wrong. Nobody ever showed up in my office because they were having a good day.

But every PI has a specialization, even if they didn't advertise it. Mine was magic. Not the using of it - I'm no Talent - but the problems that came from it, the use and abuse. And for her to be sitting in my office first thing in the damned morning, that was trouble with a capital T and that spelled Talent.

"My husband has gone missing," she told me.

"Off the roof of your house, yes." I placed the file down on the surface of my desk which, unlike Ellen's, was clear of everything. My citations and clippings were framed and hung on the wall where everyone could see them and be reassured, and my pens and notebooks were secured in the drawer underneath my laptop, to be taken out when I needed them. I'd been raised to Navy standards, and some habits died hard. "He's been missing more than twenty-four hours, according to this. And the cops aren't interested?"

"They came to the house and looked around this morning, but there was no evidence of foul play, so they took down all his information and basically washed their hands of the matter. They told me to wait for him to come home. Or contact a divorce lawyer. You were a member of the NYPD yourself,

Mister Hendrickson. You know how it works. He's a grown man, there was no sign of foul play, no ransom request or particularly odd behavior. They'll look, because we're well-off, but they won't look very hard."

Unfortunate, but not unexpected. I had no doubt my former brothers-in-blue were running all the usual searches, but her husband, at least on paper, wasn't wealthy enough to be worth ransom, he wasn't important enough to have serious enemies, and unless a background search turned up something else, he was just another person gone walkabout. Kids, yeah. Kids and women, someone tended to take it personally. Middle-aged married white men, not so much. Not enough money to buy top billing, not cute enough to grab heartstrings, not ethnic enough to make good copy.

Unless this was a Talent thing. If the Cosa Nostradamus was involved, the cops up in Westchester wouldn't be much use, anyway.

"Do you have any reason not to believe that he simply Translocated off the roof, and hasn't thought to contact you?"

Not every Talent could Translocate, use current to move themselves from one place to another. I didn't understand the whys and wherefores of it at all, but apparently you needed a strong sense of self, plus what amounted to an internal GPS to get you there in one piece.

"Al couldn't have Translocated himself from the bathtub to the toilet." Her words were fond, not frustrated or disparaging. "He isn't high res at all - neither of us are, really. I suppose that's why..." and she made a vague, slightly helpless gesture I took to indicate her encounter with the coffee maker. She hadn't been expecting it to happen.

High-res was someone like Wren Valere, or Benjamin Venec, who led the Cosa's only crime scene investigation team. Or my Girl Friday, sitting calmly outside doing filing for minimum wage and pizza every Friday. You couldn't ever tell from the outside. But strong emotions could do serious damage, even at a lower level.

"Had your husband been upset, or worried about anything? Money problems? Personal problems?" The next question involved sexual problems, so I wanted to get everything else squared away before I had to go there. If there was a cause that didn't require me to hear the backdoor confessions from a client, I'd prefer that. Not that I'm a prude - pretty much impossible, considering my parentage - but Mrs. McConnell wasn't my type.

"No." But she didn't sound certain.

I'm a good investigator. I'm well-trained, detail-oriented, and trust both my brain and my gut. I also have an advantage that most other investigators and cops don't have. People *want* to like me. They *want* me to like *them*. It's nothing I do, nothing I've learned; it's just there, encoded into my genetics. Not being an idiot, I use it - carefully, but I use it. It's not tricky. Lean forward, look them in the eye. Basic moves that make the subject feel that you're engaged, that you do care. And then I loosen the torque a little, ease the hold I keep on myself most of the time, and let some of that natural, damnable faun charm leak out. Just enough - like I said, she wasn't my type.

"I can only help you if you tell me everything."

"He... we've been married almost thirty years," she said. "And I know he's cheated on me. Not often, and never anything serious. They're one-night stands. He loves me."

She wasn't making excuses or justifications: these were things she *knew*.

"But I think…" She swallowed hard, and her forehead drew in, careless of the wrinkles it might leave. "I think one of the times he screwed up. I think there was a child."

"You think, or you know?" Had the mother - or the child - come sniffing around, looking to cause trouble?

"I think that he thought there was a child," she clarified.

"He hadn't ever said anything, but there was a look on his face, sometimes. And he tried to find someone, once. Recently."

My finely-honed and trained investigative instincts, not to mention my basic bullshit detector, told me that we'd gotten to the meat of it. "Someone?"

She reached into her bag of holding, and pulled out a plain gray folder. "He hired another investigator to find someone. A woman. I found the files a few weeks ago, when we were doing a renovation of the study. It didn't seem worth bringing up, then. Now, though… I thought it might be connected?"

I took the folder and flipped it open. He'd gone to one of my colleagues, another ex-cop who'd hung out his shingle. Keith Hartman. Hartman was a decent guy, good at his job. Not in my league, but decent enough. They'd been looking for a woman who seemed determined to stay just out of reach. Hartman's report went back three years: she'd lived in a rental apartment for the first year, then disappeared for a while, and then came back on the radar briefly, this time showing up on hospital records. And then she disappeared again, a little over eight months ago. About when our missing person starting asking about her. And that's where the trail apparently ended.

"Hospital. Maternity ward. And you think it was his?"

Mrs. McConnell gave an elegant, if helpless, shrug. "I think that he thought it was possible. But all he did was what you have; he didn't push them to look more."

And then he disappeared off the roof of their home. Taken alone, that was odd. Together with a mysterious woman and an unknown baby both disappearing off the face of the earth, it was odd enough to make my horns itch.

"You realize that, once I start looking, I might find things that are uncomfortable?" The kid, yeah, but also the fact that he had probably gone off of his own free will, without caring what his wife thought or felt. Or at least, not caring enough to clue her in.

Mrs. McConnell was a classy dame. She met my gaze square, and nodded once. "I understand."

The door opened, soft on its hinges, and Ellen tilted her head slightly, waiting to hear if she was going to be asked to run an errand, fetch a file, or clean up ex-former-client off the floor. Instead, Mrs. McConnell shook hands all around - even Ellen's which surprised Ellen a little, but she liked it - and nodded when Danny told her they'd email a contract that afternoon. They meaning he: she wasn't allowed anywhere near his laptop.

Then their new client was gone, and the boss exhaled once. It wasn't an unhappy or exasperated sound, more like he'd been thinking too hard to remember to breathe. Then he turned and went back into his office, leaving the door open. That meant she was supposed to follow him.

"So," she said, standing in the doorway. "So."

Danny was sitting at his desk, his feet up, leaning back in the wooden chair at an angle. Every time Ellen saw him do that, she was convinced that he was going to fall backward and crack his skull open. It hadn't happened yet, at least not when she'd been around to see. She took the seat the client had just vacated, and tried to match his casual position, without actually putting her feet up. She thought that might be a bit much.

"Missing husband," he said. "Off a roof."

He waved a hand airily, dismissing that aspect. "Either he was snatched off the roof by something winged, in which case we're probably not going to find him except as jumbo-sized pellets, or he went on his own. If he went on his own we have a chance."

"There are things large enough to take a grown man off a roof?" Ellen wasn't sure if he was joking or not. There were still things about this world, about the Cosa Nostradamus, that she didn't know, didn't understand. That made it painfully easy for others to punk her.

Not that Danny would. She thought. No, she was sure.

"Rocs, although they're not native around here. There was a native bird that could have done it but I'm pretty sure any still around aren't nesting in the suburbs. Dragons, natch, but if a great worm, or even a lesser one, took him, we're done."

Dragons she knew about. Not quite first-hand but close enough. A distance of about two miles – the distance between Madame's townhouse in Harlem and their office - was close enough.

"So where do we start?" They'd taken a missing person case before, but that had been a pair of teenagers who'd run off together, what Danny had called good starter material. This sounded like it would be more complicated.

"With what our missing man was looking for. Or rather, what he was rather carefully not looking for."

She really hated it when the boss got cryptic. It meant he was making shit up as he went, again.

---

WHEN ELLEN HAD FIRST STARTED WORKING with with Danny Hendrickson, she'd been relegated to following and watching. His shadow, he called her. This time, though, she had gotten handed her assignment and sent off to do it. Alone. That made her feel triumphant for about ten minutes.

Most investigation work, Ellen had quickly learned, was incredibly boring. On the other hand, it could be worse; at least she got out of the office. Danny took all the on-line research, because he was less likely to short out their entire office with one misplaced burst of frustration. Bad enough they were going to have to buy a new coffee maker: if they had to buy a new printer and laptop, the budget would be fried, too.

Doing legwork wasn't exactly glamorous, though. "So, what's this guy's name again?"

"Alfred McConnell," she said, trying not to lean away. Chadwick was a good guy, as things went. Human, Talent, and generally happy to help out, he was her first stop not because she thought he'd know anything pertinent, but because talking to him wasn't particularly stressful, and she needed all the confidence-building she could get.

She just wished he'd stop trying to look down the neck of her sweater.

"Huh. Nope. He's local work?"

"Westchester."

She might as well have said Mars; Chadwick shook his head and pushed the photo back to her. "Sorry, Ellen. You know me, I don't work much above 96th Street."

"Yeah, I figured, but you're the first stop on the list, as always."

He took that as a compliment to his knowledge, and preened a little. Ellen kept her expression professional-tough, but inside she felt a giggle shake free. The first time she and Danny had come to see Chadwick, she had been terrified; other Talent were still a mystery to her, and men - especially older men - way out of her league. But then Danny had introduced her as Wren Valere's mentee and the other man had practically bugged his eyes out, and said '"ma'am," until she'd rolled her eyes and told him to call her Ellen.

She knew Genevieve was powerful and well-respected - and with reason. She also knew that she herself was, by the standards of the Cosa Nostradamus, and as Talents judged things, almost as powerful. But she didn't *feel* powerful. And Ellen's real power, the reason other people were cautious around her, and treated her with respect, wasn't anything she could control, or consciously use. Her StormSeer sense was external rather than internal, someone's intense need reaching out to her through the natural strands of current, a ley line, or thunderstorm.

This case had none of that; she had intentionally walked through Central Park, over a known ley line, to make sure. Not even an itch of foreboding, not a single vision.

Ellen knew that she should be thankful: her visions tended to end badly. And yet she felt somehow useless, like *not* seeing their client in imminent mortal danger meant she'd let Danny down somehow.

Sergei, Genevieve's partner, said she suffered from a Surfeit of Insecurity Syndrome. He had smiled when he said it, but he hadn't been joking, not really.

"The person you should talk to," Chadwick said thoughtfully, almost unwillingly, "is Madame Haddad."

Haddad. Ellen sat back in her chair and considered the other Talent. She knew of her by reputation, but had never met the other woman. She was a power-broker, a matcher. Genevieve had never worked with her because she had Sergei, but had said she was good at what she did, matching Talent up with clients who needed their particular skills.

"You think-" she started to ask, when Chadwick spoke over her.

"I'm just saying that she's got a finger on the pulse of everything that goes down. If this was anything more than a guy taking a flying leap into nowhere, she'd have the skinny."

"Ellen Bint al-Genevieve"

Getting an appointment to see the woman had been as simple as showing up and asking the receptionist if Madame

Haddad was in. She hadn't even given her name; she hadn't thought it necessary. She'd been right.

Mahiba Haddad was tall, elegant, and very old. Her suit was perfectly tailored, her headdress a delicate length of silk that covered her hair and draped loosely around her shoulders. Her eyes were the same dark brown as Ellen's own, but her skin was paler, olive-toned, and deeply wrinkled.

"Madame Haddad." There was an awkward pause, and then Ellen sat down in the chair opposite the desk, folded her hands on her knee, and waited. She didn't know the phrase the other woman had used, but in connection with her mentor's name, assumed it was some variant of "daughter of." Genevieve was only about a decade older than Ellen, and not exactly mother material, but from what Ellen had learned, the mentor/mentee relationship trumped everything else, with Talent.

"Call me Mahiba, please," the older woman said now. "I had not thought to see you here, in my office. Certainly not for many years yet."

"I am not here for myself," Ellen said carefully, wary of accidentally making any agreements. "Merely as proxy for another." If there was going to be any cost to this, financial or otherwise, Danny could cover it. That's what the boss was for. "A man named Alfred McConnell has gone missing."

"And you are searching for him. What makes you think that I might know of this man?"

Both Danny and Sergei said: listen more for what someone doesn't say that what someone does. Mahiba hadn't said no, or she didn't know, or that she couldn't help. "Mr. McConnell went missing while searching for another. But he was not the sort to dig into dark corners on his own."

Ellen heard herself falling into a more formal voice, echoing the other woman's speech patterns. Sergei had taught her that, and Danny encouraged it. Echoing showed respect, attention.

That was the theory, anyway. Ellen was always afraid that it would come across as mockery.

Mahiba did not seem to feel mocked. She nodded gravely, and reached across her desk to pull a great leather binder toward her. Ellen immediately felt a surge of envy: Danny had his computer, but she had been working in cheap spiral notebooks and lined pads.

"McConnell. Talent, yes. Male, white, searching for someone who had been lost to him. I gave him three names. Hartman, Louis, and Hendrickson."

Ellen started and Mahiba smiled grimly. "No, he did not choose your partner."

"It would have simplified things considerably if he had. He also might've found who he was looking for."

"Why do you assume he did not?"

She smiled at Ellen's expression, then picked up a pen and wrote a series of lines, gently pulling the sheet out of the book and passing it to her.

Ellen took it carefully. The ink glinted wetly on the page, drying as she read it. And then read it again, and said, under her breath, "Oh *hell.*"

This was important enough to take straight to Danny, and not wait on their scheduled check-in. The problem was, going back to the office would be half an hour at least on the subway, and he might not even be there when she arrived. So she stood on the street, new information in her pocket, and frustration building in her. Stupid, *stupid,* not to have planned for this.

She chewed on a fingernail, and tried to think of a solution.

Once upon a time, she'd been told, there were working public phones on the streets in New York City. Now, the booths were mostly dismantled shells turned into charging stations, because everyone had cell phones. Everyone except Talent, anyway, because current at her core would short out any cell phone carried by a Talent, over time. And "time" could be anything from a year to five minutes, depending on the Talent.

"Stay calm, Ellen." That had been Genevieve's first lesson. Stay calm, and make sure you're in control of your core, where the magic rested. A Talent who couldn't control her core was a danger to everyone. Bad enough if she shorted out a city block, or set something on fire, but to do so now would shame Genevieve, too. The idea that people thought she was worth training, worth hiring, was still so new that she'd rather lose an arm than embarrass any of them, most especially her mentor.

As soon as she thought that, she had her solution. *genevieve?"*

It wasn't a word, exactly, or even a thought. It was more, if she had to describe it, like the *sense* of her mentor: the visual remembrance and the sound of her voice and the taste of her current crackling in the air, shaped into a dart that she launched into the faint eddies of current that swirled around them all the time. It was called "pinging," and it was the closest thing Talent had to texting.

Some people were better at it than others. Some could send a ping that seemed as though it were typed on a page, clear and crisp. Most people, though, it was more muted, more generalized, an emotional push of "are you okay?" or "meet me here." Ellen didn't have enough control or experience yet to manage anything more than a vague sense of her message, and only to people she knew well enough to "find."

*what's up?* came back immediately. Genevieve was alert but not worried, a sense of ready-to-act rather than in-motion-already.

*danny* Ellen sent back, focusing on the need to talk to him, rather than there being a problem. Most of what they did was confidential. She couldn't share what she'd learned, not even with her mentor. *can't call.*

A sense of comprehension hit her in return, and the knowledge that Genevieve was passing the buck to Sergei. Her partner was a Null, and could - and did - carry a cell phone.

Ellen sent back a ping of relief, and gratitude, then *going to grab coffee at the dog," a coffee shop in the area. She'd wait until she heard back from Genevieve, or Danny found her.

---

WHEN I TOOK Ellen on as my assistant-slash-student, I'd also added Sergei Didier's phone numbers- both his private one and the gallery's main line - into my cell phone. It wasn't any kind of premonition, just common sense. Having it appear on the display for the first time today, after sending Shadow off on her own, nearly gave me a heart attack, though. Considering his first words were "nobody's dead," he'd known what my reaction would be.

"We need a better set-up." I said as I slid into the booth opposite Ellen.

Ellen looked up from the laminated menu she'd been studying, and gave me a Look. "What, carrier pigeons?"

The girl who'd first approached me six-seven months ago, nearly shaking and ready to shrink away from anyone or anything that looked at her harshly, wouldn't have snarked like that. Or rather, she would have, but it would have been a defensive move, a deflection, a way of showing armor and warning away would-be predators.

Now, she was snarking because she could, and it was fun. Despite my exhaustion, I smiled. Long way to go, still. But progress.

"It couldn't be any less awkward than having to relay everything through those two," I said, but I didn't have any brilliant plan to offer, either. "You could have borrowed someone's landline, you know. Go into a store and ask if they've got one. But buy something, first."

Even as I made the suggestion I knew it wasn't going to fly. Ellen could snark at me, but she *knew* me. Walking into a strange place, and asking for what was, in effect, a favor? She'd grown up in a house where she was considered odd, if not outright crazy, and everything she said or saw was doubted and ridiculed. Talking to strangers, people who might judge her, was still a trigger, even now that she knew that magic was real, the fatae were real, and she wasn't crazy at all. Or at least, no more so than the rest of us.

I wasn't her therapist or her mentor, anyway. Just her boss. "So what have you learned?"

"I have a lead. On the person our missing person was looking for, anyway."

I waited. There had to be more to it than that, some kicker that had made her haul me out here, rather than waiting. She shook her head, and pushed a sheet of paper across the table toward me. I took it, unfolded it, read it.

You learn to roll with the punches, the jobs I've had. Never show what you're thinking, much less what you're feeling. Even when they know they've gut-punched you. Maybe especially then.

"So," I said, when I could finally trust my voice again. I lifted my hand, summoning the waitress over. "Coffee, black, and a plate of rye toast," I ordered. It might be iced coffee season for everyone else, but I'm an old-fashioned boy.

"So," Ellen echoed, waiting on me. "Our missing woman was fatae," I said. "Yep."

"So our missing man has a cross-breed daughter."

"Looks like."

Cross-breeds are rare. Trust me on this, I know.

My coffee came, and I wrapped my hands around the mug. The toast my stomach had been grumbling for minutes earlier didn't seem quite so appealing, but I knew better than to put more coffee on an empty stomach, so I lifted a piece, and took a bite. I should have stopped for lunch three hours ago, especially since I hadn't been getting much in the way of results.

"It's all there, everything Mahiba knew," Ellen went on, her voice soft, like she thought I was going to tell her to shut up at any moment. "She gave birth at St. Luke's, before they shut it down. She checked out without the baby."

Not unusual. St Luke's used to handle a lot of the fatae in town. The unusual thing was that the fatae had gone through with it at all. No, what was unusual was that she had caught, and *then* that she had gone through with it. Maybe she hadn't realized the baby had a human father? Who knew. Sometimes, fatae could be such careless sluts.

I didn't realize I'd said that out loud until I heard Ellen's indrawn breath of reaction.

"We are," I said, ruefully, and took another bite of the toast. It was pretty good, with just enough butter to soften the crunch. "God knows, my father.... Well, fauns are fauns. Probably not the best example. Do we know what breed she was?"

"Not in the notes."

"She was human-shaped, at least, or even St. Luke's might have noted something was up when she walked, and called in the Cosa, which would have put this on my radar." Like I said, cross-breeds were rare. Someone would have made sure the only other cross-breed in the city would have known, if only to be the first in with gossip. Although what they'd have expected me to do with that knowledge, I don't know.

"Right. So, what do we know? Only that our client's missing husband disappeared off the roof, after, how long ago?"

"Eight months," Ellen supplied.

"Eight months after he went looking for what we now know to be a cross-breed infant, presumably his, because why the hell else would he care?" My issues were showing.

"Presumably his." Ellen still had that scrunchy look going between her eyes. "Is this going to be a problem, boss?"

"No." It wasn't. "If anything, I mean, the guy's actually looking. Yeah, he's late, but at least he's making an effort now." The older I got, the more I understood that sometimes you just… couldn't do anything right away. It never got easier to *accept*, but you understood.

She played with the spoon in her hands, thinking. I let her be. Part of learning is figuring stuff out by yourself. When she had a question, she would ask. I finished my toast, and then ate what was left of her share. I was the boss, I was picking up the tab, I could eat all the toast if I wanted to.

"Do you think he knew? I mean, that she wasn't human?" "Yeah. You can pass -" I did all the time, just pull on a base- ball cap and turn my head so my features seemed softer, more human, that sort of thing "- but once you're that up close and personal, it's pretty much impossible to hide."

"Do you think it's connected? I mean, the woman, the baby, and him going AWOL off a roof? There's almost a year between the two things."

I wiped my fingers, and crumpled the napkin and dropped it on my plate. "Second law of disappearances: if something unusual happened in the missing person's life in the year previous, odds are high it's connected."

She nodded, taking that in. "And a cross-breed offspring is unusual."

My usual response would have been sarcasm, but I couldn't bring myself to it. "Considerably higher on the weird-o-meter than disappearing off a roof without any sign of climbing down." The first law of disappearances was that the nearest and dearest almost always had the motive with the mostest. Although that was the first rule of pretty much everything.

"Boss, what are we getting into? I mean, is this a two-person-missing case, or…"

Or what, was the question. It seemed to always be the question. I should have listened to my mother and gone into the

Navy. At least there you knew the shape, color, and requisition form for whatever shit you were handed.

"Damned if I know, kid." This was why I never promised the clients anything except my best effort; because every job inevitably went pear-shaped in its own special way. "Focus on what we know, and what we were hired to do. Find our guy. He was chasing the baby, so where did the baby go?"

I watched as she hauled out her spiral-bound notebook and flipped to a fresh page, ready to take notes - or, as I'd learned was more probable with Ellen, to sketch a flow chart. She thought in weird ways, even for Talent.

"If the mother walked out without the baby, she didn't want it," she said. "So it's unlikely that she went back for it later. We can probably rule her out, either as a problem or an answer."

She started with a box connected to a triangle by a dotted line, then a line from each to a circle. Mother and Father and Baby make Three. Then a line away from Baby Circle, with a question mark. "The baby wasn't adopted - would it have been an obvious fatae? Is there a fatae adoption board, or something?"

"No. A fatae baby's always taken in by its family, extended or otherwise. Or, it..."

There was a very uncomfortable silence. "Or it's left out to die?" she asked softly.

I'd promised not to coddle her. "Mostly, yeah. Although not often, I'd think. Population shrinkage means most babies are wanted, even with human blood."

Most, not all. And a cross-breed? If the fatae parent didn't want it, the human parent had some hard decisions to make. For one: how did you deal with it if Junior or Princess didn't look human enough to pass?

Ellen was either reading my mind, or thinking along painfully similar lines. "Your mom..."

"My mother was pretty amazing," I admitted, not looking at

her. From what little I'd been told, and the little I'd figure out on my own, Ellen's folks hadn't been amazing. Not for her, anyway. This case was going to open up some holes underfoot, no matter what we did.

"And...your dad?"

"Never met him." The burn that should have caused had died out a long time ago; I didn't even twitch any more. "My mom was in town for Fleet Week. He was a good-looking bartender. She shipped out without knowing she was pregnant, and..." And then came me, and the rest of her career behind a desk.

"Did she know he was..."

That made me laugh, and it felt surprisingly good. "There's no way you can't know. Horns, hooves, tail... and, apparently, endless stamina." She hadn't told me that part, I'd learned that one on my own. "Yeah, she knew. I think she thought you couldn't cross-catch."

Ellen shook her head, looking compassionate and disapproving the way only a woman can. "There should be PSAs."

"Absolutely. There should."

And that was as far as we were going to go into interpersonal traumas as they related to this case. I finished my coffee and pulled out my own notebook. Across the table, Ellen was still sketching out her own thoughts. Her notebook was a lot neater than mine, with colored tags and clearly lettered lists from previous jobs. My handwriting was still a disgrace. Of course, I got to enter most of it into the computer at the end of the day: she still had to read hers a week later.

"The missing guy's last few weeks visible were normal? Nothing unusual, nothing downright weird?" I knew already, but I was learning that bouncing questions off Ellen sometimes got me, not new answers but new questions.

"By various parameters of weird, no. He was retired, did a lot of puttering around, the way retired people do. Spent a lot of time at the hardware store, which I guess is normal for a guy planning on cleaning out his own gutters and doing some repair work? I don't think-"

She stopped talking, her normally sleepy-lidded eyes going wide, looking at something miles past my shoulder. Her lips opened slightly, as though she were going to say something and then forgot, and her dark skin went ashy underneath.

I'd never wanted to be a Talent. In fact, I'd occasionally given thanks that I *wasn't*. But maybe, if I were, if I could feel the current moving the way they did, I'd feel less helpless when Shadow had a vision.

I picked up my jacket, ready to shove it under her if she started to slump, and waved off the waitress who was coming over with more coffee, but otherwise, all I could do was wait.

Ellen had come to me in the first place not because she wanted to be a PI, but because she saw dead people. People who were going to die, really, but by the time someone found them.... She wanted to improve the odds. Get to them before they died. And I needed to keep people from coming to bad ends. It had seemed like a good match.

The problem was, the visions came when they did, and weren't much concerned with anything else Ellen might be doing.

As quick as it hit, it seemed to leave. Color came back to her skin first, like her heart had paused pumping blood and was only now picking up again. It took another minute before that glassy thousand-yard stare started to fade. Then she blinked, exhaled, and came back to now.

I had already flipped to a new page in my notebook. She'd only had one vision since the first one that brought us together, at least that she'd told me about, but you followed the same rule of interviewing any eyewitness; you wanted to get them talking before they had time to think about what they had seen, putting their own spin on the facts.

She focused on me, and started talking. "Two men. One black, one...white? Maybe. Similar, but different. Younger than you, but not by much. They're scared. So scared, and something's coming for them, something casting a shadow, a huge shadow from above."

I wrote down everything she said, exactly, even as my own brain was putting a spin on it. Two men, different races, some- where in their early thirties. Probably. I aged more like a faun than a human, so to outside eyes I passed for late thirties, even with the silver showing up in my hair. Human - Ellen knew to identify if they were fatae or not, unless they were so human- shaped they had no distinguishing characteristics, and there weren't many of those. As we'd just been talking about, even I couldn't pass, not if you were looking close. And a large shadow, from overhead...

That could be anything, I warned myself, focusing again on what she was saying.

"They're not dead yet. Their skin is warm, they're breathing."

One of the things we'd been working on was teaching her to separate herself from the vision, to pick out details without losing the overall sense. But all the dry runs and tray-tests in the world won't tell you how it will work in practice. So far, so good.

"And there's this sound... dry. Dry and fast. Like..." She squinted her eyes shut, trying to recapture it, and I flipped the notebook closed. Nothing she said after this would have the clarity of her first words.

"Like cicadas," she said. "Like a thousand cicadas."

It was the wrong season for cicadas to flock. But I knew what else made that noise.

"All right. Let's go check that out."

Ellen gave me another Look. "We're on a case."

"And you had a vision. The missing take second place to those in imminent risk of death."

The missing might also be in danger of imminent death. She didn't point that out. We had an understanding. Or rather, I had an understanding, and she understood that she didn't have a say in the matter.

"You need to go after-"

"It's one thing to run down separate leads. Another entirely to split up cases. You're not ready yet to do this on your own."

I'd nicknamed her Shadow for a number of reasons, part of which was because that's what she was supposed to be doing. Shadowing me, learning. Not haring off with her heart askew and her brain still vision-fogged.

"Alfred McConnell can wait," I told her, and hoped to hell that was true.

CART HOLLOW WAS one of those suburban New Jersey towns that you only knew about if you lived there, or knew someone who lived there. Bedroom communities, nothing more than houses and schools, no reason to go there if you didn't already live there. Most of the residents worked in the city, commuting on a daily basis and bringing their considerable paychecks home to spend. People were nice, polite, but they weren't accustomed to strangers walking up to their door and ringing the bell, especially mid-morning on a weekday.

The man waiting at the door had thick black hair that was running heavily to silver, the face underneath handsome enough but starting to show signs of wear. If he'd been wearing a suit and tie, he could have passed for a lawyer, or maybe a banker, the kind that dealt with individual clients, managing money rather than making deposits. But he had on paint-splattered jeans, sneakers, and a red Rutgers sweatshirt, instead.

"Please," he said. "Let me see her."

"Her who?" The owner of the house shook her head, holding her body between the doorframe and the door, just in case he tried to rush her, to get inside. "Man, I don't know what you're talking about."

"Please. All I want to do is see her. To make sure that she's all right."

The door closed in his face, not roughly but firmly, and he stepped back off the stoop. The house was a nice one, a narrow, four-story rowhouse, still zoned for single use. The steps and front yard were small but well-maintained, the paint was fresh, and the woman who had answered the door looked like a college professor type, no obvious tats or scars, or any indication that she was holding anyone against their will.

Not that a baby could have much will, and facades were deceptive. He knew that for a fact.

"I just want to see her," he said to the house. "I wouldn't take her away from you, not if you love her." He was too old to raise a child now, even if Christine were willing - and she probably would, he'd lucked out and married a woman with enough heart to deal with him. He just wanted to see her, to *know*.

He turned to his companion. "Are you sure that she's here?"

It nodded. It was sure. That was why it had brought him here.

"All right. Then we'll keep trying."

He owed it to the child's mother, if nothing else. He'd failed her before, hadn't known about the child, hadn't been there when the child was born. He had to make sure the child was safe.

Stepping back onto the sidewalk, so the residents couldn't complain that he was on their property, Alfred started to walk away, his companion at his side. The fatae hadn't left him alone more than thirty seconds, including bathroom breaks, since swooping him off the roof, as though it were afraid the human would run.

Where would he go, if he ran? Even assuming a sixty-something human could outrun a winged fatae - unlikely - where would he run to? Back home, where the creature had found him in the first place? This creature was, for whatever reason, also interested in his daughter - and the word was still so impossible, so unexpected, it made his heart clench when he thought it.

No. He had gotten nowhere eight months ago, hiring a detective, had gotten nowhere playing the usual bureaucratic phone tag. If this fatae who had not given him a name, who had not told him anything other than it too had an interest in finding this child, could help...

Then he would do whatever it asked. Even if it did seem, so far, to involve harassing the alleged adoptive parents until they could prove that the girl wasn't there.

"Sir?"

He looked up, and up. Two of New Jersey's Finest were in front of him. They didn't look happy.

His companion was gone, of course. Alfred hadn't heard it leave, any more than he'd had warning when it swooped down on him, feathers glinting in the sun.

"Is there a problem?" The moment he said the words, he knew they were the wrong ones. "Can I help you?" would have been better, an innocent citizen with nothing to fear. Asking about a problem implied that there was one.

"You don't live around here?"

"I...no." He lived well north of here, in another state entirely. And he didn't have a car to get into, to leave, couldn't point to the mass transit he'd used to get out here, had no excuse for being here that wouldn't land him in trouble. Sixty-plus years of being a law-abiding citizen, and he had no way out of this one.

"Do you have some identification on you, sir?"

"I..." he made a motion for his back pocket, but knew it was useless. He'd been working on the roof, who brought their wallet with them when they were doing home repair chores? In his old workboots, weekender jeans, and sweatshirt, he could have been anyone, from a comfortably-retired banker doing chores to a homeless person.

One of the cops looked up and down the street, obviously looking for something. The other one took a step back, indicating their patrol car. "If you'll come with us, sir?"

He went with them.

They were very polite, asking him again what he was doing there. He shook his head, and couldn't tell them. How did he get there? He shook his head again. He waived his phone call - what would he do, call Christine and tell her...what? No. Better to wait. He would say nothing about feathered companions, or stolen changeling babies. He hadn't done anything wrong.

Eventually, they would decide he was harmless, if a little crazy, and let him go.

Eventually - after they gave him a half-stale turkey sandwich and a decent cup of coffee - that was what happened.

"You want a ride to the station?" Officer Breibart asked him.

"No, I'm good," Alfred said. "I think I'll walk."

He knew Breibart was watching him. They had pointed out where the train station was, only a few blocks away. They had given him a schedule, and a twenty dollar bill to get him home - or somewhere that wasn't their town. He couldn't fault them in any regard.

He also knew that there was no point in going back to the house, even if he could find it. If the child had been there, she was gone now. It had been the pattern at the last three houses they had gone too, as well. His companion - captor? guide? - could scent the child somehow, although it had a beak rather than a nose, but it could not gain entrance to the house. It needed Alfred for that.

So he kept walking, and waited for his companion to find him again.

Ellen tried to stare her boss down. It was doomed to failure - she couldn't meet anyone's eyes long enough to win a contest like that - but she gave it the best shot she could.

"You're getting better."

"Fuck you."

That she could say that, mutter it really, still surprised her. She wouldn't dare say that to Genevieve, or Sergei, or anyone else. Well, she might say it to PB, the demon who was her mentor's best friend, but PB took that sort of thing as his due.

Danny pulled out his cell phone and told it to call someone nicknamed Bookpusher. Ellen didn't exactly slide across the bench to get away from the phone, but she might have shifted a little backward. Instinct: the more current she used, the more a menace she was to electronics, and cell phones were among the most sensitive.

"'Pusher, hi. How much do I owe you, right now? Yeah? Okay, add to the pile." He pulled the sheet of paper toward him and fact-checked himself, then said "St. Luke's, between six and twelve months ago. All female infants born there, no matter what happened to them after. Yeah, preemies, stillborns, Apgar 10s and everything in-between. Can you do that for me?" He paused. "Woman, if I had a name, I could do this myself."

Bookpusher had something to say to that, apparently. Danny leaned his head against the back of the booth, the phone held to his ear, and tried to look like he was paying attention.

"All right, okay. Yes, you're brilliant, you're wonderful, and we're now up at the fly-you-to-Rome for that dinner stage of IOUs, I get it. Just compile the names and who they went home with, if they went home. Yeah, if they didn't go anywhere I need to know that, too."

Ellen thought that maybe Alfred McConnell would have known if his daughter died at birth. But then again, he hadn't hired Danny. So maybe he didn't even know where she'd been born, to check. It must be awfully easy to lose track of a baby, if you didn't even know where it had been born.

"You're, as always, the light in my research darkness. Talk to you soon."

He hung up the phone, turned it off, and put it back in his pocket, muffling the jangling chiming noise it made as it shut down. His hand came out again with something else in his fingers.

"Tell you what. We'll flip a coin. Heads, we keep on with the case. Tails, we hunt down your vision. Deal?"

That was insane. But Ellen just shrugged, having used up her store of protest already.

He flipped it elegantly into the air, catching it flat on the back of his wrist. Heads. Danny tilted his wrist, and the harsh overhead light caught the metal, making it glitter.

"So, right. Vision it is."

---

THE SUBWAY TOOK us into Brooklyn, letting us off a few blocks from our destination, and we walked the rest of the way to the cemetery in silence. I avoided the main entrance, skirting to the side. The arch overhead was massive, easily three times as high as a tall adult, and wide enough across for two cars to pass, one going in the other heading out, without risk of scratching. It was marble, what looked like one single piece, and deeply carved with images that had been worn down over the past two hundred years to where they were only lovely shadows.

"The main entrance is worse," I told her. "I mean, glorious, but worse. And too many people. It's better to slip in quietly."

"This is the back door?" Ellen looked up at the archway as we walked under it, and shook her head. "Once you're dead, you don't much care, so why-"

"It's not for the dead. Cemeteries are for the living." There was no other reason the grass on either side of us was trimmed as lovingly as a golf course, or the huge trees ringing each section were so gorgeously placed, creating a dappled oasis of shadows and cool even on the warmest summer days.

"It feels like it should be a college campus, or park, or something."

"It used to be. Well, sort of like a park. Back when, people came here every weekend for picnics."

"Ugh."

"Yeah well, not to my preference either, but green spaces are green spaces, and hey, why not come to visit grandma while you were at it?"

We'd been walking along one of the side paths as we talked, skirting around a funeral in progress down at the bottom of the hill. I had a destination in mind, but was taking the indirect route. It was polite, when dealing with certain sects of the Cosa Nostradamus, to make like you'd stumbled on them by accident, rather than taking the straightaway.

We heard them first. Or, I heard them, and from the way Shadow stumbled on perfectly smooth grass, I was guessing she did, too.

"That's..."

"What you heard?"

"Yeah."

I could see her gather up her courage, and stick it into place. Ellen doubted herself, but I knew better. Guts of steel and nerves of whipcord, even if she didn't know it yet. Like any rookie, she had to learn.

"What is it?" she asked.

"Fatae."

"I figured that out already," she said, her voice terse. I shouldn't screw with her, not when it came to her visions. Most Talent I know, they're happy to be what they are. Ellen, burdened with the extra "gift" of being a storm-seer, wasn't there yet. She would be, eventually. There was too much that was glorious in magic for her to resist it, even I knew that. But not yet.

We crested the hill, and had a choice of paths when the one we were on branched. The left-hand choice went back down the hill at a slant. The right-hand choice turned into a series of steps, and led not into the valley, but to a rocky alcove set in the hill, complete with benches carved out of the rock. It was pretty, but not where we were going.

"Left," I said, but Ellen was already heading down the path. Her rough-tread hiking boots were better for this than my cowboy boots. I should have changed before we came out here, but neither of us had wanted to take the time to go back to the office, much less my apartment uptown. The trip out here was a pain on mass transit, and I wanted to get here before night.

Not that I hadn't spent time in cemeteries at night, but never willingly, and this one... this one had a reputation. Both good and not-good.

The noise got louder as we went down the hill. It wasn't loud, in and of itself; you wouldn't have heard it if there was heavy traffic. It was like walking under a tree full of chattering birds, except it was coming from ground level, and it sounded...worse.

I should have warned Ellen, but how the hell do you prep someone for this?

"Ack!" She jumped back, damn near into my arms, and I caught her as gently as I could. "Steady..."

The figure in front of us was about four feet tall, and barely a foot wide, and looked a hell of a lot like a bulked-up preying mantis, if preying mantis' had unnervingly human faces behind the mandibles. Exactly who I'd hoped to run into.

It clicked at us, and tilted its head.

"Sorry to interrupt you," I started to say, but those pop-set black eyes looked past me, right at Ellen, and chittered at her. I turned to look, just in time to see her shock slide back behind her usual poker face. Good girl, you don't ever let them see you be shook.

"You are not dead," it said, almost accusingly. "Only the dead come to us."

"We are not dead," I agreed. "But we have an interest in the dead. Not the same interest you have," I hurried to clarify, just in case it thought we were competition. "Only in knowing if you have recently..." encountered? Eaten? "If anyone new has been brought to your attention."

"There are always new, always old." It couldn't seem to stop staring at Ellen, which was making both of us uneasy. I realized that there were others gathering, a few feet away. All right, I'd known they would be in a pack, or whatever they called them-selves, but knowing that and seeing it up close and personal was a bit much. Normally I could handle anything the city threw at me with a certain level of calm, but this... These things would strip the flesh from my bones, when my time came, and crunch the bones into dust. It was what they did, it was their purpose in the circle of fucking life, but I hadn't expected to ever actually face it while still breathing.

"These would be...two men," I managed to say, keeping what I thought - hoped - was a calm, cool note in my voice. "Humans. One black, one white?" I had no idea if it could even differentiate, with those eyes. "Still alive."

"The living do not interest us." Its gaze was still stuck past my shoulder.

"Yeah. Could have fooled me about that." I shifted so that

Ellen was entirely behind me, and tried to catch its attention again. "If you saw these men, would you tell me about it?"

"If you came and asked me after I had seen them."

Took me a second to puzzle that one out, and I suspected that was as good as I was going to get. Doubtful they'd have access to telephones, much less the internet, and none of them were going to leave the grounds. Specifically, they *couldn't* leave the grounds. Old story, of which I knew only the base legend: turf war; they lost.

I didn't bother to say thank you: carrion-eaters weren't notorious for their adherence to Ms. Manners' finest, and I wanted to get Ellen - and myself - away from them soonest possible.

The slope back up seemed steeper than it had coming down, and neither of us stopped to talk until we were at the ridge again, and then back over the other side.

"The *hell*?"

I flinched. My mother used to have that same tone of voice: not shouting, but strong enough to break a ten-year-old's nerve. "They're called Direlings. They're categorized as mostly harmless."

"Unless you happen to be dead. Or me. That thing wanted to touch me. What is it with fatae trying to *touch* me?"

"It's all that current you have coiled inside you," I said, remembering my informant down the seaport, who had wanted very badly to touch my Shadow, too. I couldn't think of any others, offhand, but she sounded like there had been a few. I frowned. I'd never felt any urge to touch her, not like that, but I spent a considerable about of time around Talent, and I knew better. If Valere didn't chop my hand off, Bonnie would. "They - we - can feel it, like electricity on our skin. And some of 'em," and I looked over my shoulder, an instinctive gesture, to make sure nobody was following us. "Some of 'em are just damned creepy."

"Yeah, creepy as fuck. You take me to all the best places,

boss. I want to go home and take a long, hot shower. With a scrub brush."

We caught the subway just as it pulled into the station, slipping into a half-full car as far away from a noisy bunch of teenagers as we - and the other adults in the car - could manage. It had been a long day, and Ellen had done well, but there was something in her eyes that I didn't think was just because she'd gotten ooked out by the direlings. Or not only because. I kept silent the first few stops, then leaned into her personal space just enough that we could keep the conversation semi-private.

"The guys you saw, they were alive. And you heard the sound when they were still alive. So whatever was going to happen to them, it happens there. Direlings have no reason to hurt the living, so maybe now that they're aware of it -"

Ellen stared at one of the ads telling us in English and Spanish that the only way to get ahead was to learn radiology skills. "Do you really think those things will stop someone getting killed? Why should they interrupt someone giving them more to eat?"

"Shadow, you know how many fatae die every day in the city? No direling has ever gone hungry." All right, maybe that wasn't the best thing to think about. I gripped the pole and let myself sway with the movement of the subway car as we pulled out of Brooklyn and headed under the river to Manhattan. "You need to trust your instincts." This was an on-going argument: she trusted her instincts about as much as I trusted the Mayor's office. That is to say, we trusted them to screw it up.

"Okay, you need to trust me that I trust your instincts. How's that?" It felt like dirty pool, and not what I was supposed to be teaching her, but if it got that look out of her eyes, I could let her go home to that much-needed hot shower and hopefully a decent night's sleep.

The train curved around a corner and she got a minute as everyone shifted to adjust before having to answer.

"Okay?" I was pushing. I could hear myself pushing. Ellen was starting to turn into a solid investigator: she had an eye for details, the ability to think on her feet, and a deep-seated suspicion of everyone's story. But she doubted her own, too, and that was a problem.

Most PIs are assholes not because we're assholes, but because we've learned that the only thing we can trust us our own gut. And the gut, as my old partner used to say, is directly connected to the shitter. Ellen still tried to please and placate as a way to stay off everyone's radar. I should be pushing her to fight me, to stand her ground... but not today.

"All right," she said finally. "Yeah." And then with a little more certainty, "Yeah, you're right. But what are we supposed to do? I mean we can't stake out the cemetery, not and follow up on the case, too." She tilted her head at me, and I was struck again by the lines of her face. Most young women would be self-conscious about that strong a nose and jawline, but Ellen didn't seem to even notice. Cleopatra herself would have been proud. Now to get the rest of her to follow suit.

"I don't know, kid. That's why we only take one client at a time. You can't spread yourself thin and expect to make a real difference." It wasn't a consoling thing to say, but if I'd bullshitted her here, she'd know. She'd heard me talk about focus often enough before.

"My visions are-"

"Your visions are important." I headed that one off at the pass, before she started to wonder about a certain double-headed coin in my pocket. "If we need to call in help to cover all the corners, we will. It's not like we're alone in this. The PUPS would love to have a chance to out-spook the spooks, given a chance." I grinned at her, and she smiled, reluctantly, back.

Venec would hop at the chance to train some of his newbies at my expense.

We split at South Ferry, me heading back uptown, her off to the tiny apartment she'd gotten in the East Village. It was about the size of my bathroom, but the building was solid - both Didier and I had checked it out - and the landlord wasn't on any of the NYPD slumlists, so it was about as good as an underemployed twenty-something without a trust fund was going to get without leaving the island, and Valere had been clear that she was to stay within reach. The mentor-mentee thing used to involve fostering as well, I'd been told, but Ellen's case was slightly beyond that, considering her age.

It was funny, really. To look at us, you'd think there was only about a decade's difference. She'd had to grow up fast, and I'd... well, fauns age slower than humans. My hair was still dark and my bones didn't creak, but there were days I felt older than dirt. Today, staring a carrion-eater in the mandibles, I felt every grain of it.

---

ELLEN SLOGGED her way up the three flights of stairs to her apartment, unlocked the door, and fell inside, shedding clothes as she went. She hadn't been joking, entirely, about needing that shower. The way the direling had looked at her, its hand-claw-things opening and shutting like it wanted to measure the density of her bones just before it crunched into her...ugh.

It wouldn't have touched her. Danny wouldn't have let it. Her boss might come across as being sort of laconic, maybe a little slow, with the way his body slouched and especially when he pulled the baseball cap down low over his face, but she knew that there was muscle under that jacket, and an inhuman strength that could throw a full-grown human off its tracks without breaking a sweat. Plus, he had the seriously overprotective thing going on, even when he tried not to let it show.

Genevieve had warned her about that, months ago. "Danny's a good guy. But he's got a thing."

"About women?"

"About throwaways." Her mentor was a lot of things, but subtle wasn't one of them. That was why she left negotiations to her partner. "He wants to save the world, especially the underage part of the world."

"I'm not underage." She hadn't been, mentally, since she was around twelve, and started seeing things out of the corner of her eye, making her parents think she was crazy. Since she'd manifested as a Talent, in a family that didn't have a clue magic existed.

"You know what I mean." Genevieve had given her that Look, the one that said she'd expected better, smarter, from her mentee, and that had been the end of that conversation.

The shower was hot almost to the point of scalding, and at this hour, when most people were just heading home or making dinner, there was actual water pressure. Ellen would have been content to stay there for an hour, except that ten minutes was about as long as she could count on the water staying hot.

She debating washing her hair, and then decided it didn't need it yet, and she really didn't have the patience needed to deal with it, after. Pulling on sweats, and tossing her day's clothing into the hamper, Ellen curled up on the sofa on her living room/dining room/work area, and reached for her notebook.

Danny had done his Q&A right after the vision because he thought the first reactions were the best, the clearest. Ellen didn't disagree, exactly, but she was starting to think that what lingered was important, too. Like in a dream, the details that sunk in and stayed were often pointing toward the thing you needed to remember. Or what might trigger an understanding of the dream.

She shivered, and pulled a blanket up over her legs, even though the apartment was a reasonable temperature. The problem with that theory was that visions weren't dreams. They didn't come from her subconscious, but someone else's energy getting caught up in the current and arrowing in to her. They called her a storm-seer because storms picked up and tossed current around like whoa, and she caught the brunt of that every time, but once she'd gotten a little of her own current stored, the visions started finding her whenever there was the slightest surge.

Most of them were small twinges, a sense of something being wrong, but not enough information to act on. Enough to wake her up in the night, but not enough to tell anyone about. She held the fragments close, and tried to remember what she could, knowing that she might be the only person in the world to know that someone was in danger.

But she couldn't control them, that was the problem. She couldn't close the door and say "sorry, busy." Danny had taken her in to make use of those visions - both Genevieve and Bonnie were right, he couldn't say no to someone in need - but she was distracting him from someone else who needed help, now.

That...sucked. That more than sucked.

And yeah, they could get one of the Pups to stake out the place - stake out a cemetery, ok the jokes just wrote themselves - but that felt wrong. Not that they wouldn't do a fine job but the visions came to her. She was the one supposed to do some-thing about them. It was her responsibility.

"Tomorrow, we need to be focusing on Mister McConnell," she said, staring down at her open notebook. "Danny shouldn't be stressing over this, too."

So what did she have? The vision had been quiet, except for

the chittering noise. And not-bright. Not dark, exactly, not like it would have been at night, but red-shadowed, like…dawn.

She knew where, and now she knew when. She just didn't know who, or why.

Only the who mattered.

She was off the couch and pulling a clean pair of jeans out of the drawer before she realized that she'd made a decision.

And she wasn't going to call Danny. This was her deal. She was going to watch, and shout an alarm if needed, and that was all. Easy-peasy. Let the boss sleep.

Despite the urgent feeling driving her, Ellen was smart enough - despite what some people thought - not to just rush out to the cemetery, especially at night. She dressed carefully in layers, so that she wouldn't get cold while she was waiting, and brewed a thermos of coffee to take with her. She packed that in a backpack from her days living in Central Park, threw in the leftover half of a deli sandwich from the day before, and a pear, just in case she got hungry, then reconsidered and added a chocolate bar, too. She'd been hoarding it for a bad day, but she thought sitting on cold grass all night waiting to see if someone got killed, qualified.

Her mother's voice sifted through the back of her head where she usually kept it locked down, reminding her that sitting on cold grass all night wasn't required. Her mother had been not the best mother in the world, maybe, but it hadn't been because she was a stupid woman. Ellen went into her closet and pulled out the folding beach chair she'd bought on the off chance that she might have a day she wanted to go to Coney Island, and put that by the door, too. Collapsed into its carrying case, it was a small enough profile that she shouldn't get too many dirty looks.

In fact, she did get looks, but mainly because she caught the tail end of rush hour, and there wasn't really enough room for both her backpack and the collapsed chair, crushed in with so many other people. She made herself as small and unimposing as possible, but she wasn't Genevieve, who could disappear even when you were looking at her. Ellen was tall, with broad shoulders and sharp features, and people *saw* her, even when she didn't want them to. Especially when she didn't want them to.

Slowly, the train emptied out as they got further into Brooklyn, and Ellen was able to exhale slightly, letting her shoulders slump. Genevieve was always telling her to listen to the subway cars, feel the current running with them and learn how to pick up a little of that, siphoning it off in a slow but steady trickle. It was hard, though, when there were so many other people around. She couldn't relax enough to feel it, wasn't comfortable opening her own core to take it in. But she hadn't done a full charge in a while, and her mentor hammered into her head enough times that the moment you ran down was when you'd need to pull up something massive. Ellen had the advantage over most other Talent for being able to find and use ley lines easily, but you couldn't count on there being a line within reach. So: trickle charge, whenever and wherever she could.

Grabbing an open seat, she set her bags between her knees for safety, then leaned her head back and closed her eyes, trying to feel the thrum of current sliding around her. It was faint, like a dry tickle in her throat, but she found it, touched it. Her breathing slowed, and she tried to remember what Genevieve had taught her. Find, touch. Open. Everyone visualized it differently, everyone handled it differently. In Ellen's mind, her core was like her mother's yarn stash, if the yarn were alive. Different colors, different textures, mostly either wrapped in a skein or coiled in a ball. It was hard to imagine closing or opening it the way Genevieve talked about, but she could unwind it, slip the end of the new current in, and rewind it into the appropriate skein...

Distracted by what she was about to do, worried about how

she was going to sneak into the cemetery, and what she might face, thinking that she should have packed something that could act like a weapon, Ellen almost didn't notice when the first thread of train-current wound itself into her hands, her hands automatically feeding it into the existing ball of current, where it wound itself around and curled up inside her core like a contented cat.

A surprised "huh" escaped her, once she realized what had happened. She didn't feel any different, but there was a sense of well-being that silenced her worries, just for an instant. "Not bad. Not bad at all."

By the time they reached her stop, Ellen was humming under her breath, and as she left the train, she patted it once, like saying thank you.

Aboveground, night had already descended. She walked toward the gate, trying to remember everything Genevieve had ever told her about no-see-mees, the cantrip she used to keep people from seeing her. Her mentor was a natural Retriever; the cantrip merely enhanced her skills. Ellen would be starting from the opposite end. And Wren had the advantage of being white, which generally meant less unwanted attention from authorities.

In the end, though, it was anticlimactic: there were no guards, and the wrought-iron gates closing the arch were designed to keep cars out, not people. Ellen slipped between the gates without too much trouble, then pulled her bags through after her.

It took what seemed like forever to find the path Danny had taken, but there were signs at the intersections of the roads, just like real streets, and she remembered that the hill they'd climbed was marked by a squat marble tomb with a marble cat perched on the roof. She paused at the ridge, squatting down so that she didn't stand out if anyone where looking that way, and considered her options.

There was no way that she could patrol the entire cemetery - it was huge. But she didn't need to: Danny had said that the direful, direlings, whatever, mostly stayed in one place, where the city's fatae were taken to be disposed of. So the guys in her vision would have to be there, if she'd heard that much of their noise. But what-

"Hey, Ellen."

Ellen turned, still squatting, and almost busted up her knee, crying out in shock and pain.

"Whoa, hey, sorry," and hands caught her, holding her up. The other person squatted next to her, hands still on her shoulders. Male, slender build, pale skin smudged with dirt, a black watch cap pulled down low over his forehead, and eyes....

Calm gray eyes that she knew. "Damn it, Pietr." She sat down hard on the grass and stared up at one of the senior PUPs. "What the hell are you doing here?" She kept her voice low, so it wouldn't carry, but shoved as much annoyance into the words as she could manage, too irritated and embarrassed to be afraid.

"Your boss asked us to keep an eye on the place tonight. He didn't send you?"

"No." She glared at him, then relented. He hadn't meant to spook her like that, probably. And Danny... The boss could be a bastard sometimes, but it was so like him to do this. Like the two-sided coin he thought she hadn't figured out yet. "It's not his case," she said. "It's mine."

Pietr had been there when she'd first learned what she was.

He'd understand what she meant.

"Oh. Huh. Okay, you're the boss, then. What're we looking for?"

"Two men. One's black, I'm pretty sure the other one's white, but he might be Asian. Same height, broad-shouldered. I didn't see their faces."

"And they're coming here, why? I mean, generally the only

folk who come here are dead folk, people burying dead folk, and people planning to unbury dead folk. Different bait needed for all three."

"Your world is a terrifying place," she told him.

"Yeah." Pietr didn't smile, but she heard the humor in his voice. "Yeah, it is."

---

PIETR APPROVED OF HER CHAIR, his muttered "Wish I'd thought of that" giving her a brief glow of satisfaction. He had scouted the area before she arrived, and determined that the rocky ledge on the left hand path actually had a nice overlook of the slope, and the area where the direlings gathered. "If that's where you think the guy will come, then that's where we should set up."

And by "we," he meant her. Pietr disappeared into the shadows, almost as easily as Genevieve did. His plan was to go closer, make sure that they didn't miss anything. "If anything happens - anything at all, you hear me? Ping. I'll be there in a blink."

From anyone else she might have thought that meant he'd come running, but Piet was a PUP and that meant he'd probably learned to Translocate pretty well, especially after he'd taken a good look around her location, practically memorizing the space.

Ellen might have felt slighted, put in an observer's position, but she was just as thankful to not get any closer to the carrion-eaters than she had to. It wasn't only the way their leader had looked at her; there was something about their smell that made her uneasy, as though her visions had somehow tainted her, made her smell like death, too.

She settled into her chair, pulled out the thermos of coffee, and lifted Pietr's binocs to her eyes, scanning the slight valley below.

Nothing happened. Ellen let her senses open as wide as she could, the way Genevieve taught her, but there didn't seem to be any current moving at all; she couldn't even sense Pietr. Her legs went to sleep, and she got up to pace, waking them from pins and needles. She got bored, and reached for the nearest ley line, finding it a few miles to the north. She wondered what would happen if they built a cemetery over a ley line and decided that's when you got zombies. She did a few yoga moves, then went back to her chair, suddenly worried that she'd missed something.

"Midnight."

Ellen jumped out of her chair, turning in the direction of the voice.

A huge black bird was perched on the stone bench, staring at her. Ellen blinked, slightly nervous. The thing was huge, with a wicked beak, and it was staring at her, way too intently. Like she was dinner.

"Did you say that?" she asked.

The bird - a raven, she thought, or the biggest damned crow she'd ever seen - shifted on its legs, back and forth, and kept staring at her, not saying anything.

"It's not midnight, bird," she said finally. "It's got to be closer to 3am." She hoped, anyway. The thought of having to sit here another five hours made her want to cry.

The bird made a noise that wasn't words, but Ellen thought uncomfortably might have been a laugh, like it knew what she was thinking. "Look underneath," it said, and then spread those huge wings and flapped off, disappearing into the darkness.

"What?" She didn't know if she was asking the now-departed bird, or the dead around her, or a God she wasn't sure was paying attention any more. Either way, she didn't get an answer.

The coffee had gotten cold and bitter, but Ellen drank it anyway. She thought about pinging Pietr, but decided that she'd sound like a spooked kid if she did so.

"So, a talking raven. Happens all the time in New York," she said, trying to mimic Pietr and failing miserably. She thought she sounded more like Sergei with a head cold. "So yeah, a talking raven. Who said midnight, maybe, and look underneath, probably."

No, definitely. She hadn't been paying attention when the first noise came, but she'd been listening, the second time.

Ravens talked, she knew that much. Or, they could mimic words. Did the words actually mean anything? Once, she would have assumed it was a hallucination, just another bit of proof that she was crazy, her brain constantly playing tricks on her.

The fatae existed. Talking, advice-giving ravens? Not so much a stretch, after that. But did it *mean* anything?

"Coincidences happen." That had been one of the first lessons Danny had given her. He meant that sometimes you could look so hard to find a connection, trying to solve a case, that you forgot that the universe was random, and sometimes shit just happened. No deeper meaning or pattern, or at least, none that was relevant to the question at hand. On the other hand, it wasn't as though she had anything else to do, just then.

"Look underneath what? Under the ground?" They were in a cemetery, so that would make sense, she supposed. "Under the skin? Ugh. Under the hat? Undertow?" She picked up the binocs and went back to searching the landscape. "Stupid bird. What was wrong with "nevermore," anyway?"

*almost dawn. looks like tonight was a bust*

Pietr's ping was as stealthy as he was: she barely realized it was someone else's impression in her head, not just her thinking the same thing.

*the light was iffy in my vision* she sent back, not so much the words as the memory of the vision. *not giving up until the sun's up*

*fair enough* a sense of understanding, and a hint of a salute. Ellen shook her head: Pups took orders from no-one except their boss, Benjamin Venec, and not always even then, from the stories she'd heard. Genevieve admitted that she wasn't sure what to make of the Pups - they were the only ones who'd ever been able to track her down, even if they hadn't been able to stop her, and that colored her opinion - but Ellen liked them. Bonnie had been the one to step forward when Ellen fell in with the wrong crowd, and who had matched her with Genevieve. And if it was Bonnie and the other Pups who'd also shown her what she was, what her visions meant...well, it was better than being scared she was losing her mind, wasn't it?

That thought tickled another one, some connection or correlation. Ellen looked again through the binocs, then rested her eyes for a moment, and looked again. The thought slid closer, almost within reach, and the vision unfolded in her memory, delicate as dandelion fluff and just as likely to blow away if she disturbed it.

Two men, black and white. Same build, same height, same...

Same.

*Losing her mind. Twins? Look underneath.*

She tucked the binocs into her backpack and slung it over her shoulder, but left the chair behind as she moved down the stairs, down the left-hand path, following some instinct -- no, not even an instinct, a whisper of a thought. She knew she should ping Pietr, tell him where she was going, but she didn't know, and even the second it took to form the ping and send it might lose the whisper.

She followed the path mainly by the sense of *rightness* drawing her, since this area of the cemetery was dimly-lit, at best. Bushes rustled and things crackled, but Ellen summoned a thread of current and let it glimmer under her skin, and whatever it was decided to leave her alone.

She heard the chittering off to the left. Whatever was drawing her was drawing them, too. Ellen looked up. The light was shifting, just like in her vision. The clouds had cleared and the moon was bright on the horizon, even as the faintest pink was starting to creep into the eastern sky. Up ahead there was the glint of water, and her breath caught.

"Here and now," she whispered, and finally paused long enough to ping Pietr

*here and now* and a sense of the water in front of her, a single huge tree just ahead, the path curving to the right, even as she was walking faster, and then running.

Not two men. One. He was cast in shadows, standing by the water. Too-close, Ellen could see-sense the presence of direlings. Not approaching; waiting. Ghouls at the feast-to-be. The chittering was faint but she could hear it, raising the hair on her arms.

"They don't eat the living," she reminded herself. Where the hell was Pietr?

"Hey." She spoke softly, the way she used to when she lived back home and was never sure what kind of reception she'd get, what she'd done to piss people off this time. It was only one guy, she reminded herself. One guy, wrapped in shadows, his posture broad-shouldered yeah but somehow slumped in on himself. She exhaled, and counted back from three into mage-sight, trying to find out what about this guy drew her.

Human - a Null, without magic - but there was something funky about him. His silhouette wouldn't stay tight, shifting from a normal misty-black to this intensely annoying glimmer, too harsh to look at directly, like staring at the sun. He moved, and the double-image moved too, like...

Like two men, not black and white but sharp and muted. She didn't know why or how, but there were two of him in the one. Her mind flitted through a race of ideas, discarding them almost as quickly. Possession was a myth, ghosts were rare, and chimeras manifested outwardly, not like this.

"Go away."

His voice was low, too, but not soft. The shifting sharpness she saw was in his voice, scraping at the air.

"Can't do that. What's wrong?"

"Everything. Nothing." His edges almost connected, then shifted apart again. Ellen was having trouble keeping track of both magesight and the conversation, but was afraid to let go of either. "I'm just too tired to keep it together, that's all. Why do you care?"

She swallowed. Where the *hell* was Pietr? "Because I do. This... this isn't the answer." She didn't know how he was thinking he'd kill himself; the pond couldn't be all that deep. But it was clear that was what he was planning. "It's really not."

There was a tingle of current, like a flash through the air, and she heard obvious footsteps behind her. Pietr, finally. *this is him* she pinged. *i don't know what to do*

*he's alive* Reassurance and reminder: whatever was going to happen hadn't, yet. She was in time. But could she *do* anything? "Please."

"I'm tired," he said. "Tired and crazy and why the hell were you even here? Nobody here except us dead men."

The chittering in the distance go louder, as though his words made them anticipate. *Fuck you* she thought, fiercely desperate. *You don't get him yet.*

"It's my choice."

She glanced at Pietr, but he'd taken a step back, and she knew he wouldn't interfere. It was up to her.

"I saw you. That means you're supposed to live."

"What the hell does that mean?" His outline shimmered and almost clicked, then fractured into painful sunspots again.

*wildly bi-polar* Pietr pinged, the actual thought like a

lightning flash in her brain. *or split personalities? Something that's causing him enough pain he can't handle it*

"You can get help. There're doctors, medications…"

The stranger's voice held an undercurrent of savage laughter that unnerved her almost as much as the direlings gossiping to themselves behind them. "You think I haven't *tried*?"

"You're not crazy." He was, he absolutely was, but she'd thought she was crazy too, probably was crazy, after everything, after getting dying people shoved into her head, and she wasn't sure what the hell crazy meant any more. "No more than anyone else. Don't do this. You're supposed to live."

"You're as crazy as I am. You don't know that."

No, she didn't. Too many she Saw were dead already. But not this one. Not yet.

"It's your choice," Pietr said quietly, "but you don't know she's not right."

"Not today," Ellen said. "Not this way. Not face down in a pond, stripped to your bones by carrion-eaters. Do you hear them? They're waiting for you. They won't even give you the decency of a proper burial. Screw them. Walk away." She shoved every certainty she had into her voice, and prayed it would be enough. "I wouldn't have stayed out here all night, freezing my ass off, if you weren't supposed to walk away, after. *Alive.*"

"All night? Why the hell were you sitting here all night?" He turned, and she could see, in the growing graying light, that he was older than she'd thought, maybe even in his fifties, and the expression on his face was one of disbelief, and - worry?

"So I could be here when you needed me," she said, as though it were the most obvious thing in the world. And right then, to her, it was.

"Fuck." He turned back to look at the water, and she let go

of the mage-sight, knowing somehow that she'd won, that he wouldn't do anything now.

"Go the fuck away," he said. She nodded, then turned and walked away. He'd done as she'd asked, she could do as he'd asked.

Pietr and Ellen walked back up the path to where she'd left her chair, then turned to look again, the light enough to see clearly, now. He was still standing there by the edge of the water, a rough shadow, but as they watched, he turned and walked away.

"He's someone's dad," Pietr said. "Probably a daughter. He wouldn't - couldn't - do anything while you were there."

"He could still do it again tomorrow," she said.

"He could. It's his choice. But you gave him something to think about today. You gave him someone who cared."

She wouldn't see the sharp-and-muted man again; the visions didn't work like that. At least, she didn't think so. She'd never know what happened to him, because she didn't think he'd be dumb enough to come here again, to try.

She'd won. For this one moment, she'd won.

"C'mon, kid," Pietr said, even though he couldn't be all that much older than her. "Let's get the hell out of here. I'll buy you a cup of coffee."

Coffee. She didn't drink the stuff, but she needed to pick up a new coffee maker for the office. And take a shower. And get to the office. And...

Yeah," she said, folding up the chair and shoving it into the carry-bag. "Getting out of here sounds good."

<hr>

"Jesus Look what the cat wouldn't bother dragging in." I'd seen Ellen tired before - we'd worked some insane hours - but this took the proverbial cake, and a cupcake beside. "I hope you left the other person or persons in similar shape?"

She put a brown shopping bag on the desk, and tried to glare at me, but a yawn caught her off-guard. She'd tied a bright blue scarf around her hair. I liked it. It made her seem funkier, younger.

"And you're late," I went on, making a show of looking at my watch, a clunky wind-up that had survived more than a decade of working around Talent.

"Yeah well, I got us a new coffee machine," she said, indicating the bag. "And I solved the vision."

"Oh, good," I said, although I'd actually made a pot at home, before heading in, and filled a thermos. "And wait, you did what?" I squinted at her. "Shadow, tell me you didn't go back to the cemetery last night."

"Okay." She started to unpack the bag, taking out what looked like a basic but shiny espresso machine. Well, that would be classier than our old Mister Coffee, for sure.

"Okay you didn't, or okay you won't tell me?" Jesus, I was starting to sound like my mother. Although there were worse people to sound like, given the situation. "You went back to the cemetery." I wanted to yell at her but despite all sound-alikes, I wasn't my mother, and the visions were hers, not mine.

"Pietr was there," she said, heading off my next question. "So it wasn't like I was alone."

She hadn't known he'd be there when she went, though. I decided not to push it. Instead, I took the bits and pieces of the coffee maker out of her hands, and started assembling them on the counter. "So tell me what happened."

She told me, complete with shifty-eyed looks when she left something out, and expressive hand gestures I didn't think she was even aware she was making. Normally she kept her body still and quiet when she spoke, like someone had told her it was impolite to fill the air outside your own personal space.

"I'm still pissed that you went back out there without arranging for backup," I said when she was done. "That was incredibly stupid." Even when I was working alone, if I was going into a potentially hazardous situation, I called for help. Most of the time. Enough that I felt justified scolding her. "But you did good. I'm proud of you. And no, you're not getting a raise. Like you pointed out, this was your gig, your time."

I fitted the last piece of the machine together and frowned at it. We'd need better coffee to go with this thing.

"And now we're back on the clock with the McConnell case. You going to be able to stay awake?"

I turned back just in time to see her pull a two-liter bottle of Dr. Pepper from the shopping bag. Question answered.

"So, what's on the agenda?"

She was being far too cheerful. If someone else had come in and announced that they'd stayed up all night and cracked the case, I'd expect more than a little ego-puffing and outward satisfaction. But I was starting to figure my Shadow out, a bit. She had an ingrown sense of responsibility for shit that wasn't her fault, and when it was her responsibility she went a little overboard. So yeah, she cracked the case, but she'd only saved the guy once, and he sounded like there was way more than walking off the ledge to be done to fix his head. She was smart enough to know that, too.

But if she was going to pretend she wasn't thinking about that, I was willing to let it go. My promise had been to teach her, and help her find the people in her visions, that was all. Knowing that she was repressing the worry...well, indulging in the worry wasn't much better. To each their own emotional management techniques.

"We need to follow up on the most viable leads, which would be the possible connection between our missing man, and the possible offspring. So it's time to visit mom. Or mom's people, anyway."

That got her attention. Ellen had spent the past ten years being told that the not-humans she thought she saw weren't real, and she was still torn between fascination and unease around the fatae - at least, new breeds. She was used to me by now, and PB was so overt you almost forgot about him. Demon were like that.

"How do you know what she is - or who she is? The report Mahiba gave us only had a name."

"Names are chock full of information, if you know what you're looking for," I told her, picking up my coat and waiting for her to do the same before escorting her out and locking the door. She added a quick cantrip to seal the lock - I never bothered before but it made her feel better, and was good practice.

And a little extra protection never hurt anyone. "Names?" she prompted.

"Right. It's like human cultures, where different names are popular at different times, and in different countries. You won't find many guys named Jesus in Scandinavia, for example, or women named Mary-Margaret in Jewish families, right?"

"Not unless they married in. But yeah, okay. So what does "Kerrieon" tell you?"

I paused outside the elevator, and sighed. "Lilin."

Some of the breeds prefer to live alone, mingling more with outsiders than their own kin and kind. Others gathered in enclaves, usually somewhere like Central Park, or - in the case of some of our less social types - in the tunnels below the subways. The Lilin, not unexpectedly, went upscale. Their enclave was out in one of the better neighborhoods of Brooklyn, in a pre-war building that had clearly been updated to modern standards while still retaining the charm of the original. Say what you will about Lilin, and history certainly wasn't quiet, they had style and taste.

The rain had cleared, but it was still damp and warmly miserable outside. We found a place to park the rental car a few blocks away, and walked down the street in silence. There had been discussions about how to approach this, but none of them had seemed guaranteed to win friends and influence confessions. We walked up the brownstone's steps without a clue how we were going to proceed. Not that something like that had ever stopped me.

"Well, hello."

The woman who opened the door was wearing jeans and a heavy sweater than hit her mid-hip. She was in her early fifties, at a rough visual, with blond hair cut short, and faint wrinkles around the eyes. Her voice didn't ooze sensuality, and she wasn't particularly va-voom, but every part of my body stood up and took notice. It wasn't personal on either side, so we both pretended it wasn't happening.

"We need to speak with your elders," I said, giving the courtesy of assuming that wasn't her. She didn't blink or show any sign of surprise, but stepped back into the hallway and let us come in.

"May I take your coats?" she asked. "You'll need to wait a bit, before they are able to see you."

We handed over our jackets, and let ourselves be escorted into the parlor on the first floor. It was a comfortable room, cozy in a way that made you expect to see a cat draped over one of the sofas, and a paperback book left on the end-table, half- read. There was in fact a cat, opening one sleepy eye to assess us and then going back to sleep, but the end-table held a series of cell phones and an e-reader, instead. The fatae had adapted quite easily to the technological age, thank you very much.

Ellen sat down next to the cat, who deigned to uncurl and let itself be scratched behind the ears. It blinked at me, and I blinked back from my chair on the opposite side of the grouping. I like cats fine, but I could see the door from my position, and that was more important to me. We waited a few minutes, maybe ten, max, and then the door swung open again and two Lilin walked in.

The woman at the door had been sexy. These two were seduction personified. I regretted letting Ellen come with me, even though I knew it was better that she encounter them first with me to look out for her. Despite whatever you've heard about succubi or incubi, Lilin don't intentionally go out to seduce mortals. In fact, most of the time they don't even crook a finger. They just happen to be deeply sexual beings, and human chemicals respond to that.

So do most fatae, if we're being honest, and faun genetics are predisposed to like anything that sparks of a good time. I ignored my dick with the poise of years of practice, and offered my hand in greeting to the elders.

"Thank you for your time, so unexpectedly," I said. "My name is Daniel Hendrickson, this is my associate, Ellen." She had refused to give or use her last name - given her family history, I could understand that - so I went traditional. "Ellen *Ychna bat* Genevieve." I handed the woman my card, and she took it with grave, graceful formality.

"I am Alineon Layil," she said. "This is my brother Simeon. How may we aid you?" She gestured for us both to be seated again, and took chairs of their own. The cat climbed back into Ellen's lap and went to sleep.

"It is in the matter of Kerrieon Lavil," I said. "And her infant."

"Infant?" That got Simeon's attention; he sat up out of his previously indolent drape, and leaned forward, intent as a mouser spotting movement. "Kerrieon had no infant."

"Simi. Pause and let the faun speak."

"She is on record as having given birth nearly nine months ago. To a half-human child." All right, we didn't know that for certain - there were no medical records. But she'd named a human as father, so that was what we were going on.

"Impossible," Alice retorted.

Hardly impossible, with me here as witness. I didn't say that, though. "Is the girl here to speak for herself?"

"No." The woman didn't flinch from my question. "She has not lived here in several months."

"A year," Simeon said. "If the laundry comes out, at least let it all come out. She left us a year ago."

"And went where?"

"We don't know. What happened to the infant, Mister Hendrickson?"

"We were hoping that you could tell us that."

"No. As I said, we did not even know that she was pregnant. Had we known -'

"You seemed taken aback that she gave birth to a cross-breed."

That caused Simeon to let out a bark of laughter that wasn't even remotely amused. "Taken aback, yes. But - no. I see where your thoughts go and no. Never. We would have taken the infant in, no matter its parentage"

I believed them. Like I'd told Ellen, babies are rare enough. And it wasn't as though Lilin hadn't proven they were cross-fertile, millennia ago. Rare, but not impossible. They'd been reacting to the fact of their not-knowing, not the impossibility of the act, then.

"Does she have friends here?" Ellen spoke up for the first time, one hand still petting the cat. "Sisters? Best-friends-forever kind of friends, that she would have confided in?"

"Rachel, perhaps. A human girl she went to school with. But Kerrieon was not the sort to confide. She was..." Alice paused, and my bullshit detector gave a faint tremor. "She was not a girl prone to belonging, if you understand my meaning."

Ellen raised her eyebrows, and I almost laughed. Of all the Cosa members in this city, they were talking to two people who could *absolutely* understand that.

"Do you think she's all right?" Simeon said. "Both of them - the baby and Kerrieon?"

"That's what we're trying to find out, sir."

"If there's anything we can do to help, please let us know. And if you find the infant..." He looked to Alineon for permission, first, and when she nodded faintly, went on "it will have a home here. If a home is needed."

The infant, not the mother. Interesting.

"Oh *god*." Ellen barely held her reaction to the Lilin until the door closed behind them and they were back on the street. Danny laughed a little - at her, she thought. But fair enough.

"Yeah," he said. "They're a bit much, aren't they."

"Are they succubi? I mean, succubi and incubi?"

"Ugly nicknames for a perfectly respectable breed," he said. "Don't use those terms in polite company. That was good thinking about the boon companion. Do you think they were lying?"

"Yes," she answered without hesitation. "Or, they think there might be someone, and they didn't want us talking to her. Or him."

"To what purpose?"

Danny did that, asked questions in the middle of a job, made her say what she was thinking, verbalize her thoughts no matter how dumb they sounded. Sergei laughed when she'd complained, said Danny was making her self-actualize, whatever that meant. But he was right: if there was a flaw in her logic, it was more obvious when she said it out loud.

"Because they want to deal with it themselves. They live all together, you said, so they probably aren't used to trusting outsiders. If someone screwed up and a member - and a baby - disappeared, they're going to want to handle it internally."

"Reasonable." They had reached the car, and Ellen scanned the windshield for a ticket. There was none, so she unlocked the door and got in, waiting while Danny got in on the passenger side. "And also reasonable to assume that they didn',t take the baby, since they didn't know about it. Unless they're playing a very deep game to throw us off their tracks but that's unlikely. Most people just aren't that complicated, and too many people in that house would have to know about it, and keep silent. Things like that, someone breaks, and usually sooner rather than later. We're just not designed to keep secrets."

"So some unknown person took the baby," Ellen said, and swore at a driver who tried to cut her off, edging her way into merging lanes toward the bridge. "Or it's dead. Already long long dead."

"Maybe. If so, then why would our guy disappear, too? If the baby's gone, and momma's off the map…"

"Because whoever deaded them, deaded him too?" Ellen had never been a delicate flower, despite Sergei's occasional hapless attempts to protect her from the grimmer aspects of life. "Fact: momma seems to have gone missing, no forwarding address. Fact: baby is missing. We have no idea if the baby is with momma or not but since she checked out beforehand without a diaper bag, probably not. When mommy and daddy and baby make all missing, they're either together, or all dead. Right?"

"You've been listening." Listening, and reading. Danny handled mostly missing person cases, and a lot of them, she'd discovered, didn't end with happily ever afters. "All right, let's assume that there is a connection, because the coincidence required for them to *not* be is too large to start with."

They passed back into Manhattan, and she glanced at him, waiting for instructions on where to go, even as she was cutting off a cabbie who tried to cut her off. Danny winced, and she grinned. There wasn't much she felt a hundred percent confident on, but the ability to drive in city traffic was one of them. If all else failed, she'd go to work as a cabbie.

"First, we disprove what's disprovable. Go visit Rashada in the morgue, see if anything came his way in the past eight months. I'll man the phones, see if baby-girl Doe was dropped into any foster homes or orphanages."

"You think that might've happened? I mean, wouldn't someone notice, or..."

"Yeah, it's doubtful, which is why I didn't bother before. But sometimes human cluelessness trumps out. And the child *might* be entirely human, on the outside..." He sighed. "At least until she hits puberty. It would be better if we found her before then."

"If she's alive."

"Yeah. If she's alive."

Ellen focused on driving, then. She'd saved someone last night. Was it too much to hope that they could save this one, too? Maybe. She tried not to think about it, as though that might distract fate from one tiny baby.

Alfred was exhausted. His feet hurt, his eyes felt like they'd been washed in sand, and he could only imagine how frantic his wife must be, assuming that she hadn't finally gotten fed up and tossed all of his things onto the front lawn.

No. She wouldn't do that. She'd put up with so much, she'd put up with this, but she'd be worried. He should call her, he should have taken the chance when he was in the police station to call her, but back then it had seemed like a bad idea. Now, twenty-four hours later, all he could think about was her sleeping alone in their bed, her hand stretched out to where he should be, and finding only a cold mattress.

His companion set him down on the sidewalk, and inclined its head toward the house on front of them.

"What makes you think the baby's here, more than any of the other places? How can you even know it's anywhere near here? That this isn't a wild goose chase?"

"I know. Go. Talk to them." Again, it was saying.

Alfred had been given no choice in any of this. There had been a mysterious note on his desk one morning, reminding him of a one-time affair that he'd almost forgotten about, with a woman young enough to be his daughter, with the smoothest skin he'd ever touched, and eyes so pale brown they seemed nearly yellow.

"Your child is lost." the note had said, the handwriting spiky but readable. "You owe a life." Nothing more: no name, no return address, nowhere to start even looking. So he'd done the only thing he could, he'd hired a professional, told him the little he knew, and waited.

That hadn't been good enough, apparently, and the next thing he knew he'd been knocked off his feet - literally - by this creature, who insisted that the child be found *now*.

"I'm going to get arrested again," he muttered, trying to smooth down his hair and checked to make sure his jeans weren't any more stained that before. "And this time they're not going to let me go with a warning."

"I sniff. You ask."

Alfred cast an uncertain look at his companion, still not sure how well that beaked nose could smell anything, but since it could easily tear him apart if he pissed it off, he did what he'd been doing: obeying orders.

A young woman answered the door, giving him a puzzled but friendly look. By now, he didn't really believe the infant was here - especially since the woman looked barely old enough to have sex, much less be caring for a baby - and when she shook her head and said they had no infant, he thanked her for her time, and left.

"They're moving her," his companion said. "One step ahead, all the time." It clacked its beak in frustration, and drummed its talons on the side of a postal box, making a heavy, metallic thrumming echo.

"Why is she so important?" Alfred asked, for what seems

like the hundredth time. "If she's with good parents, why not leave her there? All the houses we've checked have been nice, with people who seem decent enough." He had wanted to find her, out of responsibility - he wasn't a total shit - but a pair of young parents, people who *wanted* her? That was better than anything he could give her. And why the hell was this creature so determined to find her? It wasn't from any nasty impulse; the creature seemed legitimately worried.

"The child needs to be found," his companion said, likewise for the hundredth time. "They will not tell me. They will tell you."

No matter how long it took, hung unspoken in the air between them.

I WAS TRYING to get the new coffee maker, which I'd already dubbed Podzilla, running, when the office door creaked open cautiously, as though the person on the other side had been surprised by the door being unlocked, and wasn't sure who was on the other side.

"Boss. Did you sleep here?"

I hit Podzilla's start button, listening to its hiss of steam with a possibly erotic shiver of anticipation, and ignored the question as being beneath notice.

"Boss."

She'd been taking lessons in that voice from someone else. Either that, or she was developing a strong streak of Mom, too.

"No, I didn't," I reassured her. But I hadn't slept well, either. I finally gave up around four in the morning, and spent the rest of the night wandering the streets. It was weirdly soothing; half my genetics might crave green hills and free-running water, but in everything else I was a child of concrete and steel in general, and New York City in particular. There was an energy to the pre- dawn hours that had nothing whatsoever to do with magic and everything to do with magic, if that made any sense at all. Even the darkest streets still felt the quiver of neon in the air, solitary traffic speeding and slowing to the lights, echoes of late-closing bars and early morning hustle, punctuated by trucks rattling in for pre-dawn deliveries and running through it all the constant awareness of life. New York wasn't the city that never slept so much as it was the city of overlapping shifts, where one person's bedtime was another person's wake-up call.

I'd given up and headed toward the office as the clouds were starting to lighten to pink. Ellen was here early, too, but a quick glance confirmed that she was neither bright-eyed nor bushy-tailed. She didn't drink coffee: I wasn't sure how she was still standing. I said as much.

"I'm young and resilient," she said. "But you will forgive me because I brought breakfast." She held up a bag, but my nose had already told me.

"Give. And talk." I fished out a brioche and put it on the counter next to the coffee maker, then put the bag down and waited.

"So yeah," and I could hear her taking off her coat and dropping it on the wooden coatrack, then sitting at her desk, the chair squealing slightly as she swiveled around. "I went to see Rashada, like you said. And then spent the next five hours going through her files, which are not, just so you know, digital. I have paper cuts on my paper cuts. But I can tell you that no newborn died that week coming from that hospital, and no non-human infant was brought into the morgue in the past nine months." She paused. "Rashada said she'd know if the baby wasn't human. Even half. Yes?"

"Maybe." The coffee machine let me know it was ready, and I pulled a double shot into my cup, and slammed it back. "You saw, Lilin can pass for human unless you're looking close." Like me. "I don't know what their insides look like, and never wanted to ask. But yeah, there'll be some differences that would ping for someone like Rashada." She'd cut into every fatae db in the past five years, no matter when they hit the slab. The local Talent Council had made sure of that. They wanted to know what was happening when, why, and to whom. The fatae mostly weren't thrilled with the Council's nose poking into our business, but we'd learned the hard way we couldn't prevent it. Not entirely.

"That doesn't mean the baby's alive, through," Ellen said. "Whoever took her, they might have just dumped her."

I turned fast at that, a hot comeback on my tongue until I saw how miserable she looked at even mentioning it, and how she flinched a little when I moved. Easy, boy. This is Shadow, you can still spook her way too easy. And what she'd said was true. Ugly, but true.

"If so, we may never know. But until we can prove all other leads are kaput, we don't assume that."

He was angry with her. Ellen knew she was too sensitive, too quick to assume she'd done something wrong, too fast to apologize. You spend ten years with everyone thinking you were crazy, a burden, a problem, you learned all of that. But she knew anger when she saw it, even when he was trying to bite it back, not take it out on her. She forced her breathing to stay even, soothing the static-jangled core inside her so she didn't destroy the brand-new coffee maker, or worse, his laptop in the back office.

"Don't assume anything." He was still lecturing her, his body tense like he was trying really hard not to yell, or throw something. Not that he would - not at her, anyway - but it still triggered every protective reflex she had, to make herself small, invisible, inoffensive. She placed her hands palm-down on the desk, taking comfort in the heavy wooden weight of it. It wasn't the same as grounding, where she'd tie herself into the energy of the granite underfoot, letting it hold any sudden sparks or snaps in her current, but it was enough for now. She *knew* she wasn't in any danger, she just had to convince her body of that.

"You know I won't," she said mildly, and he sighed, all of a sudden the air going out of him. He ran his hands through his hair, the small, curved horns appearing briefly, then hidden again. She still had never seen him shoeless, so she didn't know if his feet were hoofed or not. She couldn't imagine his usual cowboy boots would be comfortable if they were, but...

"Yeah, I know," he was saying, and she forced her attention back into focus. "Sorry. This case..."

"Is it because," and she lifted one hand cautiously, making a vague gesture with it, "because, you know..."

"Because the baby's a cross-breed like me? No. And usually I'm better with infant abductions, there's less chance of something going wrong." He must have seen some expression change on her face, because he elaborated. "Teenagers, they're at risk. Young kids, seriously at risk. There are a lot of fucked up bastards out there who consider them easy or preferred prey. But babies? Most times, they're stolen for the breeder biz. Adoptions for profit. So they're well taken care of, relatively speaking, and mostly given into good hands. I still want to get them back, but there's less..."

Ellen had seen enough to know what he wasn't saying. Less risk of the bad stuff. The kind of stuff you couldn't ever rescue someone from, not really. But something was still bothering him.

Danny flipped back to business. "So the mother's gone missing, and soon after the baby goes missing, and we've got no leads on either one of them. If the Lilin find anything, they'll tell us, if only to keep us from poking into their business any further. So we go back to focusing on daddy for the moment. Specifically, how he got the hell off that roof."

"Something winged took him." It was the only reasonable explanation, for Cosa levels of reasonable. "Unless we have a helicopter that's so silent that the woman inside the house doesn't hear it hovering over her head?"

"What, like a hang glider?" He shook his head, even as Ellen tried to figure out how a hang glider could swoop a full-grown man off his roof. "All right, so what? Not a great wyrm, they'd be too noticeable, even in the 'burbs. What else was large enough? And wouldn't be noticed?"

"How do you not notice something winged flying through your back yard?" But Ellen knew the answer to that already. The same way her family had not-seen any - all - of what she had gone through over the years. Because they didn't *want* to see. All the things that had happened to her, around her, they had just not seen so they wouldn't have to deal with it. You had to see before you could—

"Underneath."

Danny tilted his head to the side. "What?"

"Check underneath. That's what the raven said."

Narrowed eyes joined the tilted head. "A raven talked to you? Shadow, you need to *tell* me these things. Seriously. Maybe Talent don't think about it, but every fatae knows: when a raven speaks to you: pay attention."

Ellen bit the inside of her cheek to keep from responding. He was right, she hadn't known, hadn't thought about it that way. She'd been thinking of the bird as a bird, not... well, any of the things it *might* be. She had also thought that it was about her vision. But what if it wasn't?

"Underneath what?" she wondered, turning it around in her head.

"The roof," they both said at the same time.

Ellen hadn't returned the rental car the night before, extending their reservation through the end of the week. I wasn't sure if she was developing a twitch of precog, or just playing a hunch. The difference between the two was millimeters in my experience, anyway. If she was able to find consistent free street parking, we might have a new revenue stream in the making, through. Hire-a-parker could be seriously popular, especially around the holidays, and-

"We're here, boss."

The house wasn't anything particularly special: a well-maintained Colonial on a street filled with an assortment of similarly well-maintained houses, all built around the same time, probably mid-fifties. There weren't any white picket fences visible, but you could practically feel their ghosts running along the lines of every lawn.

"And why didn't we come here first?" I asked. Ellen glanced over at me as she scouted for a place to park, then decided this must be a Teaching Moment, because she just shrugged. "Because you hate coming out to Westchester?"

"I don't hate Westchester. I just find it pointless. No, we didn't come out here because by the time the client contacted us, she would have had time to set up anything she wanted us to see, and anything actually relevant would have been tidied up and put away, intentionally or not."

Ellen tapped the wheel with her fingers, frowning. "Is that pragmatism, or bitter cynicism?"

"A little of both, neither unwarranted. They're Council members, so she had the right to go to them for help, and instead went first to an outsider, and then to me. What does that tell you?"

"That our client wants us to find her husband, but she doesn't want a fuss. She knows the baby's half-fatae?"

"Or, more likely, she knows that the girl was young, and Lilin. Having a husband who cats around is one thing. Having one who gets off with a succubus... that's just tacky. I did do an Internet search on the neighborhood, though. God bless the Internet."

Ellen made a face, and I laughed. Yeah, all right, I wasn't above rubbing it in a little, occasionally. On the other hand, I couldn't move from one place to another by thinking about it, or any of the other things I'd seen her use current to do, so I figured we were about even.

She parked around the corner, and we walked back to the McConnell house. There was no car in the driveway, and a quick look inside the garage revealed empty space. Good. I hadn't planned on ringing the doorbell, but this made things easier. There was a ladder leaning against the side of the house, and I walked over to it, testing its sturdiness with a rough shake. "Seems safe enough." Even to me, my voice didn't sound convinced.

"If a sixty-something guy could climb it, you can too," Ellen said. I didn't point out to her that I wasn't much younger; I had enough vanity to maintain the illusion that I was still in my late thirties, thank you very much. But I set my foot on the first rung, and started climbing. It was a little nerve-rattling, but I made it to the top and hauled myself onto the roof, looking over the side to see if Ellen was going to follow me.

"Nice view."

I didn't quite fall over the edge, but it was close. I turned and glared at Ellen, who was standing next to me. "Cough next time you Translocate, okay?" The line of sight from ground to roof must have been clear enough that she'd felt she could manage it without a spotter. "All right, we're up here. Now where do we actually *look*?" Trust a raven not to be specific, and there were a lot of tiles.

"Where had he been standing?"

"Over there," I said, pointing to the area near the chimney. "According to the police report, he'd been looking at the flashing around the chimney, to see if they needed to have someone come out before winter started."

We did a crab-crawl over there, neither of us trusting our balance enough to walk upright on the slightly-slanted roof. If any neighbors happened to look out their curtained windows to see us, they weren't inclined to come out and raise a fuss. God bless suburbia.

The tiles around the chimney looked intact, but we started lifting the edges with out fingernails, anyway, searching for something, anything that might explain the raven's words.

"You know the raven might -"

"Keep looking," I said. "Ravens elsewhere might be anything. A raven in a graveyard, in *that* graveyard, at that hour of the morning? Even if it was screwing with us, which is always a possibility, we can't ignore it."

It took us about fifteen minutes, and several splinters under fingernails, before Ellen let out a surprised, somewhat worried, "oh."

"What?" I turned carefully, letting the shingle I'd been testing go back into position, and looked over at her. She held up her hand, and I heard myself go "oh," too.

She was holding a feather in her hand, the quill's point between forefinger and thumb. There wasn't any breeze, but it moved gently, the cloud-muted sunlight catching it just enough to illuminate the silvery tone of the vane.

"Fuck," I said. "Oh, fuck."

"What is it?" Ellen's voice was still worried, but I could tell she was fascinated by the feather, too. It was small, maybe six inches long, max, and could, if you weren't thinking about it, be mistaken for, well something ordinary, fallen from a dove's wing, maybe. But that particular shade of silver, the deep red of the shaft, clearly visible? That came from only one place.

"That's a gryphon feather," I told her, my mouth dry, but going for my best teacher-tone, rather than the flipped-out awe I was feeling. "The only fatae with silver feathers are gryphons. They're generally solitary, more than a little cranky, and pretty damned rare."

"So why was one so interested in our missing human? I mean, other than the missing child, there's nothing particularly unique or odd about Alfred. Why would a gryphon be interested in a cross-breed child that wasn't one of theirs?"

"I don't know." But even if Ellen didn't have any precog, my spidey senses were tingling.

They'd ended up at the edge of a park after the last house was another no-go, the owner there an older woman who truly seemed to have no idea what Alfred was talking about. The fatae claimed it was following a trail, but Alfred wasn't sure he believed that any more. The child had been in all of these places? How long ago, and for how long, and why did they keep moving her? None of this made sense.

It was late afternoon, and the park was deserted except for a couple at the far end, snuggling on a bench. He wanted, suddenly, to sit down, even on a cold bench, and just not move. He was beyond tired; he was weary. His core, never all that strong to begin with, was near-depleted, and the thought of reaching out to restock made his bones turn to ash. There was only so far a human could push himself, and he was nearly there.

The creature reached for him, clearly intending to hoist him into the sky and off to another house and another dead end. Alfred stepped back. "No. No more. Not again. I can't do this anymore. It's insane, we're not getting anywhere, and I don't think you're right about where the infant is, anyway, because there's no way they can be shifting her like this, even with the best translocation skills ever. So no, no more."

"You must. You owe a life."

"I don't owe jack-shit. I don't even know for certain this child's mine, only just what you've told me. What happened to Kerrieon? Where is she? Why did she abandon the child like that? Why didn't she call me?"

"I didn't know."

That was the first actual answer he'd gotten from the creature. The problem was, that wasn't actually an answer at all.

"What the hell do you mean, you don't know? You knew to find me, so you must know something." He'd been on this insane hunt for three days, which was two days longer than he'd thought it would take when the fatae landed on the roof and told him he was needed. Three days without decent sleep, without a bath, without a decent cup of coffee. He wasn't thinking straight any more, and he wanted it done.

"The child must be found."

"You keep saying that but you won't tell me why. Fuck that. Take me home." He was pissed, but not so pissed off that he forgot he was, effectively, stranded here in this town.

He needed to find a phone, call a cab. Turning on his heel with near- military precision, he walked away. Or tried to, anyway. The fatae's claws had been nearly gentle as they held him in flight, keeping him safe so far above ground, but now those talons dug into his flesh, the jacket and shirt no barrier.

"You owe a life."

Alfred stared across the park, seeing freedom out of reach. "What the hell is your problem? You haven't shown me any proof that she's in danger! That was the only reason I came with you, the only reason I went looking, because I thought she was in danger. But so far, nothing. If she's in one of these houses, which by now I doubt, they're well-off enough to give her a proper life. But if you don't know *where* she is, how do you know she needs me?"

He couldn't shake off that claw, so he turned into it, uncom- fortably close to that fierce beak, and the deep golden eyes glaring over it. "Unless you can tell me, right here and now, that you know for a fact that she needs my help, that she's in danger, and not being perfectly well cared for by whoever took her home from the hospital, then this. Is. Over."

"The child is not in danger. The child *is* danger." Those golden eyes were too wide, the pupils too small and black.

Alfred felt he was in danger of falling forward, falling into them and never getting out.

"What?"

"The child. It is an abomination. It must not be allowed. Only humans thought it could be saved, should be saved. It should have never happened, should have been allowed to die."

"What?" Alfred knew he sounded like an idiot. He felt like one, too. "You're insane. Never mind about taking me home. I'll call Christie and deal with the fallout the way I should have two days ago."

Just saying it made him feel better, a little stronger. Yeah. He should have told Christie at the start. She was a clear thinker, she might have figured out a way to find the baby - or understood that it wasn't their matter to meddle in at all, that the baby was already with good parents and this crazy fatae was only trying to stir up trouble. He'd go home and tell her everything, and he could finish fixing the roof before winter hit.

"No."

"Yes." He stared at the fatae, his own eyes narrowed. "Enough. Whatever you think needs to be done, whatever you're planning to do, I'm out." If the creature needed him to find the baby, walking away was the best thing he could do, for both of them. Even if the kid wasn't his.

There was no warning, only the clack of the thing's beak, before a talon hit him across the face. Then again, the blow of one feathered arm against the chest, and another blow to the side of his head. None of them were made with any sort of precision, but the sheer force behind them made that less important, and Alfred went to his knees, his head ringing and his vision already starting to haze over.

He hoped the kid was his. He'd like to think his last act had been protecting his own.

ELLEN WAS SITTING on her desk, legs crossed under her, the gryphon feather in her hands. Or rather, hovering just above her hands, the quill's tip balanced pointing down onto her palm but not actually resting on the flesh. Little sparks of current flickered around it, which made me think that there was a hell of a lot more current actually in use, if I was able to see that much.

Fatae couldn't use magic, any more than a Null human could. But it ran in our bodies, according to all the reading I'd done, making us more attuned to it than non-Talent humans. I always - almost always - knew when it was being used around me, and it would take a skilled Talent to use it against me.

Damnable thing was, I seemed to know a lot of skilled Talent. Even when I was back on the force, it seemed like half the guys I knew on the street were high res. Just lucky, I guess.

"Anything?"

She shook her head, letting the feather come to rest. "No. I mean, there's a sense of it there, the guy himself, and definitely a guy, but... I don't know if its because I'm not strong enough, or because I don't know enough about gryphons. When Genevieve taught me this, we used a strand of PB's fur and a drop of Sergei's blood, and I was able to identify them right away, but..."

"But you know them both. All right, get yourself settled down, and come back into the office."

Any current-use she did, she did out here. It would be easier to replace another coffee maker and a mini-fridge than it would my laptop, lead-lined drawer or no. But it would take her a little while to shake down her current and smooth it out, or whatever it was they did. I left her to it and closed the door behind me, taking a moment.

Ellen had been right: this case was shaking me a little. It wasn't the baby-in-jeopardy part; I knew my weaknesses and was used to dealing with them. Kids in jeopardy hit all my buttons, yeah. But it wasn't that, and it wasn't that this was a cross-breed, either. I didn't think that was it, anyway.

I sat down at my desk and pulled the laptop out of its drawer, booting it up at the same time and checking email. The formal reports from Rashada, confirming what she'd told Ellen. A note from Fagan at the precinct, confirming that no known female fatae bodies had shown up anywhere without clear I.D. Now that I knew what breed she'd been, I could guarantee that she'd be a Jane Doe: Lilin who ended up in bad places generally didn't have soft landings.

"Boss?" Ellen came in just as my cell phone rang. I held up a hand for her to stay where she was, just in case. Static was a natural by-product of Talent.

"Hendrickson. Yeah, I got it." I waited. "Really? All right." I didn't insult Fagan by asking if she was sure: she wouldn't have called me if he wasn't. "Yeah, I should be able to confirm. Can you send - all right, thanks. Yeah, take care."

I hung up the phone and gestured for Ellen to come all the way in even as I was checking to see if the promised email had come in.

"They found our missing man. He's at Mother of Mercy." "Hospital, not morgue. He's alive?"

"Only just. No ID, but they're pretty sure it's our guy."

"So what happened to him?"

"That's the question, isn't it? I've got a file coming in now." I paid extra for high-speed internet. I would have been better off spending the money on beer and pissing it away. But eventually the file downloaded.

I clicked on the attachments, and grunted.

"What?" Ellen came all the way into the office, leaning over my shoulder to see better. I could feel the gentle static hum of her core for a moment, like standing next to a portable genera-tor, then it was locked down, still and cool.

I touched my hand to the screen, tapping one area of the

photograph. "Those look like claw marks?"

"Yeah," she agreed. "There, and...there." She didn't touch the screen, but I saw what she was looking at. "The bruising, he was beaten?"

"By someone, or something with a very heavy hand." Or wings. "McConnell's in no position to answer questions; they're not sure he's going to remember anything when he wakes up, assuming he does wake up. We need to find that gryphon."

There was a heavy weight of silence over my shoulder, and I could tell she was thinking. Technically, the case was over. We'd been hired to find the missing man, and we'd done that, more or less. But there were questions that needed to be answered – a missing child to be found – and nobody else was going to do it, if I didn't. If *we* didn't.

"Boss, you're awesome at finding people, solving puzzles, that overt, detail-oriented stuff. Given time, you could learn where a gryphon hangs out. But getting it? I mean, laying hands on it? If you need something retrieved..."

"As a Retriever. I know." I shut the lid of the laptop, and stared at the matte black surface. "You're injuring my professional pride, Shadow." She wasn't wrong, though. I could find the gryphon, but it would take time, and odds were I'd never get anywhere near it. But Wren... The Wren could.

"Call your mentor. Let's see how well she plays with others."

I'd barely had time to put the order in for two large pizzas - Talent ate like horses when they were using a lot of current - before I heard voices in the outer office. Wren must have Translocated, which meant no Sergei. I was outnumbered.

"Hi." I stood in the doorway and looked at the two women standing there. If you didn't know, you'd think Ellen was the more impressive one, tall and broad-shouldered, with glossy dark skin and hair, while the woman next to her was slighter, mousy-brown and seemingly insignificant. The emphasis would be on "seemingly." Retrievers, by their very nature, deferred the eye and muddled memories. Had Wren chosen to become an assassin.... Fortunately for everyone, she was at heart a kleptomaniac, not a killer.

"I hear you've got a job that needs my delicate touch."

"We getting the mentor discount?" Sergei wasn't just her partner, he was her business manager, too. He'd have a suitably pithy comment about her working for free.

"I'll call in a favor at a later date," she said, and I nodded without argument. As much as I hadn't wanted to call her in, she'd be at death's door before she asked me for help, and at that point I'd have given it anyway. We were just saving face, here.

"I have a feather from the gryphon's wing, I think." Ellen said. "I already used it to try to trace him, but I wasn't able to get anything."

"Underwing," I said. "From the size, probably close to the claws."

"Nothing else?"

"Photos of his victim. The guy's in the hospital now; if you needed to be in contact with him..."

"Huh." She considered that. "No. Let's try without, first. I'd be able to slip in unseen but it would take some time, and it might not be needed." She held out her hand, and Ellen placed the feather down on her palm.

"Yo, wait." I went back into my office and shut the laptop down completely and put it in the shielded drawer, and then turned off my cell phone and put it in the drawer as well. I'd heard stories about what happened to electronics around Wren, and my replacement budget was already stretched to its limit. Then I unlocked the drawer below it, and took out my service pistol, and loaded it.

"All right. Do you need anything?"

"For you to shut up and stay out of the way?" Wren's voice was low, sweet, and utterly focused on the feather in her hand.

"I can do that."

This was the first time I'd seen Ellen interact with her mentor. My Shadow wasn't a Retriever, that wasn't her skillset. But she was a Seer, and I was guessing that they were going to

use that to tie into Wren's own skills. But it was only a guess. Actually using current was beyond my pay grade. I leaned against the wall and, as per orders, shut up and stayed out of the way.

"I'll be able to work a seeking cantrip, I think. It's the same thing I use when I'm scoping out a site, doing a little advance research. You've seen me do it."

Ellen nodded, intent on her mentor's words. "I should follow along?"

"No. I want you to go into your core and open up. See what I stir up."

She said "see" but even I knew she meant See.

"All the way open," Wren said, glancing up from the feather to look at Ellen directly. "I'm here, and this place is as grounded as anywhere in the city. It's an old building, solid foundations, built on bedrock. You can ground all the way down, brace yourself that way. And goat-boy over there will watch over us physically, right?"

I hefted the pistol in my hand. "Anything that comes in, deals with me, first."

"Try not to shoot us while you're doing it." "If I yell duck, don't quack."

Pre-fight nerves, even though there wasn't a fight brewing. Ellen was looking back and forth between us, then down again at the feather, and I wanted to do something say something to bolster her courage. I didn't. This wasn't my place; Wren was her mentor. I was just her boss.

"Breathe, ground and center." Wren's voice was soft, steady, and Ellen exhaled and then drew a fresh breath, her shoulders softening, her hands resting against her thighs.

The feather rose off Wren's palm, hovering in the air between them, dancing slightly as though tugged by a thread. The air was thick and electric, and I could practically hear the new coffee maker shorting out. I hoped Ellen had thought to unplug it, but I wasn't going to interrupt to check.

"Feather, fly Return to the bone But remain."

I hadn't expected spellcasting to be quite so…poetic. The sense of static in the air increased, and the feather spun around frantically, turning quill-side up and then pointing back down again.

"Let me See." Ellen's incantation or whatever they called it, was simple, but heartfelt. She reached up a hand and closed her fingers around the feather, stopping its movement. Her entire hand, underneath the skin, was alive with a pulsing yellow-green neon, like… like nothing I could describe. I felt a little ill, watching, so I looked away. Wren's hands were blue-green. The feather was sparkling with a paler silver glitter, turning faster and faster within Ellen's grasp.

"He's dying. He's hurt so bad inside, and he was so tired, he's dying."

My first impulse was to grab my notebook and write down her words, but that would have required putting down the gun. I listened as hard as I could, trying to remember.

"Feather, fly," Wren repeated. "Return to the bone, to the bone."

The feather quivered again, and Ellen cried out as though the quills had suddenly got hot, but she didn't let go. I kept my grip loose on the grip of my handgun, and breathed out, trying for my own form of grounding, the way we'd been taught to do before a raid or during a standoff.

"In a building, an old building. It's built a nest but I can't see where it is, can't…oh."

This was the first time I'd seen her try for a Seeing, rather than having one come on her, and as far as I knew, the first time she'd consciously tried to scry for someone we knew was still alive. The only difference I could see was the play of current-light under her skin; that was new. She was facing away from me so I couldn't tell if the glazed look in her eyes was the same. The shiver in my horns and the back of my neck was less for what was happening in front of me than the potential even I could feel, working beneath the surface.

When I'd first met Ellen, I knew that others were wary of her. I'd understood why, intellectually - but now I *knew* why, bone-deep. A Storm Seer wasn't just a high-res Talent. Ellen was a perfect conduit, a lightning rod that could *use* the lightning that hit her. If she was trained.

That was why Wren was her mentor. And some day, maybe, the student would be more powerful than the teacher.

I was, weirdly, calm about that. I knew Ellen. She was a good kid. Careful, cautious, and maybe a little too cautious, yeah, after the life she'd had, but that was no bad thing, either. Power corrupts, but only so far as we let it.

"I have the nest," Wren said, her voice thin but steady. I'd known her for years, but never seen her when she was working. I realized I was holding my breath. "An abandoned building, yes. Not a warehouse; maybe an old school? Further west... Trenton, maybe, one of the older, smaller cities. Smart, to stay the hell out of Madame's territory."

Gryphons were fierce, but you didn't fuck with the centuries-old Great Wyrm who claimed Manhattan for her own, no.

"I think I've got him," the Retriever said, finally. "Nice lead, Ellen. We can-"

"There's something else," Ellen said. Her face had lifted toward the ceiling, and I half-expected a bolt of current-lightning to come through the roof and hit the tip of her nose. Maybe it did; this Null couldn't see it. "There's a connection."

She held the feather again, this time so tightly the edges were crushed. "The man and the gryphon...blood."

"Spilled blood, from the fight?"

Wren glared at me, like I should shut up. I glared back.

"No." Ellen shook her head, and her hand shook, too. "Contained. Shaped, formed...."

Wren lifted her hand as though to touch Ellen's hand and the feather, but stopped. Yeah, I didn't think that would be a good idea right now, either.

"New form. New life. Three swirls of blood, swirling together."

Wren looked confused. I, on the other hand, knew exactly what my Shadow was saying. The baby wasn't a cross-breed, she was a tri-breed. Alfred's daughter...the gryphon's granddaughter.

"Fuck me," I said, half-awed, half-horrified. "That's not good."

Wren frowned at me, a truly terrifying sight. "Is that even possible?"

"Possible, sure. Probable? Likely? Good? No and no and no."

"Why?" Ellen asked. "I mean, why's it a bad thing?"

"People - and by people I mean fatae, specifically - flip out over cross-breeds. It's like, oh god, like miscegenation in the last century. Cats and dogs, living together, end of the world etc etc. Except for a tri-breed... that could actually happen. End of the world, I mean. Not in the Mayan prophesy way, but people flipping like mammals and doing incredibly stupid shit in reaction."

I didn't have a high opinion of most fatae, when it came to hard-wired speciesist reactions. I didn't have a high opinion of humans, either. Even a year on the force of any major city will burn optimism out of you.

"So why—"

"We need to find the gryphon, if we're going to get any

answers. Wren, can you Translocate me there?"

Her eyes narrowed, then she shook her head. "Third-party transloc isn't my thing. I've done it, but it's...iffy. And Ellen isn't skilled enough yet to risk that distance, to a place she's never been."

"Fuck." I could feel the timetable running out on us. Yeah, the guy we'd been hired to find had been found, no thanks to us. But there was still a baby out there, and none of us believed that the gryphon had its best interest at heart, not after the beat-down it had presumably given daddy.

"What about Pietr? I mean, since you felt comfortable enough to call him in for other stuff."

Wren looked at me. I looked at the ceiling. Ellen didn't sound pissed, but that didn't mean she wasn't. I needed to remember to tell her when I did things like that going forward, clearly. "Yeah. Ask him."

There was a moment of blankness in her eyes, and a couple of minutes later, the soft sucking-pop noise of someone Translocating in.

"I don't suppose there's any way to lock you people out?"

Pietr, being a PUP, took the question seriously. "There is. I'll teach hot-stuff here when we get back. Where are we going?"

"Not we. Me."

"What?" Ellen started to protest.

"Just me." I stared Ellen down, which only took a minute. Valere, wisely, kept her mouth shut. I considered tucking the pistol into my waistband, then decided keeping it in my hand was the less-stupid move. "This is my gig, Shadow. You're not trained for it. Yet."

The "yet" placated her. For now.

I hate being Translocated. It's roughly akin to being blind-folded, thrown into one of those sideways carnival rides, and then dumped out somewhere other than where you started, with no idea of what's waiting for you on the other end. No, actually, that's *exactly* what it's like. Also, it makes me want to throw up, which isn't the best way to come into an unknown situation.

Especially when the unknown situation contains a pissed-off, bloody-taloned gryphon.

I landed square on my feet, but facing a bare, brick wall. Behind me, I heard the rustle-whisper of feathers against feathers, and made sure the gun was secure in my hand, barrel pointing down, before I turned.

"It's more polite to call ahead, rather than drop in unannounced." The voice was dry, with an undercurrent of clacking to the consonants.

"Your number was unlisted," I said, letting my wrist loosen. It didn't sound like our suspect was about to attack any time soon, but I wasn't letting down my guard entirely. The gryphon was about ten feet away, seated on a wide sofa, its long, tawny tail curled around its hindquarters, the barbed tip twitching slightly. The wings were folded, shifting occasionally the way someone might tap their fingers, and the head was...

I hadn't been prepared for how gorgeous that falcon's head would be, great golden eyes and sharply curved beak not at all alien, or even unfriendly. But dangerous, absolutely dangerous.

"You can put the gun away, faun."

"If it's all the same to you, I'll keep it out," I said. Without my usual cap, my horns were probably obvious enough to give away my fatae blood, but it was entirely possible that he could sniff it, too. Which meant he knew I was human, also. Considering his behavior so far, I wasn't going to assume peaceful intentions, faced with that fact.

"Oh...that." The gryphon didn't really have facial expressions - it didn't have much of a face, period - but there might have been a hint of apology in his voice. "I lost my temper."

"Just a bit, yeah." I kept my breathing steady, and my gaze direct, but unchallenging. Every confrontation with a perp had this moment, where they had to decide how much trouble they were in, and how much more trouble you could bring down on them. "So now you're looking at, what? Kidnapping, assault, maybe first degree manslaughter…"

The gryphon didn't drop its gaze, but the feathers on the top of its head smoothed enough that I figured it wasn't going to attack, at least not just yet. "You can hand me over to the Council later," it said. "We need to find it."

"It?" I wasn't playing dumb, exactly, just waiting for the gryphon to come clean, and maybe tell me something new.

"The offspring. It should never have existed, and it must not fall under the wrong influences."

"The offspring, as you call it, is…what, your child, too? Grandchild?" Clearly it didn't have any paternal feelings going on.

He tilted that beaked head, and looked at me like I'd just said the dumbest thing in the history of dumb. "It should never have existed. Someone did this intentionally. Manipulated. Caused."

Great, a gryphon with paranoia and delusions of conspiracy. "Why?"

"Prophesy."

Oh for the love of Mike. I took a step back, scanning the room for another chair. The only one I saw, I wouldn't trust to hold the weight of a coat, much less a person. "Founder Ben broke us of that, centuries ago. Nobody believes in prophesies any more."

"Perhaps they should." And by they, he clearly meant me.

"Right." I'd talked crazies out of their corner before, just not recently. I was out of practice. "Any particular prophesy in mind?"

He clacked his beak, and sighed. "Choose the poison you wish to ingest. The whisper, the *threat*, of many bloods in one flesh resurfaces with regularity. But the most recent was specific enough to reference a human child with wings on her back and original sin in her...heart."

I was betting heart wasn't the original placement. The jokes were too easy to make about the Lilin, which probably had as much to do with their reclusiveness as anything else. Some folk can't help hating what they want, especially once they discover it doesn't always want them back.

"So you think you were manipulated into sleeping with the... the Lilin was your daughter, right? You didn't put the beat- down on your own son?" Nobody had suggested our missing man was anything other than human, but hey, people have been wrong about me, too.

"The girl was my offspring." He didn't seem happy about it. I couldn't tell if he was a bigot, or just embarrassed at having let his feathers down with a Lilin. "I did not know she was with child, or with what. Only after the fact was I informed."

And then he'd decided to get his grandbaby back himself. But why? Wait, he'd said influence, that the kid shouldn't fall under the wrong influences. So he was the right one? Or he thought daddy dearest would have been, before he beat the crap out of him? I hate dealing with crazies.

"So the folk who've taken her, their plan is...what? To raise the child as some end-of-times priestess? To sacrifice her? To..."

"To study her," he said, and damned if you couldn't sneer with a beak. "To see if there's a way to bring all the breeds into one."

"Well, it's nice to know we've tempered our magical fatalism with science," I said, wryly. Still, no matter how crazy they were - or weren't - if they intended to study her, or god help us, breed her, they were going to keep her alive and healthy, at least until puberty. That was one relief. But we needed to find her, and get her away from crazy people - and I was including grandpa in that category for now.

"So where is she?"

"If I knew that, do you think I would be wasting time with that idiot human?" An agitated gryphon's wingspread was impressive, and my hand may have tightened around the grip of my gun just a bit, even as I recognized the soft pop of an incoming Translocation. This loft was starting to get a bit crowded.

"I know." Ellen, her voice firm, like it was no big deal she'd just shown up in the middle of a gryphon's temper tantrum. "I know how to find her."

I spun around, and glared at Ellen, utterly forgetting - without actually forgetting - about the irate fatae behind me. "How the hell-"

"I know you well enough to follow," she said, answering the question I hadn't asked, and I filed that information away for later use. Right now I didn't want her hopping around to unknown spots but...yeah, that could be a definite plus, in sticky situations. And come with some potential problems, too. "We'll talk about your hop-skotching-into-danger later," I said out loud. "You said you can track the baby?"

"It's...not simple, exactly. But yeah, I think I can track her."

"With current?" The gryphon seemed torn between scorn and annoyance. Clearly, he didn't have much use for humans. Or Talent.

"With current," she said, echoing his tone. "Yeah."

I held up a hand, to get a word in edgewise. "What're the others up to?"

"They went home - but they're listening in case we need back- up." In other words, waiting for a ping. She gave the gryphon a glare. He glared right back, that tail lashing again, and for a moment I thought I was going to have to break up a hissing match. "Children. Focus, please. So what's the deal with the kid?" I said to Ellen.

She gave the gryphon another glare, as though warning it to keep its claws off the two-legs, and turned to me. "It's simple, really. Most cantrips are, when you break them down, it's...." She looked at me, then the gryphon, clearly realizing that neither of us gave a damn about the make-up or break-down of her spell, only if it would work or not.

"Okay. I um... I need a feather. Please?" She looked at the gryphon, and I could sense her trying not to flinch or squeak. I couldn't exactly blame her.

The gryphon - whose name we still hadn't got - studied her and then, with a single lash of its tail, reached up and plucked a long, silvery feather from its left shoulder. It didn't come out easily, and I winced, even if he didn't.

She took it carefully, almost reverently, and that seemed to settle him down a bit.

"I'm Danny, by the way," I said. "That's Ellen."

"Faosullvaant ."

I wasn't sure I could say that without a beak to clack, so I just inclined my head in acknowledgement of the information. "I'd say it was a pleasure to meet you, but not really. No offense."

"None taken."

"Both of you, hush." Ellen pulled something out of her jeans pocket, unstoppering it with her teeth and spitting the cork into the corner. She then dipped the quill into the vial. It came out stained a deep black.

Blood. She had blood in the vial.

"Do I want to know where that came from?" "We needed the connection."

So, while I was chatting up Winged McLoon, Wren - I was presuming Wren - went into the hospital and took a blood sample from a comatose man. At least I didn't have to worry about anyone seeing her. And any worry about morality got left behind somewhere in my second year on the force. So I let it slide.

"You can do this, with that?"

"I'm a Seer. Seeing is what I do, right? This will help me focus on what I want to See."

"Right." Bonnie had explained to me once that Will was the most important thing when shaping current. Will, and Control. I didn't doubt Ellen's Will...

She held the feather up at eye level, dipped the point into the blood just enough to darken the tip, and turned it slowly, the way you would a key in a lock you weren't quite sure of, or if you were trying not to make any noise. The gryphon leaned forward, apparently interested despite himself. Well, it was his feather, after all.

"Generation to generation, blood to bone. Show me."

It didn't have the poetic nuance of Valere's cantrips, but from the sparking around her hand, I was betting it did the trick. Words were mostly showmanship, from what Bonnie'd said, more than a few times. You put on a show to convince yourself you knew what you were doing, and impress anyone who might likewise doubt.

The feather quivered and then - in a snap of sparks - disappeared.

"Where..."

Ellen's face had that look again. The one that said she was Seeing something.

"Wheels. A sea of wheels, and pavement, and shoes. People walking...standing. Glass and chrome."

I waited, but that was it, nothing specific enough to identify.

But I had a hunch of my own.

"Look up," I directed her. "Lift your gaze."

Her chin tilted up, but her eyes were looking somewhere else. Hopefully, up.

"Streets, storefronts. Large glass windows, filled with things." Her head tilted to the side a little, and I was amused to recognize one of my own physical "don't bother me I'm think-ing" quirks in her body. Well, I did call her Shadow... "A large sign, overhead. Green. Hanging down. A name? A... fruit?" Her face look puzzled for a moment, her own personality cracking through the Seer. We weren't going to get much more, if she didn't See it now.

Green sign...name... plate glass .... A fruit... I ran it through my own knowledge of the area, hoping against hope they hadn't gone out of the city, or into one of the remote pockets I hadn't wandered, or hadn't been too damaged or gentrified beyond recognition.

"A name of a fruit," she said, decisive now, and I laughed in relief.

"The Upper East Side. She's seeing the Upper East Side."

J.G. Melon, home of one of the best burgers in New York City, and possessor of a large green sign hanging from the side of their building.

"I have her," Ellen said. "I know where she is. But it's right *now*."

The gryphon got up from his bench, and I was suddenly aware of how thickly-muscled that body was. Not huge, maybe eight feet tall and five across the shoulders, but *solid*. "Then let us go," he said, extending one wing down, a clear invitation. I was beyond dubious, but Ellen stepped forward without hesitation, and considering the alternative was to haul out on mass transit - which would take forever - or be held in those claws....

I got on.

One of the things I love and despair of about New York City - and Boston and Chicago, for that matter - is how a fatae can walk down the street and people look right at him and don't react. Maybe a flicker of an eyelid and then it's "oh, well, okay then" and they move on. In Los Angeles, people gawp. Down South, they do a faint *oh dear* and turn away. Outside of the cities... it can get ugly. But the big northern cities? Yeah, whatever pal, I get weirder than you in my breakfast cereal.

Then again, if you saw a gryphon, twice as big as a linebacker and three times as cranky, would *you* stare, much less get in his way?

Ellen stopped on the corner, and lifted her chin, pointing not to the restaurant, but the French cafe across the street. "She's in there."

"Hide a stroller in a sea of strollers," I said, looking at the rows of baby carriages that probably cost as much as a months' rent on the office, parked outside the cafe. "Smart. Also pretty much impossible to find…"

"Without magic. Yes." The gryphon flicked one talon, unhappy at being shown up by a Human, Talent or otherwise. "So now what?"

"Now we steal a baby," Ellen said. "Let's see if I've learned anything useful from Genevieve. You guys stay here and make a distraction."

Before I had a chance to say anything, she had gone inside. I knew what she was about to do, and she was right, it was the best chance we had. But having someone in my employ use the same tactics I was usually investigating made me slightly nauseated.

Our best chance at a distraction would draw the Council's attention. But with luck, it would draw it away from the kid, not towards.

"Do something really obnoxiously impressive," I told Faosullvaant. "Ideally without actually hurting anyone."

The gryphon looked at me like I was an oversized and not-particularly-tasty rabbit, then turned away, his wings coming out and extending. I got out of the way - barely - as he turned. The wings were large, but they were as graceful as a ballerina's arms, and hit exactly what he intended them to.

I flinched as the fire hydrant's top burst open, a heavy stream of water rising a few feet into the air before turning into a fountain. Okay, that was impressive, but it wasn't going to get a lot of people anything more than wet and pissy -

And then he launched himself into the air, his lion's body in full leap into the air like a carousel carving, catching the full brunt of the water on the underside of his wings.

And what had been ordinary water, shaken off those silver feathers, became a kaleidoscope of rainbows shimmering from his shoulders to his tail, magic in motion, a thousand liquid hummingbirds before they splashed back down to the pavement. Everyone, and I mean every. Damn. One. On the block stopped, and stared.

And then he was gone.

*"Did you see that?"* "

*That was awesome."*

*"Are they filming the new Marvel movie here?"*

*"Dude. I'm fucking soaked."*

And then the moment was over, and everyone went back to whatever they'd been doing, shaking off the water or shaking their heads and messaging their friends, but walking away and not looking back. That was when I realized that Ellen had walked past me, something bundled in her arms. She kept moving, not looking back or around, her stride steady and sure as though she had every right to be carrying that baby in her arms.

I stepped into the street and hailed a cab.

Ellen walked away from the cafe, her heart pounding hard enough to break a rib, her ears ringing from alarms that hadn't gone off. The baby was surprisingly heavy, but easy enough to carry, almost as though she *wanted* to be taken away.

Ellen thought about trying to cast a cantrip to keep the baby quiet, or keep anyone from stopping her, but the main thing Genevieve said about retrieving - the few times her mentor would even talk about it - was that the best way to hide is to be exactly like everyone else in a crowd. So, no more current than she'd normally use, and the stress and relief mixed in her expression could be any new mom, trying to get through her day, her shoulder bag passing for a diaper bag, if needed. Hopefully.

"Hush darling, we'll be home soon," she told the baby. The little face screwed up for a moment, as though about to cry, and then a tiny fist knocked against one soft, entirely human-looking cheek, and she soothed back into sleep.

Ellen exhaled, and headed for the next subway entrance.

Head down, feet moving, and if getting her subway card out of her pocket was more effort with a baby in her arms, nobody gave her a second look. She couldn't relax enough to recharge, though, and she could feel her muscles starting to shake with exhaustion. How did Genevieve *do* this?

Despite all of her fears, they made back to the office stop without anyone stopping her, or the baby starting to cry. In fact, the infant was so quiet she kept checking, nervously, that it was still breathing. She'd always heard that infants cried all the time, but this one seemed to prefer sleeping.

Surprisingly, the gryphon was waiting for her on the street. How he knew where to go, she didn't know, and she wasn't in the mood to ask, either. She glared at him, daring him to do something, make one move that she didn't like. Current moved in her core, alert to her mood.

The feathers on the top of his head, and the side of his neck fluttered slightly, but that might have been the breeze. Maybe.

Ellen wasn't happy with the fatae hanging around, but she acknowledged that he had as much right - maybe even more, being a relative - as she did. And if anyone came after her, or the baby, it would be some defense, anyway, even if just the "it's not kidnapping, look, here's grandpa" sort.

But Danny had better show up, *soon*.

The three of them made an odd grouping in the elevator; the gryphon barely fit, even with his wings furled tightly around his body. Once inside the office, the wings relaxed a little, and he took up the far corner of the front room, his golden eyes watching them carefully. Cautious, alert to anything that might happen.

"It's a baby," she said in disgust. "Just a baby, not even a toddler, which is when they get really scary." She'd babysat enough of them when she was a teenager to remember that. The gryphon just lurked, and watched, and didn't say anything. "Yeah, all right. The coffee's on the counter behind you, if you want some. There's soda in the fridge. Just... Don't talk to me right now." Not that there seemed much chance of that.

She pulled her sweater off the back of the chair, and created a nest of sorts on the desk, weaving current into it so that it stayed in the right shape. If there was a small protection charm woven in as well, it wasn't as though anyone would be able to tell. The baby scrunched her face again, and let out a little sigh, and a tiny bubble of spit formed at the corner of her mouth. Ellen wasn't sure if that was adorable, or disgusting.

"Hello, sweetie, aren't you a sweetie?" She unwrapped the blankets, wondering if maybe the boss had stopped to pick up diapers and formula, because otherwise someone was just going to have to turn around and go out again. "You look human... ten fingers, ten toes..."

The door opened behind her, the sound of Danny's cowboy boots a familiar noise against the linoleum. She risked a glance away from the baby, and saw that he was carrying a bag from the drug store down the street. Good.

He put the bag down on the floor with a soft-sounding thunk, and looked over her shoulder just as the baby opened her eyes.

"Huh. Well, there's that then," Danny said, an odd tone in his voice.

"Definitely not human," Ellen agreed. She lifted the now-awake baby in her arms, and turned, stepping away from Danny as she did so. "Your granddaughter," she said to Faosull-vaant. "I don't suppose you know her name?"

The gryphon looked like he wanted to be anywhere but there, but Ellen didn't let him escape, stepping forward just enough that the baby caught sight of him. Chubby little arms flew out to the side, fingers working as though she was trying to grab at him.

The gryphon looked at her then, two pairs of golden eyes meeting for the first time. Something in him seemed to break, quietly. "Her grand-dam's name was Marciad."

"That'll work. Hello, Marciad"

"Still think she's an abomination?" Danny was leaning against the desk now, watching all three of them.

That beak clacked again, and Ellen though that maybe she was starting to "read" gryphon, because she knew it was thought, not irritation, that was behind it. "Yes. But it is not her fault that she exists. My daughter bears the blame for that, and she has gone beyond responsibility."

Dead then, or somewhere out of reach forever. Ellen wasn't sure which might be worse.

"She can never know what she is," the gryphon went on. "No-one should be able to use her, ever."

Danny nodded immediately, although she suspected he had his own reasons that had nothing to do with whatever grandpa was afraid of. "Agreed. Although if she starts to show—"

"A problem for another day?"

"Yeah, okay."

"Great, now that you've got her life all planned out for her, where's she going to go?" Ellen would have called them on their typical male BS, saying what Marciad could or couldn't be, but the chubby little hand trying to grab her nose now had all of her attention. "Don't do that, baby-girl. Stop. Help?"

Danny removed the fingers from Ellen's nose, and lifted the child away from her. "Hello, sweetness," he cooed at her, and she went right for his horns. He laughed, like they were ticklish, but didn't remove her hands. "You're going to be a handful and a half, aren't you darling?"

"What are we going to do with her? I mean, I don't think grandpa there wants her, and her parents..."

"Mom's gone, and dad's not really set up to handle this, no." Danny coaxed the baby into settling down, letting her grab at his own fingers. "Her mother's people said they'd take her. She'll be safe there." Kept ignorant, he meant, and she heard, even unspoken. "And they always have kids running around, so one more won't raise eyebrows. If our gryphon buddy says she won't manifest feathers or a beak, I'm willing to take that on trust, but other breeds mingle a little less obviously, and those eyes are always going to be a question mark.

"Besides, she may not seem very Lilin-like right now, but better she be there when she hits puberty, just in case."

Danny went into the inner office, baby still in his arms, and she heard him sit down, and pick up the phone. Presumably to call the Lilin House. Or maybe to order pizza...it was Friday, right? She checked the calendar: yeah it was Friday.

They'd managed a happy ending, despite the odds. Their missing man was home, and Lilin House would take the baby in: they'd said so, knowing what the baby was, and Danny thought they were telling the truth. Whyever she'd been born, whatever her mother might have thought would happen, whatever she grew up to be, they would take her in, protect her. They'd make sure that Marciad doesn't spend her life being looked at oddly, as a freak, forever out-of-place. Danny would call that a win.

Ellen walked past the gryphon and reached down to pull a soda out of the fridge, taking it back to her desk and sitting down to sort through the mail. She slit open the first envelope, smiling to herself. Boss might call it a win, but she called it a promise, kept.

# THE WORK OF HUNTERS

*It was night, but the immediate scene was lit with neon flickering against the walls and bringing up bluish highlights on faces and hands. Figures in dark clothing moved back and forth, talking quietly enough not to be overheard, while others bent to various tasks.*

*A crime scene. A city. Any city, in the just-before-dawn darkness there's not enough to identify it, save the cars are American, the figures mostly male, a mix of white and Hispanic, some black, a few women, almost all of whom are black.*

*Something about it says New York. There's a familiarity to it she can't quite name, can't quite catch, but she knows.*

*Then suddenly the sound was turned up from 1 to 9. Someone yelled — "bring it over here!" — and another someone in a gray jumpsuit hurried over, carrying a bulky object in both hands, like it's a precious thing. He set it down, knelt beside it, and fiddled — and the area was filled with a grey-white light.*

*There is a dumpster shoved against one wall of the alley, purple-green in the illumination, letters stenciled in white on one end, but all focus is on the body being removed from it, gingerly, by white-coated, white-gloved technicians. It is male, the skin grey, the face mangled and bitten beyond recognition. Bare feet bloody, bare chest, the jeans covered with stains that could be anything, after time in a dumpster.*

*"Two in two days," a voice says, tired and frustrated. "You boys are going to start catching some heat on this."*

*She knows that voice. She knows it very well.*

ELLEN HATED it when a vision came in public, especially on public transit. It's not that people noticed, or tried to do anything — at most they got uncomfortable that the person next to them had gone rigid and staring, and moved away as quietly and quickly as possible. But sometimes she'd come out of it, trying her damnedest not to shake or scream, and there'd be someone staring at her, like it was all for their own entertainment, or worse yet, like they wanted to help but didn't know how to, or were afraid to.

All she wanted to do then was be invisible, to get off the subway, find a place to sit and process, write down what she'd Seen in the notebook Danny insisted she carry, and remember how to breathe. Kindness, just then, made her want to break things.

This time she got lucky: it was 11am on a Tuesday and people were either already at work or in school, or off doing whatever it was they did. The only other people in the subway car with her were a couple more interested in each others' tonsils than anyone around them, and an old woman wrapped in a leather coat who'd clearly given up giving a shit what anyone else was doing a few decades ago.

Being ignored was good. Her arms were trembling, like she'd done one set too many pushups, but that was normal. She folded her hands in her lap and breathed, waiting for the train to pull into the next stop. It wasn't hers, a stop too early, but she got out anyway. Her legs felt rock steady, carrying her up the stairs and out onto the sidewalk, although she had to hold onto the side rail the last few steps, and was glad that she was wearing sensible sneakers, not heels. A white man heading down into the subway gave her an odd look as he passed, but didn't try to talk to her. She thought he might have been another Talent, but she couldn't spare enough energy to do the tendril-touch thing Wren had taught her, to be certain.

She was blocking the stairs, she realized, and moved to the side. Leaning against the rough brick of the building, she kept breathing, in and out the way her mentor had taught her. More people went past her, up and down the stairs, and there was a comfort in the normalcy, the routine of it all. Ellen was a big fan of routine. She had a schedule, and she liked to keep to it. This had *not* been in today's schedule.

When the trembling stopped, and she didn't feel like a squirrel in a too-small box, she walked down the street until she found a bench outside a Le Pain Quotidian. Sitting down, she reached into the battered leather case she never left her apartment without these days, and pulled her notebook out.

"Do it quick, without thinking." Danny's voice in her ear, even though he'd said it more than a year ago. She clicked the pen, and started to write. Automatic writing, not thinking about grammar or punctuation or even making any of it make sense, just the images she'd seen, the things she'd felt, any impressions made, before it drifted away.

Not that she was ever lucky enough for it all to disappear.

She'd remember. She remembered all of them. The ones they'd saved, and especially the ones she hadn't.

---

TUESDAY MORNING STARTED BAD, and went worse. I'd been working a stalker case all weekend and through Monday, and was running on too little sleep and too much caffeine as I sent my conclusions and final invoice to the client. The last thing I needed right after that was a deceptively calm Talent not-quite-yelling in my ear. When Talent get too worked up, things tend to explode around them. The woman I was talking to was high-res enough that she could explode things in *my* area, and I'd replaced enough coffee makers and cell phones already this year, thank you very much.

"For the third and final time, Valere, no, I have no idea... do I look like her keeper? She's not supposed to work today, you've got custody, so why — "

I heard the external door, the one that led in from the hallway, open, and shut my mouth, trying to hear who was out there. We were, technically, open for business, but would-be clients tended to knock. Anyone who didn't knock, but came right in, quietly enough that a human probably wouldn't have heard the door over the sound of his own voice? I moved to the desk, and unlocked the drawer that housed my handgun. Call me paranoid, but you can also call me still alive, so it's a wash.

Then came the unmistakable, and familiar, sound of keys dropped on the wooden desk outside, and I exhaled, my fingers easing away from the blued metal, pushing the drawer closed again and hearing it lock. I tested the pull anyway, just to make sure. "Yeah, I think your duckling just walked in the door. I'll call as soon as I know something. Do me a favor and don't freak any more until there's something to be freaked out about, okay?"

I hung up with her still protesting in my ear. Once upon a time Wren Valere had sworn she'd never act as mentor, that it wasn't her thing — she didn't want to be responsible for anyone other than herself and her partner. That had lasted about ten minutes, when Shadow was dropped in her lap.

But then, I really didn't have much room to mock. I'd sworn never to take on an apprentice, and yet here I was. Here we all were.

I leaned in the doorway between my office and the main room, trying not to carry any of Wren's agitation with me. "Hey," I said, making a quick scan for bloodshed, mayhem, or any other reason to panic.

The outer room looked a hell of a lot better than it used to, when I worked alone. There were a few semi-flourishing green plants there, now, and several framed prints on the wall,

weirdly soothing art I couldn't identify at gunpoint. The desk was still the same beat-up wooden monstrosity it had always been, but the chair behind it was the most ergonomic money could buy — and I knew, because I'd paid the bill.

Shadow wasn't sitting in the chair, though. She was standing in front of the desk, hands resting on the wooden surface, staring at her chair like —

No. She wasn't staring at anything. She was just staring. I'd learned what that meant, the hard way.

"You wrote it down."

"Yeah." It hadn't been a question, but she shook her head, then nodded, and looked at me. "Yeah, I got it."

I did a quick once-over while her head was up and facing me. Her dark eyes were too wide, the pupils still blown, but her skin tone was good, and her breathing was steady. She'd handled it — but she'd come to me, instead of meeting with her mentor as scheduled. That wasn't good.

It was never good. Ellen was a Storm-Seer. She didn't see happy-go-lucky yay fun visions. She saw violence. Death. Murder.

"Valere called," I told her. "She was a little wigged out when you didn't show up on time, and weren't responding to pings. You might want to — "

"Oh." Anyone who says that Black women don't blush doesn't know what the fuck they're talking about, because the dark red on her cheeks was clearly visible. Her eyes got that look that Talent have, and I knew she was reaching out to her mentor, letting her know what was up.

Talent can do that. I'm not Talent. I get to deal with Valere over the phone, and pray her static doesn't take down the line while she's on it, and I get to deal with Ellen, who was at least as powerful, and pray she didn't fry my synapses if she lost control. Lucky me.

"Ideally, in the future you'll loop her in *before* she attempts to send my ass out looking for you," I said calmly, years of walking the beat giving me plenty of practice in staying cool. "Or answer her when she pings?"

"Yeah boss, I know, I'm sorry. I was so focused on remember- ing, I didn't hear her." Ellen hit send, or whatever it is Talent do when they're pinging each other like some kind of psychic instant messenger, then sat on the corner of her desk, long legs crossed at the ankles like a dame out of a Bogie movie, and stared at me until I started to wonder if I'd left some break-fast on my face. I pulled the visitor's chair out from where we stashed it against the wall and hauled it over so I could sit in front of her, close enough that my hands could rest on her knees.

Her eyes were starting to ease a little: it had been at least half an hour since the vision, then. If she'd been heading uptown, she'd had to've turned around and come here, so prob-ably closer to forty minutes. I owed Valere an apology: she had waited a reasonable time before starting to panic.

"What level?" I asked her. "I... don't know."

We have a scale, one to nine, to pinpoint the urgency of one of her visions: is this something we have minutes to deal with, or is it days or weeks to come? She's not accurate to the hour, but usually we get a sense of the timeframe.

"Yes you do," I told her, not to be an ass but because I knew that she did know. She just didn't want to commit to anything, not yet. My poor Shadow, still half-convinced, deep down, that if she voices an opinion someone's going to tell her she's wrong, she's crazy.

She's about as far from crazy as anyone I've ever met.

"Come on." I kept the pressure on her knees soft and steady, something for her to focus on, come back to. "What level?"

She nodded, listening as much to herself as me. "Okay, yes. It felt urgent, really urgent, but there was a sense of... of not having to rush, too. That's what threw me, I think. It was like... the vision itself wasn't sure?"

That had never happened before. Usually the urgency is the one thing she's really clear about, and everything else we have to figure out.

"What was it sure about?"

"It was in the city, not Manhattan though. Queens, maybe? Tall buildings, wide alleys. And a dumpster, and a body."

"Time of day?"

"Night." She reached down and patted the bag at her side, as though reassuring herself that something was still in there, and continued. "No, early morning. Really early. The body was in the dumpster. Hanging feet-out, bent at the knees. It was barefoot, shirtless. The feet and face were bloody."

Live as many decades as I have, see as much as I have, and you get pretty hard to shock. But every word out of my Shadow's mouth was making something deep in my brain start to spaz out, like a huge white space as expanding in my brain, pushing out all rational thought. "Black or white?" My voice was a croak, but I couldn't be bothered by that right now.

"Black." She said the word, but she wasn't entirely convinced of that; I could hear it in her voice. "Maybe Hispanic? It was hard to see. Not-white, though. And something had messed up his face, like it'd been scraped off?"

I'm a grown-ass man with full control of his body. I don't faint, or pass out, or lose consciousness without losing at least two pints of blood, first. But just then, I was fair to making a real good impression of it. What she was describing... it was impossible.

"B$_{\text{OSS}}$?" Her voice had gone from the distant remembering tone, to a sharper, more worried one. She'd picked up on my reaction. Damn it.

I wanted to ask her if she was sure, if she'd remembered everything perfect, but I knew she had. I'd been the one to talk her through most of her visions, I'd been the one who taught her how to recall details before she could contaminate them. If she said that's what she Saw, then that's what she Saw. The last thing she needed was me throwing more doubt on her.

I nodded, forcing the dizziness away. We didn't have time for this. "You said it wasn't right-now urgent?"

"Maybe a... two? Or three? Soon, but not right now."

I had to stand up, move. There wasn't enough room in the front office to pace, but I did my best attempt anyway. "You always see the future, don't you?"

"You know that." Her voice was sharp. She had gone from being confused to being worried, and when Ellen got worried she got angry. I couldn't complain: it was better than how she used to react, pulling in and trying to hide. I'd rather she yell at me than go back to being Shadow.

I knew that. I knew that Ellen always Sees the future. Always. She's never seen the past, not once since we started working with her, and not before then, far as she knew. But what she was describing happened nearly thirty years ago.

"Tell me everything," I say. "Every damn thing."

---

ELLEN HAD SURVIVED ADOLESCENCE by keeping a weather eye on the people around her, and working at Sylvan Investigations had only honed that skill. So even in the middle of her own trauma, she knew something was wrong.

"Boss?" She watched as her boss paced back and forth, his hands shoved into his pockets, face blank. "You're making me nervous."

That wasn't a good thing to do to a Talent. The first lecture she'd ever gotten was that the ability to manipulate current — what people used to call magic, back before Founder Ben codified the connection between current and electricity — came with a price, and part of that price was that if they slip up on their control, or pull too much power, they fry things nearby. Computers, mostly, but also people, if the Talent in question is high-res and nervous enough. Ellen was, she'd been told, high-res. And she was getting very nervous.

"Boss?" She tried again. Normally, Danny was already forming a plan by the time she'd finished telling him about a vision. He was smart, and he was quick, and he was pretty much unflappable. Part of it was a career in the NYPD before she'd ever met him, part of it was that fauns just didn't get flapped by much. He was only half-faun, but he'd said once that he got the useful part — the stone-cold liver, and the ability to take weirdness pretty much in stride.

She'd never pointed out to him that he'd also gotten the quirky charm-and-looks combo that made most fauns such cocky sons of bitches. He knew, he just tried not to use it.

Her words finally reached him, at least enough to make him stop pacing. "You saw the cops already there? So we can't stop it. The person's already dead, or he's going to be dead. I'm sorry, kid."

He only called her kid when something was wrong. Shadow, when he was worried. Ellen, or Miss Ellen when he was in a particularly good mood, the courtesy he said his mom had drilled into him coming to the fore in a weirdly playful way. But 'kid' was "I have to tell you something bad" territory.

"Do you think that's why it felt urgent but not urgent?" Like the merfolk she hadn't been able to save. No. When she saw dead people it still felt urgent, because there was someone else at risk, someone *alive*. She looked at him, her face scrunched in a frown. "What aren't you telling me?"

"El — "

"I may not have Sergei's bullshit detector — " her mentor's husband was a Null, but he could smell a lie before you even thought it — "But I know you pretty well now, and you're not telling me something."

Two years ago Danny Hendrickson had terrified her. Two years ago, everything had terrified her. Her entire life, people had told her she was crazy, that her visions were hallucinations, that everything that happened around her wasn't normal, that *she* wasn't normal. Discovering about Talent, about current, learning that she was — not normal, maybe, but that everything that happened to her had a name and an explanation — had been like breathing for the first time after a life of holding her breath.

Now... her visions still scared her. But that was okay. Anyone who saw people getting hurt, killed, and knew it was about to happen, and wasn't scared, was an idiot. The difference was she knew what it was, now. And she knew that she could do *something* about it now. That was why Genevieve had sent her to Danny in the first place. So she could *do* something about it, so she didn't feel so helpless.

But if he was going to hold something back, if there was something so bad he couldn't tell her....

"Boss." She swallowed, fought back the old bad habit of fear, and forced herself to meet his gaze squarely. "Whatever it is, I need to know."

He didn't want to tell her, but she waited, and waited him out. He was the one who'd said they were partners. Partners told each other what was going on. Right?

Five long breaths, and he exhaled, giving in.

"What you saw." He closed his eyes, and ran his fingers

through his hair, flattening the brown curls so that the tips of his horns showed, briefly. "It happened already. Years ago."

"No." She shook her head. That couldn't be right. "I See things that are *going* to happen. That's how it works."

"I know, kid. But you need to trust me on this. The murder you're seeing? It already happened."

His certainty made no sense. Unless.... She remembered the thing she'd almost forgotten. That she'd recognized a voice in the vision. "You were there."

"What?" He froze, his hand halfway through his hair again, and glared at her, his face like stone. "No, that's not possible."

Possible or not, she knew what she'd heard. Her hearing might not be as acute as his, but she knew what his voice sounded like. "I heard your voice. I didn't know it was you, it didn't sound like you, but it was."

He knew better than to argue about what she saw in a vision: she might not understand what she saw, not at first, but she *knew*. She scowled at him. Danny had been a cop, long time ago. Had she seen something from his past? But she didn't *see* the past. All she could think was that everyone said being a Seer was rare, maybe there was something they didn't know, something—

He stood up, shoving the chair back with the violence of his movement, and stalked to the door to his office, then stopped, both hands on the door like he wanted to shove it away. "So it's going to happen again," he said. "Fuck."

<hr>

ELLEN WAS STARTING AT ME, her nostrils flared and her eyes too wide, the stink of fear and uncertainty like expensive perfume, tendrils reaching delicately into the air. A predator would be salivating: I just felt sick, my gut hurting like I'd been punched from the inside. What Ellen had described wasn't possible on half a dozen levels, but the two most important were; the murder she'd described to a T had happened decades ago, and I hadn't been on the recovery site. I'd made a point of staying far the hell away, in fact.

So if she'd heard me in her vision…. Either she was wrong, or I was going to be there. At an event that had already happened.

My brain joined my gut in hurting.

Ellen was never wrong. Sometimes she didn't interpret what she saw correctly, but her Sight was never wrong. And while I'd seen a hell of a lot in my life, I hadn't seen anything that said time travel was possible. So we were left with one final option: that she'd Seen something about to happen, and that it overlaid the thing that *had* happened, somehow, to almost perfect detail.

Which, logically, meant that the same killer had left both scenes.

That wasn't possible. I knew that, knew it for a cold hard fact. But every gut instinct I had told me to trust Ellen.

Believing that deeply in two contradictory things might break some people, and it was doing its best to break me, too. But I'd seen enough impossible things happen in my life — hell, I *was* a near-impossible thing, or at least highly improbable — to know that thinking 'that can't happen' was a pretty damnsure way to have it happen.

"So…?" she said, clearly waiting for me to pull a brilliant plan out of my ass.

Maybe it was a copycat. Maybe it was coincidence. "You said we had time?"

"A little. I think." She didn't sound at all certain.

We could go to the scene, but I couldn't be sure it was the right *where*, and without a clear idea of *when*, we had as likely a chance of getting there too late, or, worse yet, just in time to be considered suspects. This might be a case where we were the clean-up crew, not the heroes.

"I saw them dead," Ellen said, echoing my thoughts. "Right at the beginning. It was all about the aftermath."

I turned on the police scanner, made another pot of coffee, and pulled out the chess set, to try and fill the time while we waited.

Half an hour later, halfway through a game that was probably going to be stalemated, we heard a callout on the scanner, units responding to a too-familiar location I'd never — to the best of my knowledge — been.

"That's it," I said, bile rising into my throat.

Twenty minutes later we were out of the office, trying to hail a cab — the subway would take too long to get where we were going, and I wasn't in the mood to deal with my fellow New Yorkers.

I raised my hand and a cabbie slid into place, which on a normal day would have been cause for self-congratulations and a little smugness. I opened the door and ushered Ellen inside, then gave the cabbie his direction.

***

WE DIDN'T TALK, the entire trip. That only left me more time with my thoughts, none of which were good.

And it didn't help that Ellen was sitting next to me, practi- cally vibrating with her need to know what was going on, what I hadn't told her yet. Even if I couldn't read it in every bone of her body, she was a normal, intelligent twenty-something with an unhealthy dose of curiosity and probably more compassion than was good for her, and she knew what she'd Seen bothered me far more than I had admitted, more than just a blast from the past echoing in our present, for reasons I hadn't — wouldn't — explain.

I didn't tell her anything. Partially because you don't prejudice the scene before you've had a chance to look it over, and partially because the last thing I ever wanted to do was talk about that. Ever. My male genetic donor might be higher up the list, but just then I couldn't have said for sure.

And having daddy undearest suddenly show up at my front door would have been less a shock than this.

We arrived before she actually imploded from impatience. I paid the cabbie by credit card — this might not be a case, officially, but I was going to claim it on my taxes anyway — and escorted Ellen by the elbow down the street to where my former co-workers had gathered.

Cops, tape, flickering lights... walking into that alley between two 1950's-era brick houses in Maspeth didn't make me feel twenty-nothing again. Not much could — except the sound of Scott's voice, booming over the softer voices and radio static.

"Hendrickson!" He didn't have the decency to sound surprised. "Get your ass over here."

That was enough to get us under the tape, although we got more than a few sideways looks. Most of the cops here didn't know me from Eve, and the ones who did, I was just 'the PI who's not entirely an asshole,' endquote.

Scott was listening to a short, balding uniform when we reached him, and it didn't look like he was enjoying what he heard.

"Great. Wonderful. Tell Marge if she misses a single hair I'm busting her back down to lab assistant. Or gopher. Hendrickson. Why am I so fucking not surprised you're here."

The uniform grabbed his dismissal and ran with it, back, one presumed, to tell Marge to be careful.

"Sir."

He glared at me. "Don't fucking sir me, you pointy-headed bastard. What do you know?"

Scott had been in my class at the academy. We'd been

bright-eyed and eager, that first year on the force. Now Scott was a captain out in Queens, graying and bitter, and me… well, thanks to my fatae genetics, I looked like I could be his son. The fact that Scott could joke about it, tried on occasion to set me up with his actual daughter, was one of the reasons we were still friends.

Most people outside the Cosa, once they figured out I wasn't entirely human, backed off and forgot me, out of self-preservation. And I didn't blame them.

"This is Ellen," I said, and waited while Scott sized my girl up. On the surface she looked impressive enough: tall, with mid-scale black skin, a regal nose an Egyptian queen would be proud to claim, wide-set eyes and otherwise even features, her hair close-cropped after an inebriated dryad tried to grab at it during our last case. If you were Talent, I'd been told, she was even more impressive, her core of current strong enough to be sensed by anyone paying attention.

What she was, Valere'd told him once, kind of whispered itself in your ear — if you were Talent. I wasn't, neither was Scott. Scott had been able to accept the fatae, the supernatural creatures of the world, but humans who could use magic? That was more than he'd wanted to know, and I'd respected that. He was an intuitive bastard, though. He knew there was something about her, something more than the surface.

"Heard you picked up a sidekick," was all he said, now. Normally, under other conditions, that would be followed by a wisecrack, a challenge, a poke, to see how she reacted to being razzed. But not today. Scott was all business, and so were we.

"Yeah. You know what's over there." I was asking, but it wasn't a question.

"I took a once-over when we hit the scene."

"Is it…" The words stuck in my throat, and I forced them out. "Is it the same?" Scott had been around for it, too, had heard the briefings. It was just a momentary blip in a long career, an ordinary atrocity that gets overlaid with others soon enough, but you still remember. You remember all of them.

"Far as I can tell, carbon copy. That's why you're here? You think our boy's resurfaced after thirty years?"

No. No I didn't think the killer had resurfaced. But I had no proof one way or the other, so I kept my mouth shut. "Okay if I take a look?"

"Yeah sure go ahead. Fuck anything up and I'll shred your license myself."

"I should...?" Ellen lifted her chin in the direction of the activity, then cut her eyes sideways to look at Scott. It was a tossup which was a worse idea, taking her to see the body, or leaving her here with the old man.

"Come with me. If you think you're going to throw up, back up ten paces and turn around before you let fly."

She nodded, and swallowed, then followed at my heels.

The sound and motion around us wasn't soothing — there's no way a crime scene can ever be anything other than jarring, unpleasant — but not enough had changed since I left the force for it to not be familiar. This far in, people assumed I had a right to be there, and let me pass, Ellen keeping close.

The dumpster was standard issue, the lid flipped open and the regulation scent wafting out. Nowhere near as bad as it had been in the late 70's, but nothing you wanted to bottle and bring home, either.

"I could have gone the rest of my life without ever smelling a decomp again."

"Picked the wrong line of work then," someone responded automatically, then did a doubletake. "Er, sorry, sir?"

If a guy out of uniform shows up at a crime scene, even wearing jeans, especially if he's a white male with a female, Black companion at his heels, assume he's either brass or a politician. Cop 101. I waved him off — accepting his apology would bring too much attention to myself, trying to reassure him would make things worse. "How long's the body been there?"

"Guestimate's twelve to twenty — stiff's still stiff."

Inappropriate humor, the hallmark of...pretty much everyone in this city, actually.

"Who called it in?"

"Union's finest," and he lifted an elbow to indicate the men in grey coveralls, standing just outside the tape, leaning against a wall in a pose best described as "tired of this shit."

"They getting overtime to wait on you?"

The shrug indicated that it wasn't his problem. Not mine either, come to think of it.

"Danny..."

I turned, expecting Ellen to be making a break for the tape. I needed to stop underestimating her. She was a little green around the gills, but she was holding steady. "This is it."

"Yeah?"

"Yeah."

"Okay." We tried not to say things like "seen" or "vision" around Nulls. It tends to freak them out. "Come on." We went closer, and the smell got worse. Another uniform handed me a tube and I swiped some balm on my top lip, then handed the tube on to Ellen, who used it and handed it back to the cop with a murmur of thanks. The obviously artificial pine-lemon scent doesn't really help, but it gives your nose something nominally less disgusting to focus on.

The details clocked in my brain: the body was adult, male, the skin bloodless enough to suggest it had been stored feet-up since being dumped. I was going to guess he'd originally been a dark-skinned Hispanic man. The first victim had been lighter-skinned. I went close enough to look at the toes. Ignoring the bloody mess where his toeprints would have been, there were ragged nails, ridged and slightly yellow. Not someone who went for regular pedicures. Then again, a guy with hooves shouldn't point fingers.

The flashes had stopped, and only one suited-up tech was lingering by the dump — they were going to remove the body soon. "Look quick and deep," I told Ellen. "Don't look for things that are similar, look for anything that might be different. Anything that jumps out at you."

She gave me a sideways glance, a clear *"yeah boss, I know,"* then redirected her attention to the scene, circling around slowly, keeping out of the cops' way. Hard to believe, watching her, that two years ago she didn't know crap about this business, and a year before that she didn't know crap, period.

I'm a pretty good teacher, if I did say so myself. And yeah, maybe having a partner again wasn't all bad. Not that I was ever going to admit to Valere and Torres that they'd been right.

***

DANNY'S REMINDER lingering in her ears, Ellen studied the scene, letting her gaze flick over everything exactly like she'd been taught. If you looked for something, you might miss something else even more important. If you let the scene speak for itself, that's when you saw what was important. Or, like Danny had said, what was different, what stuck out.

The menthol rub under her nose was distracting, and she almost wiped it off before remembering what it was covering up. Ugh.

Body, check. Dumpster, check. Big bastard, high up enough that the killer would have to be tall to throw the body in, or have a ladder... or help. She looked down at the ground, but it was bare pavement. Any evidence that had been there, the cops would have already bagged and tagged, right?

Danny wasn't telling her something, either about this murder, or the one that had happened before. Not that this was new — he'd usually held stuff back. Sometimes it was because he wanted her to figure it out herself. Sometimes he just thought she didn't need to know. But this...this was different. Because she'd seen him in the vision? No, she'd seen him before, had seen him *dying,* before. It wasn't that. It had to be what had happened before.

The problem was, her gift only told her when people were at risk of dying, or about to be dead. It didn't give her any hints about the living. That she had to do the old-fashioned way, and Danny was way better than her at body language, both reading it *and* hiding it. There was —

She stopped, not turning her head, not staring, just letting whatever it was creep into clearer focus.

The cuff of the pants, fallen back away from the ankle. That was different? No. Her vision had the same dark jeans, fallen away from the same ankle, the same bare, bloody foot...

No. "His skin was different."

"What?" Danny came closer, close enough to keep their conversation private. "Whose skin was?"

"In my vision?" She frowned at the body. "No. Yes."

Hadn't it? Looking down, now, she wasn't as certain. She'd never been that confused about a vision before. The surroundings, sure, and once even the time of day, but the victims she always saw clearly, their fear and panic reaching out to her through the current in some way nobody'd been able to explain, yet. She knew what she saw, even if she didn't understand *what* she was seeing, yet. She saw the future. That was a thing she clung to, when everything else was too much. She saw the future and she could *change* it.

The body she'd seen in her vision had to be the one in front of her now. Nothing else made sense. But the skin had been different. And she hadn't heard the words she'd heard Danny say. Had she?

Ellen reached for the memory, but it was melting away, running and blurring.

"Is there... " Was there a fatae that looked human, but could change its skin color? She couldn't ask that out loud, not here. Danny had said that there were Talent in the police force, but not many fatae any more, not since the rules changed — that was why he'd gotten out, years ago. And you didn't talk about stuff like that around Nulls, especially not Nulls with badges and training to be suspicious. "There's no way skin can change? I mean, not..."

"Not even with all the blood loss in the world." His voice was tight, thin, and usually Danny had the best voice, like a slab of bittersweet chocolate. "You have enough?"

"I... yeah." There wasn't anything to get: the person she'd seen in danger was dead. She didn't know who'd done it, and there wasn't anyone here who was going to hire them to look into it — it was, as Sergei sometimes said, 'a matter for the cops,' only with no sarcasm, this time. But she didn't say any of that, just nodded her thanks to the nearest cop, and followed him back out under the tape.

The old guy they'd talked to when they arrived was gone, as were most of the squad cars, making the alley considerably quieter as two people wheeled a stretcher past them, she guessed to take the body out and to the morgue.

"Why did I... " She changed tactics. "What happened, before?"

"Not here," he said.

---

THE CAB RIDE home was as quiet as the one out to the crime scene. Ellen — knowing that 'not here' meant 'wait until we're back in the office' — stretched her legs out in front of her as best she could, and pulled her notebook out of her bag, staring at the open page, and the handwriting she barely recognized as her own.

"Let me see," Danny said, and she handed it over, trusting him not to flip pages beyond that one entry. She didn't write anything she was ashamed of, but there were personal things there, too. But he marked the spot with his finger, reading only the day's entry.

She leaned back against the seat, and closed her eyes, exhaling and letting her barriers down, less from relaxation than exhaustion.

*Okay?*

The ping was a bare sensation in the back of her thoughts, a scrape of concern and worry, mingled with annoyance, the 'tone' of the sender as familiar as her own breathing, now: Genevieve, checking up on her. She closed her eyes to block out any distracting stimuli, and shaped a pulse of confirmation and reassurance, then sent it back.

Some Talent could ping actual words, not just emotions or sensations, but it took more out of her than she had to spare just then. She wasn't supposed to be in a cab, smelling of trash and dead person. She was supposed to be in her mentor's apartment, being put through some new test or another, or getting a lecture on ethics — which would be funny, coming from The Wren, the best Retriever on the East Coast, if Wren didn't take it so seriously — or some other new torture thought up to see how grounded she was, how much control she had over her core.

Core. It was still unnerving to her, even though learning about it had been the best thing to ever happen to her. That she could not only manipulate magic, but it was part of her? That it was real? Her hand went to her stomach involuntarily, even though she knew that her core wasn't actually *there,* that was just her mind trying to enforce some kind of normality on magic.

Not magic, she corrected herself, though she still totally thought of it as magic. Current. The Talent called it current. Magic was old world and fussy and using the word made both her mentor and Sergei wince, even though Danny laughed.

Danny was old-fashioned too. She had asked him once how old he was and he'd ducked the question, but Pietr said that Danny'd been a cop back in the 90's, so that meant he'd been in his early twenties back then, which would make him late-fifties or something, now.

She glanced sideways at her boss. If he'd been a hundred percent human she'd have tagged him for mid-thirties, max. Hair still thick and dark, lines around his eyes but nothing extreme, and while he wasn't her preferred type — she liked them bulkier, and a lot darker — he filled out jeans and a t-shirt respectably enough to get second looks on the street.

Danny was half-faun. She didn't know much about the fatae yet, despite meeting many of them in the past year, but she thought fauns might be one of the long-lived species. Her boss might look middle-aged until he was a hundred. The thought still boggled her.

He wouldn't die any time soon. The thought was not as soothing as it normally was: death could come to anyone, at any moment.

She must have leaked some of her exhaustion and worry, because Wren's second ping — a harder, more worried *what?* — demanded a more detailed response. Ellen tilted her head back against the upholstery and formed actual words in her head, shaping them with deliberate care, then wound a thin tendril of bright blue current around them, imagining them lighting up like a Broadway marquee.

*Person in vision already dead. Heading back to office. Need to stick around a bit.*

She didn't add any of her confusion, the weird echo of a previous death, or the fact that Danny was upset. She loved her mentor, and depended on the older woman for a lot, but the work she did with the P.I... They were partners. Partners protected each other.

Even if they were keeping secrets.

When she looked at Danny again, he had tilted his head, watching her, a look of amused patience on his face. "You clear the rest of the day with Herself?"

"How do you do that?" Most fatae couldn't sense current, or only vaguely. But Danny always knew when she was dipping into her core, somehow.

"You get this look on your face," he told her. "Somewhere between constipated and pissed off."

"Oh, great." She felt herself flush, and crossed her arms across her chest and looked out the window, refusing to acknowledge his faint chuckle.

He paid the cabbie — technically this wasn't Sylvan Investigations billable time, but they'd agreed that any follow-up they did on her visions fell under the 'training' portion of their agreement, until such a time as they actually acquired a client, so he covered expenses like this rather than taking it out of her very small paycheck.

Just as well: she'd expected to be working with Wren today, so hadn't bothered to take more cash out. The more core she gathered the more likely she was to erase a credit card — as well as destroy the innards of small electronics — so she had a credit card only for special purposes, and rarely carried it with her.

Sometimes it made her feel helpless, dependent on others, to not be able to carry a cell phone or use a laptop without worry. Then Wren would remind her that it was a side effect of her own core, because she was powerful in other ways, and that made it better. A little better, anyway.

She needed all the little better she could get, just then.

They got into the elevator, sliding the gate closed behind

them and feeling the jerky movements as the cage started to glide upward. "Now will you tell me what's going on?"

"You're certain that the man you saw in your vision wasn't the same man as the scene?" He wasn't doubting her, she reminded herself. He wasn't questioning what she Saw. He was trying to determine why she was seeing two different things... and how it matched with whatever it was that he knew.

"Tell me," she said, instead, and he looked away.

⁕

SHE WANTED to know what was going on. So did I. But I didn't want to talk about it. I wasn't sure I could talk about it. You pack something down deep enough, for enough years, and the words won't come with chisels and hammers.

"Tell me," she said, and that was the first tink of a hammer, the first bite of a shovel, trying to unearth what should have stayed buried. When I looked away, she pushed. "The older cop, he said something about this being a carbon copy of something. And you said what I saw, it had happened before. The exact same thing, everything I saw. That's why you flipped, because I see the future, but you knew it was the past."

I'd trained her to listen, to *hear*, and to remember. And to put the pieces together. Hollow victory when she used those skills against me, but I couldn't help feeling a rush of satisfaction.

"Thirty years ago," I agreed. "But the victim was black, then."

I hadn't been there when they pulled it from the dumpster, only read the report, later. Fingertips and toes shredded, face destroyed, wearing only a pair of pants, with no identification or identifying marks. Back then, there hadn't been a way to identify the body, not if they weren't already in the system.

"And they never caught the killer?"

"No." Regret caught in my throat, tasting like bile. Never caught the killer. Not that we hadn't known.

Ellen didn't let go. "You worked the case?"

"There really wasn't much of a case," I told her as we reached our floor, holding the cage open as she moved past me, down the hall toward our office. Nobody else was around; it was that kind of building. "No identification meant nobody yelling to get results, meant it got shoved down the priority list. And no other bodies surfaced in the same way, so we weren't dealing with a serial killer." Just homicide.

"And he was black."

I sighed. "Yeah, and he was black." Not even the black community had rallied around that body, though. He'd been nobody in life, and remained nobody in death.

But now, thirty years later, someone else had been killed in the same way. And Ellen had Seen it. And Seen me, there.

I had to figure out why.

I unlocked the door to the office, and ushered Ellen in, closing the door carefully behind me and making sure to lock it. We didn't have any appointments scheduled for today, and I didn't want to be disturbed by anything new. "I want to try something. If you're game."

Ellen perched herself on the edge of her desk again, crossing her arms across her chest, game, but uncertain. "I'll try anything once," she said, which was a total lie: She was a conservative beast, until she'd scoped out all the angles.

"I want to try and invoke a vision."

Her entire body tensed, but not in a flight-or-fight way. "Wren and I do that," she said. "Only she sources wild to do it."

Wild sourcing — pulling current out of the atmosphere, usually through a hovering lightning storm or up out of a ley line. Made sense, since Ellen was a storm-seer, triggered by those same natural currents.

"Yeah well, not an option for me." Thank any god you

wanted to name, I wasn't Talent. My mother had been a lovely woman, but Null. And fatae *were* magic, but very few *used* it. "We'd be doing this Null-school," I told her. "No current, just your brain. And I'll be here to walk you through it."

She thought about that for a bit, then nodded. "Okay."

It took a few minutes to set up, most of which involved unplugging anything electric, and having Ellen kick off her shoes and untuck her blouse, getting comfortable.

"Just breathe naturally. Keep your eyes closed lightly, don't force it, like you're ready to fall asleep."

Ellen was in her chair — mine might be more comfortable but her body *knew* hers, and that was more important right now. Her head was tilted back, chin dropped just slightly, the faint lines that were beginning to form around her eyes and mouth eased as she went through the breathing exercises.

"Let me know when you feel ready," I told her, watching the turn of her elbows, the lines of her neck. She would tell me when she felt ready, but her body would tell me when she *was* ready. Slowly, a breath at a time, the sharpness of her elbow softened, her neck relaxed, and when she said 'ready' in a quiet, still voice, she actually was.

"You're standing next to a dumpster," I told her. "It's right in front of you, but you're not looking at it yet. Your arms are at your side, you're calm, there's nothing there except you, and the dumpster."

Some like to set the stage completely, control everything except what they want the subject to recall. I always thought that bled over into the recall, that it was better to leave the subject to fill in those blanks on their own.

"It's warm," she said, like reading off a placard. "Summer-warm." It wasn't warm today, the weather still clinging to spring's fresh chill. The first body had been found in the late autumn. No match either end. I didn't know if that was good or bad. Her nose wrinkled, her upper lip rising in an expression of distaste. "It smells. Bad. Worse than trash."

A corpse, heated by warm metal. I didn't have to imagine: I knew the smell too well.

"Are you ready to look, now?"

Normally when we walked someone through this, it was their memory of an actual event, something they'd seen; trying to get them to recall all the details that fled the conscious mind. But when I asked Ellen if she was ready to look, it was with a capital L.

"Not yet," she said, her voice soft, almost lethargic. I waited while she took another breath, then another, still drawing in through her mouth and out through her nose, despite the smell she was 'remembering.'

"It's warm. And my feet hurt." Her voice hardened a little, taking on almost a whining edge. "I hate this part."

Alarm ran through me. That was her voice, but it wasn't her *voice*. The accent was wrong, the intonations off. But I waited: working with Talent always threw a few wrenches into the plan, and the worst thing I could do right now would be to startle her.

"Taking out the trash. That's all this is." Her hands lifted and clenched, her head tilted, and then her eyes were open, too wide, the whites around the pupils visible, her nostrils flared, and she was lurching out of the chair into my waiting hands, even as I heard the sizzling noise of the lights overhead popping and blowing out.

The office plunged into darkness, and I suspected even unplugging the coffee maker hadn't protected it, even as my hands were running down her arms, using the familiarity of touch and scent and the sound of my voice to bring her back to Now and Here.

"Ellen. Ellen. Come on, open your eyes sweetheart, look at me. You see me?"

Slowly, her eyes focused again on me, and the trembling of her skin stilled.

"That wasn't me," she said. "Don't make me do that again."

"I won't, sweetheart, it's okay." I let my hands rest at her elbows, not holding so much as cradling the sharp joints, waiting for her to make the decision to move away.

I had no idea what had just happened.

---

It took Ellen nearly half an hour to move away from Danny's hold, thankful that he didn't protest, or ask her how she felt. She thought it was probably pretty obvious: she felt like she wanted to throw up, or throw something. Or both.

"Sorry about the lights." He was up on a step-ladder in the gloom, a flashlight in one hand, replacing the bulbs that had blown out.

"Standard office supply deduction" he said, finishing the last one, and stepping off the ladder. "Hold your breath... " When he flipped the circuit breaker back on, the room filled with light again. He turned off the flashlight and put it on the desk.

"That wasn't me." She had to say it, before anything else, had to affirm and confirm that the *thing* she had felt wasn't her, hadn't come from her. It felt like curdled milk, smelled like sunburn, and if she could scrape it outside of her and burn it to ash, she would.

"No. I'm pretty sure it wasn't. I just don't know *how*..." His voice trailed off.

"That was the killer."

He nodded. "From what you said, yeah I think so."

"How? And was it the one back then, or now?" Danny seemed certain the killers couldn't be the same, but there had been no sense of time in what she had felt, no visual she could connect with. Nothing except the *feeling* of it, leaving her sick and disoriented. "I don't ever want to do that again. Okay?"

"Yeah. Okay."

He had already agreed, but she needed to hear it again. "Promise?"

"Solemn oath," he said, and that was what she'd needed.

She had a headache, though, and her mouth tasted like the vision had smelled. She got up and pulled a soda from the little fridge: it was still cold, even though the fridge had been unplugged. She plugged it back it back in, but the condenser didn't start to hum. "Damn it. Coffee maker dead?"

"Can't imagine it survived." She wanted to hide her head: bad enough to blow light bulbs, they were easy targets. But that coffee maker had been nice — and Danny was impossible without his morning caffeine.

"You were a little stressed," he said. "You're probably going to need a new ATM card, too."

"Damn it." That she did carry with her, and it would be the second one this year already. Never mind that the bank manager at her branch was Talent and wouldn't ask embarrassing questions, it was still embarrassing. "I hate that part of this. And yes, I know, every gift has a price tag, even if we don't see it." That was Sergei's favorite saying, and she and Wren would both roll their eyes when he trotted it out, even though it was completely true.

Nothing came without a cost. To help people, she had to See bad things. But when the person was already dead... The theory was that the current- surge picked up strong emotions, things that were so strong even a Null could project them, and her skill was strong enough that she picked them up out of the storm, siphoning them off automatically along with the current. Lucky her.

But this vision... there hadn't been a victim's distress. Only the killer.

"There's too much overlap in the way the bodies were disposed of for me to think they're two utterly unrelated killers," Danny said, and his voice was the one he used when he was puzzling out clues, smooth and weirdly disinterested-sounding. He didn't shut his emotions away, he said they were his most useful tools, but he didn't let them get tangled in the facts. She tried to match that.

"The same person, thirty years apart? Wouldn't they be too old, now?" She thought about Danny's age. "Unless they weren't human?"

"People kill well into their seventies and eighties," he said. "But generally not with the violence that required." He started pacing again, one hand running through his hair, scratching lightly behind the nub of his horns, mostly-hidden under his curls.

"If the visions somehow overlapped, if you were feeling what happened in the past, too, reading the echoes or something, we'll leave that to the Pups to figure out how, that's another point saying they're connected, too. But this second one... " He hesitated. "I hate to ask this," and for Danny to say that he really didn't want to ask, "but when you were in his thoughts... did he know you were there?"

The question was like running nose-first, eighty miles an hour, into a brick wall. She couldn't even imagine the look on her face, but it was enough to make Danny sigh, and run his hands through his hair again. "We need to talk to Valere."

<hr>

MY MOTHER RAISED me reasonably well: I'm confident in my own skills, but not so arrogant that I think I know everything or can handle everything. So I sent Shadow off to wash her face and shake out the last of the vision-tatters clogging her brain, and I called her mentor back and told her to meet us at the coffee shop down the street from us, stat.

Wren Valere. There were any number of retrievers in the Cosa Nostradamus, but when someone in America said the Retriever, there was never any doubt who they were talking about. If you had something that needed to be reclaimed by means less-than-legal, and you had the funds, you went to Wren Valere. Or you used to, anyway. I studied the woman across the table from me, by now used to the way my gaze slid over her features, never really taking anything in. That was part of her success, that utter — and apparently natural — invisibility.

Five foot-ish, brown hair, brown eyes, white skin... as a trained observer I should have been able to tell you the exact shade of her eyes, the tone of her skin, if she had high cheek-bones or a mole over one eyebrow. I couldn't have said with any certainty if her face was round or square. She was...unmemorable.

She was also the one who had, not quite singlehandedly, brought down a highly-funded not-as-secret-as-they-thought anti-fatae organization, helped save the Cosa from tearing itself apart, and probably saved the entire city from burning down in the aftermath. All before she was thirty-five.

She also put too much sugar in her coffee. My teeth hurt just watching her.

I drank my own coffee, and waited. Ellen had just caught her mentor up on all the details since this morning, with the occasional assist from me.

"I've been reading up on Seers, since Ellen landed on my doorstep," Valere said. "Most of 'em, something like this, I'd say no way. They See the future, not the past, and that's all there is to it. But El's a Storm Seer. And that's... there's less specifics on that, mainly because there are so few."

Few, powerful, and slightly terrifying, all the more so

because Ellen's skillset focused on the dead or dying. Nothing is feared so much as the person who brings that inevitable news.

"So it's possible? That I saw something that had already happened?" Ellen clearly wasn't sure if that was a good thing or not.

Wren gave her a Look they must teach you in mentor training — my first partner'd had it in spades. "The moment you say something's not possible, someone will do it. But it's not *probable*."

"You've been with Didier too long," I told her, because that was a line right out of his mouth. She gave me the finger without taking her attention off Ellen, but the exchange seemed to have drawn some of the tension out of the both of them.

"But it happened today," Ellen went on. "I saw that, too? But the details weren't right. And when Danny invoked a vision..."

"Yeah, we are going to talk about that," Valere said to me. I nodded. She had a right to be pissed, but I still thought it had been a risk worth taking.

"I think what happened in your first vision was an echo between the first murder and the one ... today? Last night?"

"Earlyish in the morning," I said, "going by what the scene looked like. That's not a drop site you can use much after dawn." Not unless you knew exactly when the garbage trucks would pull by, and being wrong by ten minutes could mean getting caught with your hand in the till. "And that's when the weather was acting up, according to the weather daily site, so it would make sense." I'd done my research when Ellen first came to me, too: Storm Seers didn't need an actual storm to pick up their signals, but atmospheric disturbances did seem to up the oomph, as it were.

"An echo?" Ellen was mulling that. "So it wasn't that I couldn't see or remember the vision clearly, it's that there were..."

"Overlays," Wren said. "Or maybe a reflection in a mirror of another reflection. One of the PUPs could explain it better, and given half an opening probably will, at length. But it makes sense, why the details were off."

"Except it doesn't." I didn't want to be the one to point it out, but there was a major flaw in the theory. "It doesn't explain *why* — and why her last vision was from the killer's point of view. Why would she be catching echoes from *him*, not the victim, like usual?"

That stumped both of them, from the silence I got in return. "And," because the devil's in the details, "Ellen said that it was warm, in her third vision. It wasn't warm last night, and the first one happened in the autumn. So is this a third killing we don't know about, or one that's yet to happen, or..."

There couldn't be a third to come. There couldn't even be a second one. Except there had been.

I looked up, and Valere was giving me a side-eye — not accusingly, more of a 'what aren't you telling us?' consideration. I wide-eyed back at her, lifting my eyebrows to ask 'What? You have something to ask me?' She looked away, and the question was dropped. For now. I was going to have to tell them, though. It was pure D stupidity not to, stupidity to not have told them from the start.

But my mouth stayed shut.

"There's always a logical reason, some kind of connection." Ellen was clearly parroting one of her lessons, the way Valere was nodding along. "Maybe it was because we tried to force it, coax the vision, instead of it coming naturally? I might have gotten the echo of the first murder on the second, because there were so many similarities, and then... I'd seen it and I'd been there, so when I reached back, I hooked into the killer, not the victims? And maybe he was thinking about another kill, one that took place in the summer?"

"How?" Everything they'd told me was that it was the victim

who triggered the vision, that their imminent death — realized or not — plucked whatever strings Ellen was tuned into.

"If the killer was Talent," Wren said slowly. "And not just Talent, but a Seer, too."

That, I hadn't been expecting.

---

"I THOUGHT SEERS WERE RARE."

"They are. Maybe one-in-fifty-thousand rare, maybe a hundred thousand. Or maybe there are more, and most of them never know what they are, or make an actual fuss about it, so nobody ever knows."

We'd moved on from coffee to desert, a huge plate of baklava the waitress had brought over, with three forks. A refreshing thing, working with Talent: current burned calories, so there was no "oh I'm watching my diet" among the more high-res folk. In fact, I had to stab a few hands to get my fair share.

"So someone could be a seer, and never show any sign of it?" I didn't blame Ellen for sounding dubious: her visions slammed into her like a semi, and there was no way she could pretend they didn't happen. She'd been called insane — and worse — by Nulls before she understood what was happening to her, because she couldn't just shake it off.

"You're exceptional, El. Most seers aren't anywhere near as strong as you were even without training, and now..." Wren Valere was many things, but modest wasn't one of them. "And now" clearly meant "and now that I've gotten you trained up, you're awesome."

"So a low-res Talent, who also happens to be an equally lo-res seer, kills someone, or plans to kill someone, maybe thinks hard about the next time they plan to kill someone, and tangles their stream with Ellen's?"

"It's a logical explanation."

And whatever Nulls might think about current — magic — it was, above all, a logical phenomena at core. I nodded, trying to rejigger my brain to fit that into the puzzle.

"Unless there's something else you'd like to add to the discussion?"

"Seriously, you need to spend some time away from Didier, your mimicking is getting creepy," I told her, and swiped the last bit of baklava from under her fork, distracting her from that line of questioning.

Ellen, younger but smarter than both of us, asked, "If you're right, and the killer's Talent — is it the same killer from thirty years ago? Or a copycat with a really strong visual sense?"

Wren looked at me. "How much evidence was gathered at the first killing?"

My utter and absolute lack of desire to think about it, much less talk about it, didn't matter a fuck any more. "The usual." I shrugged, trying to reach for a casual indifference. "Wasn't my case, but there was some talk about it. Photographs, mainly, and the original reports, on the scene and post-mortem. So yeah, someone could have got hold of the old file. If they were turned on enough to replicate it, they'd have to have a strong emotional reaction. Pre-deed jollies?"

Ellen made a vague noise of disgust.

"Sorry, Shadow, but that's how people like that roll. You want to get their reasons for doing something, you gotta deal with that."

"I just.... That person was in my head," she said.

I thought about what she'd said and what it meant, and winced. "Yeah. Sorry."

Wren had started drawing something on the table with the tip of her finger. She might have been using current to make a mark: if so, I couldn't see it. "It would make more sense for it to be the same killer."

"Except like I said to Ellen, the guy — or woman, not to make assumptions — would be at least fifty by now, probably older. Not to be ageist, but there comes a time when beating someone's face in and hauling them to a dumpster disposal takes more upper body strength than most mid-life crisis have. And his being a Talent rules out fatae involvement."

His being Talent would also rule out it being the same killer. But I couldn't tell them that, or how I knew. I rubbed my face and shoved my fingers through my hair, trying to stave off the headache pushing its way in. I needed to tell them, but the thought of the words it would take made my throat squeeze shut.

"Maybe a partner," Wren said, trying the idea out. "A younger partner, picking up where he left off?"

"No." Ellen frowned, then shook her head. "No." She seemed certain, and she'd been the one in the guy's head, however briefly, so we didn't push it.

"The new killer's Talent, then. At the risk of going all shrink-like, maybe they read about the original killing, and it triggered something in them?" I wasn't going to comment on the link between Talent and crazy, not where Ellen could hear, but I was thinking it. The proportion of slightly nuts was consistently higher in the Talent community, be it an effect or cause of Talent, nobody was saying.

"We tend toward power-mad, not bloodthirsty," Wren said dryly, knowing damn well what I was thinking, and we left it at that.

---

"THERE'S nothing we can do right now, without more information," Danny said. His hair was sticking up in all directions, the tips of his horns barely visible through the dark curls. Ellen raised an eyebrow at him and he reached down to grab the baseball cap on the bench next to him, jamming it on his head. Most people in New York — everywhere — ignored what looked bizarre, or assumed it was a costume, but Danny tended to keep his differences hidden, when he was out in public. The fact that he'd been so careless told her something was going on — more than just the question of what was going on with her vision.

"You two go do whatever it was you were originally going to do," he said. "Let me work my own magic, see what I can dig up about today's incident."

"All right," Wren said, shutting Ellen's objections down with a sideways glance. "Call when you get something."

They left him to settle the bill, and took the subway uptown, neither feeling the need to fill the silence with words while they were in public.

The thought that the killer was Talent — and a seer! — lingered in Ellen's thoughts, all the way back to her mentor's apart- ment. Talent killed. She knew that, knew it firsthand, but it still felt *wrong* somehow. It didn't fit with what she's seen, or what she'd Seen. Bonnie — one of the paranormal investigators who'd first explained to Ellen what she was, what her skill set did — had said once that when Talent kill it's generally a crime of passion, and usually they use current to do it, because that's their natural, instinctive weapon. They don't beat someone to death.

And the dumpster? That was... specific. You toss a body in the trash, you're saying it was trash. Garbage. Something to be disposed of, rather than buried or cremated.

Was that significant? Yes, she decided, following her mentor off the subway, and up to the street. Yes, it was. But was it significant to the first killing, and carried over by the copycat? Or did both killers feel it?

Walking into Wren and Sergei's apartment, surrounded by the familiar sense of current-grounding and elemental locks, was a relief. Ellen sank into the sofa, but the tension didn't flow out of her the way it usually did. She closed her eyes, and listened to the sound of her mentor in the kitchen, opening the refrigerator and taking something glass out. A snap, and the sound of something being poured.

When she opened her eyes again, there was a tall glass of ice water waiting on a coaster on the coffee table in front of her, as well as a familiar white plastic binder. Wren sank into the chair opposite her, but didn't seem relaxed, either.

"He knows something."

Ellen didn't roll her eyes at the statement, only because she respected her mentor too much. Also because Wren would make her pay for it somehow, eventually. "Yeah, I know. Danny likes to think he's subtle as shit, and he's really not." He could be sneaky and cajoling and persuasive, but not subtle. Probably the faun genetics; she'd heard enough about his father's people to know that 'subtle' wasn't even in their dictionary.

"But I don't think it's anything really relevant. He's not subtle, but he's also not stupid. He wouldn't keep anything back that could give us" and she almost said answers, and at the last minute said "solutions."

She didn't know why she was defending him. No, she knew why: because Danny was holding something back and Wren was going to poke at it, and that meant conflict, and she didn't like the feeling of being torn between mentor and boss. She hadn't even heard about the Cosa Nostradamus until she was an adult, long past when she should have been in mentorship, but she knew that the relationship between them was supposed to trump everything. But Wren — and Bonnie and the rest of the PUPs — had decided that working with Danny Hendrickson would be part of her mentorship too, to give her an outlet, the chance to *do* something with her abilities, give her some kind of hope, she guessed, and now....

And now Danny was as much her mentor as The Wren, in

some ways, and most of the time it worked and sometimes it didn't.

Now was one of those "not" times, maybe.

Wren, thankfully, let the topic drop. Mostly. "Maybe. I'm still going to have Sergei put out some feelers, see if there's anything more known about this morning's events — or the one thirty years ago. And if Danny is hiding something... we're going to find out."

Ellen knew why Wren was telling her this. No secrets, she'd promised, that first afternoon when they'd been thrown together. If something was going to cause a blow-up between Danny and Wren, Ellen wouldn't get caught by surprise.

"If there's anything to know, Sergei will know it, eventually," Ellen said neutrally, not commenting on the second half of what her mentor'd said. "Now I'm guessing I get to make up the lesson I missed this morning?"

She guessed right.

<hr>

I WAITED NEARLY HALF an hour after Ellen and Valere headed back uptown, ordering another cup of coffee and paying the bill they'd stuck me with, before I reached for my cell phone. There were three messages waiting — you turned your cell phone off when you were lunching with high-res Talent, even if they *weren't* upset — but I ignored them, and instead dialed a landline number that had been beaten into my memory over the past few years.

"PSI Central. This is Pietr Cholis speaking, what miracle do you need us to perform today?"

"The snark-meter is redlining over there today, I take it?"

The exasperated sigh on the other end was answer enough. "What do you need us to do for you, Hendrickson?"

"You wound me," I said. "And it's a simple informational

request. There was a killing this morning, male, dumpster dumped. Was it one of yours?"

If there'd been the killing of a Talent, the PUPs would know about it. Especially if Valere was right, and the killer had been a Talent, too. That was what the PUPs did; they dealt with current-related crimes within the Cosa Nostradamus, the things the traditional police couldn't — couldn't even *imagine*, most of them.

"Hang on." There was a rustle of papers, and then a beeping noise. I still didn't know how they managed to use computers in that office, and wasn't dumb enough to ask. "Nothing's on the agenda," he said. "Is this something we should be paying attention to?"

"Nope," I said, forcing something that almost sounded like cheerfulness into the words. "Just wanted to make sure that you weren't going to swoop in at the last moment and steal all my glory when I solve the case and you take the credit."

"Fuck off and die," Pietr said. "We see you at the poker game next week?"

"Wouldn't miss it. Uvidimsya pozzhe."

"Show off," Pietr groused, and hung up.

It didn't quite make me smile, but it was close, and after today? I'd take close. I pushed my coffee mug toward the center of the table, and left a decent tip. It was warm and sunny outside, so I decided to walk, rather than taking the subway. I needed time to think, and walking familiar streets always worked well for that.

It was entirely possible and highly probable that this morning's killer was Talent. It explained too many things, and I'd discovered over the years that when something fit all the pieces, odds were it was because it was the missing piece.

But that meant we were definitely dealing with a copycat, because the killer thirty years ago hadn't been Talent.

The killer thirty years ago was dead.

Everyone involved with the murder back then was dead. Except me.

I dodged around a clump of tourists huddled over a map on their tablet, and crossed the avenue at the light, cutting through the waiting cars rather than bothering to go all the way down to the crosswalk. How can you tell a New Yorker? We don't lift our heads when we jaywalk.

Thirty years ago. I'd been a rookie. And an idiot, although the two together are redundant, according to my old sergeant. Wet behind the ears and filled with a desire to do something positive, to prove I was more human than faun. If they hadn't changed the regs, made it harder to hide my genetics, I probably would have dyed my hair grey and retired when I got my twenty, and felt that I'd served my time, made my difference.

It hadn't ended that way. And I'd walked away from the NYPD carrying secrets.

The case hadn't been mine, and for that I thanked fate on a regular basis.

But fate — and those secrets — seemed to have caught up with me.

The woman passing me heard my muttered curse and looked askance, although I suspected it was more my tone than her knowing Greek. Then again, this was New York, so who knew.

I didn't bother going back to the office. Nothing I needed was there; it wasn't a case file or tax-related. No, what I needed was in a small grey lockbox in the back of my closet, under the matching lockbox that held my original birth certificate and my retirement papers.

PEOPLE ARE SOMETIMES TAKEN ABACK when they walk into my office. "Sylvan Investigations" makes them think that I'm awash in nature, maybe, or that I'm at least making an effort to be Green. But the office is work, and work needs to be straightforward and focused, giving the impression of competence as much as compassion. And, anyway, I have a black thumb. We only keep the plants we do have alive because of Ellen.

My home, though. I'd painted the walls and ceiling a pale blue, and covered the windows with a thin scrim that changed daylight to a faint green haze. The furniture's wood, the upholstery dark brown Ultrasuede, and the rugs thick and green. I can feel my blood pressure lowering the moment I step through the door, and kick my boots off.

This is my refuge, my home. My bower, if you use faunish terms, which I try not to. I didn't even meet any of my cousins until I was a teenager, and spent the next decade or so trying to not be like them. But in the end, some genetics will out. Living in the city is my choice, but my soul needed the glades.

I touched the display set into one wall, and the faint strains of Clapton's guitar seeped into the air. That's another reason I tend not to invite people over: most of the folk I spend time with are Talent, and I'm not letting any of them near the obscenely expensive and incredibly high-tech audio system I set up. The music suited my mood, so I let it play, and headed directly for the bedroom. No point putting this off.

One slender manila envelope, the paper slightly discolored now, the original seal unbroken, untouched. I'd sealed it myself, saliva and dark red security tape, as much to keep myself from it as anyone else.

I'm no Talent, and any connection I have to current is muted, sketchy enough to not exist at all. But even I could feel the tension stretched in the air, drawing across my fingertips where they touched the envelope. Opening this could mean nothing. Or it could mean... what?

That was what I needed to know. I'd spent my entire life protecting people, finding the ones who got lost in the edge between worlds, who wandered unknowing into danger. The fact that I knew these particular shadows so well changed nothing.

I was going to keep telling myself that, all the way down.

I cut open the tape and lifted the flap, letting the contents slide out onto the bed next to me.

Three photographs, two glossy black and white, one color. One sheet of paper, typewritten, the marks almost hard to read after so long using computer printouts. A carbon copy of the coroner's report. That was it.

I looked at the color photo, then at the matching one in black and white, comparing the scene to the one I'd seen that morning. I hadn't been wrong: it was identical. The only difference was the color of the victim's skin, both photos making that clear.

A flitter of panic tried to shape itself in my gut, and I forced it down. It happened thirty years ago. It had been a one-off, my only connection to it a badge and a uniform I'd put away nearly two decades ago. And there was nothing to connect me to this, no reason it should come back to haunt me now.

But the third photo stared up at me, the closed eyes and grey-toned skin a silent reprimand.

A fragment of a poem came to me, the lifetime legacy of my mother's bedtime reading habits, a line about hunters taking apart a stone wall to get at a fleeing rabbit, and the farmer who had to come after them and repair the damage done.

The rabbit was long gone, the hunters long gone, but their handiwork remained. The damage had never been repaired.

I'd promised Ellen I'd never lie to her, not even for her own good. It was the basis we'd formed our relationship on, that I would trust and respect her.

Even if it might break her trust in me.

I reached for my phone and dialed the number for her

answering machine, a low-tech piece of junk that probably only her mother and I ever called.

"Hey. When Valere lets you loose, come by the office. I think I might have a lead on this morning's case."

Case, even though we had no client, technically. Lets you loose, not when you're free. If I'd trained my Shadow properly, she'd know that meant *not* to share this with her mentor.

I slipped the evidence back into the envelope, and tucked the flap under, then got up and took my rarely-used briefcase down from the closet shelf and slipped the envelope inside, snapping the latch shut with an almost-reassuring snick of metal on metal.

You could tape things up, lock them down, but things escaped. Always.

ELLEN HADN'T GOTTEN Danny's message until late that night, staggering home half-drained and wanting nothing more than a hot shower and cool sheets. But she always checked her answering machine, and she always went when Danny called. Especially when he left a message like that, cryptic as fuck.

Their office building was creepy at night. Never mind that Ellen was pretty sure she could hold her own now against anything human and most things fatae, it was still unnerving to walk into the lobby after midnight, when the air was filled with shadows and silence. The only light came from the emergency exit signs, and the elevator console. They never turned those off, Danny said; security risk balanced against safety risk, since there wasn't a night guard, just an empty desk in the narrow foyer.

The elevator was even creepier inside, rattling and humming to itself, the light here slightly bluish. She looked down at her arm, watching the way that light chased across the skin, making her flesh almost disappear into the shadows.

Was this how Wren felt, always somehow slipping off the radar, even in the middle of a crowded, well-lit room? She'd never asked; it always seemed too personal somehow, too private a thing.

After those shadows, it was a relief to see clear, warm light coming under the office door. She turned the key, and pushed inside. The outer room was empty, but the door to Danny's office was wide open; the light was coming from there.

"Hey." He didn't even look up; then again, who else would be showing up at ten-thirty at night? "Sit down."

There were two chairs in front of his desk. Client chairs, padded to be comfortable, comforting. She sat down in the nearest one, and waited.

"Good workout?"

"She had me running control sprints." It was about as exhausting as anything you did holding completely still could be, all the effort happening inside, in her core. But there was no way she could explain it to Danny; he wasn't Talent.

"Mmm," he said, his thinking clearly elsewhere, then pushed back in his chair, leaned back, and sighed.

"What?" and she knew it was the defensive, bracing-herself what, the kind she'd promised not to do, but that sigh brought it out involuntarily.

He pushed some papers across the desk to her. She leaned forward and took them. Three photographs, old-style glossy paper, and two sheets of a formal report from the New York City's coroner's office, on copied letterhead.

She bit down the urge to ask what all this was — if he wanted to tell her he'd have told her — and looked at the photographs. She'd never seen them before, but felt a shock of unwanted familiarity. "This is evidence from the first murder?"

"Mmm."

She looked at the report, but the typewritten letters were hard for her to make out, the photocopying blurring them even more, and the few words that leapt out at her were unfamiliar medical terms.

"You had evidence from the first murder. You *kept* evidence from the first murder." Because even with his contacts, he couldn't have gotten them this quickly. Could he?

"Mmmmhmm."

She narrowed her eyes at him. "You said it wasn't your case."

"It wasn't."

"Did you kill him?"

That surprised a harsh laugh out of him, and he sat up again, a half-quirked smile on his lips, like she'd said something unintentionally funny. "No. Although it's interesting that was your first thought." He waved away her stuttered apology. "I didn't kill him. But I knew who did. And I protected him."

Ellen sat back in her chair as though his words had slammed her in the gut.

His voice was thin again, distant. "I was a kid. A little older than you are now, but even with human blood, that's still young for a faun. I should've been frolicking in the country-side, causing havoc, not carrying a badge and a gun. But I was curious, wanted to know everything, be as street-smart as the guys around me. And I overheard things I shouldn't have heard."

He rubbed his hands over his face, and for an instant she could see the years on him, then they were gone, and it was just Danny again. "The guy who was killed was scum, El. The kind the world's better without."

She knew the sound of those words: they were the sound of someone who'd repeated something over and over again, so they'd believe it. She'd done the same thing, telling herself the things she saw weren't real, the things she could do were just hallucinations, that everyone was right and she was crazy, not that the world had gone crazy around her.

You did what you had to do, to survive.

"Okay." She wasn't going to argue with him about that; he already knew that was bullshit. "And someone decided to do cleanup?" She tapped one of the photographs with her forefinger. "That's why the dumpster. It wasn't convenience, it was... a message?"

"More a statement," Danny said. "They took the trash out." She nodded, his words connecting with her own thoughts just hours earlier.

"Who was it? You can't protect them this time, Danny, they've killed again, and — "

"They didn't." He cut her off sharply. "They couldn't. They're dead. Have been for years. And so's everyone who knew about them."

"You're sure?"

He gave a single sharp nod. "On my mother's honor."

His mother had been a Navy officer, and he adored her. He meant it.

"And yeah, I know, that makes me the connection," he said, beating her to the punch. "If there is a connection, and it's not just some sick Talent who found a mention of the old murder and decided to play copycat, and Christ, when that's our best option we're screwed."

Ellen looked at the photographs again, splaying them out under her hand and forcing herself to really *look* at them. Her vision was blurred by now, the memory softening and washing out around the edges, but there was enough there that she *knew*. "There's a connection. Part of what Wren and I were doing tonight, trying to identify any threads that could have tied me to the killer, made me pick up both murders and not just the new one, connect me to their thoughts rather than the victim's. But we couldn't. Because we were missing a piece."

He met her eyes then, his jaw twitching slightly. "Me."
"You." She felt ill.

GETTING things out into the open, even only partway, always
hurts more thinking about it than actually doing it. That didn't
meant doing didn't hurt like a bullet. But it felt good to be able
to dig into the problem, instead of just worrying at it. "What's
the first rule of the PI biz?"

"Twenty percent retainer before we do anything."

"Wiseass." But if she was snarking at me, she was recovering
her balance, and that was good. I only wished I could say the
same. I was running on fumes, both physical and emotional,
and that *wasn't* good. I needed to watch myself. "The first rule is
to know what you're investigating. So strip out the emotional
crap, any personal twitches, and look at the facts."

Friends would laugh to hear me saying that — I might have
a slight reputation when it came to people in distress — but the
rule was true. You couldn't be effective if you were hamstrung
by personal emotions.

"Even though— " she started to ask, and I nodded. "Especially because." I leaned back in my chair, swung my feet up on
the desk — my normal working pose — and asked the ceiling,
"So what do we know to be fact?"

She fell easily into the Q&A. "Someone — an unknown
male — was killed and left in a dumpster between midnight
and six am yesterday morning. Fact. His face was beaten, and
all identifying marks were violently removed. Fact."

She'd gotten a bottle of water out of the office fridge, but
was using it more to gesture with than to drink from. I didn't
know if she was using current to keep any water from sloshing
out, but it was impressive nonetheless.

"And," she went on, "the display of the dump site was

exactly the same as one that occurred thirty years ago, fact, where the only thing that was different was the race of the victim. Fact."

"The only think we are currently aware of being different," I corrected her.

"Right. Currently aware of. Also a fact: I saw the dump site." She frowned. "I saw the dump site," she repeated. "I don't see dump sites."

The only sound in the office was the thump of the other boot dropping. "No?"

"No. You know I don't. I see the victims, sometimes the moment of death, sometimes the scene of the death, but not after they're dead, not like that, in so much detail." She set the water bottle down carefully on my desk and sank into the chair opposite me. "You think my skillset's... expanding?" She looked horrified at the idea, and I didn't blame her.

"That's Wren's area of expertise, not mine." I'd lived this long not getting directly tangled in Talent matters, and I intended to continue that theme. "More likely it's what she said, that the killer in the current case is Talent, maybe a seer of some kind, and that you picked up their bad vibrations, not the victim's." Which would also explain why poor Shadow saw the poor bastard too late to save him. It wasn't his death-fear she was picking up, but the killer's... what? Anxiety? Glee?

How many seers were there among Talent? Was this something she was going to have to deal with, along with the dying putting a claim on her? If so, it was a nasty move on part of the Universe and I did not approve.

The Universe and I hadn't been on good terms for a long time now, though, and it didn't seem to bother it a bit.

"So, a possible fact," I said instead. "The vision had bad recep- tion, hooking you into the past event as well, reason possibly because the killer was also a Talent and was projecting their own sick connection to that past crime into the current."

She nodded, her expression a mix of resignation and hope. "Wren's got a call in to the PUPs, see what Bonnie can get her."

"If there's anything to get, Bonnie will have it." I didn't say anything about my own calls: since nothing had come up, better to wait and see. Too many hands in the pot just got fingers burned. "So we have a seer with a muddled vision, and a dead body, killed with violence at the hands of a single perp and left in a manner that echoes the dump site of a murder three decades ago. But it wasn't the work of the original killer."

"You're sure that's a fact?"

She wasn't challenging me, just clarifying.

"First, he wasn't a Talent. Second, I went to his funeral," I said. "Full honor guard and bagpipes."

Her eyes widened. "A cop?"

I don't know why she looked so horrified. She should have gotten over any idea of cops as better-than-average long ago.

"A cop," I confirmed. No need to name names, the dead were dead.

Ellen licked her lips, rubbed the back of her hand across the tip of her nose, then finally asked, "Can ghosts... can they kill?"

"Not like that. Not with that kind of physical violence." And I'd only heard rumors of ghosts who had enough oomph to interact with Nulls at all. There had to be an impressive level of unfinished business to tether a spirit to the physical world, once the flesh fell away. Or so I'd been told. "It wasn't him, Ellen."

I'd trained her too well, to accept reassurances that vague. "How do you know?"

"Because if it was, he would have gone after me, first." Nothing personal; he'd just been that kind of a bastard, and my outliving him would be proof that I wasn't entirely human. And that was all he would have needed while he was alive, much less dead.

"Oh." She pursed her mouth, digesting that.

I shook my head, and rubbed my own nose, which was starting to itch. "Look, it's late — hell, it's gotten past late and around again to early. Go home, get some sleep. Or kip here if you're too tired to slog home." We didn't have a sofa in the office, but there was an air mattress I knew firsthand was reasonably comfortable.

"But-"

"The dead are already dead, Ellen. I'm more worried about you right now, and I know firsthand what happens to overtired Talent." More to the point, what happened *around* overtired Talent, but she took my point.

"Yeah, okay. And no. You might be able to sleep on an airbag but I prefer actual padding and a pillow." She stood up, stretching to her full height — which was a few inches more than mine, not that she lorded that over me more than once or twice a week. "Regroup in the morning?"

"Wren and Didier might have something for us by noon, so let's say 11?" I could and had gone on no sleep for a few days, if I needed to, but six hours of shuteye was optimal if I wanted brain cells. "Back here, unless we get a call — "

The phone rang.

We both stared at it. "Phone calls at 2 am are never good news," but I answered it anyway.

"Sylvan Invest — what happened?"

Phone calls from Scott at 2am were only ever bad news. "Yeah, all right. Yeah. I'm on my way. Thanks, man." But he'd already hung up.

"They found another body," she said. "They found another body," I confirmed.

Thirty years, nothing. Now two dead bodies with the same probable cause of death in twenty-four hours.

Ellen's skin had taken an unhealthy, ashen look. "Boss... is it a good thing or bad, that I didn't see this one happening?"

Honest to god, I didn't know.

---

"ANOTHER DAY, ANOTHER DUMPSTER" The uniform who'd been told to show us to the scene had at least a decade under his badge, and the attitude of someone who'd retire out of a squad car, not behind a desk. But that was a point in his favor, honestly, and he didn't give back any gruff about Ellen tagging along, or make a snide comment about private dicks. I'd heard them all before, even made a few myself, but two in the morning, when you're stone cold sober and standing in a dingy Queens alley over a bodythat's only a few hours dead.... Yeah, not the time to appreciate dick jokes.

"White, from the shape of his gut I'd say mid-forties. Face, feet and hands disfigured." The uniform's tag read Miller, B, and he recited the info like he was reminding himself what to buy at the supermarket.

"Bald," I noted, looking over the edge before a tech shot me a glare for getting in their way.

"Yeah. Or his hair got bashed off." Miller smirked, and got the same wattage of stare from the tech, who was getting awfully possessive of the body. I moved back a little, bringing Miller with me.

"Two in two days. You boys are going to start catching some heat on this."

Off to the side, Ellen jerked, like she'd been poked with something sharp, but she didn't say anything, so I didn't call her on it.

"Maybe. Probably not. First guy, not in the system, nobody's come looking for him. Bet you my first year's retirement this guy's the same."

"No bet."

While we were talking, Ellen had moved closer to the

dumpster. She must be taking lessons in sneak from her mentor, because the tech barely glanced at her before going back to work.

She hovered a minute, her hands lifted just a little over her hips, like she was trying to resist the urge to touch something. I watched her indirectly, keeping my focus on Miller so he kept his focus on me.

"Think there'll be a third?"

I shrugged. "Depends on how bad the weather gets."

The crazy rises when the temperature rises. More accidental deaths in winter, fewer spree killings. Historically, anyway. And Ellen had said it was warm, in her last vision.

Speaking of whom, Ellen had turned away from the dumpster. I could see her face in profile, like the bas relief of a coin or some ancient sculpture, giving nothing away except a regal sort of sternness. But if you knew what to look for, the stress lines were there.

"Good luck," I said, not meaning a word of it. I didn't want the NYPD anywhere near this, out of sheer self-preservation. Fortunately, Miler was probably right. Nobody would raise a stink about these victims, and the cases would get back-burnered until they were ice cold.

Just like the first one. Nothing had really changed.

Milled just grunted at me as we left, but other eyes watched us until we were under the tape and back in civilian territory where we belonged. Scott may have vouched for us being there, but we weren't wanted.

If I let that bother me, I'd never get any work done. "You all right?"

"I was looking for trace." Ellen licked her lips, then rubbed the back of her hand against them. "If the killer had been Talent, there might have been something left on the body."

That sounded like a PUPI-trick. Useful. "And?"

She shook her head. "Nothing. Maybe they washed it off,

Bonnie says it can be done, but killing with current usually needs a lot of... passion. That's hard to scrape off, after."

"So maybe we have the world's first dispassionate Talent killer. Lucky us." I was only partially being sarcastic. "Or they were in such a cold rage that their core just locked down." It could happen, theoretically, and if it did we'd have no way to know. You can't prove a negative, only presume it. "But something's got your brain twisted around. What?"

"What you said, back there."

I nodded, although I wasn't sure what I'd said, specifically.

"It's what I heard you say in the first vision. You were here. So I got that much right. But I *saw* the last murder, not this one." She didn't look at me, but studied the street in front of us, frowning slightly. An early-morning jogger went past, swerving out of our way without missing a step. "Why didn't I See this one? And why did I feel him, in that last vision, and not the earlier ones?"

"Maybe because it was invoked? You were reaching out, not letting it come to you, and that made the difference? We're not going to do that again, either," I added, before she could say anything. "If you felt him he might have felt you, and that's a no-go." I used my no-argument voice, and she nodded once. "The visions are all screwed up, we got that. You're seeing past tangled in future mixed with now, and trying to untangle it's probably impossible, except after the fact." I didn't want to tell her how often that was true with any case. "So that's what we're going to do, take what we have, and see what it tells us. Old school Come on, let's get out of here."

Three minutes later, an Outerboro cab prowled down the street, and slowed in front of us. Ellen stepped off the curb, and I followed. There weren't many Talent cabbies, but if one was in the area, having Ellen ping them was a hell of a lot faster than trying to flag one down in a residential neighborhood, or summon one via an app.

"Where to, boss?" he asked Ellen, and she looked at me for a response.

I give them Valere's address. If nothing else, she'll have coffee made by the time we get there.

---

Sergei me them at the door. He was wearing a suit, his silk tie beautifully knotted, and an air of annoyed distraction. It was impossible to tell if he'd just gotten in, or he was just going out.

With Sergei Didier, it could be either, and Ellen knew better than to ask. "Second pot's just about done," he told them, "and Wren's in the workroom."

The workroom was a heavily-warded practice room, specially built when they'd bought the condo. Most times they went outside, or up onto the roof, because both of them were more comfortable there, but when winter hit, or it was too hot, Ellen could appreciate being inside.

Danny veered off into the kitchen to score a mug of coffee. Ellen went down the hallway and knocked on the workroom's door, a sharp shave-and-a-haircut rap.

*In/safe*

Inside, Wren was sitting cross-legged on the floor, her shoulders relaxed and her eyes closed. Ellen waited, not bothering to close the door again: Danny would be coming to join them, and they wouldn't be doing any practice runs today, anyway.

"Another body?"

"Uh-huh." Around Wren, despite her best efforts, Ellen always felt herself reverting back to the awkward, self-conscious self she'd been when she was first dragged into the Cosa Nostradamus. She'd gotten past the fear, finally, and the last lingering voices telling her she was crazy had been smothered under the reassurances of her mentor, her boss, and the

PUPs, but next to Wren's smooth-limbed gracefulness and sheer competence, it occasionally all came flooding back.

If Wren noticed, she didn't say anything about it. "You didn't sense anything this time? No visions?"

"No."

"Good." Wren opened her eyes, and looked up at Ellen. "I know you want to use your skills to get to the bottom of this, and I respect that, but you also need to stay safe yourself. No more soliciting visions, okay? Let Hendrickson throw himself into white knighting all over the city, that's not your job."

"As always, your concern for my welfare is breathtaking." He was carrying two plain white mugs, and handed one to Ellen.

"Boss?" Ellen looked at him, and raised her eyebrows significantly. He sighed. "I can at least have my coffee?"

Wren looked between the two of them, then rose to her feet with the grace Ellen had just been envying. "I'm going to be needing a chair for this, aren't I?"

"Probably," he said, turning to let her go past him through the doorway, then following her back to the main room, where two loveseats flanked a low table, and the far wall of windows opened up to a view that probably cost more than Ellen could even imagine, the décor an odd mix of modern art and homey clutter. Danny had said once that the betting odds on them moving in together had bankrupted half the bookies in town, and he was pretty sure that's why they'd finally done it.

Wren took a seat, and Ellen sat on the opposing sofa, but Danny stayed standing.

"Hendrickson?"

"There was another murder, similar to this, three decades ago." His shoulders were straight, his chin up, and for an instant Ellen could see the overlay of the young cop he must have been once. "Dumpster dump, identifying marks scraped off, shoeless.... Pretty much a replay except for the race."

"And he was never identified?"

"Oh, he was identified." Danny gave a short, humorless laugh. "The victim was... word was, he had been assaulting homeless people, just for kicks. Sexual assault on some of them. And not all of them survived."

"But none of the survivors talked? And with no evidence to arrest, much less convict, someone laid down homemade justice?" Wren didn't even sound surprised.

"Back then... no. Nobody was talking. And yes." He looked at Ellen, briefly, then locked gazes with her mentor. "I knew who was behind the killing. And I knew who covered it up." He swallowed, but didn't drop his gaze.

"Did you help cover it up?"

"No. But I knew it was happening." Guilt, and disgust writhed in those words. "They're all dead now, Valere. They have been for years."

There was something going on in the stare those two held, but Ellen couldn't read it. Finally, her mentor dropped her gaze, and sighed. "Ghost?"

Danny's mouth twisted like he'd sucked a lemon. "You've got more experience with that than I do. What do you think?"

"It takes an awful lot of rage to keep a ghost around, plus some physical remnant for them to latch onto — usually their bones."

"The original killer was cremated," he said. "And the other two, the ones who covered it up... they held a lot of things inside, but not rage." He cared about those people, Ellen realized. Was that why he'd kept quiet? Because he'd judged one man's life not worth ruining two others?

She didn't think she'd make that choice, she didn't think he'd make that choice again. But she wasn't *certain* of it.

Wren was still asking questions. "And none of them were murdered themselves, or died violent deaths?"

"Not unless you call cirrhosis of the liver violent."

"Then probably not." Wren didn't look unhappy to have the possibility of a ghost shot down, and Ellen made a note to ask her mentor about her experiences some time. Or not.

"So we rule out the original participants," Wren said. "That means starting from scratch. When you're planning a retrieval, the trick is to go for the simplest, laziest approach, and work backwards from there. I can't imagine murders are much different — people are lazy."

Danny made a 'can't argue with that' face, his shoulders relaxing a little, and gestured for her to go on. "So the simplest explanation is...?"

"Copycat," Ellen said. "Like you said before, someone who found a record of the original murders, and it triggered something in them, made them want to repeat it, or outdo it. I mean, they've killed two, not one, and I think — " and she shuddered "— they're going to do it again."

He reached out and touched her knee. It was faint, just a brush of his fingers across her jeans, but it helped.

"Would anyone be able to access that kind of record?" The question was directed at Danny, as the ex-cop.

"Hell if I know. It didn't get much newspaper coverage at the time but I'm sure there was some. And a thirty year old cold case? Not exactly the most protected data in the world. You get someone going through the archives, they tell someone else the story as a curiosity, or maybe a reporter looking for a 'this crime before your lifetime' story to shock the kiddies..." He was ticking things off on his fingers, when he paused. "I bet they're digitizing the back files, finally," he said. "Odds are they're using an outside source for that. They're all supposed to be discreet, lips zipped, all that, but supposed to and are don't always even live on the same street."

"So what you're saying is we have no way of telling who might have gotten their hands on the story, and that anyone could know it by now."

He shrugged. "Cold cases. Sometimes someone talking about it is how you shake a new clue loose, so...."

"So trying to track down the how is probably a waste of time. Okay. But the details of these newest murders is exactly the same?"

"Enough that someone had to have access to the details, yeah. Or it's the largest coincidence since Harry met Sally." Danny started pacing again, holding his coffee carefully so it didn't spill as he moved. Ellen watched him, trying to see what he was thinking in his body language. She was getting better at it: from the tension still in his back and shoulders and the way he was holding his mug, he was frustrated, and worried... and guilty. Although she could have guessed all that just from knowing him.

"It's not your fault," she said.

"Isn't it?" He wasn't looking at them, staring out the windows, his mug cupped in both hands. "I knew about the first killing and never said anything."

He'd given her the opening. "Why didn't you?"

He sighed. "Because it would have raised too many eyebrows in my direction, and I couldn't afford that, not if I wanted to have a career. Because it would have been my suspicion against the word of people with more backing, more reputation. Because.... Because I didn't see where the world was any worse for not having that scum in it. I'm not a saint, Ellen. I'm not even a particularly good person."

There was a snort from Wren, who clearly disagreed. "You fucked up," she said. "We can play my sin's worse than yours some other time. Right now, the only solid link we have, other than your guilt, is that this killer has a connection to Ellen, however that happened. By the terms of your agreement with each other, that makes it Sylvan Investigations' problem, right?"

Ellen looked at Danny, who lifted his mug at her. "Right."

"And which because it involves Ellen, is going to also make it my problem." Wren took a deep breath, and added, "and the fact that it involves a Talent also makes it a problem for Venec's people."

Danny's body language changed in an instant, back to the more familiar slump-shouldered slouch. "Oh, give me a break, Valere. We don't actually **know** the killer's a Talent. Isn't there any other way that Ellen would have picked up on *him*, in her vision?"

"Not really. Come on, Hendrickson, get over your control issues and admit that having a PUP along isn't going to hurt."

"Bet it does," he grumbled, then sat down next to Ellen on the sofa, stretching his legs out in front of him. "Fine. But before we call them in, I'm going to need some Irish in this coffee."

I NEVER GOT MY WHISKEY.

Fortunately for all concerned, it was Pietr who showed up at our office, bright if not early the next morning. I could deal with Pietr: he was the mellowest of the team, not that that was saying much, considering they were all hired for get-to-it-iveness and a high level of ego. But he and Ellen got along well, and he was used to being second dog in the sled after Bonnie — and probably after Venec, too, although the surviving founder of the so-called Private Unaffiliated Paranormal Investigators didn't do much in terms of day-to-day investigating any more, getting stuck in a suit and politics more often, poor bastard.

We'd agreed that Wren should need to be somewhere else, for this. She and Bonnie were friends, and Ellen was her protégé, but there were still pretty clear divides between what the PUPs did and what she might still do for a living to make it potentially awkward.

"I brought donuts." Pietr held up a familiar red and yellow cardboard box.

"You're aware that I haven't been a cop since you were still in diapers, right?"

"Fine then, I'll eat them all myself."

Ellen snagged the box out of his hands before he could pull it away, and put it on the sideboard next to the coffee maker. The *new* coffee maker. "Play nice, boys," she said. "Or I'll eat all the donuts myself."

She could, too. I didn't know her workout routine, but Ellen was a solid wall of muscle naturally, and since she'd started working with me she'd clearly taken the "occasional physical exertion" part of the job seriously. Whatever she was doing, she burned calories in a way that was impressive even for a high-res Talent. I'd leave most of the donuts to them.

"So," Pietr said, metaphorically rolling up the sleeves of his button-down, "Bonnie briefed me on the situation, much as she knew — we've got a Talent going around replicating an old crime scene?"

I nodded, snagging an old-fashioned for myself. "Valere's pretty sure it's a Talent, anyway, and possibly a low-level seer, too. Which means odds are good that more than one person knows about what's going on, because you people are not the silent types."

Neither of them objected: I wasn't wrong. The Cosa gossips like grannies on steroids, and while some fatae are worse offenders, the human members don't slack in that department.

"And if two people know about it... " I trailed off.

"Then so does a third and a forth," Ellen finished for me. "So, knowing your methods, that means we get to go poke a few hornet's nests and see if we get stung. Great."

Pietr frowned, and held up a finger. We waited. "You said a Talent and possibly a seer, too?"

"Low-level," I confirmed. "Valere thinks that's why Ellen

tapped directly into him, when we went looking; because they're on the same wavelength."

"So he might know we're looking for him?"

I looked at Ellen, who gave a faint, damned-if-I-know shrug. "She says he didn't notice she was there," I said. "And Wren thinks he's low-res, so hopefully he's so focused on getting his jollies that he's not paying attention to anything coming in on the wires. That's the best we can hope for."

Pietr wiped donut crumbs off his mouth, and slicked back his already smooth hair. "You guys always have the *best* parties."

I shook my head sadly at the Pup. "Weren't you the sane one, once?"

"Only relatively," he said. "Only relatively." True enough.

---

ELLEN REFUSED to worry about the killer being a seer, too. She knew better than the others what that meant, and it generally *didn't* mean you ever knew what was coming in your own life. Her main worry right now was seated across the table from her, giving her an 'are you kidding me?' look. Ellen had questioned people before, even though Danny had always been there with her before. She'd even questioned people who looked like they didn't want to talk to her and might actually get violent if she poked too hard, so if Danny thought she was fine to handle a few interviews on her own, she was.

"You're sure there's nothing you can tell me?"

It annoyed her that she still took Danny's opinion as more valid than her own, but her annoyance was probably a healthy step away from assuming she *wasn't* capable, and doubting anyone who said she was. Probably.

"For once, the city's been quiet, and you want to stir things up?" her companion asked. "You need trouble that badly?"

"I can't help it," she said, forcing what she hoped was a

cheerful grin, a la Hendrickson. "I just get twitchy when everything's quiet."

The Talent — an older man, maybe fifty or so, snorted and shook his head at her. "Your mentor is a bad influence on you. She gets twitchy if the city's not falling apart under her feet."

That was unfair: Wren actually preferred it quiet, so she could work. The Retriever just always seemed to end up knee-deep in the chaos. Which was part of why they'd asked her to mentor Ellen in the first place, and she was getting introspectively distracted again, she realized.

"Anyway, I haven't heard anything out of the usual but — hey Pauly!"

A heavy-set Indian man behind the counter turned and glared at the older man. "Told you not to call me that."

"Cabrón, I've known you since you were eleven, I'll call you whatever the hell I want. Come here and talk to the girl."

"Why should I do that? I'm working here."

"There's nobody else in the damn shop, take five minutes and sit down. If anyone needs a muffin, I'll get it for them myself."

It was a kind of ballet, the bickering the two men exchanged, even as Pauly was taking off his apron and dropping it on the counter, coming around to join them at the table. There were in fact other people in the bakery, but nobody seemed to even notice that the counter was now unattended, busy with their coffee, newspapers, and cell phones.

"This is Ellen," the older man said, gesturing at her. "She's got a couple questions you're more likely to know than me, seeing as how you see everyone come in and out, and probably hear all the latest."

"Even when I don't want to," Pauly agreed gloomily, sitting down in the third chair at their table and studying Ellen. "Who're you and why should I tell you anything?"

"Manners, Paul. That's Valere's mentee."

Ellen hid her wince, and Paul did his best to hide his flinch. There was a lot she loved about working with Wren Valere, but this wasn't part of it. Her mentor had a — rightfully earned — Reputation among the Cosa Nostradamus. In fact, Danny Hendrickson was probably the only person who never seemed bothered by it, which was probably why they'd sent her to him in the second place.

"I'm not here on her behalf," Ellen said. "I work with Danny Hendrickson, of Sylvan Investigations? We're trying to track down something that might have happened over the past week."

"Something what?" Paul was still guarded, but his body had eased a little in the chair, and his constant eye-flicks back to the counter could just be normal watching-the-job nerves. She scraped a tendril of current off of her core, watching as it flickered from deep green to a paler neon blue, and let it rise gently, stretching toward the other Talent.

His own core didn't react, sitting solid and calm. Either he was so low-res he couldn't sense the overture, or he was the calmest bastard she'd ever met, and his visible nerves were just for show.

There was no reason for him to be trying to play her, but Danny's head in the back of her voice joined Wren's, urging caution.

"Ah, if I told you that, it would color your responses," she teased, instead. She wasn't comfortable flirting with strangers, but Danny said to just imagine that it was him, and give as good a sass as she could, that being female and young meant she could get them to underestimate her that way. She wasn't entirely comfortable with that, but if it worked, it worked.

Paul's eyes narrowed, and then she felt his own touch of current rising, prodding gently at her. It still felt rude, testing another person's defenses like that, but Wren said that everyone did it, at some level or another. It was like sizing up someone's watch, or their car, to establish status.

Paul's current was sluggish, the strand thicker than it needed to be, and she deflected it gently, a polite rebuff, without showing anything of her own core. High-res got more respect, but it also made people cautious. With luck, he'd think they were evenly matched. He grinned at her when he felt the push-off, the tension still there, but not quite so... tense. "Okay then. Ask away."

---

WE'D AGREED to meet mid-afternoon. I got there a few minutes early, but Pietr was already waiting. He looked almost impossibly clichéd, sitting on the bench in his perfectly pressed khakis and shirt, his hair still neatly combed, a newspaper open on his lap. I resisted the urge to ruffle his hair, knowing that his slender frame hid a grab bag of martial arts tricks, not to mention some of the best physical control of current I'd ever seen.

That didn't mean I couldn't indulge in some verbal jabs, though. "Is it a law that you have to dress like a prep school dropout, or is that really your style?"

He closed the newspaper and folded it, placing it on the bench next to him as I sat down. "It's self-defense," he said. "The rest of my team have very specific styles, you can pick them out of a crowd at a distance. This," and he gestured down — is bland enough not to get noticed."

"So you can spook through a crowd while they peacock."

He waggled his eyebrows. "Exactly. It wasn't intentional, originally — I just tend to be blander than they are. Even Sharon, yes."

I grinned. Sharon could pass for a VP of any small corporation, her suits were so unremarkably well-cut. Even I, who broke out dress shoes and slacks only under protest, could admire her style.

"And did the bland avenger discover anything?"

He snorted through his nose. "Nothing. Nobody's heard anything, nobody's seen anything, nobody's spooked to anything. Not that they were going to admit to me, anyway. You?"

"Maybe. I dig a little lower than your usual class of informants, put my ear down to the street." And I meant that near-literally. "Nobody came out and said anything, but they're pairing up and doubling down — " I paused, realizing that Pietr had no idea what I was talking about. "They're going to the buddy system for sleeping, where one person naps and the other keeps guard, then they switch off. Ditto for when they have to leave their safe-spots, always having someone watching your six."

"Homeless people?" He wasn't judging — well, the quick glance at my torn jeans and ragged-ass sneakers might have been a little judgy.

"Homeless people, hookers, dealers. The elite of the street." Single women and homeless people were, I'd discovered, the best true judges of what's going on. They'd had to develop gut instincts and the ability to place a person in a glance, for their own safety. It wasn't nice, or fair, but it was damned useful to a cop — or a PI. "Anyway, when they do that, it means something's up. They're jaded as hell, and don't spook easy, after a few years."

I could practically see that sink into his brain and start to cook. "That would match up with my usual informants coming up empty. And you think this killer is taking people off the street?"

"That's the theory. Neither new victim came up in any database, and nobody's reported them missing...although with the amount of damage done to the bodies, they could have been.....

But yeah. I'm pretty damn definite they're either homeless or near-as, in terms of being invisible." That fit with the first murder, too. He'd been off-radar, intentionally invisible to polite society. Too many echoes to be coincidence.

"I should've asked before: any sign of abuse or malnutrition?"

I did like working with professionals. "None. They weren't perfect specimens, and like I said, there was considerable damage done, but no obvious signs of drugs or violence, and reasonable health for dead people. But get over your assumptions: not everyone on the street is a druggie or diseased."

He drew in a breath, as though he were about to protest my assumption of his assumptions, then exhaled and nodded. Again, I like working with professionals.

"Noted. So the probable target community knows they're being targeted. Do they have any idea by whom?"

"None. Like your people, nobody's seen anything, nobody's heard anything, and nobody I spoke to personally knew anyone who's gone missing. But they're all on edge. Like gazelles who are damn sure there's a pride of lions over the hill."

"Nice image. And you're planning to go back there tonight and blend with the locals, see if a lion bites at your heels?"

"Yes, and no. If the killer is focusing on the pattern of the first murder, then they're targeting humans who are not only out of the mainstream, but have done so for less than savory means. Pimps, pushers, abusers... basically, un-nice people. So odds are, whoever it is won't go after me. I'm many things, but unsavory isn't one of them."

I wasn't being entirely truthful: there was a pinprick in my thoughts, that my original connection to the first murder's cover-up might be unsavory enough to draw attention. But there was no need to mention that to the PUP.

If the killer went for me, so much the worse for the killer. "Plus, all three vics have been human," Pietr pointed out.

"You probably smell wrong, or something."

"Yay me," I said, less than enthusiastically. But he was right, and I'd stupidly missed that: so far, this had been an all-human affair. "Ping Ellen, see if she's on her way. She never has her phone turned on when she's working, and I need lunch before I fall over."

And, if we were lucky, she'd found some other parts to the puzzle we could use.

ELLEN DIDN'T RESPOND to Pietr's ping, but she showed up about five minutes later, out of breath and slightly flushed from more than her fast-paced stride.

"Sorry. I didn't want to risk putting them off by looking at the clock, and I didn't want to rush them, either, so — "

"I take it from that you got luckier than we did," Pietr said, cutting off her flustered explanation.

"Maybe. I don't know. Paul, he's the counter guy at LaLa's — it's a bakery," she explained to Danny. "Really good one. Anyway, it's where a lot of Talent who work night shifts hang out. Wren took me there a few times to meet, um... "

"People I should officially take no notice of?" Pietr said dryly.

"Yeah. Them." She shook off the moment. "So, I asked around and managed to get ... one of the employees there to talk."

She paused, and on cue Danny said "attagirl," and grinned at her. "And by 'managed' I assume you mean 'bribed them with a favor to be named later?'"

She made a face at him. "I don't make that mistake twice, thank you very much. And no, I didn't have to promise anything. I think he wanted to talk, he just didn't know who to talk to."

"And you were it?" Pietr sounded almost hurt.

"And Wren Valere's protégé was it," she corrected him. "Once I reassured him it wasn't one of her jobs I was working, anyway. First time I've ever played on her reputation."

"How did that feel?" Danny asked.

"Unpleasant," she admitted. "But useful."

"Good," Danny said. "So you'll use it when you need to, and not lean on it."

"Everything's a teachable moment with you, boss, isn't it?" He made a face back at her. "Report, Shadow."

"Right. So he and some buddies were out one night, doing things we're not talking about, and were heading home around two, three in the morning, crossing past Fourth Calvary cemetery, pausing to pay their respects. Because that's what you do at three a.m., apparently." She sounded deeply dubious of that. Considering their last experience in a graveyard at night, neither man contradicted her.

"Anyway, they were coming off work, so none of them had been drinking, he swears it on his mother's name. And all of them saw the same thing exactly." She paused, holding it long enough for both of them to give her 'get on with it' gestures.

"Ball lightning, forming over a gravesite."

"That's odd, but — " Danny started to say, then stopped when Pietr held up a hand.

"Did they notice a color to it?"

She nodded. "It was several shades of green."

Danny looked from one Talent to the other. "And that means something?"

Pietr gave a half-shrug. "We're still not sure what the colors current manifest mean, but —"

"Wait, current?" This time Danny interrupted him. "On its own? Admittedly I'm not Talent, but it's that unusual?"

"That's what freaked them out, boss. Wild current running alongside lightning or a ley line is one thing, we know how to deal with that. Or, I do *now* anyway," and she gave him a rueful look. "But it has to be sourced from something; it doesn't just appear on its own."

Basic stuff. Current ran alongside electrical energy, like well-mannered twins. A Talent was a Talent because they could siphon off that current with their bodies, filter it into raw and manipulatable power, where a Null — an ordinary human — would become a crispy critter. Some of the fatae could interact with current, but mostly on an autonomous level; they couldn't direct it.

"On its own." Danny was having trouble processing that, and Ellen felt a twinge of sympathy. She had probably looked much the same when Pauly had told her what he'd seen.

Pietr, meanwhile, was already thinking several steps ahead of them. "Did they mark what grave it was forming over? Was it a new burial? Maybe the body was releasing its core after the fact. It's rare, but it does happen."

"The grave was an old one, in an older section," Ellen said. "No new residents in that entire row, they said. Just the ball of current, swirling and snapping."

"And?"

"And they ran like hell, assuming that the entire thing was going to implode. But nothing happened, that they heard or heard about later. I think they've been waiting for the other shoe to drop, ever since."

"And when did this happen?" Danny asked. "A week ago."

Her boss lifted an eyebrow. "The same week since the first body was found?"

"That week, yeah."

"I don't suppose they took down the name of the stiff in the grave they were observing?" Pietr asked.

"They did not." She'd asked, and gotten an 'are you insane?' look in return. "Not everyone has the stoic determination of a PUP, you know."

"And thank god for that, otherwise I would be out of a job.

So what now, Hendrickson? We go graveyard-hiking?"

Her boss nodded glumly. "Might want to bring a shovel, too."

WALKING through a graveyard in the daylight is an oddly soothing thing, green leaves and green grass and a relative silence in the middle of a city. People used to picnic in cemeteries once up on a time. Hell, Pietr had greeted my suggestion of a shovel with a suggestion that I remember who I was talking to, so we even *looked* like picnickers, carrying nothing more potentially distressing than a thermos.

My thermos, specifically, that I'd filled with holy water before we left Manhattan. I had no idea if it would be useful against anything we might encounter, but my mother raised me to consider the angles and cover my odds. Then again, tossing holy water onto wild current might blow half the city up. It's uncertainty like that that makes my job fun.

"Could be worse, boss." Ellen said, walking by my side, while Pietr strode ahead of us on the path, checking each row of headstones as he went. He'd spent half an hour back-and-forthing with Bonnie while we were in transit, and come back with what they called a cantrip that should lead us to where the current-burn should be.

Might. Should.

I turned my attention back to Ellen. "Oh?" That hadn't been a very Ellen-like thing to say; she wasn't a natural optimist, nor did she generally embrace sarcasm.

There was no snark in her voice or in her expression when she said, "No missing kids."

That was a nasty gut-punch, both the thought and the truth of it. I hadn't planned on specializing in missing teenagers, it was just that kids tended to fall through the cracks between official and not-official more often than adults, and too often the not-official involved the fatae. Impressionable teenagers and some of my cousins… bad mix.

"Yeah, just some unknown Talent killing random adults and leaving them in dumpsters. So much better." But it was, and if that made me a bad person, well, I'd come to terms with that a long time ago.

"Over here," Pietr said, interrupting the moment, and calling us over. He then ruined the brief burst of adrenaline by adding, "I think."

"You think? That's reassuring." Too sharp: 'think' was better than we'd had before. Without a name to search on, finding the right place would have been impossible except for the fact that PUPI didn't accept impossible. Either their cantrip had worked, or it hadn't; we had to trust that it had.

We caught up with him standing over a grave that looked pretty much identical to every other path in its row: plain headstone, the carving still fresh enough to be readable, without any particular design.

"A cop," I said, because that was the first thing that caught my eye, even before the guy's name. "A Talent?"

Pietr gave me an epic side-eye. "You think I know the name of every Talent in the city aboveground, much less under?"

All right, it had been a stupid question. "You can find out?" "Yeah." He got that unfocused look, and I figured he was pinging someone back in the office. They could say it wasn't actually telepathy all they wanted, if it looked like telepathy and got results like telepathy, it was telepathy in my book.

"David Kovar," Ellen said, tracing her fingers over the headstone, then looking down at the grass covering his mortal remains. There was nothing I could see that indicated anything other than mediocre groundskeeping, and nobody visiting to care.

I'd already arranged to be cremated. Graves were just depressing.

"You picking anything up?" I asked Ellen, who had cocked her head as she studied the grass, like she expected it to tell her something. Maybe it was, who the hell knew. I shifted, and looked around to make sure we weren't being watched by a suspicious groundskeeper or legitimate mourner.

"I'm not that good," she said reluctantly. "Scraps, maybe. Aftertaste. Definitely current," she added, lifting her chin, her nostrils flaring like she was catching an actual scent. "And definitely wild-sourced. It... tastes different. Or not different, but, like the difference between the wind coming off the ocean versus a breeze over a lake?"

"Got it." She'd learned to use nature metaphors with me. I might be a city boy down to my boots, but there're some resonances that are bone-deep and bred in.

"But it's gone now," she said. "It went somewhere else." She looked up at me and frowned. "Current doesn't do that. If it's not gathered, it just... finds the nearest line to connect with." She looked around, then down again. "There's no obvious man-made electricity out here, and there isn't a ley line for miles....

And we haven't had a half-decent storm in weeks. So where did it go?"

She was asking Pietr more than me, for obvious reasons. He had that same pose; like a hunting dog trying to pick up the scent in the wind.

"I'm assuming it couldn't just get up and walk away?" I raised my hands when they both shot me looks, the kind that asks if you were dropped on your head as a child or just naturally stupid. "Hey, you ask me how to track down a gnome or out-annoy a piskie, I'm your guy. Current? Really not my thing."

"For god's sake, don't even mention piskies," Pietr said, swallowing hard. "That's the last thing this day needs."

We may or may not have paused long enough to listen for

the unmistakable chittering sound of piskies snickering in the underbrush or tree branches overhead. Nothing.

"Yeah, sorry about that. But my point is, you guys are the experts, not me. So...what causes a ball of current to form, and what could carry it away?"

"Another Talent, maybe," Pietr said. "Someone who could handle it. Or maybe several someones. Venec could. Valere. Maybe a few others."

"Not you?" Ellen asked.

"Not me. I'm reasonably high-res — " Understatement, since no PUP was low-res, it was a job requirement to be powered-up, but I took his point — "but something that hot would burn me significantly. You could handle it though," he said to her, eying her appraisingly. "Probably even better than Venec."

"Me?" Ellen looked slightly nauseated at the thought.

"You're a Storm-seer, Ellen. Natural affinity to wild current, remember?" He shook his head. "You, and Valere, and maybe Solange, but that's about it. But it's none of you, and if someone that supercharged had come into the city, we'd have heard about it by now."

'We' meaning the PUPs, not us.

"So, what carried it out, then? And I'm still waiting for an explanation of *how* it formed." I didn't like the idea that wild current could just suddenly spark into life in the middle of a graveyard. What if it had happened somewhere more popu-lated by people who were actually breathing? Odds were, even the nullest of Nulls would notice something weird going on, and the last time that happened, the entire Cosa paid the price.

"Yeah. I don't know. I mean, we have theories but..." Pietr studied the ground. "I need to run some tests."

That explained the dark blue case he had slung over his shoulder; he'd brought his lab with him. "You do that. Ellen, you said it went elsewhere, Pietr says you can handle it. The question is, can you track it?"

She blinked at me, thinking. "Maybe?"

"If anyone could, she should be able to," Pietr confirmed. "Gather the scraps and braid them together," he said to her. "That's what I'd do."

She nodded, looking thoughtful, and more than a little nervous.

"Even if you can't follow it," I told her, "anything you learn will be useful." Even if we couldn't find where our suspect went, there was a lot you could tell about someone by *how* they went. And you never knew what piece was going to suddenly make the puzzle complete.

———

ELLEN WASN'T QUITE sure what she was doing, but one of the first things Bonnie had told her, and Wren kept repeating over and over, was that half of using current was letting your body do what it did naturally. The other half was *controlling* it.

She'd almost died before, because she hadn't known how to control it. Now she did. Grounding had been the first and hardest lesson she'd learned, those first few weeks with Bonnie and the PUPs, but she *had* learned it.

Focus. Be aware of the body, aware of the core inside her, the strands of current coiled loosely around some place that *wasn't*, that might have been at the base of her spine, or the pit of her stomach. Ground. Keep the current controlled and calm, the static energy ready but not active, waiting but not anxious.

She'd spent the first twenty years of her life being anxious without knowing why: it was still odd to know it had a cause, that she could control that cause, soothe it.

Focused and grounded, she opened her eyes and looked

with what Wren called *magesight*, where she could *see* the flickers and flares of current running through *everything*. Even now, it was still slightly terrifying, and hypnotic, but she managed to narrow it through focus, until the flares specific to the wild current came clear, and everything else faded slightly.

Red and orange. Vibrant, neon sparkles, some of them barely large enough to see, others snapping like firecrackers, swirling in a tight ball like... well, like ball lightning, she guessed.

"Which way?"

The boss' voice was quiet, controlled, and that made it easier for her to maintain control, too. She turned her head, and watched how the flickers moved — no, not the flickers, the echo of flickers. Ghost sparks, the current strong enough to linger as trace, even now.

She didn't want to think about how powerful the original had been, then. Or what it must have taken, to control it.

"That way. I think." She took a step forward, then another, and the trail remained, giving her confidence. "It moved this way."

It was easier to stay focused inward, but Danny needed information, too, and maybe he'd figure something out from what she was seeing. "It's about waist-high," she told him, feeling rather than seeing him staying a pace behind her, giving her room to work. Her fingers and elbows tingled, the current in her core stretching out, intrigued by what she was following. She kept herself contained: she couldn't risk contaminating the scene with her own trace, Pietr and Bonnie would never let her live it down. "And it's staying to the walkway... well, mostly," she amended, as it led them off the path and onto the grass for a short time.

"It's staying off graves," Danny said. "That suggests sympathy, if not intelligence."

"Mmm. If you say so." She zigged, and they were back on

the path, heading for the gate... and the sparks of current went *through* the gate. "Boss? Are there fatae that can pass through metal?"

"Gnomes. Maybe some others. Don't tell me.... " There was a pause. "None of them could carry current." He sounded definite on that, so she took him at his word.

"Humans?"

"No human can pass through metal. Even using current. If they could, you think Wren wouldn't already have taught you?"

"Fair point." Her mentor wasn't actively teaching her retrieval skills, but a few had come up in practice, anyway. "We need to circle around, see if we can pick the trail up on the other side."

She felt a hand come down on her shoulder, steering her away. "Keep focused," he told her. "You're navigator, let me do the driving."

This was similar to some of the training exercises she'd done with Wren, and similar to the trailing-a-suspect tricks she'd learned from Danny, but combining them was more difficult than either alone. It took them almost half an hour to make their way back to where the current-trail had disappeared, and for her to pick it up again, at which point Pietr pinged them to say that he'd called in for reinforcements, and would let them know the results later.

She hadn't even realized that the PUP had left.

"Pietr says he'll send us a report later," she told Danny. "This way. The trace is fainter here, but...." She squinted. "It's like it... compressed? No. Intensified. It... " She shut her eyes for a second, but the residual image remained, dancing against her eyelids. "It got stronger here. What happened here?"

She opened her eyes again to find Danny looking not at her, but the corner, where a pile of flowers and a narrow candle in a glass holder had been placed against a signpost.

"That's a memorial," he said. "Someone died here." He

frowned, and she could imagine the puzzle-pieces sliding around in his brain, slotting together. "Lots of power, a probably already unstable Talent, and a trigger. Boom?"

She reached out a finger, as though she could touch the echoes of current. "Boom," she agreed.

---

Hearing Ellen say 'Boom' shoved something else in my brain, but it wasn't quite ready to come out of hiding. I knelt down to look at the photo and laminated card attached to the memorial. An older woman, struck by a hit and run driver the day before our unknown Talent started to play. Was that enough to trigger someone into violence? Probably not alone, but I wasn't a psychologist, it wasn't my job to understand why, just figure out who, and how to stop them.

I walked a safe distance away from Ellen, and turned on my cell phone. Two messages, one from an unknown number. I listened to that one first.

"Hendrickson."

I didn't recognize the voice.

"My name is Elizabeth. I work for a friend of yours."

That covered a small but significant group. I waited, assuming Elizabeth would get to the point at some point. "Word has it that you're going after a small problem that's come up in the city recently. I've been told to tell you that whatever you dig up needs to be reburied when you're done."

And that narrowed the group down considerably. The message ended without any more detail. I deleted it, and went to the next.

"Call me."

That voice I did know. I hit the redial and waited until Meg picked up.

"Megadeath Funeral Services, what's your death wish?"

"You never actually get funnier," I told him. "What's up?"

"Word is, you might be looking into the dumpster deaths."

"Word has a way of getting around," I said. "I hope it wore a condom."

"You never actually *got* funny," Meg told me. He was a satyr, a distant Greek cousin according to the tangled fatae bloodlines, but unlike me, he couldn't pass for human even on a bad day under an overcoat. Meg more than made up for being a shut-in by establishing himself as a serious digital player.

"The Underbridgers are twitchy. They say that something's been prowling, the past few nights, near some of their camps. Map of complaints looks like it's a clean overlay around where your bodies were found."

The trick to being a successful investigator isn't being brilliant, or even working your ass off, although both those things are useful. The trick is to know people who like to know things you didn't know. "That's useful, Meg. Thanks."

He didn't say goodbye, or you're welcome, just hung up. "Ellen." She looked up when I called, but I could tell that

her thoughts were elsewhere, probably trying to figure out where our human-shaped ball of energy had wandered off to. I thought maybe I had an idea.

"How do you feel about camping?"

"THIS WASN'T EXACTLY what I thought you meant," Ellen said an hour later, as we picked our way through the debris that partially blocked the underbridge passage. Technically, the DOT was supposed to make sure these underpasses were cleared at all times. In reality, there were a lot of bridges in New York City, and they didn't have the manpower nor the give-a-shit to worry about anything that wasn't likely to flood or catch on fire — or get any news channel notice.

"Yeah well, if you want we can dig out the tents and the rucksacks and go for a weekend hike in the Catskills," I said, and I half-meant the offer, if only to see her freak out the first time a mouse tried to crawl into her sleeping bag, or a spider dropped into her hair. "When you're on a hunting trip, you need to go to where the game is." I stepped over a particularly rusted-looking spoke of something long-abandoned, and looked back at her shoes again, just to reassure myself that yes, her footwear was sturdy enough to be doing this. Ellen might own a pair of impractical, open-toed shoes, but if she did, I'd never seen them.

I looked forward again, and came to a sudden stop as a figure appeared in front of us. It had moved quietly and stayed upwind, apparently, since the moment it came close, I could smell the miasma of stale human sweat, old dirt, and dried food stains that wove around it, clinging to the skin.

"Got any spare change?" Its teeth were horrible, its hair knotted so badly I couldn't tell how long it was or what color, and the skin was the sallow shade of someone who hadn't seen a vitamin in any form in way too long.

"I got some, if you've got time to talk."

"Talk?" It cackled, and moved closer. I managed not to flinch. "I can talk. What do you want to know?"

When I'd been a uniform, I'd done my share of street person interviews. The badge and the gun had actually made it harder: they flickered between being scared and being pissed. The trick was never to lead the conversation, but make them take control of it. The more in control they were, the more they'd tell you.

"Heard there was some disturbances, lately. Unofficial ones."

"Here? Who'd come here?" He — and it was a he, I finally determined — spread an arm wide to indicate his kingdom. "Who'd come here who didn't have to?"

"A good point," I admitted, and waited.

"Tell 'em." Another figure approached. Less filthy, but thinner, younger. Someone who hadn't been out quite as long, or hadn't embraced it so hard. "Tell 'em, Sam."

"You tell 'em, you're so determined to talk," Sam said, but didn't back off.

"Something's been sniffing around," she said, with a glare at him for putting her on the spot. "Thought it was a dog at first, big dog. That kind of sniffing. Or maybe coyote, they say some of 'em are in the city now. But it wasn't. No dog *stares* like that."

"I thought it was one of them," Sam said, and there was a capital T to his them, even spoken. "The night-walkers."

Fatae, he meant, although I wasn't sure if he had a specific breed in mind, or just the vague fear humans had for the unknown.

"But they ain't never hurt us," Sam went on. "We got nothing they want, and too much cold iron."

I didn't have any desire to break it to him that cold iron didn't faze a full two-thirds of the fatae — how could it, if you lived in the city? Better he sleep feeling secure. He was right, anyway; most of the fatae would have no interest in him, and the ones who did prey on humans generally preferred them younger. And cleaner.

"So what was it?" Ellen hadn't come any closer, but neither of the Underbridgers started; they'd seen her, and decided she wasn't a threat.

"Dunno. It snuffled at us a few hours, then went away." "Rose saw it, too." The woman jerked a shoulder vaguely behind her. "Rose camps over there, couple-three miles off. She doesn't like company, though."

"She's too mean for anything to bother," Sam said.

A woman alone? I wondered if they'd seen her recently. But so far, all the victims had been male. "And nobody's gone missing?"

"Nobody we know," Sam said. "That don't mean much. Some folk are here and gone and you can't say what happened for sure." It wasn't that he didn't care, he just didn't care. I got it. I didn't like it, but I got it.

"You can show us where you saw it sniffing around, exactly?"

Sam waited, and I reached into my pocket, pulling out a fold of bills. Three tens and a fiver; small enough to be used easily, large enough to look impressive. Giving him a handful of singles was more likely to put his back up than appease him.

The bills disappeared into an equally grubby hand, and he turned and started walking away. I followed, with Ellen at my left shoulder. The woman hung back, either because she didn't want to get closer, or because someone had to watch their things, I didn't know. I didn't see anyone else moving in the shadows under the bridge, so maybe they'd fought off everyone else to claim this space as their own.

You can't save everyone, and some people don't actually *need* saving. I try to focus my energy on the ones who not only needed it, but had asked. Even if they weren't aware they'd asked us, specifically.

"Here." Ellen stopped dead behind me, and that one word locked my knees in place. Ahead of us, Sam turned to look back. "No, up ahead."

"Here," Ellen said again. Her eyes were round, too much white showing around them, and her mouth was open a little. I knew what that meant.

"Hang back," I told Sam, who probably didn't need telling. Then her entire body shuddered once, violently, and something passed over her face, a spasm just under the skin, a twitch of pain and shock and horror and fear there and gone again, as her eyelids closed and her skin flushed.

"El?"

Her right hand lifted, just the fingertips, but it was enough to tell me to wait. So I waited. Eventually, maybe four-five minutes later, her fingertips relaxed again, the muscles in her neck eased, and she opened her eyes.

"Another body?" Three in two days was a spree killer. That would mean there would be more bodies piling up.

"No. Not yet?" She was always a little woozy after a vision hit, but we'd managed to work past the panic that used to hit her, too. Knowing what it was, and that she could do something about it, had made that part easier to bear. Or maybe she'd just seen too much to panic, now. "It was the killer. Again. Same... same details as before. I.... Why am I seeing through their eyes?"

The expression on her face was too close to the one she'd worn when we first met: too proud to beg, but desperate enough to do it, if that would ease the pain and confusion. So I did what I couldn't do back then and reached out, pulling her into a loose hug, arms over her shoulders, her face tucked down against my shoulder.

"I don't know, Shadow," I told her, ignoring our audience. "I don't know but you're not alone. You don't have to do this alone."

---

IT SHOULDN'T HAVE MADE Ellen feel better, but it did, knowing that Danny was next to her, and that he was armed. He didn't talk about it, never made a big deal of it, but she'd seen the pistol he kept in the locked drawer in his desk, the box of bullets next to it. She knew he didn't go out on cases without it.

She had felt it pressing into her side, under his jacket, when he'd hugged her.

The hug probably had a lot to do with feeling better too. She wasn't touchy-feely, had a distinct aversion to being held or restrained in any way, but Danny's hug hadn't felt like that. She wasn't really surprised; for all that he had the facade of tough guy, she'd figured him out early on. Genevieve had only gotten part of it, when she called him a white knight. He didn't just make a career out of helping people; he actually *liked* people.

He liked *her*.

Despite all that, the snap and crackle of the killer's... *glee* was still in her, trying to reach her own core, trying to... She breathed deeply, dropping into fugue state as she walked, making sure that her core remained still and calm, the tendrils of current resting, not restless. Control. She had it, she would not give it up, no matter how invasive the visions became.

"You okay there, Shadow?"

"Fine."

She'd told him what she'd seen in that brief vision, more an aftershock than something new: the sense of future-time-not-now familiar enough that she was certain that it was the killer anticipating, not actually doing, and he'd handed another bill to the homeless man and hauled her back into Manhattan via subway, never letting her get more than a step from his side.

They knew where the killer was planning to be, now. Where, and a vague sense of *when*. They'd solved cases on less. She knew that, but uncertainty still made her skin prickle.

"You're sure he didn't get anything from you?"

"Yes." She'd told him that three times already. Wren had taught her how to keep herself separate from the visions. After the first time the killer had caught her off-guard, she'd focused on using those lessons to wall herself away from intrusions. She hadn't been sure it would work, but she was reasonably certain it had.

Certain enough that Danny thought they had a good chance of catching the killer off-guard. If they got there first. She'd described the surroundings, and he'd nodded like he knew.

"And when we get there... " He'd told her this three times already too, but she needed to hear it again.

"I bluster, and you whammy." He'd gone into more detail the first time, although not by much. She tried to relax, listening to the hum of the subway rails, the fine lines of current running along the tracks, throughout the city. She siphoned off just a hint, less to refill her core than to reassure herself, like double-checking you had your keys.

The day and time was displayed on one of the subway monitors, and the sense of uncertainty and unreality increased. Two days since she'd had the first vision, and barely enough sleep to matter. Had Danny slept at all?

You made mistakes when you were tired. They couldn't afford to make mistakes.

And then it was their stop, and it was too late to second-guess or raise doubts, even if she'd known what to say.

---

THE KILLER'S glee shuddered through her again, the *satisfaction* it took, and she took hold of Danny's arm, feeling the rough cloth and muscle under her palm.

"Hang in there, Shadow," he said, and they were pushing through the mid-day crowds and walking up the stairs, coming out on a little side street that looked too narrow and crooked to belong in Manhattan.

She kept her hand on his arm. "Where are we?"

"Pine Street," he said. "What you saw, it's down this way."

"This way" led down the street several blocks, past a Dunkin Donuts where they stopped to get two coffees, and then on to a small plaza built around what looked like a several-stories-high glass pyramid, surrounded by office buildings on all sides, and lined by a rack of rental bicycles. There were metal benches scattered at angles around the plaza, and Danny led her to one, urging her to sit down.

"Drink your coffee," he said. "Look natural."

He set his coffee down on the bench next to her, and started to add sugar. If you didn't know him, or weren't looking carefully, it seemed like he was devoting all his attention to making sure the right amount of sugar went in. But she could see his eyes, the way they scanned across the plaza, seeing things — noting things — that she could probably look for an hour and still miss.

He wasn't only an ex-cop and a trained PI. He was fatae.

Impossibly, she forgot that sometimes.

"You okay?" he asked, and she started to give her 'fine' response when she realized he was asking something different.

"I... yeah." Did she sense anything, he meant. Was the killer nearby. "I'm okay."

They were here before the killer, just like Danny'd hoped. They had time to set the scene.

She dipped slightly into her core, letting a tendril test the area, to see if there were any other Talent around. A few, passing by, but none of them with the same flavor of hot sparks she'd felt from the killer. These were people with their cores calm and under control.

"Nothing yet," she said, and licked her lips as a thought occurred to her. "What if they're not coming now? Didn't the murders happen at night, before? How long —" She stopped, and her mouth opened again but no words came out. She looked sideways at where Danny had finished preparing his coffee and was standing up now, seemingly without a worry in the world. "You son of a bitch."

Danny didn't quite smile, but there was a definite flicker of satisfaction on his face, like she'd just passed a test. The bodies had all been killed at night, and dumped somewhere isolated, not in the middle of a plaza, when the sun was still up. If they were coming here, it was for something else.

A seer sees things that are to come. If a seer sees something a seer sees.... Who saw it first?

It didn't matter, if they had a faun to twist it to his benefit. "All right." She wasn't going to give him the satisfaction of arguing. First, because it would waste time and energy, and make them conspicuous, and second, because as pissed as she was at him, it was a damn good plan.

If it worked.

---

THE COFFEE WAS CRAP, but it gave me something to do with my hands. It had taken Ellen a while to figure out what I was planning, but considering the pressure she was under, it was still a decent job. She figured it out, considered objecting, then accepted it as the only workable plan we had: I could see it all flicker across her face.

I could also feel the nerves coming off her like heat off a radiator. I wouldn't have blamed Ellen if she'd told me to take a flying leap, or something even more physically improbable. I probably would have done the same, if I'd told me what I had in mind. But she was a smart girl, with good training. Once she saw the pieces she knew how they had to go together. I still deserved a lot more than that muttered 'son of a bitch,' though.

I consoled myself that she wasn't being used as bait, exactly. Not entirely, anyway. It's not being bait if you're also the trap, is it?

"It's a risk," I admitted. "What you saw, and felt, it didn't match the evidence of the other killings, so there had to be something else. A low-level seer might not be able to pick up all the details you do, but there might have been enough to, I don't know, throw a line in your wake." To draw him here, to the place where she'd seen him. It was convoluted as hell, but the kind of convoluted that might appeal to a crazy person.

Ellen, not being crazy, looked dubious.

"So. How do we — how do I do this?" She was still sitting on the bench, her coffee in her hands, more as something to hold onto than something to drink. She was watching a couple across the plaza from us, leaning into each other on their own bench. I shifted, drawing her attention back to me. Those dark eyes and arched nose, tight-drawn mouth, everything about her face was determination, not fear.

Nobody else would die, if she had any say in it. I felt bad for depending on that, except she wouldn't be here if it weren't for that determination. And we were back to the complicated knots visions tangled us all in.

"We can do this, kid." Ideally with minimal bystander inter-action, but we don't always get what we want. Fortunately, most people were good at not seeing what they couldn't explain. "I'd feel more comfortable if we'd some information on *how* the killer gathered and held all that current," I said, "but with our usual run of luck, Pietr's going to call just after we wrap things up on our own."

There, just a tiny twitch, a hint of a curve, but it was there, before her mouth flattened again. "Probably," she agreed. "Without backup or further information, what's the plan? Do we stand in the middle of the plaza and bellow out a challenge?"

"Do I look like Nick?" Pietr's teammate was a damn solid investigator, which I'd never say to his face, but he had all the subtlety of a garbage truck. "No. I want you to sit here very quietly, and wait. "

Truth was, I didn't actually have a plan. I had a scrap of an idea, a thread of a suspicion, and the only person I knew of who could identify the killer. That would have to be enough.

Eventually I drifted off to the side, leaving her there, seemingly unprotected. Seemingly, because I'd seen Ellen shut down a would-be masher with a flick of her eyes and a single, firm 'no.' And if anyone pushed, they'd find out why most wise people left Talent alone.

There was a food cart down at the other corner, one of the classic Halal lunch trucks. I drifted in that direction, and bought two gyros, one without tomatoes, two bottles of water, and an extra packet of pita with a container of tzatziki sauce. It was going to be a long wait, and I didn't know if we'd get another shot at food, after this. And you couldn't overfeed a Talent.

As I was starting to drift back toward her, I was aware of something shadowing my heels. Literally: it was about the size of a cat, sinuous as a snake, although it looked more like a badly—designed marionette.

"I'm going to sit down over there" I said casually, dropping my voice low, and changed direction to suit my words. The bench I'd chosen was slightly shaded, with greenery behind it, and had a clear line of sight both across the plaza and of the street in front of us, while the glass pyramid behind us prevented anyone from getting a drop from behind.

'lynau were paranoid bastards, and it was rare to see one out before nightfall. More to the point, they hung with gnomes and gnomes and I didn't have a very good relationship, having to do with me having cheated them out of a prize — said prize being a teenaged runaway — a number of years ago. So if they were searching me out, that was either very good or very bad.

I opened the packet of pita, and left if on the bench next to me, with the tzatziki. It wasn't a bribe, that would be tacky. This was two Cosa members, sharing a meal. If the offering was ignored, it was bad news. If the offering was shared... well, it could still be bad news, but possibly useful, too.

When I looked down again, half the pita was gone, along with all of the sauce. All right, then.

"What's shaking, cousin?"

There was a muted burp, then a scratchy voice said, "thank you. That was very good."

I waited.

"The cold ones have a message. Something came into their tunnels two nights ago. They could not chase it away, could not stop it."

"Did it harm any of them?" Shit. We'd been so focused on the human victims, the established MO, I hadn't even thought that it might go after the fatae, too.

"No. It... stared at them. But in the end, it went away. But the cold ones told me to tell you, it smells of blood and hunger."

I took a bite out of my own gyro, careful to put Ellen's on the side away from the 'lynau so it wouldn't get any ideas. I had no idea why the gnomes would tell me this, but they had, and thought it important that I know.

"Thank you, cousin," I said. "Tell the cold ones that I appreciate their sharing this with me." I wasn't going to promise them a damn thing until I knew the value — or lack thereof — of the info, but this was the most civil we'd been to each other in years. I wasn't going to be rude.

There was a rustling of paper, then a used napkin landed on the bench next to me, and I was alone. I packed everything back into the bag, and went to join Ellen.

"Lunch? Excellent." She ate like a teenager — worse, she ate like a teenager in mentorship, burning calories at a terrifying rate.

"Got some new information," I said, as she ate not only her gyro but what was left of mine as well. "Our suspect paid a visit to some cousins of mine. Spooked them, considerably."

That made her pause, mid-bite. "Nobody was hurt?"

"No. Didn't seem interested in them. Or no... was definitely interested, but took no action." That tickled one of the pieces in my brain, but didn't move it anywhere.

"You're sure it was our suspect?"

"Good question," I said. "No, I'm not sure, but my cousins were. They're not very nice, in fact they're not nice at all, so they wouldn't bother to tell me anything unless they thought it was a threat..." My words trailed off, and I stared up at the sky, the pale blue starting to shade darker as the sun passed behind the western skyscrapers.

"Shadow, *why* would it be a threat?"

She couldn't read my mind — every Talent I knew swore up and down that mind-reading wasn't a current-skill — but she read my mind.

"Because they're not very nice." Her voice was flat, not with a lack of emotion, but with a pipeline of repressed emotion, the kind where you want to jump up and punch the air but you can't. "Because the first victim, way back when, was someone not very nice. And the ones who were sniffed at and left alone and unbothered were nice — or at least not not-nice — and your cousins were left bothered because they're not-nice."

We had our victimology.

"And the trigger point was a hit-and-run. Pretty much the definition of not-nice. Someone's raised wild current to become a vigilante? That's... "

"If you say brilliant I may disown you," I warned her, busily shifting puzzles pieces to fit this new theory.

"I was going to say extreme," she said, mildly reproving. "Have you ever seen Wren pull down a storm?"

"No." That was something I'd like to keep an entire city between myself and the event, if possible.

"It's amazing. It's like cocaine, probably, the minute it hits your system. Like one of my visions a thousand times, except it all feels good. But... When you pull down tame current, something that's already been running with electricity, something manmade, it's already gotten used to being controlled, diluted. You can weave it into your own core without too much difficulty, once you know what you're doing."

Talent were normally trained in their early teens: Ellen'd come to it nearly a decade late, her training still fresh in her mind, and hard-won.

"But wild current... it resists, and it... it surges. Like thinking you're going to take a sip of water and getting hit in the face with an ocean wave. And it can drown you — well, burn you out, actually — if you're not careful."

"And if you're not high-res enough?" Both Wren and Ellen downplayed their strengths, unlike certain PUPs I could name.

"Yeah." She looked pensive. "That would explain why I felt them, rather than the victims. If they're that strong, and surging — working off wild current alone — they'd be incredibly powerful. And scary-close to wizzing out, to losing control. And if they're also a seer.... They'd be able to tell, if someone they ran into was planning to do something bad?"

I didn't have a clue about what a Talent could or couldn't do, and she knew that. But I did know a thing or two about getting inside a killer's mind, even though it left me feeling filthy, afterward.

"They were trolling the ...my cousins," I said. "Drawn by their particularly nasty little minds. But they didn't kill them. Because they were fatae?"

"Maybe," she said. "It would make sense? Whoever's doing this, they're focused pretty tight. Not-nice, and human. Like you said, victimology." She made a face. "They think they're cleaning up the city. Like.... That's why you didn't say anything the first time. Because one fewer creep on the streets, and where's the bad? That's what they're thinking now, that there's no downside to what they're doing, that it's... maybe not right, but Just."

I felt my body still, almost afraid to breathe. Ellen's voice had taken on a weirdly gentle hardness totally unlike her usual tones. This wasn't her thinking things out; this was her bringing up what she'd gotten from the contact, all unknowing, siphoning off some of the killer's own ... not thoughts, but emotions, intentions. There was a reason I preferred to do all our brainstorming indoors, in our own office. Most humans were Null, often to the point of not being able to see current-work or recognize a fatae right in front of their nose, but all it took was one would-be supernatural hunter, or worse yet a gossip rag writer with a camera and a recorder, and a Talent losing control, and we'd have another mess on our hands.

I was trying to think of a way to snap her out of it, bring her back to center, when her hand reached out blindly, and grabbed at my sleeve. Ellen wasn't a toucher, not like that. "Boss, we had this all wrong. It's not a someone. It's a some*thing*."

<hr>

DANNY WAS, as a rule, unflappable. But when he got flapped, he did it with a seriously impressive level of swearing, in languages Ellen didn't recognize. Another time and place she might have sat back and listened to him go, waiting for the stream to dry up before getting back to the matter at hand.

They didn't have that luxury.

Other people might say that bad luck was just negative expectations catching up with you, or sheer chance, but Ellen not only believed in bad luck, but was pretty sure it was sentient, and had a nasty sense of humor. Because the instant after she told Danny what she'd realized, she felt it again — not stirring in her thoughts this time, but racing full-on toward her, a bolt of current-energy practically screaming with rage.

They'd been right: it had been aware of her. Had been following her, sniffing around the way it had sniffed around the others. But when she'd recognizing what it was, she'd gone from not-of-interest to Threat.

"Boss, down!" she shouted, and a lash of current slipped from her, wrapping around his knees and pulling him to the ground, spreading quickly into a thin curtain to keep his face from hitting the pavement. She heard the startled "ommmph" as he went down, and then it was all she could do to protect herself as a howling rush of current slammed into her.

Not a storm-seer: a *storm.*

*Help!* The ping was punched out of her by the blow, its usual tight-focus blown wide by the impact, and she didn't know if it would reach her mentor, or be scattered into silence, but she didn't have time to worry. Having failed to take her down with the first attack, the killer had regrouped, shaping itself again into something human-formed.

In the falling dusk, it looked like an art installation, performance art with neon. Deep yellows, almost gold, twined with electric blue and hatchmarked against an eye-watering green, a scarecrow of a figure, with no face but deep holes where eyes would be, the lack of light there more shocking than anything else as it lifted its head to stare at her.

It wasn't human. It wasn't fatae. It wasn't a single killer but many, the wild current not taken within itself but *making* itself. Ellen had no idea how such a thing was possible, but she couldn't give a damn just then, too busy fighting down both anger and panic.

Her own core surged under her fear, and she pressed mental hands against it, not to soothe but to shape and control it, tendrils slipping along her bones, coating her, covering Danny, who was wise enough to stay down until he figured out what was going on. She hoped that anyone else lingering in the plaza had the sense to run, or if they were Null, that that would protect them. If they weren't a threat to the entity, didn't read as whatever it decided was 'bad,' it should ignore them.

Should.

Another shock of wild current hit her, and she fought to hold control, even as her core surged at the challenge. Current-duels were deadly; Wren had told her that when she first learned what a core was, and how to use it. Current was all about control, about using only what was needed, and not over-loading yourself, or you'd blow just like a transformer, and with just as bad a result.

Another strike hit her, and she reached back along it instinctively, found what she thought was a weakness at the other end. She focused, sending an arrow of her own current toward it, and shrieked with vicious, if silent, glee when she felt it hit. The current-figure staggered back, black sparks dancing where the blow had connected.

But it wasn't going to be enough. She was only human, only flesh, and this thing was impossibly pure current. They'd underestimated *everything*. If help didn't get here soon....

Then it pivoted, its attention directed away from her for a second, and she saw in the corner of her eye that Danny had rolled onto his side, was reaching — had pulled out his gun and was aiming it at the thing.

Her ferocity turned to panic. What did he think he was doing? Bullets wouldn't touch it, but it would make it think he was a threat, too!

***

I MIGHT NOT BE Talent but I was still half-fatae, and there was no way not to feel the change in the air when the thing arrived. Every short hair on my body lifted away from my skin like I'd been hit by lightning, and the slap of Ellen's current against my legs was a comforting cuddle, by comparison.

I hit the ground, but not hard. I had no idea how she'd kept my face from scraping pavement but I'd remember to thank her later. Right now I was more concerned in getting up to see what the hell was happening.

Then I felt the roll of current overhead, and thought it might be wiser to stay down, just now. I'd have called for help, but I knew from experience that my cell phone was now probably a chunk of expensively fused plastic and electrodes. But my gun was low tech, intentionally, and it would work....

A little voice in my head, ever-practical, pointed out that shooting something made of current was about as smart as pissing into the wind, but I had to do *something*. I was as useless as teats on a bull. Worse, I was a liability, not even —

Of all the bad ideas that my mother ever despaired of me having, this one might have been the worst. Or the best. Probably both, wrapped up in one suicidal bow. But even as it hit me, I was pulling the pistol from my holster, rolling onto my side and up on my hip and elbow, and aiming the muzzle directly into what looked like the 'chest' of the current-figure, not because I thought it would do any damage there but because it was the widest target.

My senses are nowhere near sharp enough to actually see the bullet's trajectory, but my imagination fills in the gap in the instant between pressure on the trigger and when the current —thing realizes something's passed through it.

I'm pretty sure that the bullet was destroyed the moment it hit, not going all the way through and out to endanger any possible rubberneckers, sure enough that I don't waste time in guilt, but pull the trigger again. I had four bullets in the chamber, so two more to get it riled enough —

But only two were needed.

"Fuck me." Never mind that I'd wanted this result, now that

I had it I really didn't want it. Too late, now. I felt the current wrapped around me shiver in reaction, as the killer sent a lash of electric yellow straight to my chest. And I was pretty damn sure it knew that a bolt to the heart *would* do damage there. Ellen's protections held — but that wasn't what I needed. So I scrambled to my knees, still staying low, and shot again.

This time, the neon-yellow bolt hit me in the shoulder, knocking me flat on my back, all the air in my lungs vaporized.

"Boss!"

I wanted to raise a hand, tell her I was okay, but I wasn't and I couldn't. Damn, that'd hurt. But I managed to lift my head enough and open my eyes to see the blurry shape that was Ellen, backlit by the fizzy sparking shape beyond her. She was trying to look at me and it at the same time, and I wondered how badly I'd mangled her fight training, that she was doing that.

Being unable to move didn't stop my brain from working. Current. Not a someone, a some*thing*. If I'd the strength to do it, I would have smacked myself in the face. In my defense, that's what I keep people like Pietr and Bonnie around for, to tell me what current can or can't do, and Pietr had missed it entirely, too. Only Ellen, connected to it, had figured it out. But that was no excuse.

Current, wild current. It hadn't been taken from the graveyard, it had formed there. Too many Talent buried there, maybe dead from violence, or unjust means? I'd leave the how to the PUPs, that was their area, I just needed to know the why, because the why was the solution, it always was. Motivation made motive. What fucking motivation could a ball of current have?

What connection did it have to the first murder?

The poem I'd been thinking of earlier came back to me, my mother's voice reciting it from memory, decades past. I hadn't understood the poem back then, but the images had always stuck with me, the idea of a wall being built up and taken down, the idea of a wall as a natural thing, a *good* thing, the kind of walls we saw as we drive up the throughway, low stone walls covered in moss, aging slowly, marking off land and territory: mine here, yours there.

If you took stones out, the way the hunters did, to chase after your prey, you weakened the wall, took down the barriers between those neighbors. There was a wall marking the division between life and death, too. If something picked at it, scraped at it, dislodged a few stones....

It might not have been what Frost meant, but I grabbed at that, and ran with it. Figuratively speaking, since I was still flat on the ground and not planning on getting up any time soon.

There was another clash of sparks, bright enough that I squinched my eyes shut again and dropped my face back to the ground — or the weirdly-soft pillow of current that was keeping me off the ground, anyway. The gun was under my fingers, and I closed my hand around it, even though I knew it wouldn't do any good — or worse, I might hit Ellen.

Guns were tools of violence, designed to kill. Taking out the trash, the gang kids used to say when they took out an inter- loper, dumped him back on his own turf. Current took the impression of its holder, after long enough in the core, I knew that much. That was how Talent used it, were able to command it. If we could replace the violence... repair the wall?

"Boss!" Ellen's voice, tight and worried. "I can't hold it much longer."

Of course not. She was only one girl, even high-res. How could she hold out against the combined energy of rage, hate, fear? It would dismantle her, piece by piece, in its determination to take out what it saw as the trash, its natural prey.

"Rebuild it," I told her. "What?"

"Rebuild it. The wall. Put the pieces back, bits of you."

It seemed perfectly reasonable to me, if I could just get her to understand....

And then the black slipped around my eyeballs, and took me back under.

---

ELLEN HAD no idea what Danny meant, but she could feel the snap and sizzle of the thing's current coming closer each time, and once her defenses broke, it would reach her — and it would reach Danny, too, who had slumped boneless on the ground. She could tell he was still breathing, but not how badly he'd been hurt. She needed to protect him, get him out of this. Idiot, he could have stayed safe, the thing only saw her as a threat, first, it —

It clicked, then. Not a chain of therefore-thus, but knowing Danny Hendrickson, working with him, listening to him think out loud, and she understood why he'd shot at the current-shape, even knowing damn well it wouldn't hurt it. To draw it away from her, protect her.

It picked things out of their heads, read their intent. Had read her, even as she read it, connected by the wild current. And then she thought, maybe, maybe, she understood what Danny'd meant, about rebuilding a wall....

Or, she had no idea what he meant, but the image was clear in her head anyway, a shimmering wall of bricks, carefully placed and cemented, two bricks thick and insulated between. Not the current battering at her, wild and angry, but her own: controlled, protective. She Saw the wall, shaping it and building it piece by piece like Danny'd said, blocking the current-thing away from them with her own bricks, turning around it, blocking its escape, turning again, walling it into a corner, and then closing the corner, the wall rising higher, over her head, the shimmer of the bricks fading as the insulation took hold, turning solid dark red, like a schoolhouse, or a prison.

But a prison could be broken out of, walls could be shattered, if you left too much power inside.

The thought of touching it directly, of allowing that *glee* to touch her again, made Ellen sick. But she bit her cheek hard enough to bleed and reached inside the last open section, latching onto it with current-shaped claws even as it struggled to slide through, pushing it back at the same time she reached for a jugular, pulsing with power, and dug her claws in.

So much power. So. Much. She was blinded by it, the shock-sparks dancing under her skin, diving for her own core, wanting in, in. The temptation overwhelmed her, how strong she would be, how easy it would be to destroy the creature then, to....

Overrush. The single word, Wren's voice in her head, was enough to dampen the urge. Too much current, too fast, flooding your core, and you overrushed. Death would be the best part of that, Wren said. If you were unlucky, you went mad, first. Wren's mentor had died that way.

And she didn't want that current inside her, angry and vile as it was.

Her claws dug in deeper, siphoning off the current, but instead of drawing it into her own core, she let it slide out, using her arms as a straw; in at the fingers, out at the elbow where it jutted just outside the second wall.

Releasing this much current, shaped to such rage, into the city was the equivalent of letting toxic fumes hit a schoolyard, but she didn't know what else to do, not with the current-shape struggling under her claws, trying to get hold of her, to draw her own current down to feed itself, to tear open her face and obliterate her fingerprints, to wipe every trace of her from the world.

"I'm not a bad person!" she yelled at it, willing it to stand down, stop attacking her. "I'm not!"

It didn't believe her. It didn't have the ability to; it wasn't human, it didn't have rational thought, only sense and memory. If she was lucky, once torn from the consciousness it did have, the current would disperse enough to just cause some bad moods or crankiness in whomever it hit. If she was unlucky....

Another burst of current seized up her arm, bypassing the exit at the elbow, aiming directly for her brain, and she fought it back, cold sweat slicking her body. An entire war waged between her elbow and shoulder, the pain incandescent, the only thing keeping her from dropping to her knees and howling was the knowledge that the moment she did that, she was dead.

And after her, Danny. Dragged and dumped like trash, a warning nobody else knew how to read.

"I won't. Let. You hurt him," she gritted out between clenched teeth, her tongue stinging where she'd bitten it, the sweat dripping into her eyes and burning like tears. They protected people from things like this, that's what they did. People were oblivious, they didn't know, didn't want to know, or even if they did know they couldn't do anything. She could. That was why she'd seen this. Not because it shoved into her brain; she Saw it so she could stop it.

With her free hand, she shaped the final bricks, slotting them into place, then slipping her arm out and slapping the final piece in.

Her arm still stung like an entire nest of yellowjackets had munched on it, but the pressure was gone, the malign-shaped current swirling away, what wasn't locked behind the wall. There was another swirl of current behind her, and she twisted, her heart racing at the thought that it had escaped, or there was something else, another one, her current rising again, sluggish and sore, to face this new threat.

"Whoa, down," a voice said, even as a familiar reassurance pinged against her awareness. Pietr, and the broad-shouldered shadow of Nifty behind him, translocating in from somewhere else, the taser-like weapons they wouldn't let her try in their hands and their eyes alert for a threat.

"In there," she said, waving a hand vaguely behind her, not sure and not caring if they could see the wall she'd built. From the way their eyes widened, they could.

"Good going, kid," Nifty said, stepping forward, an over-sized metal briefcase in one hand. "We got it from here."

Normally she would be offended at being dismissed; here she had other things to worry about.

"Boss?" She dropped to her knees, her undamaged hand going to Danny's shoulder, the current that had been protecting him sliding back under her skin, coiling down in muted tones of blue and green to her depleted core, like a cool drink of water after too much sun. "Danny?"

"U'ky shhhh" he said, and blinked up at her. "Ow."

She collapsed all the way onto the ground next to him, relief making her eyes water. "Yeah. Ow."

***

"Ow."

Ellen's face collapsed into a soft, happy-but-going-to-cry-anyway expression. "Yeah, ow." She'd flopped down onto the ground next to me like someone'd cut her leg-strings, and I wanted to pat her on the shoulder, tell her she'd done good, but my arms didn't want to move just yet.

We'd done it. I wasn't quite sure what we'd done, because it had mainly been El who'd done it, but we'd done it. I squinted, and identified Pietr and Nifty doing the cleanup work, while Ellen starting patting gently at my side, I guess making sure I was still there and all in one piece.

Everything hurt. That's usually the result of being current-whipped — like being hit by lightning, but with more malice — and thrown into the pavement. Fortunately, there was no need to move. It wasn't like either of us were in any shape to deal with mass transit, and my credit cards were a useless slag of plastic in my wallet, after being exposed to that much current. The PUPs would have to pack us into a cab when they were done, in repayment for getting here after all the fun was over.

Once she determined that I wasn't about to die or bleed out anything I needed, Ellen disappeared for a bit, coming back with soda from a grease cart that had either missed the entire foofah, or — more likely — had come back once it was clear that nobody was going to get killed. The ginger ale felt good against my throat, and the can was cool against my forehead, where a headache was threatening to erupt.

It took a while before the guys were certain that the entity had been secured, and they'd figured out, more or less, what Ellen had done to contain it. That was what I was guessing from the way they'd gone from circling an empty space to opening their kits and doing something to the empty space. Ellen could probably see whatever it was they were working on, but I didn't bother asking her for a play-by-play.

"I didn't know current could do that," she said softly, drinking her own soda. "Be...directed like that."

I hadn't known either. Maybe nobody had. "You people are a work in progress," I said. "You think those guys," and I lifted my chin in the direction of the PUPs — "had any clue what they were doing when they started? But we know now."

"Yeah." Not quite a sigh, but not quite an agreement, either. It took a while, and a couple of false starts, with Ellen chewing her lip and fiddling her fingers, before she finally asked the question that I knew'd been burning a hole in her gut.

"The current-shape... it came from dead Talent? All their

anger, their fear, it siphoned off their current, mixed with the natural current around the graveyard...."

"Sounds logical" Logic was all we had to go on, here: it wasn't as though we could question it. I shuddered at the thought. Maybe Venec and his band of crazies would try that. Not me, and not Ellen. Our job was done.

"And it just happened to pick up the memory of that particular killing, out of all the ones ever to fixate on?"

"Digital scanning." It was the only thing I could think of. "Remember, I said, they were transferring all the old cold cases to digital? I checked; they had to put it on hold a few days ago because of a power outage, blew all their scanners."

Current played merry hob with electronics. An upset semi-sentient current?

She considered that theory, her entire face shadowed. "Why now? All that anger, outrage, why did it take form now?"

I'd laugh, except I was pretty sure it would hurt like hell. "Ask them," and I nodded toward the PUPs. "Cosmic alignment? A particularly bad storm in the upper atmosphere? Bad fucking luck? Could be anything, all of them, nothing at all. That's how shit goes down, all at once, seemingly out of nowhere. But it never is, El. Nothing comes out of nowhere."

The more you try to press things down, the harder they come back up.

"And that's why we're here." She was watching the PUPs now, frowning as they stood quietly, their hands up like particu- larly inept mimes, and I could imagine the faint prickly feel of current being worked, but that's all it was, my imagination. A couple walked by and didn't even blink at them, which was either typical New York whatever in action, or they were using so much current they were effectively invisible to Nulls.

"Do you think this is the first time it's happened?"

I shrugged, and yeah, fuck, that hurt. "How long have there

been vigilantes? How long has there been current? This isn't on you, Ellen. If anything, it's on me."

She shook her head, and I nodded. "I might not have helped with an active cover-up, but I sure as hell enabled a passive one. And never mind that I thought it was the right thing to do at the time, choosing a life that might do some good over one that wasn't. You stay passive long enough, it's the same as doing wrong."

I'd learned my lesson, but it came back and haunted me anyway. And more people had died.

I took that thought and locked it into the book of deal-with-later. And I would, but right now I had more immediate concerns. "You okay?" She seemed way too calm for everything that had gone down, even with her recently acquired jadedness. "Yeah. I think I am. I mean, that's why I'm here, right? For the people who get caught up in the bad luck and the cosmic align-ments they can't do anything about? When it's not a Talent-driven crime, not really, not what they handle," and we both looked back at the PUPs, who were now putting things back in their kit, presumably finished. "It's current-driven, though. And that's me. Us."

I could feel myself duckface, unable to argue with that even though it felt a bit like hubris. "Yeah. I guess." I'd never thought that deep about it, beyond a need to keep people from getting lost. I guess... she was right, in a way. A lot of people had gotten lost.

"So how do we stop this from happening again?"

And there was the question of the hour, maybe. "I don't think we can. People — human or otherwise — they do damage. All we can do it put back each stone, one at a time."

She frowned at me. "Yeah, about that. I still have no idea what you're talking about."

I laughed, and yeah, I was right, that hurt too. "You need to read more poetry."

And then Pietr was there, kneeling next to us. "A car's coming. Medic's at the office, take a look at you both."

"I'm fine," Ellen started to say, and he shut her up with a look. "I'm not going to explain to Wren Valere how I let you go without a full checkup, so shut up and do as you're told. And that goes for you too, Hendrickson."

I lay back on the ground and stared up at the darkening sky, the lights coming on around us from street lamps and office buildings. I was alive. Ellen was alive. Nobody else was going to die tonight.

"Yeah, okay," I said. "Okay."

# AN INTERRUPTED CRY

I scowled at the filing cabinet, a finger poking into the too-full drawers. We needed to order another one. Maybe two.

Being a PI has a lot in common with being a cop; mainly, that paperwork is the worst part of the job. Getting shot falls to second place only because paperwork happens with depressing regularity and so far, despite what certain people who will remain Wren Valere like to claim, getting shot *doesn't*.

But despite the folder of receipts and reports on my desk, I was in a reasonably good mood.

I'd cracked open the office's sole window—one of the few advantages of renting space in an older building was that the windows opened—and the faint noise from the street and the occasional wing-flurry of one of the pigeons who insisted on roosting on the ledge had a lot to do with that mood. New York City, my favorite place in the world eleven months of the year, becomes a heat sink in August, refusing to cool down even at midnight, and the air— let's just say that heat, humidity and subways aren't a good combination. Even in September, you can feel the lingering layabouts, like the heat was so lazy it couldn't be bothered to get up and move. But with October's arrival, that last taint of too-warm had fallen to cooler nights, and a crisp upper-60's was the renewed daytime normal.

Climate change would probably screw that up too, but for now, as the sun slipped behind the western line of skyscrapers and I had to turn on the overhead lights to keep working, my mood was all about counting blessings.

It didn't hurt that we'd wrapped up the last case with a win: an eleven-year-old girl, reported missing nearly a week before. We'd found her chilling with a colony of kitsune near Saranac Lake and brought her—reluctantly, with complaints every mile of the way—back to the arms of her distraught (and utterly clueless) parents.

If I had a dime for every teen who went walkabout for fairy lights and fatae glamour.... Actually, I charge considerably more than a dime. But keeping them home after is their parents' problem, not mine. I'm a PI, not a babysitter.

I tapped the paperwork, thinking about the case. Once, missing kids'd been my bread and butter—twice over when my fatae cousins were involved. But the past year or so, Ellen and I'd been hip-deep in cases where Ellen had gotten a vision of someone in dire and immediate likelihood of death, and we were the only ones who knew about it.

Not only did those cases tend to end messier, it was rare anyone actually paid us for them. We needed more bread-and-butter, much as the thought of wishing ill on anyone sat badly on my overdeveloped conscience, thanks mom. Not just for the money, though—watching Ellen's face when we reunited the kid with her parents had reminded me how damn young my protégée/assistant/partner was, and the toll this job was taking on her.

It made my stomach hurt when I thought about it. She was a storm-seer, a scary-powerful Talent, and there had to be a better way for her to make a living than this. Between her mentor and my contacts, we should be able to find something....

And that thought was followed by the same one that always followed it: Ellen would kick my ass for daring to decide what was good or right for her. She was solid muscle, that kid, and no respect whatsoever for her elders. Anyway, actively *doing* something gave her a way to deal with the visions, according to Valere, and who was I to get in the way of someone's demon-slaying?

Metaphorical, that was. I'd nothing against the one demon I'd met, and it would be hypocritical at best for me to go on a humancentric rant, considering my own genetics.

"Fuck it. She's a grown-ass adult, mostly. And we're definitely going to need another filing cabinet."

I managed to wedge the folder into the appropriate drawer without mangling it or the surrounding files too badly. "Small victories, Hendrickson. One more pile and then there's a cold beer in the fridge with your name on it."

Of course, because fuck my life, that was when the lights went out. *All* the lights. I got to my feet and pushed open the door between my office and the front room to confirm that yeah, those lights were out, too, and the coffee maker's everpresent red light had gone out.

Going back into my office, I checked and, sure enough, my phone and laptop were no longer charging, and a quick glance out the window showed me that the buildings across the street were showing only the dim red light of emergency signs. I was too high up to see if the traffic lights and street lamps had also gone off, but I had a pretty good guess as to what the answer might be.

Blackout.

I sighed, thankful that there hadn't been a power surge in the building that blew up my laptop again. That shit got old, fast. "So who did what now?"

When you work closely with Talent, the human portion of the Cosa Nostradamus, the assumption that a power outage was caused by somebody screwing up and pulling too much power from the grid was the immediate, logical, and usually correct assumption. Usually followed by mocking rights for everyone else of the hapless—and deeply embarrassed—Talent in question.

What's particularly annoying, though, is that Talent—because the magical energy they called current made it difficult for them to use most electric-powered machines—are the least affected by things like power outages.

The rest of us mere mortals? We needed our computers, damn it. And our coffee machines.

Fortunately for me, my paternal genetic inheritance had some benefits, including the ability to see better than humans in the dark. Despite the shadow-on-shadow now filling the office, I grabbed my cell phone off the windowsill without fumbling it, unplugging it from the now-useless cord, and called one of the three landlines I had in my address book.

"Wasn't me." Ellen was less defensive than resigned, as though of course that would be the first thing I'd ask her.

"If it was, would you admit it?" She might have done it, easily enough: Ellen was not only a storm-seer, she was one of the strongest Talents in the City, second or third only to the *other* numbers I had in my address book, and only because she had less experience. That fact would freak me out if I ever let myself really think about it.

A low laugh. "Not a chance in hell." Fair enough: I gave her enough shit when she shorted out just the office, couple-three months ago.

"Well, Valere's out of town, so we can't blame her, unless the blackout's spread up and down the East Coast?" The last time that had happened it was 2003, and had been caused by a group of Talents in Ohio playing an incredibly stupid game of Chicken.

"Not like I have a TV to check the news," she reminded me.

I looked up at the shadowed ceiling for patience. "So ask around!"

"Oh." There was an abashed silence, then, "Iggy says it's lights-on in Boston. Ditto Lu in Philadelphia."

Talent, in addition to being able to manipulate current to do things the rest of us can't, can use that to 'ping' each other at long distance. It's not telepathy, they insist, but if it walks like telepathy and quacks like telepathy, in my book, it deserves some Hoisin sauce.

"Just us then. Yay. And it's past sundown. It's ConEd, don't expect them to get shit fixed any time soon. How're you set for power?"

"I'm.......okay." I could hear the hesitation in her voice, though.

"Damn it, Shadow, even I know—"

"I know, grandma, I know." She cut me off, and I grinned, secure that she couldn't see my amusement. The girl I'd first met would have hidden under the desk when scolded, not sassed me back.

"All right, I'll pretend you're all grown up and can take care of yourself. Get some sleep, and hopefully they'll have figured it out by morning."

Talent might not suffer the lack of televisions and computers tonight, but they had one significant weakness in a blackout: they couldn't top off their core of current in an emergency. Lacking a man-made source, the only other ways to replenish current were ley lines or an electrical storm. While there were ley lines aplenty deep in the bedrock of New York, they were, I was told, tricky to reach. And autumn wasn't an ideal time to look for thunderstorms.

No, every wise Talent in the area would be curling up on

the sofa tonight, staying out of trouble. And the unwise ones? Well, those weren't my problem. Not until after the fact, anyway.

Unfortunately for the rest of us, it was still work as usual tonight. Mainly because the subway lines would be a mess, too, and the thought of trying to find a cab home tonight, or walking the whole way, didn't appeal at all. So I was stuck, at least for a few hours.

I let out a sigh, and picked up the next case file, figuring I might as well finish the filing, so I could ignore it again for another month or three. But, fatae genetics or no, my eyes weren't quite dark-sensitive enough to read the writing on the label. I reached into the lower desk drawer and pulled out a thick white candle in a glass holder, the kind they sell apportioned to various saints, and used the lighter next to it to bring a little light to the situation.

"Fortune favors the prepared, yeah?" Holding the folder close to the candle revealed the name. "All right, finally paid in full, Mr. Belkin, you now go in the drawer of honor.

"A lesser man would have made his junior partner do this," I told the folder. "But then you'd end up god knows where and I'd never find you again."

Ellen was getting there as an investigator, and I trusted her to have my back, but the girl couldn't file to save her life, or mine. My mother had been career Navy, and more than a few of her neatnik habits had stuck. As much as I hated filing, I liked everything to have its own place, and for everything to be in that place when I looked for it.

But as I turned back to the filing cabinet, I paused. I'd my share of horror movies watched too young and too late at night, and in my years I'd seen shit that should have stolen my sleep, but I don't creep out easily. Yeah, knowing the entire city had gone dark was unnerving, if you let it, but—

Something. Not quite the corner of my eye, maybe just

beyond that, but *something* enough to make me jerk to a halt, tilt my head, feel prickles of something uncanny on my skin.

The flash of light could have been anything. It could have been a flashlight, or a candle, or a camping lantern brought into the building by some paranoid, prepared bastard. It was probably some other poor bastard stuck in their office, trying to get work done despite the circumstances.

The prickle on my skin said otherwise, and I moved to the window, Academy training and experience keeping me to the side, rather than full-on in front of the pane.

Our building wasn't a flat square: it was shaped like a U, with a skinny courtyard in the middle, so that more offices could claim to have windows. Directly across the courtyard, maybe fifteen feet away, there was a flicker of....

No, it wasn't light. Not from a candle or a flashlight or any other emergency illumination system I'd ever seen, anyway. It was, lacking any other term, creepy as fuck; bog-orange and too dim to be useful, like one of those fish you only ever see on deep water nature shows or something. Elongated, narrow, and then it flicked out of sight not like it had been turned off but like it'd......turned sideways and was too skinny to see?

I might ignore my non-human inheritance most of the time, but when it's howling at me like a bansídhe on steroids, I listen. That wasn't someone over there, that was some *thing.*

That should have been the end of it; my mother hadn't raised an idiot. You don't go poking your nose into things not your business just because you're curious, and seeing as how more than half my neighbors would call me a thing, too, if they'd got a close look at my hooves or horns, well, I wasn't going to assume anything. Not my business, not as a PI, not as an ex-cop, not as a concerned citizen.

Not until a second figure. human-shaped, walked in front of the window—and then fell, as though he'd been taken out by a blow to the knees.

"Ah, goddamnit." Now I didn't have a choice.

---

I WASN'T a cop for very long before HR changes forced me out, but they trained us well back then, and the muscle memory stuck. My brain was calculating time and distance to the other side of the building even as I unlocked the middle drawer that held my gun and ammo. I tried not to rely on guns—there are some things lead or silver bullets can't kill—but a bullet slows even them down more than a bit, if you're a good shot.

I loaded up, shoved my phone in my jeans pocket, and didn't bother with the penlight stashed next to the ammo box: I didn't want whatever the *thing* was to get advance warning it had been seen. Hopefully, my own night vision would be up to the task.

I kept the gun in my left hand, down low by my thigh and out of sight in case anyone I shouldn't be shooting was gossiping in the hallway. There were a few open doors as I moved down the hallway, other tenants trying to wait out the subway halt, or just taking advantage of the quiet, or—in at least one office—having a blackout party, complete with off-tune guitar and, I was betting, at least one six-pack of beer.

I'd rather have been hanging out with them. Or back in my office, oblivious to everything, but my skin was still prickling, and the image of a body falling was too-sharp in my memory. I wondered briefly if I should be calling for backup, but the day I couldn't poke my nose into an office in my own damn building without help was the day I'd buy a grove somewhere and retire.

The elevator was an obvious no-go, so I took the stairs, wincing at the unavoidable clatter of my boot heels on the metal risers. The emergency lights were brighter here than in the hallway, but they reflected in unpleasant ways, and I wondered if they had to be that particular shade of red. Five turns down to the lobby, leaving me a little dizzier than I liked, and I had no idea how full humans would be able to manage in an emergency.

The lobby had yellow lights, not red. I blinked twice, adjusting.

The night guard building management had finally gotten around to hiring looked up from the security desk, saw it was me, and then went back to his tablet, the wavering white light from the screen illuminating his face almost too brightly. Nice to see he was earning his paycheck. Bastard was gonna be pissed if his battery died before the power came back on.

I considered alerting him, realized I had no idea what I'd be alerting him *to*, or how I'd even explain it to him. "I saw a light that couldn't exist, and someone falling in a way that looked suspicious?" Not enough cause to call 911, even with my creds. And if that light was fatae-related? Hauling in the blues seemed like a bad idea. There were a handful of people left at the NYPD who knew what I was, a few dozen more who knew about the Cosa Nostradamus itself, but short of an all-out clusterfuck, there was no need to bring them into this. I'd spent too many years socking away favors and goodwill to waste it here and now.

I left the guard to his reading, and hotfooted across the lobby to the other stairwell and up the stars again, this time trying to move more quietly. When I reached the fourth floor, where I'd seen the odd light flash, I paused with the fire door barely cracked open, listening.

Nothing. Not only the absence of people but the muted echo of a building that had gone dead. It was unnerving, once you paid attention to it. New York City wasn't supposed to be this quiet, ever.

As though on cue, a siren went by, five stories below, fire truck and a police car as a chaser, proof that even in a blackout, some things keep going. That probably shouldn't have been so reassuring. I used the distant wails to cover the sound of me moving down the hallway, mentally counting doorways until I reached what I hoped to hell was the right office. The doors here were the same as on my side: a beat-up dark wooden frame with a frosted glass inset. Where my office had letting on the glass, this one had a small sign by the side on the door, but the lettering was unreadable in the red-lit gloom.

Not that it mattered what they were selling, inside.

The door was slightly ajar. Any other day that could be a warning sign - you didn't leave your door open where anyone might walk in. During a blackout, it could just be someone'd done what I had—poked their nose out to see if everyone was affected, and forgot to close it again. With what I'd — maybe — seen inside, I took it as a warning sign. Gun raised to firing angle, finger sliding up the trigger guard, I pushed the door further open with my right, turning sideways to present a smaller target.

Nothing jumped out at me, nothing swung or fired or otherwise attacked. I paused, always the longest heartbeat, waiting, but nothing moved deeper in the gloom of the office. I stepped inside the doorway, glancing around, but didn't see anything in the main room except standard office furniture, a desk and two chairs more comfortable-looking than ours, and what looked like a pile of....

I stopped and, lowering my gun but keeping my finger on the ready, stepped closer, cautiously, to the pile.

My sharp exhale of relief was too loud in the gloom-filled room. Laundry. Specifically, a laundry sack, the off-white canvas kind you dropped off at the laundromat so they could wash your unmentionables for you. I'd never been that wealthy or that lazy, but I'd dated a girl once who swore by it.

I looked up again, and my relief disappeared. Just beyond the duffle-sized sack, face down on the tile floor, one hand out flung as though to stop his fall......yeah, there was my dead body.

"Not mine." I back-tracked out loud, as though disavowal now would placate any eavesdropping gods. But it was too late, I'd claimed him, and now I had to go over there and find out what had happened.

At least whatever had caused that glow seemed to be gone. Maybe it'd just been an odd reflection, an emergency light that flickered and was turned off. I'd worry about it in a minute. Even if a victim's obviously dead, you check just to be sure.

Gun lowered but still ready in my hand, I knelt at the body's hip, far enough away a sudden flip couldn't catch me, and checked for a pulse. The flesh was still warm, muscles soft enough to give under my touch, but nothing was happening underneath.

It didn't take a trained PI to figure out the scene from the evidence. Joe Doe here, stumbling around in the sudden dark, maybe blinded by whatever the light had been, had fallen over his laundry delivery and broken his neck.

I let my finger slide back to the safety, tension sliding out of my gun arm. "I knew dirty laundry could be dangerous to a person's career, but deadly? That's a new one...."

Some days, if it weren't for morbid humor, we wouldn't have anything to laugh about at all.

Because it was just then I realized I'd been wrong. I wasn't alone in the office, after all.

---

"Beer! Beer half price, while it's still cold!" The guy leaning in the doorway of the bodega on the corner didn't have many takers—most people were drinking what was in their own fridges, not running out to buy more. He'd probably have better luck trying to sell ice cream—although it was too cold, in

Ellen's opinion, for anything frozen. She shoved her free hand into a pocket and wished she'd stopped to pick up a pair of gloves as well as her flashlight before she left her apartment.

Ellen had been safe and settled for the night, shoes off and her feet up, when the power went out. There had been no reason for her to have abandoned her comfortable if butt-ugly sofa, shove her feet into hiking boots, and walk the length of Manhattan in the middle of a blackout, when her boss had told her, flat out, to stay on that butt-ugly sofa and not worry.

Except. Except.

Ellen was a born worrier. She knew it, Danny knew it, at this point people she'd never even met knew it. But usually she had enough to worry about without taking on random and probably non-event things like her boss alone in his own office. Her boss who was perfectly capable of taking care of himself, and had been doing so long before they met. Decades of taking care of himself, in fact, although she wasn't entirely sure how old he was, faun genetics mixing with human ones. But he was forty by looks, at least, and probably twice that in actuality, and he didn't need a twenty-something Talent checking in on him.

And she really didn't need the exercise, walking nearly the length of Manhattan at night—although she had to admit it was more pleasant than she'd thought: the power might be out but the city didn't stop for darkness. Nearly every street she walked past had some sort of block party going on, makeshift bonfires in tailgating grills or metal trash cans, and sometimes the occasional portable generator; instruments being played, children too wired to go to sleep playing with glow-in-the-dark Frisbees or just running wild among the adults sipping their slowly-warming beers and telling stories about past blackouts.

Unlike most of them, Ellen knew that there were other things out there, too. Things as a child she'd been told were impossible, figments of her imagination, now taking advantage of the darkness to mingle more freely than usual. She heard the chittering of piskies overhead, and refused to give the pranksters the satisfaction of notice, but nodded a greeting to the river troll who had perched on a stool, sucking down a beer he'd lifted from someone's party, and smiled at the tumble of satyrs who'd ventured from their park to see what was up—and possibly hook up. They were related to fauns, she knew that, but not how closely, and the one time they'd run into a tumble while on a job, they and Danny had oh-so-politely ignored each other. There was probably a story there.......

She didn't know much about Danny's family, except his mom had been military and was dead, and his father hadn't ever been in the picture. Since she could relate, they didn't talk much about it, where 'much' meant 'not at all.' If there was anything about satyrs she'd needed to know, anyway, Wren would have told her.

A tendril of current reached her, rising from the crowd gathered on the corner, a tentative, polite, *hey,* and she raised the hand holding the flashlight in acknowledgement. A tall white man lounging on a stoop with his friends raised his hand back, a sense of curiosity and the offer of a beer before they got too warm to drink following the ping. She didn't know him, except that he was, like her, Talent.

And for him, that was enough for the offer of a beer, conversation, company.

Ellen had spent her entire life isolated from her family, told she was insane for the things she claimed to see and feel, ignored when she wouldn't—couldn't—stop the visions that rocked her as a teenager. Now, she walked through the city and knew that she was part of something larger, connected in a way her fourteen-year-old self wouldn't have believed.

But the odd sense of urgency made her decline the offer, walking on. It wasn't particularly directed at anything, the feeling—nothing like the sharp, insistent pressure of her visions, the ones that threw her into someone else's fear and danger. Just a sense of wrongness that made her feel like she needed to be out and about.

For most of the trip, she could tell herself that's all it was about: stretching her legs, touching base with the net of Talent and fatae living in New York City, enjoying the cool air and sense of muscles warming up after a day of laziness, rather than moving with purpose toward the office. Until she was actually there.

Their building was dark as everything else, no surprise, but the doors opened with a push—she supposed with the power out, the locks were designed to open rather than stay shut, in case anyone was caught inside. It took her a moment to adjust to the dim yellowish lighting, turning off her flashlight and slipping it into her pocket to save the battery.

"Hey." She pulled her building pass out of her wallet, flip- ping it for the security guard to see. He just jerked his chin and grunted, then went back to whatever he was reading, clearly uninterested in her right to be there. She supposed it wasn't as though there was much in the building to steal: most of the offices were one- or two-person operations, not the kind of places that had expensive equipment, or cash in their safes. Other than one private investiga-tor's office—theirs—and a film agent, their neighbors were mostly accountants and lawyers, that sort of thing. Based on the building directory, anyway: she hadn't gotten around to knowing their neighbors. Danny had been in the building for over a decade; she suspected he knew the names of everyone who'd been there longer than a year, even if he'd never actually spoken to them.

*Danny.* The tension that had driven her here didn't increase, but it hadn't decreased, either. She climbed the stairs, keeping one hand on the railing, feeling her chest burn a little, hearing the soft clump of her boots on the risers disappear against the walls like all noise was being swallowed.

She grabbed at that thought and shoved it into the box she

kept for things she didn't want in her head, slamming the lid down tight. The building was safe, her imagination was a pain in the ass, and when she just happened to pop into the office, Danny was going to roll his eyes and sigh, and probably put her to work, saying, "as long as you've hauled your ass downtown, you might as well be useful."

That thought kept her company as she turned the corner and saw their office door. Closed. That was good, right? She reached for the doorknob and—

*Their faces were covered in muck, tear-streaked, eyes too wide, not the surprised kind of wide but shock, or maybe drugs, making their vision unpredictable. Teenagers, late teens, a boy and a girl, clutching each others' hands and side by side.*

*No, not side by side. Tied up next to each other, their fingers the only things loose enough to grasp, tangled with each other for comfort, for humanity in the dark....*

*And there was something near them, shifting in the shadows. Something dangerous. Something that could see them, but they couldn't see it.*

As visions went, Ellen thought as her knees hit the floor, that hadn't been too bad: quick and sharp, not the bone-grinding agony of some of them. But the sense of panic, of disaster not-yet-averted, that sank its claws into her gut, made her skin crawl and her heart beat too fast? That was always the same.

At least she knew what it was, now. Knew how to manage it. No denial, no panic, no hyperventilating. No being told she was insane, over-imaginative, doing it for the attention. Let it roll over her, let it seep out and let her come back to herself. She felt the floor underneath her, solid, the thin carpeting still holding layers of chemicals, the texture scratchy under her fingers. She forced air to move slowly into her lungs, then out again, concentrating on calming her heart, until the weird spacey feeling that always followed a vision passed, and she no longer needed to throw up.

Maybe that had been it, the feeling she'd been having. There'd never been any warnings before, but she'd been repressing them before, then learning how to handle them, so maybe...this was a good thing, right? Having warning?

"Whatever. Get on with it," she told herself. Danny had trained her to sit down and write down everything she'd Seen before it faded or got corrupted, but she was right outside the office; if she could get there, she could tell the boss directly.

Ellen pushed her hands against the floor, forcing herself back to her feet, thankful that nobody had seen her collapse. Her leg muscles trembled a little, but after that first shock seemed perfectly willing to hold her. She made it to the door, surprised to find it locked. She hadn't even thought to bring her key, but since this door had been the first she'd practiced lock-picking on, it only took her a minute to get through, even with her hands trembling slightly, still. The sense of triumph warmed her for an instant.

But the outer office, her space, was still and quiet, and there was no movement, no welcoming sounds from the inner office where Danny would have been working, no hint of candle or flashlight from under the door. She sighed, exhaustion hitting her suddenly, as she slid the pick into the palm—sized case, sliding it back onto her belt. He'd already gone home, despite the subways not running.

And now she *had* to go find him, because visions didn't wait, always sharply insistent that they move on it, *now*, before the people she saw died—or *more* people died. She would grab a cab, she'd seen them cruising the streets, looking for fares, even with the traffic lights being borked, and have it trace the walk to Danny's apartment, catch up with him that way.

"Boss?" She called out, just to be sure. Maybe he was taking a nap in the back—unusual but not unheard of.

And because Danny had trained her to be thorough and careful, she checked his office, just to be sure. It was dark, but she could see clearly enough that he wasn't there, boots propped up on the desk, chair pushed back, baseball cap pulled low over his forehead, hands folded across his midsection and making that half-whistling sound he swore wasn't snoring.

But there was a shadow on his desk that made her frown, working her way carefully over to it.

His laptop, still on the desk's surface and surrounded by a pile of pale folders, not locked in the drawer the way it always was when he closed up shop for the night. Lid up, and when she cautiously touched a key, it came back up, running on battery power.

He wouldn't have just left it like that, not when he didn't know when the power might come back up, not when he knew that the building wasn't protected—he kept all his financials on that laptop, and his current case notes.....

Her heart thumping loud enough she'd swear it had actually shifted up into her throat for real, she reached her hand down and checked the top drawer of the desk, the narrow one that was always, *always* locked.

It was open. And empty.

Danny was gone, he'd left his computer up and running, and he'd taken his gun.

---

"Fuck. Fuck Fuck and also Fuck." Ellen stared at the open drawer for half a second longer, then was out the door, running down the stars without any concern for possibly breaking her neck, sprinting through the lobby, past the still-oblivious security guard, and out onto the street. She was gathering current within her as she went, not the usual careful coaxing, but a spastic grab-and-throw, a net cast to catch the nearest Talent cabbie in the area, even as a narrower ping stretched across town, reaching for a very specific signature.

*I need help*

The response was immediate: *Office. Now. Hang on*

And Ellen had only half a second to think that what she was being told wasn't possible before she felt herself flung into a dark, cold nothingness...and out, the dizziness sending her down to her knees, the remains of her dinner rising up into her throat. She gagged, willing her stomach to settle down, to not throw up on the vaguely-familiar carpeting of the Paranormal Scene Investigations office.

"Sorry," a deep voice said, and a hand offered her help getting to her feet. A man's hand, dark skin and calluses over hard bone. Benjamin Venec, the head of the PUPs, and, Ellen guessed, the source of the translocation that had just flipped her across half of Manhattan without warning.

She tested her knees, found them steady enough to hold her upright, nodded her thanks. "I didn't know anyone could do that." Transloc was difficult enough for a Talent to do, doubly so to bring someone else with them. To grab someone like that...

Venec had the kind of steady stare that could make an honest person twitch. "I don't advertise. It makes people uneasy."

Yeah. Yeah, she could see that. Ellen frowned. And she *could* see—there were lights in the office. She supposed, if you were home base for a dozen powerful—and active—Talents in the business of poking and prodding at magical crimes, having a backup generator in-office was a basic business expense.

"And it's crap for him," a voice cut in from behind Ellen. "Go home, before you fall over." The second voice was lighter, a woman's, and offered no room for argument. Venec's poker face softened slightly and he gave his companion a weary salute before he nodded once at Ellen, and left the room.

Before Bonnie could say anything more, Ellen blurted, "Danny's gone missing."

———

ELLEN HAD, somewhere, picked up Danny's habit of pacing while she thought, and the office they'd been in was too small for real movement. Bonnie finally took pity on her, taking their conversation out into the hallway between conference rooms, where Ellen's longer legs could pace.

Finally, the PUP broke into Ellen's increasingly frantic retelling of the night's events, including her vision. "I hate to say this, kid, but you need to calm down."

Bonnie had been one of the first people to take then-teenaged Ellen seriously, who had helped her to understand that she *wasn't* crazy, that magic—current—was real, and that Ellen could see the things she saw, that they weren't hallucinations. She could tell Ellen to stand on her head in the middle of Times Square and sing God Save the Queen, and Ellen would probably do it.

Or try to, at least.

"He took his gun," she said, for the third or maybe fourth time, after taking a few calming breaths that didn't help. "But he left his laptop up and running, and he just doesn't do that. Not ever."

Bonnie did that narrow-eyed stare thing she did, some-times. "Did you try calling him?"

Ellen stopped mid-stride, and stared at her. "I...no."

Talent didn't use cell phones, as a rule—the current they manipulated did horrible things to tech carried too close to their body, and cell phones and credit card were usually the first to go. Ellen hadn't thought of it, but Danny wasn't Talent.

Bonnie steered her toward the front room, where a landline rested on a sleek receptionists' desk. "Call him."

Ellen dialed the number from memory, and listened to it ring. And ring. She hung up, and tried his home phone, and then the office again on the off chance he'd gone back there. Then she called them all again, in order, leaving a brief message on each machine: "It's Ellen. Call me."

She hung up the phone and looked at Bonnie, who held up a finger, clearly focusing on something else. Then she blinked, and refocused on Ellen. "Venec stopped by his apartment on the way home. Nobody's there, no sign of any disturbance."

Danny was going to hate that someone had been in his apartment; he was intensely private about it. But they would worry about that later, after they'd *found him.*

"He's in trouble, Bonnie."

Bonnie shook her head, her short curls — dark red this month — looking almost black in the low light. "It's still inconclusive. He could be at any of half a dozen blackout parties— okay, he's not a party animal, but he knows a *lot* of people. And his phone might have died—sorry, bad choice of words, the battery might have run down, and it's not like he could recharge it anywhere right now, is it?"

Danny *never* let his phone battery die. They both knew that. "He didn't leave me a note."

The PUP rested a hand on Ellen's arm, fingers gripping lightly; if Ellen wanted to throw her off, she could, and they both knew it. "He didn't know you were coming to the office."

Ellen let the hand stay there, feeling not restraint but support. Even so, she argued. "He's not at his apartment, and he's not in the office, and he took his gun."

It all came back to that. Maybe, maybe his phone had died, or he'd turned off the ringer, or he'd dropped it somewhere and not noticed. Maybe. But Danny Hendrickson was an ex-cop, with a solid weather eye for trouble that had only been honed in his years as a PI. He had a permit to carry, but he didn't most of the time, preferring to leave it in the safe-locked drawer. For the pistol to be gone meant that wherever he was, he'd expected trouble.

And he hadn't called her, or Bonnie, and he hadn't left a note. Ellen knew that the other woman was trying to be logical, the voice of calm reason, but she didn't particularly want to be calm or logical. She needed to find her boss.

"Ellen." The fingers tightened around her arm, briefly, getting her attention. "We're professionals. Act like it. Your vision. That we *know* is urgent, right?"

Ellen nodded.

"All right then. We lead with that. And it might lead us to him, anyway. If there is trouble around, and it involves kids, you know he's going to be mixed up in it eventually."

That got a weak smile from Ellen, because it was true.

"So. Two kids. Tell me more." Bonnie wasn't Danny, didn't have the same measured, calm voice he got when he was walking her through a vision, but she was used to questioning witnesses, dealing with some of the more flighty and uncooperative members of the Cosa Nostradamus when she was investigating a crime. She gave off a sense of patience, as though she was willing to wait forever if that's what it took, that was surprisingly soothing.

"It was too quick. There wasn't anything to work on." Ellen leaned against the wall and studied the photograph hung opposite her. It was of some bridge somewhere, mist low over the arches, but she'd never left the New York City area, so she didn't know where, or if it was some famous photo or the work of one of the PUPs, as they traveled on business—or, she supposed they did take vacations, at some point....

"Ellen. Focus."

"Right." She was exhausted: the translocation had drained her a little, and stress had done the rest, but she couldn't give into it, or let it distract her. How long had it been since she'd had the vision? An hour, two? How long since Danny had gone missing? She didn't know, couldn't know. No watch, no clocks. Their building wasn't wired for closed circuit security, so they couldn't even check tapes.

The vision. Right. Danny would kick her ass if she didn't focus on this, he'd be pissed at her worrying about him when there were kids who needed help.

"There wasn't anything for me to focus on. Wherever they were, it was dark."

"Blackout dark?"

"No.... No. Pitch dark. Like, can't see your hand in front of your face, dark." She scrunched her face as she tried to remember, as though that would job her memory. "Darker than it is now, even in blackout."

"But you could see them clearly. Interesting. But not relevant right now. What else could you see? What did you *feel* from them?"

Ellen closed her eyes, concentrated. "They were scared, but I didn't see what they were scared of. No, I *couldn't* see what they were scared of. It was really hidden, or invisible?"

She couldn't think of anything that could actually make itself invisible, but she didn't know everything yet. Bonnie might. Danny would.

That wasn't enough: Bonnie was waiting for more. "A boy and a girl, white, younger than me? But not young—late teens, maybe?" She wasn't good at judging that even in person. "The stuff on their face.... It was just mud, or dirt. Nothing special about it."

She felt the urge to growl in frustration. As visions went, it had been one of the most *useless* ever.

"Okay, hang on, keep breathing, okay?" Bonnie was using her Calm the Victim Voice now, but Ellen couldn't work up the energy to be offended by that. "Let's at least get a sketch of the kids' faces, then, okay? And I can put out an APB on them, and see if the local cops have a missing report filed yet."

"You draw?" She hadn't expected that, somehow.

"We all draw, at some level," Bonnie said, taking her elbow and leading her back into the conference room. "Job requirement. I'm more Picasso than Rembrandt, but I should be able to do a reasonable likeness. And once we've got that started, we can try and find our missing boy, all right?"

No, it wasn't all right. The need to find her boss was like walking on hot pavement, but her *job* was to focus on the vision. Save the kids, if she could. "Yeah. All right."

BONNIE HAD BEEN RIGHT; she wasn't particularly brilliant as a sketch artist, but when Ellen decided that it was close enough to the faces she'd seen in her vision, the PUP laid down the pencils, and considered what she'd created. "Yeah, youngish, and scared." There was something odd in Bonnie's expression, a twist that Ellen couldn't read, although that might just have been the lighting: it was dimmer than regular light, and Ellen wondered if the generator was starting to die, too.

"Now what?"

Whatever Bonnie had been thinking or feeling, she shook it off with Ellen's question, and looked up and across the table with a glint of mischief on her face. "Now, for the cool part," she said. "Go into mage-sight, and see if you can tell me what I did." Unlike the movies and books, watching current being manipulated was, generally, a lot like watching paint dry: only interesting when a fly got stuck in it. Ellen's mentor had a more organic, whatever-works methodology, but she encouraged Ellen to learn everything she could, especially from the PUPs. So at Bonnie's nod, Ellen let her eyes unfocus, and waited.

Ellen had tried to describe using mage-sight to Danny once

and given up in exasperation, because there was no way to explain it to someone who couldn't *do* it. It wasn't particularly magical, unless you were a science nerd. But for Talents like Bonnie and Pietr, the science of what they did was fascinating, and they expected everyone else to be just as fascinated, so Ellen had gotten a full lecture on it, of which she retained only the basics: that mage-sight bypassed the usual rods and cones in the eye, hitting the optic nerve directly, and from there straight into the occipital lobe.

What it did there, Ellen didn't know, and didn't care. It was enough for her that it worked.

Most people couldn't sense current at all—to Nulls, and most of the fatae, it was at most a faint hum in their awareness. Talent could sense it, feel it, and manipulate it—but they couldn't *see* it, unless they were using mage-sight. Then it was like watching a rainbow, if rainbows came in neon and each color demarcation twitched like guitar strings being played, or maybe like the way a piano sounded. Except nothing like any of that, really.

Aware of the urgency, Ellen put aside her usual frustration at not being able to categorize the sensation, and *watched*.

At first, she thought Bonnie was crafting a basic fixative, a cantrip the pups had adapted to keep evidence from getting washed away and the rest of the Cosa had adapted to a hundred less urgent purposes, the current flowing over the page, settling on the surface, blurring the image slightly before sharpening again. Then it was as though something in the rainbow *twitched*, and the sketch disappeared from the page, only to reappear again a split second later.

Ellen resurfaced from mage-sight, blinking dumbly across the table at the PUP. "You made it go somewhere. You...popped it somewhere else." She blinked again. "Oh my god, you recreated a fax machine."

Bonnie grinned, looking far too pleased with herself. The

trouble with current was that it interfered—sometimes dramatically—with anything that used electricity, especially in an office like this, where current was not only in use all the time, but they were constantly playing with new ways to manipulate and use it. But a fax machine *made* of current....

Ellen knew that she was powerful, but she also knew her power was a blunt hammer, and Wren's only slightly less so. Bonnie and the rest of the PUPs were surgeons, in comparison.

"So now it's in various hands, paws, and tentacles around the city, and we'll see what we'll see, hopefully fast. If these kids are ours, someone will have noted that they're missing. And if they're not, we've got spoons in those pots too."

"I feel like I should be doing something more..."

"What, running around in the middle of a blackout, trying to interrogate people who are all either sound asleep or shitfaced?"

"I... yeah? Or on the night shift, maybe." There were humans and fatae who woke with sunset, and slept at dawn. Ellen was reasonably sure she knew how to find them without Danny. Reasonably.

"Not a bad idea. Do you have any idea what you'd ask them?"

"...No." Ellen scowled down at the table, a sense of uselessness and hopelessness swamping her. "Danny always did that."

"You're still in mentorship, Ellen." Bonnie's voice went from mocking to gentle. "You're not expected to be able to take lead yet. So let my contacts do some of the work for us, while we—" She stopped, tilted her head and stared at Ellen. "You've got a tic. Did you have dinner? How's your core?"

"Yes, and not good," Ellen had to admit, her hand coming up to cover the twitch that had just started in her cheek. "Wren had me doing some trial runs yesterday, and I—"

Ellen stopped talking when she caught Bonnie's sideways

look, and made a face. "I know, I know. I'm supposed to draw down every night, just in case, but the blackout hit, and...."

"If you actually need wiring to pull down, I'm going to be deeply disappointed in your training," Bonnie said. "Come on. I could use a refill, too, before we do anything more. I think there's a coat in the closet that'll fit you, do you need a hat?"

Twenty minutes later, draped in what Ellen suspected was Venec's old leather jacket, since the shoulders were only a little loose around hers, they were standing on the northwestern edge of Central Park. Here, the lack of lights was eerie but not unnerving, the late night silence about normal. Neither of them wore watches, so Ellen had no way of telling what time it was, but the feel of the air suggested more time had gone by then she'd thought.

She waited for panic to flood her, the urgency to find Danny push against her ribcage again, but instead she just felt empty — and itchy, now that she let herself feel it, deep in her core. Not wanting to admit that Bonnie had been right, she tilted her head back and studied the spray of stars overhead. "Wow."

"Yeah, that's right, you're a city girl. We need to get you up north some time, watch a meteor shower. It's seriously awesome. But come on, get your ground on."

Bonnie had brought her to Central Park specifically for a reason, and that reason told Ellen that her mentor and the PUP had been exchanging notes about her training. Drawing down from a man-made source was a simple thing, once you understood what you were doing. Current than ran alongside man-made electricity was already thinned, tamed. Pulling current from an electrical storm— Wren Valere did that without hesitation, the wildness in the clouds suiting something in her. But Ellen's main skillset came from wild current, storm-current, and every time she reached out into the heart of a storm, a part of her braced against a possible vision, closing herself off instinctively. She might have a natural connection to storm-current, but that didn't mean she liked it, or wanted to encourage it.

But ley lines, the deep reserves of natural current that criss-crossed the planet? Ley lines soothed her. They were steady, consistent. Safe. She could let herself drop into the stone, deep into the earth, and bathe herself in the ancient current that circled and circled and never felt the need to get anywhere in particular, letting just enough slide into her bones, deep into her core, a painless drip until she was full.

And Central Park was home to one of those lines, not particularly powerful after all this time surrounded by Talent, but old and deep. Rumor had it, it had been what first attracted Madame to this place, back when it was all covered by woods, and no white person had set foot on the beach yet, not even lost Vikings.

Ellen reached out a tendril of her own current, and let it drift toward the key line, drawn by the greater strength there. There was a faint shudder, a soft *feeling* of a click, and the earth-current recognized her, allowed her tendril to pass and join.

Normally she would enjoy the sensation, like a cat enjoying a long stretch in a sunbeam. But if it was as late as Ellen now suspected, there was no time to take her time, no time to luxuriate. The clock had started ticking the moment she had the vision, and if she was going to be working without Danny, working at the level Bonnie operated at, she needed current, and she needed it quickly.

*Sorry,* she told the ley line, as though it had feelings that might be hurt by her abruptness. *Sorry,* and she *yanked* what she needed out of it, neon gravel sliding in her bones, scraping her raw before it was churned and smoothed and fitted into the swirl of current curled around her core.

Core didn't exist, not in a physical sense that a doctor could find, she'd been told, but it was how they were taught to visualize it, and she could *feel* it, a furnace of current wrapped around her spine and belly, sparking and soothing all at once.

Distantly, as she rose back to the surface, she could feel others tapping that same vein, deep and low, all across the city, spreading out into the suburbs, fading with distance. But they were slow compared to her, the skim of hummingbirds to her mosquito drinking deep.

Her eyes opened, only then realizing that she'd closed them, and her fingers slowly unclenched. From off to the side came Bonnie's voice, still that low, calm, soothing tone.

"You good?"

"Yeah." She looked at Bonnie, and for an instant could see the sharp neon haze that surrounded her, limning her auburn curls in a brighter purple, then it was gone.

"So." Ellen breathed deeply, feeling her core snap and fizz in satisfaction, tamed current pushing against her, making her feel almost impossibly awake and alert. "Now what?"

Bonnie hummed, staring up at the sky as though getting an answer from there. Whatever it was, though, it didn't seem to satisfy her. "Lacking any other leads? Now, we go find your wayward boss."

<hr>

I COULDN'T SEE.

That was my first thought, that I couldn't see, and for a heart-stopping second I was convinced that my eyes were gone, that I'd been blinded, because when you *know* that your eyes will adjust to even the faintest glimmer of starlight, pitch black isn't a concept you can understand.

But that's what I was in: pitch, immutable, darkness.

My second thought was that everything hurt. Not dying-pain, just aching sore hurt, like someone had taken a baseball bat to every inch of my skin. But not dying, that was good. Not dead was even better. *Deal with one thing at a time, Hendrickson. Can't see, so what* can *you do?*

My breathing was too fast, too harsh, and that was the first thing I dealt with. Calm it down, listen for other noises. Was I alone? Was I locked in a box, and if so, where was the air coming from?

No, abort that thought, don't think about there not being any air, don't think about....

Crap.

I forced myself to take a deep breath through my mouth, then exhale, then again until my brain stopped acting like a coked-up hamster. Then I took another breath, this time through my nose, nostrils flaring. Air. Not fresh, not pleasant, but there was a definite flow of air coming from somewhere, circulating through the space I was in. And it wasn't a small space, either, certainly not coffin-sized, which had been my first panic. I probably needed to stop watching horror movies.

*Get a fucking grip, Hendrickson.*

So I couldn't see worth a damn, but there was enough air to breathe, at least for the moment. And, I discovered the moment I tried to move, my arms and legs were tied to something behind my back. Not a pole, I determined, and not shackles. A frame, I decided. Wood, from the feel of it under my palms, and old wood at that, worn down by....

Well, probably by lots of people tied to it over the years, might as well be a pessimist. The other option was that someone had made their people-frame into a sanded and polished work of art, and honestly, that was even more disturbing.

So. Last I had a script, I was in a stranger's office in my own building, during a city-wide blackout, tracking an unknown but probably fatae-related glow, and had found an unknown but very dead body, probably but not confirmed human. And now I was in an unknown location, tied up and probably beat-up, based on the aches, and unable to see for jack shit, all the above likely courtesy of someone who did not have my continued happiness and well-being at heart.

This was why only idiots investigate without backup. Gun. My gun. Was it...?

I couldn't check my pockets, but there was no comforting weight there. So either my captors had taken it, or I'd dropped it when they dropped me. But I was pretty sure my pocket knife was still there.

Not that I could reach it. Ditto my phone, if it was even still in my pocket. And if there was any signal wherever the hell I was. No idea where I was, or when it was, or how to get loose.

All right, I knew what I didn't know. What did I know? *Put that allegedly trained professional brain to use, Hendrickson.*

I closed my eyes so I wouldn't be straining to see something where I couldn't, and concentrated.

Air, stale but circulating, check. What did it taste like? Cold. Cold but not wet, not briny... metallic? A little. Rotting wood? A little. Decaying flesh? Thankfully, no, and it was a sad fact of my life that I knew firsthand what that smelled like.

Tunnels. Underground, probably deep underground for this kind of silence, although when the subways started up again I might be able to hear the vibrations. Tunnels where no light could reach, but obviously someone had access.

How long had I been out? No way to tell. Was anyone around? Only one way to find out.

"Hooooooo" I called out, just barely under my breath, and listened to the echoes. Tall ceiling, and a long space in front of me, less so at my back. I was in a cul-de-sac of some sort. And the walls were stone, not wood or metal.

That last bit was less the echoes than my own gut instinct, but I felt pretty confident on that call.

Yesterday I would have sworn that I knew the tunnels under the city as well as any human, but this was new. So: deep, dark tunnels of unknown source, and a boglight glow that appeared and disappeared, and a dead human, who seemed to have died of natural if embarrassing causes but I hadn't had a chance to check the scene to say for sure. And someone or something possibly but not certainly related to the boglight, that cold-cocked me and left me tied up here. Had I gotten everything?

Not quite. I was now pretty certain that—unlike five seconds ago—I wasn't alone any more.

Add to the known facts: my captor or captors not only didn't need light to see, they were also silent-moving bastards. Not gnomes, then. That was good; gnomes and I had an uneasy relationship, at best. And it wasn't just the caves versus groves bullshit, despite what Rorani said: I disliked them for completely non-racist reasons. They had a bad habit of stealing preteens away from the aboveworld and not letting them go when the fun wore off. But they were also noisy bastards, move-ment-wise. All the metal in their diet didn't make for stealth.

Another mark in the unknown column, then.

Something brushed against me, running up my arm, and I would have flinched if I'd anywhere to go. The touch was papery-soft, and the smell, this close, was deeply unpleasant and completely unfamiliar.

"You have the advantage of me," I said, pleased that my voice came out without cough or hitch. "Danny Hendrickson. And you are?"

There was silence, then another pass of that papery-smooth skin over mine, down to my knuckles, and this time a full-body shudder took me. Warm-blooded, whatever my captors were, and very clearly fatae, not human, not with that smell. But what breed *were* they? I was wracking my brain, trying to remember the breeds that lived underground, were warm-blooded and smooth-skinned, smelled something like damp, moldy cotton, and didn't need even the slightest bit of light, but all I could come up with was Attack of the Mole People.

Definitely too many horror movies.

And then there were two, maybe three figures around me, from the displacement of air and where the sliding touches were coming from. Either that or a single figure with at least five arms. Dear brain, please stop trying to help.

But the multiples helped me identify the odor. Graves. This close, this many, and they smelled like old blood and graves, not wet cotton, and my mind decided to switch reels and go for *Nosferatu* instead. But there was no such thing as vampires in all the Cosa Nostradamus, no creatures that existed to feed on blood alone. Everyone knew that.

There was a puff of dry, putrid breath in my face, and a touch on my neck, just at the jugular, the heavy weight of what

have been the tip of a claw on my skin, and I was forced to accept that everyone might be wrong.

---

"WHAT CAN'T you translocate us to the office?"

"Because it takes energy," Bonnie said. "Hauling myself around is work, hauling another person around is twice as much work. And we may be topped-off with current right now, but splashing it around needlessly isn't going to do us any favors." Her voice softened, even as she stepped off the curb, raising her hand to summon a cab. "And it's not as though it's going to take up all that long to get to the office, under the circumstances."

Her hand twitched once, and a cab swerved around Columbus Circle, the lack of traffic lights making it appear like a yellow shark in murky waters. Bonnie grabbed the door, and Ellen was scrambling inside, giving the driver the address even as Bonnie crawled in after her.

They'd barely shut the door when the cabbie was off again. He clearly was enjoying the lack of traffic, or traffic lights, keeping just under a speed the cops would have no excuse not to pull him over for, barely slowing down to check for opposing traffic at street corners as they roared down West 59th. Ellen liked to think she'd become a properly jaded New Yorker, but riding the subway had nothing on this cab ride, and all she could do was hold on and glare enviously at Bonnie, who seemed as comfortably at home as if she were on her own sofa, not whipping around corners at 60 miles per hour.

Ellen had grown up avoiding cops as a matter of course, but at that moment she wouldn't have minded one pulling them over. But they made it to their destination without a ticket or an accident, and she was out the door and onto the sidewalk while Bonnie was still reaching for her wallet.

"Save the receipt," she said, when Bonnie joined her.

"Oh, I was planning on it," the PUP agreed, and gestured for Ellen to lead the way into the building.

The guard looked up this time when they walked in—a different guard, Ellen noted, and she pulled her ID from her pocket, shoving it across the desk for him to scan with his penlight.

"Elevators out," he said, handing it back to her and shoving the visitor's ledger at Bonnie for her to sign, his penlight barely enough light for her to make out the lines. "Don't break your neck on the stairs."

His concern was overwhelming. "Right, thanks."

In the stairwell, the fire door clunking shut behind them, the red lighting overhead was suddenly washed with a cooler white light. Ellen glanced at Bonnie, not surprised to see a stream of current wrapped around her hands emitting the glow. "You need to teach me how to do that."

"Valere's slacking, if she hasn't shown you already." She reached out with one glowing hand, and touched the back of Ellen's wrist. "It's just—no, Torres, this isn't the damn time," she muttered, and dropped her hand. "Later. Come on."

Ellen didn't remember going down the stairs taking this long—then again, she didn't remember much of her flight down, several hours earlier, only the feeling of bile in her throat and panic fluttering in her chest.

That flutter returned when they exited onto their floor. The hallway was silent, their steps echoing on the bare floor, knocking against closed and empty office doors. They, and the desk guard, might be the only people in the entire building.

The office door was wide open. Ellen couldn't remember not closing it, but she didn't remember not-closing it, either. When she hesitated, Bonnie pushed past her, going directly to the back office. By the time Ellen joined her, Bonnie had tweaked the current-light to shine up at the ceiling, redirecting illumination into the entire room rather than a specific angle, much more useful than a flashlight would have been. Ellen made note to *definitely* get the cantrip the other woman used, then turned her attention to the inner office, trying to see anything that she might have missed before.

"You're sure he was here."

Ellen didn't bother to respond to that with a glare, much less words. Yes, she was sure. He'd been in the office when he called her: she knew the sounds of him moving around, the wheels of his chair on the hardwood floor, the crackle of the phone lines because there was so much interference from the antennas on the building across the street. She could identify the sound of Danny in his office the way she knew the subdued hum of electricity in Wren's building, familiar and soothing.

She didn't feel soothed at all, right now. "He was working on the filing," she said, touching the papers left out on the wooden desk. "He hates filing, but he won't let me do it. Says it would take longer to teach me the system than to do it himself."

"Hendrickson is borderline OCB," Bonnie said. "Obsessive compulsive bossy. Trust me, I know the type."

"Mmmm." Ellen hadn't planned on going there, not having

an actual death wish, but given the opening and the distraction…"And how goes that?"

"Everything's great this week," Bonnie said. "Ask me again next week."

Bonnie Torres and her boss were either the love story of the century, or the soap opera of the year. Or probably both, considering how much they argued and how often Bonnie announced to anyone who would listen that she was done with relationships forever, but somehow never seemed to actually break it off. Pietr had 7-2 odds that they'd have a kid and she'd still be insisting she was a free agent in the delivery room.

"He was filing," Ellen said again, picking up one of the folders and then placing it back down again in the same spot. "And then he stopped. Mid-act?"

"He's not easily distracted, our Danny." Bonnie had known him longer than Ellen had, if not so closely.

"No. And something did distract him, because otherwise he'd have put his laptop away." Security issues aside, her boss was the kind of guy who washed out the coffee pot before he went home, every night without fail. It wasn't OCD, he just hated the taste of stale coffee. "What could distract him?"

"A noise?" Bonnie suggested, looking around as though some echo of the sound might be visible. With Bonnie's current-skills, it might have been, Ellen didn't know.

"Sound, maybe. Or a sight?"

Bonnie turned to her, frowning, the current-light making her skin seem even paler than usual. "It's a blackout, after sundown, and Danny's not Talent, so there was no light to see anything, unless he took a flashlight with him."

"He's not Talent, but he's not human, either," Ellen said. "Not all, anyway."

"Oh." Bonnie put two fingers to her lips, and huffed a laugh. "I forget that, sometimes. Fauns have good night vision?"

"Like a cat's, Danny said once. Or comparable. If there's moonlight, he can see by it, mostly."

"Moon wouldn't have risen then. But the security lights?"

Ellen shrugged, having run out of useful information. "I don't know if it would be enough to read by, red light and black print are a crap combination, but if something moved, he'd —"

She got up, and turned slowly in a three hundred and sixty degree circle, scanning the room until her gaze fell on the window. The window that had no shades, no curtains. Danny usually sat at the desk, here, slanted sideways so his back wasn't entirely to the window…. But if he'd been filing?

She stepped forward: it was two strides for her to reach the filing cabinet, so maybe about the same for Danny, who was only slightly shorter than she was—about the same, in his boots. "There couldn't have been anything in here, not if he was caught by surprise." And if he had been, there would have been some disarray, some sign one of them would have noted. "But he'd have to pass by the window. If he saw something out here?"

She tried to imagine being at the desk, at the file cabinet. This high up, what could catch his eye? The window looked out over the narrow courtyard, and a sliver of the street, but without half-hanging out the window it was hard to see down. But across….

There were three windows she could look directly into, from here. That side of the building mirrored their own, meaning three offices that also didn't have shades drawn.

She paused, imagining the scene the way Danny'd taught her to, blocking out the unknown, moving what was known into place, setting the scenario and letting possible outcomes play out, one after another.

"Come on," she said, already heading out the door, assuming that Bonnie would follow.

The other side of the building was just as still and empty,

although Ellen would have sworn it felt colder, somehow. She didn't say that to Bonnie, though, only taking a minute to get her bearings, then leading the PUP down the hallway to the first of the three offices she'd seen from Danny's window.

The first one they checked hosted a graphics designer; the office itself was empty, the door locked and showing no signs of having been picked previously, no evidence of trouble inside. Even the chairs had been squared up evenly before whoever it was left for the night.

The second office had no sign on the door, the door itself unlocked, and—based on the sheen of dust visible when Bonnie shone the current-light inside—nobody had been inside in weeks.

The third office had a small brass plate that said a CPA by the name of D. Kovar worked there. And occasionally slept there, from the state of the loveseat shoved up against one wall and the laundry strewn across the floor.

"Either someone's messier than I am, or —a struggle?"

"Maybe." Bonnie made a 'stay there' gesture, and Ellen, well-trained, froze on the spot. The PUP did something with another strand of current, weaving a pale blue net that settled over the floor in front of the clothing, dimmed, and then disappeared.

Footprints appeared, two sets, and an oddly elongated shape sprawled across the floor.

Ellen had to remind herself to keep breathing. "Is that a body?" Was. Was where a body had been. The current showed what *had* been there.

"Mmmm." Bonnie stepped around it, studying it carefully. "Too short to be Hendrickson," she decided, and Ellen let out a breath of relief.

"But who? And where did it go? And where's Danny?" She scanned the room as though he might suddenly appear, and then her breath caught. "Oh."

Without waiting for Bonnie's all-clear, she stepped forward, skirting the still-glowing prints and the body outline, and bent down to pick up the gun she'd seen glinting in the current-light. An actual gun, not the evidence of one.

"It's his," she said, something turning and twisting in her gut, current gone ice-cold. "It's Danny's."

---

THE CLAW-TIP RESTED against my skin for I don't know how long. It's hard to tell time when you're wrapped in pitch dark, an unknown distance below-ground. All the tricks I had for figuring distance, time, location—all useless. Time boiled down to that single sharp point scraping across my jugular, something deeply unpleasant leaning into my personal space in a way I didn't enjoy.

You can't make a sarcastic rejoinder to a threat that isn't talking. That isn't making any noise at all. I tried not to breathe through my nose again, and let my muscles go as slack as I could, to be of as little interest, as little threat as possible.

Eventually, the *creatures*—and I hated using that term, but not knowing what breed it was or even if they were a known breed at all, I didn't know what else to tag them in my brain—left. Not that I heard them go. I was aware of the sharpness now resting just under my left ear, and then suddenly it was gone, the pressure, the presence, all of it.

But they didn't leave me there alone. There was heavy breathing in the space with me now, the thick, slobbery kind of heavy breathing you only get when someone's trying very hard not to cry. Or panic.

Unwilling guests, then. We'd have that much on common, at least. "Hey there," I said, pitching my voice into what my old partner called the calm-and-console mode. "Hey."

The noise stopped on a choking noise and the pull-through-the-nose thing people do when they're surprised.

"Who…. Who's there? Someone's there?"

"Who are you?"

Two voices, speaking over each other. One male, one female. Human, I'd lay odds. Both young, from the sound of it. Not preteen, but they didn't carry the pseudo-authority of being legal-and-adult yet, either. I'd gotten good at estimating shit like that.

"Did they hurt you?" Important things first.

"I…not yet?" The girl spoke first.

"Knocked around a little," the boy said, reluctantly. He'd fought, and lost, and didn't want to admit it even now, tied up in the darkness. Sixteen, seventeen at most. Kids. I needed to get them out of here.

"You're tied up?" Maybe our unpleasant hosts had underestimated them, or run out of rope. Maybe.

"Hands and ankles," the boy said, sounding disgusted now, more than scared.

"We're back to back, on some kind of pole." There was a grunt, then the sound of a body moving. "I think I can get a hand free, though."

"That's gonna hurt," the boy said to her. He could see what she was doing? No, they'd been tied up together, he could feel whatever she was trying.

"I don't think they tied us up for milk and cookies," she shot back, over the sound of another grunt.

Whistling in the dark, literally. But I could use that. More, *they* could use that. Sass would keep your feet on the ground when everything else was gone, that's why it surfaced under stress. I had a flash of my old partner lecturing me, his nightstick tucked under some teenaged kid's chin to keep him still. "A perp sasses you, boy, he ain't dissing you. He's trying to show he's tough, he's strong. So you have two choices: you can beat him down and show him he ain't so tough, or you can respect the strength under the sass, and work with it, and nobody has to get bloody."

Hopefully, nobody would get bloody this time, either. "If you can get even a finger free," I told her, "do it."

There was silence, then the harsh exhale of someone bracing themselves to do something they knew would be painful, and a series of small, pained grunts. I realized that she was dislocating something, probably her shoulder, maybe her elbow. Her companion hadn't been kidding: that had to hurt like hell. Gymnast, maybe, or she'd taken up yoga young, or was just naturally agile, but either way after a few minutes of that she gave a short, triumphant bark. "Left arm free." There was a pause, then, less triumphant, she admitted, "I can't do anything with it though, can't reach my right side or my feet, there's something around my middle. More rope, I think."

"Can you reach…boy, what's your name?"

"Paul."

"Can you reach Paul? Work on his ties?"

"I… yeah, I think so." There was another silence, then Paul let out a muted yelp. "Careful where you're poking, Lisa!"

"Sorry not sorry," she said, singsong, and I updated my evaluation: siblings. "Can you shift at all, now?"

There were a series of muffled grunts, I presumed from Paul trying to shift within his bindings. If they were like mine, and he didn't have his sister's flexibility, he'd be able to twist his torso, but not much more. Apparently, that was enough.

"I can touch the ropes around his arms," Lisa said. "Just barely though. And it hurts like hell. But there aren't any knots I can find. Ugh, what are these made of?"

I'd already asked myself that, and run through a series of possible answers, based on the smooth, almost oily texture of the bindings. I didn't want to tell her what I'd determined, though. "There isn't any give at all?"

"No. In fact, I think they got tighter." She sounded pissed about that.

I lifted my head a little at that, like I'd gotten a whiff of fresh air. "It was reactive?"

I could practically hear the scowl in her voice. "I don't know what that means."

"It means the more you struggle, the tighter it's going to grip."

"Oh." There was another noise, and a grunt of discomfort. "Yeah."

"And when you slipped your arm free, the binding around it kind of slipped free?"

"Yeah," she said again. "Slid, actually. Gross."

Oh, if only she knew. My brain left that alone, though, working on possible hacks. "All right, so here's what you need to do. Don't tug or pull at the rope. Scratch it."

"Scratch?"

"Like you would a scab."

"Ick."

"Don't get girly," Paul said, sounding slightly panicked. "Get it *off* me."

It took longer than any of us were comfortable with, every ear cocked for a hint that our captors were returning set against the steady scratch-scritch-scritch of her fingernails. I tried not to think about how fortunate it was that she'd been the one able to slide free, because my nails were trimmed close, and I would bet everything in my wallet Paul's were the same, if not bitten down even lower. Even when they didn't go for talons, the females of every species seemed to pay more attention to their nails. I wondered idly if it was because they were vain, or they were aware that nails were weapons?

Probably both, I decided, as Paul let out a soft noise that sounded like triumph, mixed with panicked relief. "Right arm's free," he announced, and I could hear him shaking it loose, probably trying to work out a cramp. "What now?"

"Do the same to your left arm, you idiot," Lisa said, and from the scratching noise that started up again immediately, I presumed she was doing the same to her own. Two of them working on their own arms was more efficient than one of them getting free and then trying to free the other, but it made my own skin itch, hanging there waiting, unable to do anything at all.

It was our luck that they'd been tied up to each other. I also suspected I'd been tied more thoroughly; whatever our captors were, they'd probably made the mistake every other breed, including humans, did, underestimating the threat of a half-grown teenager versus an adult male. The young of any species are terrifying, trust me. Babysitting should be required training for evil overlords.

"Arms free," Lisa announced in a breathless whisper. "Going to try for my legs, but I don't know…"

"Do a little at a time, then lift yourself up again," I told them. If she spent too long with her head bent that low, she'd get dizzy, and I had no idea if they'd actually been injured, if she had a concussion, anything that might affect her balance and blood pressure. I took an inhale through my nose, relieved when I didn't smell fresh blood anywhere. Whatever damage we'd taken, it was dried and crusted, now.

Internal injuries would have to wait until were free and out of here, to check. Hopefully we'd get that far, where it would matter.

They'd both set back to work, the scratch-scritch-scritch making me tense with the need to tell them to go faster, and the knowledge that they were already working as fast as they could. If they could reach my knife…. well, if they could they'd already be free, and I didn't know how these pseudo-ropes would react to a sharp edge, anyway. With our luck so far, it would scream for help, or something, like a rope out of "Jack and the Beanstalk." Was it the Beanstalk legend that had the talking rope? My brain was fuzzier than I'd thought, if I couldn't remember that.

"What's your name, anyway?" Lisa, her voice sounding stronger than before, though still low. Someone had told her that whispers carried better than low voices, and she'd remembered. Good kid.

"Danny," I said. "Danny Hendrickson."

"I'm Lisa Mays, that's my cousin Paul. You have any idea what it was that grabbed us, Danny Hendrickson? Because I'm pretty sure they weren't human."

Her voice was calm, but there was an undercurrent to it I'd heard before, the desire to be reassured and told that they were being silly, that they'd misread the signs, had been hallucinating, that of course there was nothing in the world beyond what they'd always known.

I thought about lying to her, then figured the odds of them getting out of here alive on a lie, versus knowing what they were up against.

"Yeah, I'm pretty sure they weren't, either."

There was a pause that felt longer than it probably was, then, "Are you?"

I laughed, not having expected that. I probably should have. "Former NYPD at your service," I said, which wasn't really an answer, but they both took it for one, based on the sigh of relief Paul let out. They were still young enough that my having been a cop gave them comfort.

I wished I were still that young.

There was a thump, and a muttered curse. "I'm free," Lisa announced. "Can't... ow. Gimmie a minute, though."

Considering how numb my limbs were, I could imagine it would take her more than a minute or two to be able to stand and walk without pain. But tension was creeping back up my spine: we'd been left alone long enough, odds were that someone would be coming to check on us, and like Lisa, I was pretty sure milk and cookies weren't on the menu.

"Sooner would be better," I warned her, and was rewarded by a shifting of darkness within the darkness, less seen than sensed, as she crawled toward the sound of Paul's scratching.

Between the two of them, they seemed to make better progress, and it wasn't as long before I heard another thump, and a muffled curse that told me they'd broken him free. But before I could call them over, I sensed something nearby: the smooth, nearly soundless pace of invisible ninja unknowns.

"They're coming," I said, and both kids stilled immediately. "You're only going to get one chance. The moment they come into range they'll know you're down, they can see in this gloom. So you need to be ready and go. No hesitation, no stopping, rush right by them and don't stop for anything."

"But...you...?"

I appreciated the concern but it was pointless. I was still tied, hand and foot. "There's no time. Head up, every chance you get. We're deep underground, so up is your best chance."

The not-sound came closer, and I took a deep breath, ready to shout, scream, whatever it took to get our captors' attention for the second or three they were going to need.

"Danny..." Lisa, agonizing, guilty.

"Don't fucking waste time," I told her, and then started to howl.

---

Ellen was not going to cry. She wasn't going to cry, and she wasn't going to swear, and she wasn't going to throw anything. But Ellen very much wanted to do all three of those things.

Instead, she slid Danny's gun into her jacket pocket, the weight of it throwing her off-balance, and watched while

Bonnie used current to erase any sign of their having been in the office.

"Should we call the police?"

Bonnie gave her a side eye. "Really?"

Ellen shrugged. "We don't know that it was Cosa business."

The PUPI had been formed to deal with crimes by and against the Cosa Nostradamus, the kind of thing you couldn't explain to the local cops. But Danny had been a cop, once.

And this...

"He's an adult, El. And there's no evidence that he's done anything other than go walkabout. You think they're going to have time in the middle of a massive blackout, to worry about one missing PI?"

"But—" Ellen had no response to that. Bonnie was right, and worse, the idea of going back to her apartment and waiting for him to show up again, waiting for news to come about the missing teenagers—or worse, another vision—to come, seemed the worst of all possible options.

"Let's get out of here."

Another slightly less unnerving cab ride uptown, and they found Lou, the PUP's office manager, already at the desk, a faint white glow of current-light illuminating the front room.

"Why in god's name are you even here?" Bonnie asked, taking Ellen's borrowed jacket and hanging it with her own in the front closet.

"Carly called me, because hey, who needs sleep?" Lou handed over a sheet of paper. "You asked about this?"

Bonnie took a quick look at the sheet, then handed it to Ellen. "Any of those names look familiar?"

Ellen took it, squinting in the current-light. Eleven names, male and female, written in block print. "No."

"Those are all the kids of the age and basic description described, currently known to be missing in this area. It would be in this area?"

Ellen nodded. "We think so. Every vision I've had that we've been able to follow up on, it's been within fifty miles, more or less. It's like it knows where I am."

"It?" Bonnie looked intrigued, then shook her head. "A discussion we're going to have another time. None of the names strike a chord?"

"It doesn't work like that." Ellen's voice was sharp, but she didn't apologize. Bonnie and the other PUPs had seen her visions in action, but she'd never really discussed it with them, not with anyone except Wren. And Danny. "There are clues, things that tell us where to look, and then we...dig."

"But you didn't get any clues from the vision?"

"No. Just...dark. And they're dirty. That's it." She tried to remember more, regretted now that she hadn't written it all down when she should have. Was there something she'd missed, so worried about Danny? Panic fluttered, and she forced it down. Wren said that panic got more people killed than bullets ever did.

"Dark and dirty. Lou, do we have anyone on the string who's good with dirt of the actual dirt kind?"

"Alan. Geology major, did time in the oil business —" and she pronounced it 'awl bidness,' in an exaggerated drawl. "You want I should wake him up?

"Please," Ellen said, when Bonnie indicated with a glance that it was her decision. "It was wet dirt, muddy, and...." Her gaze unfocused. "Not brown? Not black. Red? Like clay."

"Clay, check. Local sources thereof. Dark less helpful, it's fucking dark everywhere."

"Oh, and we need to know more about the guy who had the lease on this office," and she scrawled something on the pad on the desk. "Come on, El, if Lou is here, there's coffee on."

The reminder that it was well past 1 am, meaning she'd been awake for over eighteen hours, made coffee suddenly the most appealing thing in the world.

The ability to light up the office didn't extend to making any of the heavily-warded electronics work, apparently, and they didn't use laptops. "Batteries are delicate," Bonnie said when she saw her glancing at the desktop computers. "It's why cell phones are so easy to fry."

Ellen licked her lips, drumming her fingers on the table in front of her. It was dark wood, gloss-finished, and made a solid noise under her hand. "We didn't grab Danny's laptop. I have the password, I could get it, maybe there's something useful on it?"

"You think you could yank it here without frying it?"

That, Ellen thought sourly, was the real question. Getting it here in one piece was pointless if it was then useless. And Danny would kill her when he got back.

"Okay, so no computer. No questioning. No...what *can* I do?" Her frustration swelled, forcing her body up and out of the chair, even as she realized that there was no room to pace in the conference room, barely large enough for the table and four chairs around it. "Kids are in trouble, Danny's missing, and I'm not doing anything!"

"Ellen. Sit. Down."

Ellen was back in her chair before she realized her body was moving. Bonnie was still in her own chair, leaning back but not looking at all relaxed.

"This is the part that sucks," the PUP went on. "When you've got a case but you don't have leads. But running after maybes and mights in the middle of a blackout is not smart time management. There are people out there who are chasing down possibilities for us. Our job is to be ready to go when they come in. Okay?"

"That's not how Danny does it."

"That's because Danny is a throwback cowboy with a two-person operation, and he's too stubborn to ask for help."

All of that was entirely true. Ellen went back to drumming

her fingers on the table, as though the rhythm would somehow make thing happen more quickly.

"I screwed up. I didn't write down the vision, I was too focused on getting to Danny."

"Wait." Bonnie sat forward in her chair, her gaze meeting Ellen's. "Why were you focused? Did you know something was wrong?"

"I..." she thought back, amazed that it was only hours before, not days. "No. But he'd called me, when the power went out. When he was in the office. I'd told him I was planning to stay in, but after I hung up the phone I was, I don't know, restless?"

"Not unusual in a blackout," Bonnie said. "We're used to feeling the thrum of the city, all that current being generated; having it suddenly disappear can freak us out a little, even subconsciously."

"Oh. Yeah, maybe that explains it. But I just started walking, and found myself outside the office when the vision hit. You don't think it's connected?"

"I think we don't know enough about how your visions work to even venture a guess. Sorry." But Ellen could see the gears churning in Bonnie's brain: the PUP might not have a theory yet, but she would, eventually. Ellen was just as willing to leave it in her hands.

"I don't—"

The door opened, and Lou stuck her head in. "Got info for you on David Kovar, CPA. No known enemies on the radar, no contacts within the Cosa that we can find, and if they were there, we'd have found them, and no reason so far as the cops or the gossip chain know for Anon to drag his bloody body parts off to places unknown."

"And Danny? Did he have a connection to Danny?" "Nothing on the radar there, either."

"So your theory is probably right—he saw something, and

went to poke his extremely twitchy nose into it. Damn it, Hendrickson.... You," and Bonnie poked a finger in Ellen's direction. "You won't ever do anything without backup, right?"

"I called you, didn't I?"

"All right." That seemed to be enough to appease her. "We're currently on hold for anything new about the kids; either wait for your boss to come back on his own, or we go hunting. You know him better than me, these days: what's your call?"

Ellen looked at her fingertips, candles, lit to conserve current, flickering odd shadows around the room. "If he could come back, he would have. Or called my home line, or Sergei's line, and left a message." He hadn't done any of those things. "If he couldn't, that means he's in trouble. Real trouble. And probably having to do with whatever did the damage in Kovar's office. " She could see it in her mind, what must have happened. Danny had been working, had looked out the window at exactly the wrong moment, and seen something that made him go investigate, armed.

Alone.

And then what? Had he been injured, dragged off, too? Or had he followed under his own power? She could imagine him doing that, but.... He would have left word, somehow.

She refused to think that he was dead and dumped somewhere. She couldn't think about that, or she'd curl up under the desk and not be able to function.

"Shake the bushes we can reach," she said. "That's what Danny would say."

"And that would mean what, exactly?" Bonnie managed not to sound exasperated, but there was a line of tension strung through her words that suggested it.

"Same thing you've been preaching to me. Play to our strengths. Use the contacts we have." A vague, very thin plan was forming in her mind, and it would worry her how thin it was, if she had time to look at it too long. So—contrary to her nature but wholly in line with Danny's—she didn't. "Keep reaching out to Talent, especially the Talent who would be out and about on a night like this. The skulkers and lurkers, the ones who normally cause problems, not solve them."

"That's more Wren's style, maybe we should call her..."

"Wren's on a job. And she doesn't poke, she goes in and grabs. We need to ask questions, not intimidate people." Ellen was fiercely fond of her mentor, but Wren Valere only had two modes: invisible, and terrifying. Neither of those would be useful just now.

Bonnie made a face that said she wasn't going to disagree with that assessment. "Skim the sewers, check. It's almost dawn, I'll haul everyone in. And where will you be, while I'm doing that?"

Ellen inhaled, held it a moment, and looked up at the inky shadows of the ceiling before exhaling slowly. "Talking to the fatae."

---

ELLEN HAD SPENT MOST of her life being told that there were no such thing as...well, pretty much anything other than humans. That the things she saw in the corner of her eye, heard in the dark, or early hours of the morning, weren't real. Imagination, they told her. Crazy, they muttered. And of all the things that had haunted her, growing up not knowing that she was Talent, the half-seen images of fantastical creatures had been the most disturbing.

The few years she'd been aware of the Cosa Nostradamus, the time she'd spent *working* for someone who wasn't a hundred percent human, the fear had been wiped away, replaced—mostly—with awe that these creatures were real.

But that awe never stopped her from being very cautious around them.

There were high-res Talent and low-res, law-abiding and less so, but all Talent, far as anyone had ever been able to determine, were human. There were certain rules that held true for all humans, in terms of what they wanted, needed, could be held to—or they would suffer consequences.

The crash course Ellen had gotten on the fatae, the non-human members of the Cosa Nostradamus, said that there were at least thirty-seven distinct breeds, or species, who stayed still long enough to be counted and named, not including demon, who might or might not be a distinct breed; the jury was still out on them. Thirty-seven, most but not all of whom interacted with their human counterparts, some of whom would be just as pleased to *eat* their human counterparts, if it weren't for the censure that would follow.

And at least half of those thirty-seven, in some form or another, had enclaves in New York City or the suburbs surrounding the city. Danny had contacts in most of them, but Ellen.... She swallowed, and firmed her chin. They knew her, some of them. They knew she was Danny's protégé, and Wren's mentee, even if they didn't know her for herself, yet. It would be enough.

It would have to be enough.

She considered asking Bonnie or Lou for a translocation directly to her first destination, but they were both busy, and some fatae took it the wrong way if you just appeared on their doorstep without proper warning. So she did it old school, and went down to the street to hail a cab.

It was still a few hours until dawn, but Ellen thought she could tell the difference in the sky; the stars seemed dimmer, the moon higher but less radiant. A cyclist sped past her, tiny red and white lights blinking as they went somewhere in a hurry, before one of the fare-hungry cabs glided to a stop at the curb.

"Hell of a thing, huh?" This cabbie seemed slightly more cautious than the one earlier, although he too swerved through an intersection, barely checking to see if anyone was coming the other way. Ellen hadn't taken many cabs, she thought maybe they were always like this? "I mean," he went on when she didn't respond, "they're saying maybe no power until tonight, can you believe it? Fucking ConEd, man. They never get their shit together."

"Mmmm." Ellen tried not to dig her fingers into the upholstery as the cab slid around another corner. Another sign that morning was coming: two busses lumbered along the right hand side, and a few other cabs and hired cars slid alongside, but the usual press of cars on the avenue seemed absent.

"People stay home, when it's all-dark," the cabbie said, clearly noticing her gaze via the rear view mirror. "Sun comes up, then people'll think about maybe going to work, but mostly we're gonna have a snow day, so ta speak. Mayor'll probably tell all non-essentials to stay home. We make out like bandits when the subways aren't running."

He grinned, and she noted that his teeth were oddly spaced, and a little too sharp for human comfort. Her gaze instantly flickered to the door handles, and her shoulders relaxed only when she saw the handles were intact, the locks unengaged.

"Relax girlie. You pay your fare square and don't mess up my meter, we've got no problems," the kelpie said. "Everyone's got to make a living, right?"

"Right" she said, leaning back with studied casualness. He had a TLC medallion, giving him the right to pick up fares; if passengers disappeared too often, they would have yanked it by now. Right? And he'd pegged her for Talent, or at least not a Null, so they were on relatively even terms.

Ellen heard a giggle escape her, and waved away the

cabbie's quick look of concern. It was just…. She was heading to a den of non-human iniquity, driven by a creature out of one of the darker fairy tales, to try and rescue her boss, who was part-faun, from an unknown danger. And people used to think she was crazy because she had *visions*?

Getting herself back under control, she asked, "You hear any rumor about the cause of the blackout? Anyone pointing any fingers?"

"For once, not a peep," he said, and both of them knew they weren't talking about generators blowing up or power lines going down. "This could be a totally natural whoopsie. Or maybe someone just fell asleep at the switch. Sometimes bad news is just, you know, the universe shitting on us."

Cabbie philosophy 101.

"And nothing else happening—nobody flipping out?"

"You mean, other than you people, like a bunch of addicts cut off at the nip?"

She made a helpless shrug: you didn't argue with someone you were trying to get information from, she'd known that even before coming to work for Danny.

"There was some squalling over by the east docks, 'bout midnight or so," he said thoughtfully. "But they're always squalling over something or 'nother, ever since they put those nets up. But you want to know about fusses, don't go to Lala's. Go ask Alice."

She blinked at him. "Who?"

Alice lived along the lower stretch of the Harlem River Drive, in what looked like a cave made of tumbled-down concrete. Ellen made her way through the darkness with the aid of the current-light Bonnie had quickly taught her, thankful for the fact that the pathway was cleared and even. Whoever or whatever Alice was, she clearly didn't mind visitors.

Hopefully, she didn't mind letting the visitors leave, either. But a quick ping to Bonnie to let her know where she was and what she was doing—and with whom—left Ellen confident that, worst case scenario, the Pups would come after her. Eventually.

Having both members of Sylvan Investigations go missing would just be bad for business.

She stood outside the cave entrance, and hesitated. There wasn't exactly a doorbell, or door knocker. Or a door to knock on. "Hello?"

The response was a thin but strong voice, echoing from within. "Come in, come in, no reason to stand outside."

"Said the spider to the fly," Ellen couldn't resist, and the cackle that replied told her that Alice had damn good hearing, too.

It took a few steps to get past the crumbled, unpleasant facade, but once inside, the concrete cave seemed more comfort- able than Ellen's own apartment: thick rugs were layered on the ground, insulating it, and there were several lanterns casting a better glow than her own current-light, so she extinguished it, curling the remaining current back into her core.

She could hear traffic distantly, the rumble of occasional trucks and emergency vehicles, she thought, and the occasional low toll on a foghorn on the East River, just a few hundred yards away. During rush hour it might get noisy, but now it was an almost pleasant white noise. There was a shadow at the back, perched on a sofa. Angular, too angular and narrow to be even the skinniest human, but Ellen still wasn't prepared for what she saw, drawing closer.

There was nothing about Alice that could have passed for human even in a crowd. From the silver-green body to the over-sized head topped with bent-over feelers—antenna?—she was clearly one hundred percent fatae. But the expression on her face was perfectly readable, despite the compound eyes and a rigid mouth: she was amused.

"I'm not going to eat you, girl."

"Good. I'm told I'm occasionally hard to swallow."

The soft clacking of forelegs was, Ellen, thought, the laughter she had heard earlier. "Only people who come here are people who need listening to. What do you need to tell me, girl?"

Ellen shook her head. "I need to know what you've heard, what others might have said."

Alice settled further on her sofa, tilting her head. "And you think I know those things?"

"I was told that if there was anything happening in this city, you would know. Second only to Madame." And, the cabbie had told her, safer to bargain with. The Great Worm of Manhattan did not make cheap bargains.

"Speak to me, then. Tell me the things you need someone to hear."

Ellen thought about trying to correct Alice again, then decided the fatae knew damn well what she meant, and was either being difficult, or really couldn't respond any other way. "My boss went missing tonight, and there was—" There hadn't been a body, actually, just the place where one had been. "And someone's probably dead. We're trying to track down what happened, if anyone saw or heard anything. If any of the fatae heard or saw anything, or were part of anything."

Alice just sat there, and Ellen had a moment of despair, that they were really going to just *listen* to her, and not actually offer anything. And meanwhile, time was wasting—why had she listed to the cabbie?

Finally, Alice shifted, forelegs touching each other to make a dry, scratchy sound. "Why would the doings and deaths of your boss be of interest or concern to the fatae?"

Ellen licked her lips, and hoped to hell that his reputation had spread this far, into this corner of the city. "My boss is Danny Hendrickson."

"Ahhhhhhhh." The forelegs stilled, and a secondary pair took up the clacking. Ellen didn't know what that signified. "The meddler. The mender."

Ellen raised her eyebrows and cocked her head to the side, but had to admit those were two words that summed him up pretty well, yeah.

"And you tell me he has gone missing. Or dead."

"Missing, in the darkness." She wasn't going to believe he was dead; belief was half a step away from being truth. The body they saw had to be the missing CPA he'd gone to investigate. "With no warning, no note. And left his gun behind." Ellen wondered at how the words spilled out: she knew she had trust issues, even with humans, but this... Alice, drew confidences from her in a way even Bonnie and Wren didn't.

"And you go after him."

Ellen blinked. "Of course." It was as simple as that.

All four legs now rubbed together, creating a sound like shallow water rushing over rocks, echoing against the concrete walls, disappearing into the muffling effect of the carpets underfoot.

"The Hendrickson. There are few who know him, here, who would harm him. Even those who hate him know he has too many friends, too many bindings, otherwise. But there are those in the darkness who know nothing, care for nothing. And the darkness below is as the darkness above tonight. Look there, if you would find him, I think, yes."

A hint, a direction—at least, Ellen thought it was a direction. "Where?"

"In the caves below the tunnels, the deeps below the shallows. Where the shadows live, but do not go." When Ellen couldn't hold back her irritated sigh, there was a moment of that soft whispering laughter-sound again. "Did you think this would be easy, little girl?"

"I live in hope," Ellen said. "Just once."

Caves below the tunnels, below the shallows. It wasn't "Seventh Avenue at 57th street, ring the bell and ask for Charlie," but she'd been over the city enough times with Danny on cases, during training runs with Wren, that she thought she knew where to begin.

---

*I don't like it*

*I don't like anything about any of this*

Pinging didn't carry exact words, but Bonnie's worry and Ellen's exasperation were palpable things, carried on short bursts of current. But even that was taking too much time.

*You follow your leads, I'll follow mine. I'll be in touch.* And with that, Ellen broke contact, pressing her current down into her core and telling it to be still. It simmered and shimmered, but quieted, like a lake after a motorboat went through. If Bonnie tried to ping her again, she was concentrating too much to hear it. She'd pay for that later, probably. But even at her most pissed off, the PUP had nothing on Wren's partner Sergei when he was irritated, so Ellen figured she'd survive.

"So go on," she told herself, pulling the loaner jacket more tightly around herself, well-aware that the chill she felt wasn't from the night air.

"In the caves below the tunnels," Alice had said. Gnomes lived in the tunnels underneath and alongside the subways, mostly the older ones, the ones that went deep into the ground, so you had to haul up three flights of stairs, or take an elevator down. Danny had never taken Ellen down into gnome territory —he had some kind of running feud with them—but he'd shown her the major entrances, in case she ever needed to know. They mostly lived out in Brooklyn and Queens, since the Bronx didn't have many tunnels to start with, and Staten Island didn't have any. And Manhattan—after they rebuilt most of the

A, C, E and R stations in lower Manhattan, word had it that most of the fatae living there had moved out.

Gentrification was a bitch for everyone.

But some were known to linger in a few spots in Manhattan, too stubborn to move. Considering they'd been hauling a solid, six-something male who couldn't weigh much under 150, she'd started with the spot she knew closest to the office, one of the three in Manhattan proper. The 2nd Avenue subway had torn up the area while it was being dug, but they'd also re-opened the tunnels originally laid down in 1929, before the Great Depres- sion put an end to those plans.

"In the deeps below the shallows, she said." The 2nd Avenue

line wasn't as deep as the A, across town. And it was newer, still being built when the exodus happened, so that would've appealed to fatae who didn't like to mingle with humans above-ground, right?

It wasn't the best leap of logic, maybe, but it felt right to Ellen. And Danny and Wren both told her, over and over, that her gut was to be trusted.

It was, Ellen guessed, about an hour before dawn. She'd been awake now for almost twenty hours, nearly six of them in the dark, both literally and figuratively. Her eyes were gritty and sore from exhaustion, but the few 24-hour bodegas in this neighborhood had probably shuttered the moment the power went down, and the single street cart she saw was selling bagels and muffins for the oh-god-early shift, but spread his hands in apology when she asked about coffee, and all the sodas he had were warm. She took one anyway, grimacing at the taste. She bought a chocolate muffin, too, and shoved it into her pocket for later.

The subway entrance was darker than was comfortable, like the toothless mouth of something rising from the concrete, and Ellen had to steel herself to take that first step onto the stairs.

"Ridiculous," she told herself, forcing her voice to above a whisper. "You run up and down stairs like this a couple times a day, and never think anything of it."

But then, even late at night or early in the morning, there were other people around, and warm, welcoming lights to show the way. She was the only person visible or audible, and the steps now leading down into the subway were dark and too-quiet, so still that she could hear the scurrying of the rats along the rails, the darkness encouraging them to forage more brazenly. She concentrated, remembering the cantrip Bonnie had taught her earlier that night. When she thought she had it right, she pulled a thread of glowing current up, wrapping it around her ankles and feet to illuminate where she stepped, while still allowing her eyes to adjust as much as possible to the gloom.

Once she made it down the stairs, there were faint red emergency lights, and here and there the clearer white of generator-run illumination, few and far between, and she used them, plus her own glow, to find the section of the wall she was looking for. Danny had said it was obvious, if you knew what to look for…

There. The mural—normally an exuberant swirl of colored tiles, now only a shadowed pattern—was set in a thick black frame that was bolted to the wall itself. She was tall enough to run her fingers over the top of the frame, then down along the side to where there was a faint bump.

"Come on, come on, don't fuck me over…."

Her handspan was too narrow, but a few inches past that, there was a section of the wall that shifted slightly when she pressed down on it, and then a crack in the wall appeared, opening just enough for someone slender—or malnourished—to slip through.

Ellen had never been particularly slender, and was nowhere near malnourished, but she knew the trick of bending and sliding, and didn't mind risking a tear in her jeans or a skinned elbow. The edge passed skin-scrapingly close to her nose, and she was pretty sure she left a strand or two of hair behind, but pulling her torso in and pushing her shoulders down got her through.

"Ugh." Ellen had never wanted to be one of those pipe cleaner girls, the ones with no butt or thighs, but they had a definite advantage when spelunking.

Inside, thankfully, the tunnel widened, giving her enough room to swing her arms without hitting the walls, and the ceiling overhead was high enough that she could walk upright without fear of a concussion. It was also lined with a bioluminescent moss of some kind, a light similar to her current illuminating the tunnel evenly, if dimly. Ellen was surprised, and then annoyed at herself for being surprised. The fatae didn't use current, not the way Talent did, but they weren't lacking in other skills, including things humans had forgotten, or never bothered to learn.

Including, it seemed, moss-lamps.

"So, where now?" Her voice sounded too spooky in the tunnel, not because it echoed but because it didn't, the moss soaking up all sound the moment it was made. She'd never gotten around to memorizing the tunnel maps—something she was going to remedy the moment she got back—but Danny had said that they were all pretty much the same, that gnomes didn't have much in the way of imagination or innovation. If so, then she was pretty sure that this tunnel would meet up with a larger one, if she went in just a bit further.

She counted off fifty-seven steps in her head, and on the fifty-eighth a puff of cooler air told her she'd reached it, even before the light showed her the second passageway, angling off in both directions, left and right.

"Of course. Just once, a signpost?" The moss ate those words, too, and she reminded herself to shut up, before she freaked herself out or, worse yet, alerted someone that she was there. Gnomes *probably* wouldn't bother her, but probably wasn't a definite. And she didn't know what else was here, what Alice had said was below.

A signpost, or a straight answer. Ellen would have given a lot, just then, for either. But that, Danny liked to say, was where the bills got paid. And it wasn't as though she had to rely on a flipped coin, either. Not in this particular case.

Ellen flexed and stretched her shoulders, trying to force her body to relax: some Talent might be able to work cantrips when they were tense, but every time she tried, it fizzled on her. Wren swore that would ease as she got more experience, but it hadn't, yet. Resting a hand flat against her breastbone, fingers pointing toward her chin, and taking a deep breath, she reached into her core, imagining tigers dipping into the swirling colors there, neon-bright and cool to the touch.

The threads she'd pulled in earlier had integrated with her own, her particular signature reshaping them for easy use. She scooped out a handful, feeling the neon shift to paler colors, sky blues and mint greens. When it felt ready, she shaped it with her memory of Danny: his voice, his appearance, his scent, the way his hand felt when it rested on her shoulder, either encouraging or stopping her, the way he paced when he was thinking and the way he rested his boot heels on his desk when he was reading, the way he dog-eared pages and the way he stood on the subway, one hand holding the rail, body swaying gently to the movement of the train. All the physical details, from the faint curl of his horns to the bend of his knees that she'd subconsciously collected, making up the sum total of Daniel Hendrickson's physical self.

It was a cantrip the PUPs had originally meant to track down physical evidence at a scene, but they'd discovered that it worked best with an incredibly strong sense of *who*, not what.

Not so good for finding evidence, but incredibly useful if you were, for example, tracking a missing person.

But—like so many of their cantrips—it took a lot of current and concentration to make it work. Even with her core topped-off and ready, she still felt her skin go clammy and her knees go weak, as though she'd not eaten for a week. But it was temporary: she didn't let that break her focus.

*Danny Hendrickson* His name, imbued with every memory, every sense of him she had, the depth and breadth of her knowledge of him.

Current swirled around her now, almost visible sparks of blue and yellow. It tugged at her, leading her a step into the tunnel branching to the left. It swirled again, as though confused, then stopped, turning right, then left. She pushed at the swirl, willing it to lead her to wherever Danny was, when the sound of something approaching her broke her concentration, and the swirl dissolved into dark sparks, and disappeared.

"Damn it."

Opening her eyes, she absorbed the remaining current back into her core before it could escape. Pivoting to face the sound —it was coming from the other tunnel—Ellen crouched low, readying her body for fight or flight even knowing that flight would be useless unless she went deeper in: fleeing back to the tight squeeze exit would be *asking* to be caught by whatever was coming. Her breath slowed, her eyes widening, the hours of training with both Danny and Wren paying off in the instinctive readiness.

The sound came closer, and she realized it was the sound of feet against stone. Not heavy, not booted. Not Danny. More than one. And that was all Ellen had time to identify before they were on her, nearly knocking her over. She grabbed, instinctively, then ducked as one of them took a swing at her.

Wren and Danny both also preached, if you can't run, and you're not sure you're going to win, try confusion.

"I'm a friend!" she said, pitching her voice low, but set to carry, even as she moved into position to counter the blow. "Friend!" Even if they weren't, it might slow them down enough for her to get the upper hand. But the flesh under her grasp felt human, and when they stilled enough for her to look, the face of her attacker was familiar, mud-stained and tear-streaked.

The boy she'd seen, in her vision.

***

ELLEN BARELY HAD time to react to that first blow before she had to pull a second body off her back, reaching over her shoulder to untangle tight-clenched fingers from her hair. "Calm the hell down," she hissed, yanking the second attacker forward with one arm, pushing her down to the ground with the boy. "I'm here to help you."

"They're coming, they're coming after us." The girl was sobbing, but at least she could speak: the boy seemed stunned into silence, eyes wide and staring.

Ellen knelt down to put her free hand over the girl's mouth, and listened. There was nothing except the sound of their breathing, harsh and raspy, before it was sucked up into the moss and muffled.

"Nobody's coming," she said, still keeping her voice low. "And if they do, I can handle them." She hoped. The kids weren't Talent, there was no hint of current around them at all, so odds were whatever fatae they'd run into had scared the bejesus out of them. If they were lucky, a scare was all they'd have to deal with.

But even as Ellen thought that, she dismissed it. The only fatae who would be lingering here would be gnomes—even human predators didn't spend much time near gnome-dens. The smell was too bad, Danny said, although he wasn't exactly unbiased. But gnomes didn't cause this kind of fear, even in

Nulls, and gnomes wouldn't have dragged Danny off, even if they'd somehow managed to get the drop on him.

And she wouldn't have a vision of someone being menaced by gnomes, they were more the annoying creeper kind of threat, not—. Her breath caught at the realization: she'd found them here, where she was looking for Danny. It couldn't be coincidence. It *couldn't* be.

She managed, barely, to let go of the girl, forcing herself to lean back, trying not to spook them while still conveying urgency. "Tell me what you saw. Quickly!"

The boy just stared at her, an ugly bruise on the side of his face, and she wondered how badly he'd been hit on the head. The girl, on the other hand, seemed eager to keep talking, her gaze so focused on Ellen in any other circumstance it would have been stalker-creepy.

"We were just hanging out, over on the Greenway, when the lights went out?" Her face scrunched up, her mouth twisting as she tried to remember something. "Yesterday?"

"Yeah," Ellen said, nodding, making note that they'd lost track of days. Not good.

"It was so dark, at first it was cool, 'cause we could see the stars, I didn't know there *were* that many stars. And then something g-grabbed us." The girl's voice stuttered, but went on. "Ugh, they were…they were all quiet and slithering and gross, and they tied us up with these *ropes* that weren't actually rope, and we were able to scrape them away, and the guy said to run, so we ran, but —"

"Guy? What guy? Where is he?" The words shook out of her without thought, her fingers curled around the boy's upper arm, merely because he was closer. "Where is he?"

She got a blank stare from both of them.

"The guy who helped you," she said more slowly, forcing each word out. "The guy who said to run."

"Oh. Back there," the boy managed, waving his free arm

vaguely the direction they'd come from. "But you can't go there, they're-"

"They're not human," the girl finished for him.

"I know," Ellen said grimly, letting go of the boy. She pulled more current up, wrapping it around her arm from elbow to thumb, strong enough for them to see the cool sparks dancing just above her skin, if they weren't completely Null. From the way they flinched away, they weren't. "But I'm not exactly helpless."

"But what do we do?" The girl again, rocking back and forth where she sat, reaching out to grab the boy's nearest hand, their fingers twining tightly enough it had to hurt.

"You keep going that way," and Ellen pointed over her shoulder, back the way she'd come. "You'll see a narrow exit—that'll take you into a subway station. Okay?" She waited for them both to nod. "And I need you to carry a message, can you do that before you freak out?"

They were both in shock, both from the experience and the fact that their captors hadn't been human, but having someone *listen* to them, who talked to them like adults rather than patting them on the head like children, was exactly what was needed to get through. They both drew themselves up, the change visible even in the dim light.

"You're going to help him?" the girl asked.

"I am."

"He helped us escape," the boy told her, his voice flat and serious. "What do you need us to do?"

She gave them the address for the PUP's office, and had them repeat her message, word for word, until she was pretty sure one of them would remember it. No matter who was in the office—even if Lou was busy, or Bonnie had been called out on another case or collapsed for a nap without leaving a note—they'd understand.

"2nd Avenue under-tunnels, unknown fa—" the girl stumbled over the word, then corrected herself—"fatae, vision-related, going in to find Danny. Situation under control. Stand by for ping."

Ellen nodded, mental fingers crossed that they listed to her, and didn't try to race in after her. If what these two told her was right, the quieter she did this, the better.

Then she shoved them on their way, and headed deeper underground.

<hr>

EVERYTHING HURT. I was used to being in motion, or at least being able to stretch, and being trussed like a roast... okay, it wasn't the first time it'd happened to me, but was heading into being the longest wait to get free.

The kids were gone, our captors lashing by me silently in pursuit. One, two...maybe three, maybe more of them, leaving me behind. I'd strained my ears, listening for some sound that the humans'd been caught, but once the pounding of their sneakers had disappeared into the blackness, the silence returned, plugging me back into solitary.

And I waited, feeling the burn starting in my shoulders and thighs, a creaking ache in my lower back. I wasn't a kid any more, that this sort of thing was fun. And my usual response—to put my brain to work—wasn't doing much for me now, because I didn't have a damn thing to work with.

I'd been around the block a few times in my life. Hell, I'd practically mapped out the entire neighborhood, over time, and talked to everyone who lived there. But I had no idea who —what—my captors were, and that was pissing me off probably more than the way kept poking my legs and arms, testing me for tastiness.

I assumed that's what they were doing, anyway. After leaving me alone a while, they were back, fingers hard and thin, coming out of the darkness at random intervals, no sound to warn me they were there, no smell beyond the omnipresent cold wet dampness of the tunnel, and by this point, no sensation in my limbs except the slight burn when they poked me, and nerve endings woke again.

I had no idea how long I'd been down here, strung up like a side of beef, but eventually—aching muscles and poking fingers or no—I got bored. And me bored, my mother always said, inevitably ended in me stupid.

"See," I told a particularly bony finger, "this is why we can't have nice things, because of breeds like you."

That earned me another poke, this time in the gut, and a lot harder.

"So you do understand English. Good." Few of the fatae breeds had their own distinct language—don't ask me why, that was a question for a linguistics grad student in search of a research topic—but not all of them picked up human speech, either. And since these guys didn't seem to be much in the way of talking....

Another poke, this time to the throat, made me gag and lose my train of thought for a minute.

"Fuckers," I said, more to distract myself than because I really wanted to insult them anymore. "Either eat me or kill me or whatever it is you're going to do, but enough with the goddamned poking!"

If they were focused on me, though, maybe there were fewer of them hunting for the kids. If anything was happening, it was beyond my ability to hear. Entirely possible, although the longer I stayed here, the more starved my brain was for sound, and the harder I was listening for it. Maybe they were out-of-sight-out-of-mind types. Or maybe their silence extended to hunting down runaway meals, too. Brain going in circles. Bad sign.

"Look, I don't even know if I'm tasty. Fauns are pretty indigestible, I've been told. Too gamey."

And then there was more silence, but at least the poking stopped.

Wait. Was that good, or bad? I strained my senses to pick up any movement at all—the bastards had to *breathe*, right? No fatae breed could go without breathing, not even trolls, although it might take several minutes between intakes, for them.

There, in the distance, the faint sound of respiration. All right, at least one of them was still there. Watching.

So they breathed, about human-normal rate. And they were warm-blooded; the fingers were boney, but definitely covered in some hard flesh, not scales. And they could see in practically-pitch dark, well enough to function.

I'd been captured by mole people. Great.

Specifically, mole people who ate flesh—human, and otherwise. Even if I hadn't been sure of their intent at the first, the putrid feel of their breath was proof enough. You didn't get that kind of halitosis from vegetables and fish, and there was a particular smell that came from eating human flesh. And I hated my life that I knew that fact.

"At least introduce yourselves before dinner," I said, but the fun had gone out of it. I was tired, numb from the constant aching, and my only comfort—that the kids had escaped—was dulled by the fact that I didn't *know* the kids had escaped.

Not for the first time I wished I'd been born Talent, not so I could blow my way out of here—we were far down underground enough it would take someone of Wren's skill to find enough current to use—but so I could send a ping out to say goodbye. Or maybe 'get your ass down here now!'

Even if the kids made it to the surface, the odds of them telling anyone—at least, anyone who might believe them—was slim. But slim was more than none. It wouldn't be enough to save me before I was cut down and served up; all I could hope was that, once they heard—and got everything two shaken teenagers could remember—the PUPs would make sure the mole people didn't nab anyone else.

I probably should feel bad about depriving a breed of their preferred food source, but not so much, actually. Let them learn how to make stew of river rats, be useful members of society for a change.

And then the single source of breathing was gone too, and I was alone.

"Shit."

Being alone was better, if only because it meant I probably wasn't going to die right away, but it also meant I had no distractions, except.... Wait. Yes. There was sound. Distant, but definite, and loud enough that it was probably human. Had Bonnie and her crew actually figured out where I was? Or was this totally unrelated?

Shit, had they caught the kids, bringing them back? Or some new poor bastard?

There was a crack of what sounded like thunder, and light flashed down the hallway, too bright to do anything other than make my eyes water and sting, my body trying to flinch away from the intensity. It was followed by another crack of thunder, louder this time, and in that instant before the light faded I opened my eyes enough to see that I was wrapped in thick, grey-green ropes of unknown origin, and on the wall next to me were a row of hooks. Literal, metal meathooks, large enough to hang a cow, and probably rusted enough to kill a sailor, but also probably still sharp enough to cut a rope against, if I could just swing myself close enough to reach.

Once-a-week yoga classes, and dislocating your shoulder is a small price to pay for being able to feel the ground under your feet again. Thankfully it was a short drop, and I was up out of my crouch and moving before my body had a chance to protest. Adrenaline was a wonderful thing.

The blackness had returned, but I'd scoped out the feel of my cage already, and knew more or less where to put my back so it was against a wall. A cold, sleek wall. Metal? A touch confirmed that—too cold to be wood, too sleek to be stone, unless someone had quarried marble down here.

I had no idea what they'd used, of how they'd gotten the hooks into it, and I didn't care. There was one exit out of this hole, the same one the kids had fled down, but it led toward whatever was making the light and sound. Which was probably good for me, but also meant that there would be more mole people there, dealing with the intrusion. Fifty-fifty chance of me making things worse, going that way. But staying here didn't seem a great choice either. I went forward.

And two steps toward my escape, something grabbed me from behind.

---

ELLEN HAD LEARNED, a long time ago, that life wasn't even in the slightest bit fair. Fair would have been her parents listening to her, not either ignoring her or pretending she had an 'overenthusiastic imagination' until she was a teenager, then letting the doctors convince them she was having a hormone-related mental breakdown. Fair would have been *someone* in her family having a lick of Talent, and recognizing her for what she was, instead of having to practically stumble over it, years later. Years too late.

But she was above all practical, and if they had, odds were she would never have been mentored by Wren Valere, never known Bonnie or Pietr, and never worked with Danny. Overall, her life now didn't suck. Even the visions she'd been gifted with — she could *do* something about them now, could help people.

She wasn't willing to say it all came clean in the wash, but there were payoffs. She'd learned how to read scenes, ask questions of people so they'd answer without meaning to, look at evidence and maybe see what other people missed.

But none of that was helping her right now, because there was no one to ask, no scene to read, and no evidence to examine. Just her, and a too-dark tunnel, and a boss who was missing, presumed clunked over the head and dragged off somewhere to be eaten.

"No. Stop that." She stared down the darkness of the tunnel ahead of her, and tried not to let herself get sidetracked, following the cantrip that sparked and shimmered dimly ahead of her. "Don't panic, *think*."

She could ping Bonnie, have her rouse the troops, have the wrath of the Cosa descend with her.... Smart money would probably do exactly that. But smart money wasn't always the right money. Her father used to say that. He meant what seemed the right move wasn't always the one that paid off. And here, in these tunnels...

*Deductive logic*, she heard Danny say. *What does basic deductive mother-of-pearl logic tell you?*

Bioluminscent moss still clung to the walls in scraggly patches, but there was no other source of light that she'd been able to find. So whatever lived down here, they had good night vision. And it was quiet. The kind of quiet that pressed against your ears and made you think someone was standing right behind you: she'd already turned several times, current crackling in defense, only to find herself alone.

No, she'd been right in her first instinct. Too many people down here would set off alarms long before she was ready. Quiet infiltration, until she figured out what was going on.

*Then* she could ping for help.

"Assuming they can even transloc down here, not being able to see a damn thing for landmarks." The words were barely more than silent mouthings, but the way even that was swallowed by the stillness and the moss made her decide not to speak again. Way too disturbing.

Silent, night-dwelling creatures that clunked people over the head and carried them off.... It really was like some bad 1950's horror movie. Except she wasn't the faint-hearted blonde scientist-girl who screamed and fainted.

*Where are you, boss?* she asked the cantrip. A thread of current flared brighter in response, and she followed it deeper into the tunnel, until she found the tunnel's residents by literally running into them.

"Holy mother of fuck!" It came out as a yelp, the moss swallowing it, but leaving an odd ringing in her ears.

Whatever she was facing, they weren't silent, either. They hissed. And they didn't like current, not a bit, she learned that when they attacked her arms before anything else, hard fingers scrabbling at her forearms as though they were trying to tear her skin off to get at the current, yank it out of her by force. She barely had time to pull her arms away, drawing the current back inside herself and plunging the hallway into darkness before she realized that had been a terrible idea: they could see in the pitch and she couldn't.

She pulled the current back out, shaping it as she did so into a dense ball, then threw it—not at her attackers, whom she couldn't see except as faint shadows in the darkness, but at the wall she could feel, to her left.

It hit and imploded, a boom of noise echoing into the hallway, followed by an intense burst of blue light, and another boom, like the sonic boom of a jet, chasing the light down the hallway.

In the split-second they were blinded, Ellen dodged around them, slipping out of those hard fingers grasping for her, and kept going, moving to the left when she sensed the tunnel split again, not out of any plan or knowledge, only instinct.

And when she heard something moving ahead of her, shuffling toward her in the darkness, rather than running away, following that same instinct, she grabbed it, thinking—she didn't know what she was thinking, if she was thinking at all.

But there was cloth under her hand, rough cotton and solid muscle and a smell she'd recognize in—well, a dark room. Surprise and relief flooded her, making her grab at him more tightly, a rough and unexpected hug.

"The hell—Ellen?" His voice was low and raspy-sore, and the best thing she'd ever heard.

"Hi boss." Ellen wasn't going to start giggling, she *wasn't*. "Don't suppose you know another way out of here?"

His raspy breath sounded near her left ear, the weight of his body a reassuring, human—mostly human—presence. "I didn't even know the first way. Do we have backup?"

"Just me." It seemed beyond idiotic, now, that she hadn't pinged for help, despite all her rational-at-the-time thinking, and there's no way the kids would have found anyone by now, if they even went through with finding the office and delivering her message.

It was like he could hear her thoughts, or maybe he just knew how she thought, because, "You know, just because I'm the poster child for do-it-all-yourself, that doesn't mean I should be your role model."

"Yes boss." He yelled when he was stressed, and even at a hoarse whisper, that had definitely been a yell. And she could fix that part of it now, at least.

*Found him* she sent, more a sensation of *Danny* and *relief* and *worry,* because she had no idea where they were or how they were going to get out of here, and there was something wet on her hand that she was pretty sure was blood, and it wasn't hers, so odds were it was his.

There was a shift of air in the tunnel—they'd been found. "Can you move?"

"If the alternative is being dinner, yes." And even in the dark she could tell he was giving her his 'don't ask me stupid questions you already know the answer to' look.

A reply came from Bonnie, distant, like the ping was trying to force its way through interference, a matching sense of relief and worry, and the vague image of a medical gurney.

*Yes* she sent back, tugging at Danny's shoulder. "Come on."

If they moved fast, they might just make it back to the opening before they were caught.

---

I HAD no idea how Ellen had found me. But I was also pretty sure I wasn't operating at a hundred percent capacity just then, so I didn't let that bother me. Also: I'd trained her, hadn't I? So go, me.

The fact that she stank of fear wasn't quite so reassuring, but I was pretty sure I didn't smell much better. No shame in being scared when something wants to eat you.

"How—"

"Don't talk," she said, her fingers curling more tightly into my arm. I'd probably have bruises but hell, right now everything felt like a bruise, and the blood slowly moving in my limbs again wasn't helping, making me feel like I was being attacked by a thousand tiny pissed-off acupuncturists. I bit my lower lip like a stoic hero, and stumbled on after her without another sound.

We moved along in the darkness that wasn't quite as dark as before. It took me too long to realize that the visibility was thanks to current glowing a dim orange in front of us. Not in front of us: curled along Ellen's arm, the one that wasn't towing me along like I was a recalcitrant five-year-old. It hugged the line of her wrist up to her elbow, just enough to show us shapes and not enough to totally disrupt our night vision, the way emergency lights worked, and wasn't my Shadow a smart girl?

And I might have lost a few more brain cells than I thought, because... oh. That wasn't sweat on my forehead. I was bleeding. When had that happened?

She was muttering under her breath, some cantrip from the sound of it, and I wanted to tell her to shut up, that they'd hear us, but interrupting whatever she was using to find the way out seemed a bad idea, too. We turned a corner, and then another one, and without thinking I pulled her to the side.

She turned to me, her lips moving, the word barely audible even inches from my ear. "What?"

"Fresh air. That way, not this."

She didn't question me, just backtracked to the last turn, and we headed that way, instead. I might be bloody and woozy and half-numb, but the nose knows: there's something in my genetics that will always turn toward open space and fresh air, or at least as much of that as we can get in the city.

And yeah, okay, maybe I was too focused on that, or keeping the blood out of my eyes—seriously, when had I started bleeding, and should I be more concerned about it?—and maybe I was trusting Ellen's sense of direction and her current-glow more than I should have, but we turned a corner and barreled into one of the mole people. And I mean barreled—it wasn't expecting us, either, and we hit at a reasonable clip, two bodies hitting one, and the one hitting back immediately.

I've been in my share of brawls—I was the half-breed kid of a single mother, and a Navy kid living off-base, so fighting was probably inevitable—and I took two things away from this, immediately. One: mole people were crap at actual fighting, and two: I had definitely taken damage earlier, because my first swing knocked me back more than it did them.

And three: I needed to work on Ellen's fighting skills more, because she should have taken a single opponent out faster than she did. But there was only the one, and they didn't seem to be in communication with each other, because there was no hue and cry after it was laid out on the floor. Low light and low-tech. Possibly anti-social, or a really low birth rate, since I'd never sensed more than three or four together. Good to know.

Four: The floor was cold. And really hard. And suddenly, I needed to take a leak like nobody's business.

Ellen was leaning over me, pulling me up by both arms. "You okay?"

"No." Honesty is the base of good communication, right? "But I can move."

We abandoned what attempt at stealth we'd been making, the glow on Ellen's wrist intensifying. I guess she figured at this point the risk of letting them know we were there was offset by the likelihood that the increased light might blind them?

Increased light meant I could see that the tunnel we were in was stone and wood, not metal, the surfaces scraped clean enough we could see tool marks and the black scrawls where long-ago engineers had left half-finished plans. Human work, which, combined with the fresher air flowing, meant we were closer to the surface now. Hopefully.

"Are the lights still out?" I'd been in the dark, literally and figuratively, for so long now, I almost couldn't imagine a world with light.

"When I came in, yeah." Ellen's voice was still low, but she didn't shush me this time. "Whole city and some of the 'burbs, rumor has it a whole line of generators blew, but nobody's admitting to anything."

Of course not. I swiped the heel of my hand across my fore-head, and came away with more blood, but it felt tackier now, like it was starting to dry up. Good. "How close to morning is it?"

"Don't know. Might be light already. Maybe?"

Not good. If we went out and it was still dark, the mole

people could yank us back again easy enough. Or maybe not: if I could shake this dizziness, and Ellen was prepared, we could take them. Probably. Maybe. And maybe they'd decided to let us go.

I listened, as best I could while moving fast, trying to hear past Ellen's ragged breathing and the pulse of my own heart, and could hear things behind us, and not far enough behind for comfort.

My heart may have pumped a little harder. "Move faster."

Ellen's fingers tightened on my arm, and her annoyingly long legs seemed to get even longer, forcing me to stretch to keep up. "What are those things?"

"Don't know, don't care right now," I said. "Less talk, more running."

We weren't actually running: I wasn't sure I could, and the current-light, even brighter, wasn't enough to tell us what might be ahead. But the closer we got to the source of fresh air, the faster I walked, until the taint of cold metal and stale water disappeared entirely, replaced by a saltier, warmer smell. Truck exhaust, and green growing things, and the smell of *people*, living too many together, all the most glorious things I could imagine, just then.

Until we hit a dead end.

"The fuck?" Ellen sounded less surprised than indignant: how dare our escape route fail us? I sagged forward, not risking collapse in case I couldn't get up. Hands braced on my knees, I tilted my head back to keep the blood from getting in my eyes, and blinked. "Look up."

"This isn't the way I came in," Ellen said, staring at the battered, metal trap door set above us.

We both heard the sounds of pursuit behind us—if you could call those slithery dry whispers *sounds*—at the same time. "You want to go back and find it?"

"Don't put words in my mouth, boss," she grumbled,

already looking for a handhold to use, so she could reach the handle. Ellen's taller than me, and uninjured, so I leaned against the crumbling stone wall and waited for her to figure out how to open the hatch. After a minute of her doing everything from jumping straight up to trying to climb the wall like Spiderman, I coughed gently.

"Maybe current'll do the trick?"

There was a shocked second, and then a grumbled, "fuck you, Hendrickson."

Laughing was a bad idea. My ribs were killing me, even before she reached a hand down and hauled me up, just as the first bony finger scraped at the back of my shirt.

---

THE METAL HATCH CLANGING down behind me was one of the most orgasmic sounds I've ever heard, even moreso when the sizzling crackle of current told me Ellen was sealing it tighter than the MTA's budget. I let my knees give out under me, then, dropping to the dirt like someone'd cut my strings.

On the plus side, the pins and needles feeling was gone. The minus side, that just let me feel how sore I was, all the way through every muscle.

Ellen staggered away from the metal hatch and collapsed next to me, arms stretched over her head, legs bent, and dug her fingers into her hair, pulling at the thick curls like she needed to relieve pressure. "Where are we?"

Good question. Her human eyes were probably only seeing shadows and smudges. The hatch led out to a small hill overlooking an abandoned factory—based on the size of the parking lot and the broken windows, anyway. The hill itself was mostly dirt and a few scraggly patches of grass, but there was a wild rosebush just behind us that filled the dark air with perfume, even though most of the flowers were still buds.

The Bronx, I thought. Maybe. The first glimmer of light was coming into the sky from our right, and when I stood up, carefully, I could see the light-studded silhouette of Manhattan behind and to our left. "South Bronx. Not my favorite place in the world, but better than where we were."

"No lie." She turned a little, looking over her shoulder at the hatch, a dark glint of metal through the grass. "You think that'll hold them?"

"They won't come after us," I said. Okay, it was more of a hope than a certainty, but I'd had time to gather evidence to support the hope. "They like it dark as possible, which means they're probably not all that fond of sunlight."

"It's not dawn yet." She didn't open her eyes to check, but she was right: there was barely a streak of dark red across the horizon. But it would come up fast, after that.

"In their skin, would you risk it?"

She thought about it for a while, then shook her head.

I hoped that let her rest better for a while. Me, I was twitchy as a selkie in shallow water: just because she or I wouldn't do something didn't meant the mole people wouldn't. I mean, I had no idea who they were or why they'd been in the city to start, much less knocking over some poor bastard in his office.

"I've called in the troops," she said, her eyes closed. "They were waiting until we had some sense of where the hell we were. They should be here soon."

"Tell them to bring coffee and doughnuts," I said, sitting back down beside her.

That didn't get the laugh it didn't deserve.

"I'm almost afraid to ask, but there were two kids...."

"About yay tall and scared out of their limited wits? Yeah, boss, they made it. Well, they made it as far as me, and I sent them on to Bonnie."

"Good move."

"If they made it. They were freaked out enough they might have just gone home, too. Boss... I saw them. In a vision."

That made my already-exhausted adrenaline leap again, before I told it to settle down—we'd already rescued them, right? "When?"

"Just before I got to the office. Would have been around the same time you were getting clunked over the head, maybe?"

Before I could dig further, there was the sound of a car horn, a damn sight closer than any car should have gotten without me hearing it, and then:

"Good morning, children." The man standing over us would have blocked out the sun if it had been up already. He had a massive flashlight in one massive hand, and what looked like a squeeze-horn on the other. "Your ride is here."

"Hey Nifty." I waved at the Pup, mentally tabling Ellen's vision-report for later. "About time you guys showed up. Do I *always* have to do all your work for you?"

He took us home, anyway.

---

TRANSLOCATION ALWAYS MADE me want to heave my cookies. This time, I made it to the PUP office bathroom before doing so. When I came out again, mouth sour but hands and boot-tips clean, Ellen had a mug of what smelled like hot cocoa in her hands, and her feet curled up under her on the sofa in the break room. And we had an audience not only of Nifty and Bonnie, but Venec and Pietr, too. Not quite an all-hands-called-out confab, but close enough to make me nervous.

I sat next to Ellen on the sofa, intentionally sitting on her feet until she pulled them away with a scowl at me.

Bonnie waited, then sighed. "So."

"So?" I knew where she was going, or I thought I did, but

since I had no idea what to tell her, I was willing to drag it out a bit.

"Ellen gave us the once-down, but she didn't know a hell of a lot. What the hell were those things, Danny?"

PUPI had been established to investigate crimes within the Cosa Nostradamus, the things regular law enforcement was incapable of dealing with, or even understanding, in most cases. They'd won a lot of support, grudging or otherwise, in the years since Venec and his late partner had fought to establish them. But they didn't speak for the fatae.

Then again, nobody actually spoke for all the fatae. That was seventy percent of our problem.

"I have no idea."

Ellen's eyes, which were starting to slide closed under the combination of safety and hot cocoa, opened wide at that, and I got the full extent of wide brown stare. "What?"

I shrugged. "I have no idea. Yeah, most of the breeds are sociable enough that we get to know them, but not all are, and it's not like the Cosa has a census bureau sending people knocking on doors inquiring as to how many arms they have and what they prefer to catch for dinner. And some things like being hidden."

"Especially if they eat other things," Pietr said. "Upright, walking-and-talking things."

"More or less, yeah." There was more of that going on than humans wanted to think about, but generally it was kept to... well, it was kept out of human sight, mostly. "Secondary

evidence, but enough to get a warrant on, if you know the judge."

"Such as?"

"Breath." I didn't have to elaborate: Venec at least knew what I was talking about, from the expression on his face. "Also, they're not exactly living somewhere with a lot of hydroponics, unless they're eating moss."

"Herbivores don't have teeth like that." Ellen had gone face-to-face with them, so she was as close to an expert as we had right now. My nose, her eyes, and a lot of don't-know. Wonderful.

"They also don't go assaulting people in apartment buildings," Nifty said. "That was what got you tangled up in all this, right? Sounds like these fatae decided to use the darkness to go grocery shopping."

"That had been my thought," I admitted. "What I saw, maybe it was hunting party. Taking advantage of the blackout. Lot of people go missing during blackouts, and we don't always find them. Maybe we know why, now."

"Maybe." But Venec didn't sound convinced, and honestly, neither was I. "What drew your attention there, Hendrickson? You're good, but you're not good enough to know something's wrong a building away, not without her visions to tell you."

Cold, but accurate. "Light, in the window. I would never have noticed anything happening if it weren't for that, and I only even saw it because of the blackout."

"What color was it?"

Good question. "Orange. Not red, definitely orange. Weird, murky, not even really light."

"Deep sea creatures use weird lights, because they see on different spectrums than we do," Ellen said. "And there was that weird glowing moss down there..."

"You should probably write your cable bill off as a business deduction, you keep learning smart things from the Discovery Channel."

"NOVA, actually. And deductions only matter if you make actual money, boss."

"Now would be a pretty damn good time to ask for a raise." I wasn't going to say I couldn't have found my way out, eventually, but the point was I didn't have to. "Only, I don't think they needed any light to see." They hadn't acted blind, when I was tied up. Although they had been pretty handsy, so maybe they used touch in absolute dark....?

Hell, deep sea vision whatsis made as much sense as anything, and figuring out the science of this was the PUPs job, not mine. I was more concerned with-

"But why was Ellen's vision tied into it?" And there was Pietr with the question I'd been wondering. "She usually sees people in imminent danger of death, but Danny here was closer to risk than they were. And he was the one who rescued them, before you even got there. No offense meant."

I didn't have to look at Ellen to know she was rolling her eyes at that.

"Maybe it wasn't them you were seeing, exactly." Bonnie glanced up at Venec, who nodded, looking even more deadpan than usual. "Maybe it was a warning of what's to come."

"That's not how my visions work," she objected.

"It's not how they've worked," Venec said. "That doesn't mean they won't always work that way. Skillsets aren't finite things; you learn, you grow, you expand."

"Oh, *great*." And in that instant, my Shadow was a teenager again. Grinning would have been inappropriate, so I bit it back, and reached over to pat her knee consolingly.

"It would make sense, though." Pietr again, his voice thoughtful, his eyes looking somewhere not in this room. "The timing.... Maybe the vision was triggered by what Hendrickson saw, and so she picked up on their next victims."

"Then why didn't she see the guy in the office they took first? Or me?"

Pietr shrugged. "We can run tests, if you'd like. Knock you over the head at random moments, see if she—"

"No." Ellen and I both nixed that at the same time. But something was starting to ache in my gut, matching the ache I'd had in the back of my head for nearly a day now. "But that's still the fucking mystery, isn't it? Not what they are, not what they intended to do with us, but *why* they were suddenly in the middle of Downtown, risking exposure by going into freaking *office* buildings. Do they need, what, a particular blood type? People who use a certain body wash? And did their usual source of food disappear, or—"

"Or they're new here." Ellen had been on the heels of my thought, finishing it for me. "They've only just come into the city, maybe just settled those tunnels. That's why Danny hadn't heard anything, why Alice only knew rumors—"

"Wait, you went to talk to Alice?" I swung around to stare at Ellen. "Are you *insane*?"

"Who's Alice?"

I waved Venec down, and continued to stare at Ellen. "Seriously? What the fuck were you —"

"Trying to find you! And Alice... liked me. I think. And she likes you, or what she knows of you."

That... was less reassuring that it should have been.

"Anyway, she helped me, okay? I wouldn't have found the tunnel without what she said."

"Who is Alice?" Venec repeated.

"Nobody humans should treat with. Let it go, trust me." He either would or he wouldn't, and if she spun him into a neat cocoon and sucked him down for lunch, it wouldn't be my fault.

"You think they're recent immigrants?" Bonnie exchanged a look with Venec, and he groaned, pressing the heel of his hand against his eyes, "All right, yeah," he said, agreeing to whatever she'd suggested to him. "You're on better terms with the Council these days, you get to ask them. I'll round up the lone-jacks. Hendrickson...."

"Not It," I said. "I'm a PI, not a diplomat. And only half fatae, in case you forgot."

You ever get stared at by four pair of eyes, all of 'em knowing you're going to give in sooner rather than later? It's the most depressing experience ever.

Danny wasn't happy. Ellen supposed she could understand that: he'd already been at the tail end of a long day when the blackout started, and since then he'd been conked over the head, tied up, maybe discovered a new breed, been threatened with being eaten, rescued himself and two teenagers, and then, when it seemed reasonable he'd be able to fall into bed for a week, sent out to snoop among the fatae community to find out what anyone else knew about the mole-people fatae who'd almost eaten him.

She'd be unhappy too. In fact, she decided, she *was* unhappy. Not that it did either of them any good.

The sun was up, but the buildings around the PUPI head-quarters in upper Manhattan were still mostly dark. The street lamps were dimmed, but the traffic lights were working, so that was one good thing, anyway. Yay emergency services. She shoved her hands deeper into the pocket of her borrowed-again jacket, and looked at her boss.

"So. Who're we going to talk to? Not Alice, I'm guessing."

"Jesus. No. And when I find out who told you to go see her I swear I'm going to take their teeth for a trophy. You just… don't do that again, okay?"

"Why? I mean, she's odd, but…"

"You ever read *Lord of the Rings*?"

"Of course."

"Alice is what Shelob has nightmares about."

Ellen opened her mouth to say something, and realized that she had absolutely nothing whatsoever to actually say. Alice hadn't seemed particularly terrifying to her, but Ellen knew enough about the world now to know that that could be as much her own ignorance as Alice's lack of menace. If Danny said steer clear, she would.

"She spoke fondly of you," she finally said, needing to get at least that much of a last word in. Danny's only response was a giant shudder.

"What are the four sources of gossip?"

"Cops, the homeless, club kids, and politicians." There were four kinds of gossip, too, according to Danny: political, religious, financial, and sexual. She didn't think sex or finances were going to help them out here—she hoped not, anyway. Religious? No, political. So....

"We're going to see Linder."

"We're going to see Linder," he confirmed.

Linder wasn't happy to see them. That wasn't anything new. The fatae glared at them, the leather jacket over their sloped shoulders crackled and worn with age, fingerless black gloves pulled over gnarled fingers just as crackled and worn. But the eyes in that narrow face were bright and sharp, and the mind behind them was even more so.

"Well, well, if it's not Dum and Dee. How're ya doing, Dee?"

"I've had better days," Ellen admitted. "Blackouts, man. They suck."

Linder cackled at that. "You Talent, you rely too much on magic tricks to stay warm and toasty. Weaker than Nulls, when the weather gets dry."

"But stronger than Nulls after a good hard storm," she said in return, and let just a hint of current rise through her skin, prickling her pores open with energy. Linder wasn't one of the breeds who could see current, but most of the fatae knew when it was being used around them.

"Show off." But it was said with amusement, and Ellen let the current subside, her point made.

"And you, Dum. Been a while since you came sniffing around my humble abode. So clearly you want something from little old me...."

Linder's abode was humble the way New York City was humble; which was to say, not at all. They were standing in a glass-walled living room in a massive apartment on Columbus Circle that probably cost more in rent for a month than she made in a year. Linder dressed like a bum because it amused Linder to do so.

"As much as I'd love to play the game, I'm working on no sleep for the past two... maybe three days, and my temper's a bit sharp right now," Danny said. "Ellen's actually here to keep me from snapping your neck if you say something I don't like."

Linder's expression didn't change, but they did run a hand through thick white hair, revealing a sharply-pointed window's peak and eyes that glinted red deep within the pale blue pupils, before gesturing to the overstuffed leather sofas at the center of the room. "Well now I'm intrigued. Sit, and tell me more."

Ellen settled into the corner of the sofa and tried to look as though she was ready and able to stop Danny if he became homicidal.

"You know where I've spent the night, Linder?"

"Hopefully somewhere scandalous, and you're going to tell me about it."

"Tied up, underground."

"Danny. We've all told you to make nice with the gnomes already—"

"It wasn't gnomes." Ellen was watching Linder carefully, and saw the slightest hint of a clench in the jaw and a twitch over those blue-red eyes. "But you knew that already, didn't you."

"I will be the first to admit that I know most of what makes this fair city tick, Daniel, but even I don't always know what's making *you* tick. I—"

"Don't waste my time or test my patience, Linder. You knew. How many others knew?"

"Knew what? Danny, honestly, I—"

"That there's a new breed in town, taking over the under-tunnels. A flesh-eating breed."

That stopped Linder dead, something Ellen wasn't sure was possible.

"Who else knew, Linder?"

Linder sighed, stretching long legs out and digging at something caught in their teeth with one dark claw, the other hand cupped politely to hide the activity. "You just want me to confirm what you already know? That's a waste of favors, Danny."

"I'm not here to exchange favors. This isn't one of those deals. You're going to tell me what we need to know."

"This one of your vision deals, Dee?" Linder looked at her then. "Are we on the clock to save some poor hapless human soul?"

"I've saved fatae too," she said, irritated.

"Truth, truth. Neither of you are speciesist... well, it would be hypocritical of you, wouldn't it, Danny? All right. Yes, I knew about our newest residents. About... two weeks, maybe. Maybe a bit more."

"And you knew they were flesh-eaters."

"Who among us isn't? I mean, of the interesting sorts, anyway."

"People-eaters."

"Ah, that. Well." Linder inspected his claw, then sheathed it.

Ellen was never going to be jaded enough not to find the smooth motion of claw disappearing into an ordinary-looking finger not-fascinating, but she'd learned enough to not stare overtly. Not that Linder would have minded, but it would have lost them points. And points were everything, dealing with Linder. "You understand, it's nothing personal. It's just human problems are human problems, yes? That's what we've been told, all these years."

"Don't bring up that bullshit with me," Danny said, sharp as broken glass. "Not that 'us against the humans and their magic' crap, because it was old and pointless a hundred years ago and even more now, on both sides. And yes I'm taking this person-ally—I was the one trussed up in slime-holds like a roast waiting for the oven."

"Ah, you're half fatae, so they weren't going to eat you. Prob-ably." Linder shrugged, waving his hand as though to dismiss the issue. "I mean, sharks take a bite out of things sometimes and decide halfway through it tastes nasty. Might be like that. But not all the way eaten."

"Comforting." Danny's voice was cold and dry, now, and Ellen felt herself start to tense, as though preparing to throw herself between them—or possibly, throw herself on a grenade, real or conversational. "And you were just going to let it happen. Sit there and not say anything. Yeah, I'm not getting over that any time soon. And neither will the Council, I suspect."

"It's not like we had a heads-up, Hendrickson." For the first time, Linder let some real emotion slip through: annoyance, and a hint of uncertainty. "These shklya slipped in, first thing we know is when rumors start someone's taken up residence in the downbelows and the gnomes are giving them scare-eyed roundabouts."

"And that didn't tell you there was something wrong?"
"Yeah, something wrong we should stay away from. We didn't know for sure they were going to eat humans. Not for sure."

"But you did know."

"Maybe. Yeah. There were rumors."

"And you didn't warn anyone. Because hey, just humans, right?" Danny's voice carried more disgust than should be possible, slick and dripping with it.

"It's not like that."

"It's exactly like that. And guess what? Venec and Torres know."

It wasn't a lie. Bonnie and Venec did know. They knew the mole people were here, and that they preferred a people-heavy menu. They didn't know that the fatae had also known, and been willing to stay quiet so long as they also stayed uneaten. Mainly because Ellen hadn't been able to convey all of that in a ping, while also following the conversation in front of her.

"Lonejacks might be able to overlook that little no-tell of yours," Danny went on. "They're firm believers in taking care of oneself first, after all. But the Council?" He made a regretful tsking noise with his tongue. "The Council won't look well on that. And you know they haven't forgotten that they put themselves on the line during that trouble with the Silence, not so many years back."

Ellen hadn't been in the city then, hadn't even known about Talent, much less that she was one. But she'd heard the stories. Wren Valere had been elbows deep in that, protecting the city —human *and* fatae. But Wren, for all that she was respected, wasn't exactly feared. Nobody wanted to get the Council riled, though. They had power, money, *and* influence on their side.

Danny had slid the knife in. Now it was her turn to twist it. "The real issue isn't even the Council," she said, trying to look as though this had just occurred to her. "All they can do is make your life hell. But how long do you think an entire community of flesh-eating monsters will be able to feed, even in a city as populated as New York, before people start to notice? An increase in missing persons, maybe a few piles of bones appearing, even *one* sighting of—what did you call them, shklya?— making it into the newspaper, and you'll think terrorism fears were a walk in the park.

"I know my species: we're dumb, panicky, dangerous animals. They're not going to stop to differentiate between any of you: it'll be kill before you're killed and eaten."

"You think we don't know that?" Linder asked, even as Danny looked at her with an expression that asked if she'd really just quoted *Men In Black* at a Time Like This. "That's what we're afraid of, a mob of angry, crazy humans! Who, I might add, outnumber us, what, twenty to one? And most of us, we're not exactly fighters!"

"So you thought staying quiet was your best protection. Well, it wasn't." Danny's voice had gone cold and dry again, and Linder was still looking nervous.

"All right. What are you going to do?"

Danny shook his head, reaching down to dust off the toe of his perfectly clean boots ostentatiously. "I'm not going to do anything. You are. You're going to go to the Council and you're going to tell them everything you know, and you're going to work with them to deal with this."

"I'm not—"

Whatever Linder saw in Danny's eyes, it was enough to silence any further words. Ellen didn't realize until then that she'd been holding her breath.

They saw themselves out of the building, leaving Linder sitting on his sofa, surrounded by gleaming chrome and leather, sunlight streaming in through the windows around him. The lobby hummed with electronic noise and energy: power was back on, New York was once again filled with neon and glare. Ellen felt herself relax a little more, sensing the stream of current running like lifeblood through the city's veins. She didn't need it right now, but if she did, it was there.

She glanced sideways at Danny. His hair was even more a mess of curls than usual, without his usual baseball cap jammed down on his head, and she could see the faintest tips of his horns peeking through, the creases in his skin where exhaustion was catching up with him, and something else, something deeper than sleep deprivation, darker than anger.

"What's going to happen now? Will the PUPs do something?" She had no idea what she thought that might be.

He closed his eyes briefly, not missing a step. "What we do, Shadow, what the PUPs do.... We're about cause and action, about laws and culpability. But that's all new. It's not how the Cosa Nostradamus worked, historically. We act, and we react."

"Danny." She reached out, her fingers curling around the rough fabric of his sleeve, halting him mid-step. "What are they going to do? The Council, and... What are they going to do to the shklya?"

He didn't answer her, and after a minute, she let go.

# ABOUT THE AUTHOR

Laura Anne Gilman's work has been hailed as "a true American myth" by NPR, and praised for her "deft plotting and first-class characters" by Publishers Weekly. She has won the Endeavor Award for THE COLD EYE, and been shortlisted for a Nebula, (another) Endeavor, and a Washington State Book Award. Her novels include the Locus-bestselling weird western Devil's West trilogy, the Cosa Nostradamus urban fantasy series, and the Vineart War trilogy, and the story collections WEST WINDS' FOOL and DARKLY HUMAN. A former New Yorker, she currently lives outside of Seattle with a cat, a dog, and many deadlines.

Join Laura Anne's Patreon here: https://www.patreon.com/LAGilman

Sign up for Laura Anne's newsletter here: https://mailchi.mp/2cc5d5547cb1/gilmanquarterly

More information, social media links, and updates can be found at https://www.lauraannegilman.net/

# ALSO BY LAURA ANNE GILMAN

*Retrievers*

Staying Dead

Curse the Dark

Bring It On

Burning Bridges

Free Fall

Blood From Stone

*Paranormal Scene Investigations*

Hard Magic

Pack of Lies

Tricks of the Trade

Dragon Justice

Lightning Strikes

*The Devil's West*

Silver on the Road

The Cold Eye

Red Waters Rising

West Winds' Fool and Other Stories of the Devil's West

Gabriel's Road

www.ingramcontent.com/pod-product-compliance
Lightning Source LLC
Chambersburg PA
CBHW070818190726
48292CB00006B/2046